Titles by Rachel Wilson

SPIRIT OF LOVE
BITTERSWEET SUMMER
HEAVEN'S PROMISE
RESTLESS SPIRITS
SWEET CHARITY

SPIRIT OF LOVE

RACHEL WILSON

JOVE BOOKS, NEW YORK

HAUNTING HEARTS is a registered trademark of Penguin Putnam Inc.

SPIRIT OF LOVE

A Jove Book / published by arrangement with
the author

PRINTING HISTORY
Jove edition / October 1999

All rights reserved.
Copyright © 1999 by Alice Duncan.
This book may not be reproduced in whole or in part,
by mimeograph or any other means, without permission.
For information address: The Berkley Publishing Group,
a division of Penguin Putnam Inc.,
375 Hudson Street, New York, New York 10014.

The Penguin Putnam Inc. World Wide Web site address is
http://www.penguinputnam.com

ISBN: 0-515-12675-6

A JOVE BOOK®
Jove Books are published by The Berkley Publishing Group,
a division of Penguin Putnam Inc.,
375 Hudson Street, New York, New York 10014.
JOVE and the "J" design
are trademarks belonging to Penguin Putnam Inc.

PRINTED IN THE UNITED STATES OF AMERICA

10 9 8 7 6 5 4 3 2 1

SPIRIT OF LOVE

Prologue

My Dearest Evelyn,
  It is with great reluctance that I put pen to paper and write to you today, but I can perceive no other course of action. The good Lord knows, I've tried to cope. Truly I have, Evelyn. You needn't think that I have run to you at the first sign of distress in our dear mother. I am certain you know me better than that. I have never called upon anyone for help before, but I fear the time has come for drastic action.

"Dear Lord," Evelyn Witherspoon whispered, her soft doe's eyes going as round as saucers.

"What is it, Mother?" Georgina Witherspoon rose from the chair in which she had been embroidering a slipper for her father's birthday and hurried to her mother's side. "Does Aunt Vernice's letter contain unpleasant news?"

Usually the family found letters from Aunt Vernice, who lived clear across the country in the New Mexico Territory, interesting and enlivening. At least Georgina did. Her parents occasionally tutted with disapproval at some of the things

Vernice wrote about. The present missive was obviously different.

Evelyn fluttered Aunt Vernice's letter at her daughter. "I—I fear it does, Georgina."

"Dear me." Georgina didn't know what to do in the face of her mother's distress.

"Good God, is it your mother? Again?" Georgina turned around to find her father, George Witherspoon, standing at the parlor door looking grim.

Georgina tried to hide the slipper in a fold of her skirt, not wanting him to see his birthday surprise. Her father's words startled her. "Grandmother Murphy? Is there something wrong with Grandmother Murphy? Is she ill?" And what was that "again" business? She didn't ask.

She was alarmed to see a look of fearful premonition in the glance her parents exchanged. It was as if they knew something she didn't.

Georgina didn't like to be left out of things. Since she was a properly brought up, well-bred young woman, she did not demand an explanation of either parent, but only watched, her insides tight with apprehension, as her mother finished reading Aunt Vernice's letter.

Something was terribly wrong. Georgina could see it in the pallor of her mother's cheeks and the glitter of unshed tears in her eyes. "Mother! Mother, please, tell me what's happened!" She'd never seen her mother thus, and it frightened her.

Her father walked over and took the letter from his wife's trembling fingers. As he read the words scripted thereon, the frown that grew on his face was forbidding to behold. Georgina put a hand to her mouth, worried about this show of consternation in her parents. She forgot all about her father's birthday slipper. It dropped from her fingers to the carpet and was ignored.

"So," George said at last, "the old bat's gone around the bend at last, has she? Ghosts, my foot." He gave a wholly undignified snort.

Georgina gasped.

Mrs. Witherspoon uttered a stifled moan of affliction.

George scowled and slapped the letter against his open palm in patent disgust. "I wondered how long it would take her to lose her marbles.'' He looked up and glowered at his wife. ''I'm surprised it took her this long, quite frankly.''

Mrs. Witherspoon began to weep softly.

Georgina was profoundly shocked.

Chapter One

Georgina Witherspoon didn't know if she was more enthusiastic than apprehensive or the other way around when the train finally chugged to a halt in the small depot of the commensurately small village of Picacho Wells, New Mexico Territory. She'd never been away from home in her life before now, except when she and her parents had vacationed together in Saratoga. In her estimation, such trips were mere holidays and didn't count.

This time, however, she'd traveled the whole way from New York City to Picacho Wells alone. All by herself. Without even Henry Spurling, her putative fiancé, to guide and guard her.

Henry had intended to come, but he'd fallen ill with the croup and couldn't. Georgina would never admit it aloud, but she'd been relieved. She assumed she'd marry Henry one day, thereby doing her duty and fulfilling her God-given destiny as a woman and a Witherspoon, but the knowledge didn't thrill her.

In her heart of hearts—that very most secret place to which she allowed no one, not even her dear mother, access—Georgina longed for excitement. She'd like at least one smallish

4

adventure to call her own before she took up the mantle of matronhood in the stodgy New York society of her birth.

So here she was. Alone. All by herself. In the vastness of New Mexico Territory. Come to help her aunt cope with her allegedly mad grandmother.

She grinned happily.

Enthusiasm seemed to be winning this battle. As Georgina picked up her skirt so that its hem wouldn't brush against the smoke-blackened floor of her train carriage and headed for the door, she felt, in fact, an unfamiliar impulse to whoop with delight.

She was free! Free from the strictures of her upbringing. Free from her very proper parents. Free from the constraints of the stifling society in which she'd operated since the day of her birth some twenty-three years ago. Free. Free, free, *free*!

She stooped to peep out of the windows as she moved toward the train door, and a smidgen of her exhilaration faded.

Goodness sakes, but it was bleak out there. She didn't even see a tree. Georgina took heart from the certain knowledge that this was the train station, and bucolic train stations always looked a trifle—well—bucolic. The trees and other scenic vistas must be elsewhere, she thought. She bucked up immediately.

Although she'd traveled the entire trip in an enclosed car, she hadn't avoided being smudged by soot. There seemed to be no way to avoid it, even in the first-class section. Since, however, a passenger riding in one of the cheaper open carriages had caught fire somewhere in Texas and had to be rolled in a blanket to be extinguished, she did not repine about the slight damage to her traveling suit. She figured she'd arrived virtually unscathed, and anyhow, the interesting train trip and its accompanying rigors had already given her something to write home about.

Her parents were very anxious about her. They hadn't wanted her to come. Using all the coercive force she possessed, Georgina had eventually persuaded them to allow her to make the trip. After all, she had argued reasonably, *somebody* had to do it. Poor Aunt Vernice was unquestionably at her wits' end and needed help, and Georgina was willing and able—eager even—to help her. She wasn't altogether sure she was going to enjoy caring for an insane woman, but any trouble encountered in that endeavor was worth it to be able to travel all this way and to see the Wild West for herself.

The Wild West.

Georgina's insides quivered with delight. She'd read so many magazine articles and novels about the wonders of this savage, untamed land full of cacti and cowboys and Indians and bandits and coyotes and so forth. She could hardly wait to meet a real brigand. She hoped it wouldn't take long.

Her first glimpse of Picacho Wells might have daunted her had she been a girl of a lesser spirit. *It's so ugly,* was her first thought. Her second thought got blown away by the wind, along with a feather from her hat. She slammed her hat down on her head, and was extremely glad she'd worn her small-bustled, straight-lined traveling skirt, or the howling wind would be showing onlookers a good deal too much of her fancy New York City patent-leather boots.

Speaking of onlookers, Georgina realized there were several of them, and they all seemed to be staring at her. Did she really stand out that much in her smart bolero jacket with leg-o'-mutton sleeves in pale gray washed silk with her tucked white blouse and matching gray nine-gored skirt? Looking around in avid curiosity, she decided perhaps she did. That was all right. Georgina intended to fit in here; she would simply remember to dress in more simple frocks in the future.

Good heavens, people dressed oddly here. And were those men actually squatting right smack on the boardwalk, leaning against that building over there? With their hats pulled down so low she could hardly see their eyes? She squinted hard against the bright sunshine, thinking she must be mistaken.

She wasn't mistaken. They were indeed. Gentlemen would never behave in so casual a manner back home in New York City. Perhaps those fellows weren't gentlemen.

Oh, dear. As much as she longed to see a real, live desperado, Georgina rather hoped none of those men was one, because they were a little too close for comfort. Perhaps this squatting-on-the-boardwalk-and-leaning-against-a-wall business was an old and established western custom.

Georgina reminded herself that her intention was to learn without prejudice. It was not her place to pass judgment on these, her fellow United States citizens—even if they didn't live in a united state.

Merciful heavens, she was now outside the boundaries of the United States! For a moment she reminded herself of her greatest hero, Theodore Roosevelt, and she nearly succumbed to the emotion of it all. Since she didn't wish to make a spectacle of herself, she swallowed her tears of delight and took in a deep breath of territorial air. It was very dry, and she sneezed. Still holding onto her hat because the wind seemed to be trying to tug it off her head, Georgina walked inside the train station's small building.

Two ladies nodded at her, and she smiled back, wondering if one of them was her aunt Vernice. Neither of them looked at all like her mother, nor did either lady move to greet her. Georgina experienced a tiny pang of dismay. If Aunt Vernice hadn't been able to come herself, hadn't she at least sent someone to meet her train? Georgina devoutly hoped so, because she had no idea how to get to her grandmother's home if she hadn't.

"Miss Witherspoon?"

The deep, drawly voice at her back startled Georgina into spinning around. She blinked at the man standing there— looming there, rather. He was an inordinately tall fellow. As far as Georgina was concerned, men shouldn't grow so tall. Tall men were too intimidating. She drew herself up to her full five feet, three inches, adopted a polite smile, and lifted her chin.

"Yes? I am Miss Witherspoon."

He tipped his hat, which was encouraging. At least he didn't seem to be a savage.

"How do you do, Miss Witherspoon? I'm the sheriff here in Picacho Wells."

"My goodness."

Georgina experienced the first real disappointment of her western jaunt. The western sheriffs she'd seen depicted in *Harper's Magazine* and on the covers of the novels she liked to read looked nothing like this man.

For instance, the illustrations by Mr. Frederic Remington and Mr. Charles Russell always showed their rugged western sheriffs as the possessors of fine handlebar mustaches. This man was clean-shaven.

And he wasn't at all squinty-eyed, as if he'd ridden hard trails in pursuit of rough characters in the harsh desert sun for days at a time. His eyes were quite lovely, actually: deep chocolate brown with curly dark lashes. He didn't squint at all.

And what about guns? She'd always understood that proper western sheriffs wore two gun belts, crisscrossing, with their lethal cargoes toted in tooled leather holsters, one per hip. This fellow had a gun stuffed into the waistband of his trousers, next to a pair of well-worn, floppy leather gloves.

He was tan enough to be a western sheriff, at least, and he was relatively good-looking. Still, he had a terrible, twangy drawl. And he'd spoken to her before they'd been properly— or even improperly—introduced. He didn't look gallant and daring at all, and Georgina suspected he was no gentleman, unlike the sheriffs about whom she'd so often read, who were molded along the lines of a modern-day Ivanhoe or Sir Galahad or one of those other knightly fellows.

"Your aunt, Miss Vernice Murphy, asked me to meet your train and see that you were all right. I've got a buggy outside the station, and I'll take you to the Murphy place." He held out a hand to her. "Ash Barrett, ma'am. Pleased to meet you."

It was the final blow. Ash must be short for Ashley, a civilized name if she'd ever heard one. He was supposed to be a Buck. Or a Kid something-or-other. For goodness sake, Georgina had attended school with men named Ashley. In New York City. She was mortally disillusioned.

There seemed to be no help for it, though. Swallowing her disenchantment, Georgina took Mr. Barrett's hand and shook it. She even managed a fairly proper smile. "I'm happy to know you, Mr. Barrett. Thank you for seeing to my welfare."

"You're welcome. I'll bet Picacho Wells is a far stretch from New York City."

"Er, yes. It is, indeed."

"You'll get used to it. We all do, sooner or later."

"I'm sure that's true."

They recovered Georgina's baggage with little fuss, and Georgina found another reason to be glad Henry Spurling hadn't been healthy enough to make the trip. Henry always became rattled in new surroundings. If he were here, he'd be putting on his fussy face, whining, directing everybody and everything, and annoying the locals. The sheriff, who seemed to know everyone in town, dealt with her luggage easily. Overall, she guessed she'd rather be taken care of by the sheriff, even if he was far from ideal.

"The buggy's right over here, ma'am," he said as he strode off, carrying two of her bags. He had a manly stride, at least, even if he didn't seem inclined to shorten it for the sake of her more constricting clothing. She hurried after him.

Georgina didn't resent being consigned to the care of a man she didn't know by an aunt she hadn't met. After all, that's what men were for. Georgina accepted society's opinions on the matter, and had never thought to question her role as an ancillary adjunct to the masculine gender. She supposed her reluctance to accompany the sheriff in this instance was only leftover disappointment that he didn't fit her picture of what a western sheriff should look like.

She glanced around Picacho Wells and realized it didn't fit her mental images of a western town, either. It seemed, in fact, to consist of nothing but dust and shabbiness. Mercy, didn't folks have access to paint around here?

Well, she refused to let appearances fluster her. She was here, this was probably the only chance she'd ever have to experience an adventure, and she aimed to make the most of it. If Picacho Wells was an ugly place, and if Sheriff Ash Barrett wasn't Georgina's idea of a proper sheriff, he was at least handsome. She decided to be grateful for small mercies and to hope things would perk up soon.

They did.

No sooner had Ash Barrett helped her into the buggy than several gunshots rang out over the windy air. Georgina looked up and was unnerved and excited to see two men with bandannas pulled over their faces. They were backing out of a building that said it was a bank, although it didn't bear any resemblance whatever to any bank she'd ever seen.

She uttered a small scream.

Her scream wasn't in reaction to seeing, at dangerously close range, a pair of dastardly bank robbers. It came out of her throat spontaneously and as a result of her being pushed by the sheriff, very hard, to the floor of the buggy. Once she recovered from her shock, which took mere seconds, she pulled herself up to her knees, sputtering with indignation. It took her another several seconds to push her hat back into place. When he'd shoved her, it had brushed against the buggy seat and fallen over her eyes. All the time she struggled with her hat, she heard gunshots, shouts, foul curses, and a couple of screams. And she was missing it!

Georgina was no fool. She wasn't about to expose her entire body, or even a small portion of it, to flying bullets. Nevertheless, she'd never been this close to any kind of real, honest-to-goodness excitement in what seemed to her to be an extremely sheltered life, and she didn't want to miss anything. What's more, she resented being manhandled.

By the time she managed to get herself positioned so she could peek through the window of the buggy, Sheriff Barrett had overpowered the villains. Blast! She wished she could have watched him do it.

Two men lay in the dusty road, one on his back and the other facedown in the dirt. A puddle of blood was spreading out from beneath the one who was faceup to the sun. A third was on his knees, his hands pressed to his head, squashing his hat flat. Georgina didn't think the hat would be ruined by his doing so, as it didn't look like a particularly handsome specimen of hathood to begin with.

The man appeared to be crying and pleading. Sheriff Barrett, clearly unmoved by the robber's show of fear and remorse, shoved him down, hard, into the dirt, grabbed his hands, and threw a rope around him, holding him still with a boot to his back. Apparently, western sheriffs didn't use the manacles so popular back East.

Still smarting from being thrown to the floor of the buggy, Georgina opened the door and got down. She had to hop, because no one was around to help her and there were no stairs available. So be it. She was no china-doll miss who had to be pampered and coddled.

Sheriff Barrett yanked the bank robber to his feet, using the rope he'd tied around his hands. The man cried out in pain. The sheriff had opened his mouth, presumably to reprimand the villain, when he spied Georgina and stiffened.

"What the hell are you doing out here?"

It took a second for Georgina to realize Mr. Barrett was talking to her. She stopped dead in her tracks. "I stepped down to see what was going on." She did not appreciate being cursed at, but decided it would be prudent to take the matter up with the sheriff later, in the privacy of the buggy.

"Well, for God's sake, get back in there. Can't you see there's trouble?"

Annoyed, Georgina snapped, "Of course, I can see it! That's why I got down. I want to see what happened."

A man with a huge nose who seemed to be helping the sheriff chuckled. "Cain't very well fault her fer that, Ash. She's a female, after all."

Mr. Barrett grumbled something under his breath. Georgina didn't catch what he said, but she was almost certain it was unflattering. She refused to be daunted. Very gingerly, she tiptoed near one of the dead villains, holding her skirt off the ground. She didn't care to get blood on her garments.

"Ugh." He was a very unpleasant sight. Georgina had never seen a dead person before. Well, except for Grandfather Witherspoon, but he'd been laid out in a coffin in the parlor and had looked fairly good, except for being dead.

She suspected this dead fellow wouldn't have looked good even after an undertaker had been at him. This was one person who fitted Georgina's mental pictures of what a proper westerner should look like. Every inch a scoundrel, he was. She was pleased.

She uttered a very unladylike squawk when she was grabbed roughly from behind.

"Get away from that man, Miss Witherspoon. It's no sight for a—ow!"

Georgina hadn't meant to slap Sheriff Barrett. She presumed the combination of circumstances had rendered her mental processes sluggish and, since she was already laboring under strong emotion, being grabbed that way had precipitated an automatic reaction. She was actually tolerably glad to know her survival instincts seemed to be keen, in spite of a life lived in ease and luxury in a civilized eastern city.

"Unhand me, if you please, Mr. Barrett. There's no need to be brutal."

"Brutal?"

It didn't look to her as if he aimed to apologize. He appeared, in fact, surprised. Georgina was offended. "Yes, brutal. All of this is new to me, and I was only curious." She swept a kid-gloved hand out in a gesture meant to indicate the entire western United States.

Mr. Barrett plainly didn't care. "Damn it, lady, do you

know who these men are?'' He, too, swept a hand out, but his gesture was meant to encompass the dead outlaws.

"Of course I don't. How could I?"

"Exactly." Mr. Barrett spoke as if Georgina had just proven his point for him. "And what you don't know can get you killed out here. This isn't New York City, Miss Witherspoon."

"I'm well aware of that, thank you."

"You're not acting like it. For Chrissakes, lady, these men are a gang of outlaws that have been robbing and murdering all over the Southwest."

"Gracious sakes." Georgina glanced again at the dead men, feeling a good deal more respect for them than she'd had initially.

"Gracious sakes." Repeating her words, the sheriff put an emphasis on them that Georgina didn't believe they deserved.

She lifted her chin at an angle calculated to depress sarcastic innuendoes. "I am ready when you are, Mr. Barrett. If you're through here." Again she gestured, indicating the dead men on the street. A crowd was beginning to gather, and Georgina believed their inquisitiveness amply vindicated her own.

"If I'm through here?"

Georgina frowned, not understanding why he should sound so exasperated. "Don't you have minions who can take care of the details engendered by such a circumstance?" She considered it a reasonable question, but Mr. Barrett rolled his eyes in an ungentlemanly fashion and snorted.

The large fellow with the huge nose who had chuckled earlier now walked up to them. He tipped his hat at her. She offered him one of her most gracious smiles, pleased to know that a few proprieties existed in this out-of-the-way place, even if they were extended by a man who seemed to have more nose than was absolutely necessary.

"I'll take care of it, Ash. You drive the lady to the Murphy place."

Mr. Barrett gave Georgina a lingering and, it appeared to her, contemptuous glare. After too many seconds of that, he said, "Thanks, Frank. I'll do the paperwork after I get back."

"Take your time," the man named Frank said. "You're dealin' with a Murphy, after all."

She was a Witherspoon, actually. Georgina almost pointed it out to Frank, but decided against it. She did have Murphy

blood in her. She presumed his comment was meant as a compliment and that Frank was telling the sheriff that the Murphys,
as a respectable family in the neighborhood, deserved consideration. She appreciated him for it, and gave him another
smile. He smiled back, giving her a glimpse of teeth that
looked more like broken pickets than any teeth she'd ever
seen. She blinked and commanded herself not to stare.

"Thank you very much," she said to Frank. Her gaze for
the sheriff was much colder than the one she'd directed at
Frank. "Whenever you're ready, Sheriff. I shall return to the
buggy now."

"I'll be there in a minute."

Georgina frowned at him. It sounded as if he were speaking
through gritted teeth. She neither understood nor approved of
his tone. "Fine. Thank you."

It was a struggle, but she managed to get into the buggy
without help. She was going to be living here for however
long it took to sort out things with Grandmother, and she
aimed to do it right. Not for Georgina any misplaced airs and
graces left over from her New York City home. No sirree. She
was going to become a proper western woman, or know the
reason why.

She had to wait several more minutes before Sheriff Ash
Barrett condescended to take his place in the driver's seat of
the buggy. Georgina did not care to be kept waiting, and she
had a sneaking suspicion he let her wait on purpose, although
she had no idea why he was being so disagreeable. He was
almost as much of a fusspot as Henry, for heaven's sake.

As Georgina waited, she observed the village of Picacho
Wells. Again, she couldn't help but be slightly discouraged. It
really was a pathetic-looking place. Her gaze swept the street,
from north to south and back again. That's all there was to it.
One street. A swaybacked boardwalk ran along it on either
side, and buildings stood like ragged schoolchildren behind the
boardwalk. A hitching rail that looked more splintery than was
seemly ran the length of the boardwalk.

And there were those men, squatting there, doing nothing,
with their hats pulled over their eyes. Mercy sakes. She directed her attention back to the buildings.

Everything seemed to be plain and brown, pockmarked, and
peeling. Windmills pierced the sky behind several of the build-

ings, their blades spinning like pinwheels in the relentless wind. The landscape appeared to her to be as dry as a bone, and she couldn't imagine what purpose the windmills served unless there were underground water sources around.

Georgina presumed most people lived beyond this one main thoroughfare, although she couldn't imagine where. For as far as her eyes could see, there was nothing but grassy, windswept plains. Were there houses out there? She didn't see any. Hmm. This wasn't at all promising.

Since she was so busy observing her surroundings, the only reason she knew the sheriff had come was that the buggy dipped suddenly, almost heaving her out of the seat. When she caught her breath, she realized Mr. Barrett was in the driver's seat. He didn't turn around to greet her or otherwise acknowledge her presence, but only presented her with a view of his excessively broad back.

Georgina frowned, then scooted forward so she could talk to him. Deciding to give him a chance to redeem himself— after all, perhaps he'd shoved her to the floor of the buggy out of concern for her welfare and a sense of misguided chivalry— she said sweetly, "Thank you for rescuing me from the shooting, Mr. Barrett."

"You're welcome." He sounded not at all conciliatory.

"Is Ash short for Ashley, Mr. Barrett?"

"Yes."

Georgina had suspected it. She compressed her lips and decided to give him one more chance. She heard nothing more from his lips but a click to the horse pulling the buggy. The buggy jerked forward, slamming Georgina against the seat cushion—if *cushion* was the proper word for so thin and hard an object. She struggled upright again, this time honestly furious.

"Mr. Barrett," she said in her most severe tone. "If in the future we should happen to be in the vicinity of one another when bandits try to rob a bank, I should appreciate it if you would *not* shove me to the floor of a buggy."

He twisted his neck so that he could look at her. It wasn't a friendly look. "Don't worry. There probably won't be a buggy handy. I'll just shove you to the ground."

Georgina's mouth fell open. It took a good ten seconds for

her to recover her composure enough to cry, "Good heavens! You truly *are* a brute!"

"A brute? Cowpats."

Cowpats? She had no idea what he meant, although she was certain it wasn't anything good.

"Yes," she said firmly. "A brute. There's no need to use force. You need merely advise me to remove myself from danger, and I shall do so expeditiously."

He heaved a huge, irritated sigh. "Listen, lady, I know you're not used to life out here in the territory but, believe me, when the shooting starts, there's no time to talk. I'm the sheriff here, and I'll do what it takes to protect my citizens." He added grimly, "And even visitors."

"That's very good of you, but you needn't do it in so rough a manner." Georgina was feeling pretty grim herself.

"You'll get over it, Miss Witherspoon. And it seems to me you ought to thank me for it, too. If I hadn't shoved you, you might not be alive to get over it."

Georgina thought she heard him mutter an addendum about almost wishing she weren't, but she wasn't sure. She opted not to argue anymore, because she realized her first assessment of him had been correct. The man was, beyond a doubt, no gentleman.

After fuming for a moment or two, however, she began to perk up. This might be an ugly place. And it might be rough and full of dastardly bank robbers and crude, ungentlemanly sheriffs. But it wasn't dull. In fact, by gum, Georgina believed she'd just experienced the first real adventure of her lifetime. She breathed in a big gulp of dusty air and felt her spirits lift.

Chapter Two

Ash Barrett was almost as disgusted as he'd been when he first realized Phoebe, his deceased wife, had possessed feet of clay. Hell, Phoebe's entire being had been molded of clay. Sticky, clingy, melty, gooey clay. The kind that got into everything and gummed up the works and ruined it so that it never operated properly again.

So far, Georgina Witherspoon was just as bad. Maybe even worse, if such a thing were possible. Until he'd met her, Ash hadn't believed another such creature as Phoebe existed on earth. He was unhappy to discover his mistake.

Yet there she sat, in his very own buggy, which he was at present driving down the main street of Picacho Wells at her aunt's request and out of the goodness of his heart, headed for the home of a crazy old lady, and she was scolding him. *Him. She,* Georgina Witherspoon, a fluffy bit of goods from the big city who didn't know New Mexico Territory from her own hind end, was sitting on the seat of his buggy, drawn by his horse, driven by his own personal self, and lecturing *him,* Ash Barrett, sheriff of Picacho Wells, about how to treat a lady.

"You'll get over it," he repeated.

"Of course I'll get over it," she said in a voice as crisp as burnt toast. "That's not the point."

Lord, he wished the Murphy place were closer to town. He

16

wanted to get this over with. He liked Vernice. Hell, he even liked old Maybelle Murphy, even if she was as crazy as a loon. But this granddaughter of Maybelle's was enough to try the patience of a saint, and Ash was no saint.

"The point is you're still alive," he said through his teeth. "If I hadn't shoved you, you might not be. For Chrissakes, lady, this isn't New York."

"Yes, I believe we've covered that point."

He turned and squinted at her. "Why are you carrying on like this, anyway? I'm sorry if we folks here in Picacho Wells don't possess the fine manners you're used to, lady, but the territory's a rough place. I figure we'll get manners eventually, after we take care of more important things, like getting rid of the hard cases and bandits."

She sniffed. "That's still no excuse."

"This is a stupid conversation."

"I don't believe any civilized conversation is stupid in and of itself, Mr. Barrett. I object to being treated like a sack of potatoes. You were the one who treated me thus. While you evidently believe you had sufficient reason to do so, I disagree. No lady likes to be tossed around."

"Lord." If he were a less prudent man, Ash might have snapped the reins and made the horse go faster. Ash Barrett was nobody's fool, however, and he didn't do it. He also liked his horse, Nestor, who, while too old and ugly to be a good saddle animal any longer, was tough and strong enough to pull his buggy. He didn't want old Nestor to stumble in a gopher hole and bust his leg.

This female in the buggy, though . . . Well, if the world were a just and equitable place, she'd be the one to step into a gopher hole and at least sprain her ankle, if not break her neck.

She was exactly like Phoebe, except that Phoebe had been dark and Miss Prissy Witherspoon was fair, with hair like spun silk, and a complexion a man might die for if he didn't know better. Ash knew better. She opened her mouth to light into him again, and he knew it was going to be a long trip.

"At any rate, I don't believe it was necessary to shove me the way you did. Nor was it kind of you to curse at me afterwards."

"Curse at you?" Ash wasn't sure he could stand much more of this.

"Yes. You swore at me when I was—" She stopped. "Oh, my goodness, what are they doing?"

Ash jerked his head up, wondering what in hell was happening now. If somebody else was robbing the bank, he might just quit his job, no matter how much he liked it. Picacho Wells was usually as peaceful as a slumbering baby. He'd never heard of two crimes happening in one month, let alone one day. When he glanced over to where Georgina's attention was focused, he was relieved to see nothing unlawful going forward.

"That's the undertaker, Corny Stonecipher. He's putting the bodies up for display." He heard her take a big gulp.

"He's doing what?"

"Putting the bodies up for display. So folks can see them."

"So folks can see them?" Her voice squeaked.

Ash peered at her over his shoulder, wondering what her problem was now. "Yeah. Folks do that out here. Shows any other would-be crooks that criminal activity won't be tolerated in Picacho Wells." The custom was a common one in the Southwest, and Ash approved of it. He considered it a deterrent.

"Good Lord in heaven! Do you mean to tell me that a respectable undertaker is actually going to prop those dead men's corpses up in those coffins, and put them on exhibition for the citizens of the town to gawk at? As if they were pieces of meat hung in a butcher's shop?"

Ash shrugged. "That's one way to look at it, I reckon."

"I've never heard of anything like it."

He noted the tone of disapproval in her voice and bridled. "Listen, lady—"

"Don't you call me *lady* in that supercilious way, if you please!"

Ash's fists tightened on the reins and he had to fight to keep from jerking them and hurting Nestor's mouth. "Listen, Miss Witherspoon, if you don't like the customs out here, you don't have to stay. Want me to take you back to the train station? I'll explain to your aunt that you couldn't take the rough life away from New York City. I'm sure she'll understand." It sounded like a good idea to Ash.

"You will do no such thing! I can, too, take life outside of

New York City. It seems to me that I've already demonstrated as much.''

"How? By getting out of the buggy and walking into the middle of what might well have been a shootout because you didn't know any better?''

"Folderol!''

Although the word itself was solid, the tone in which she uttered it wasn't. In fact, it sounded to Ash as if she hadn't thought about her earlier action in exactly those terms. The little fool.

She cleared her throat. "I did no such thing. All the shooting had stopped before I got out.''

"Right. A lot you know about it.'' He was too disgusted to talk to her anymore. She seemed to share his sentiment, because she finally shut up and sat back against the cushion. It was about time.

It took forty-five minutes to get from Picacho Wells to the Murphy place if the roads weren't flooded, the horse didn't go lame, a herd of cows or a flock of sheep didn't get in the way, robbers didn't stop you, a wheel didn't bust, and the wind didn't blow up a storm and prevent forward motion. Luck was with Ash today, and he appreciated it. He didn't want to be stuck with Miss Georgina Witherspoon a single second longer than he had to be.

As soon as he drove the buggy down the tree-lined drive and into the Murphy yard, the front door of the house flew open and Miss Vernice stepped out onto the porch, a huge smile on her face and her arms held wide in a gesture of greeting. Ash was fond of the Murphy women, even if one of them was a couple of cards shy of a deck.

It was too bad Devlin O'Rourke, Maybelle Murphy's long-time lover, had died so suddenly a few months ago, because now there was no one to keep the Murphy place in repair. No one, least of all Maybelle or even Devlin himself, had expected Devlin to go. To the best of Ash's understanding, he'd succumbed after a short, virulent bout with influenza, leaving Maybelle too stunned to cope, although Ash had always assumed her to be up to anything. Tough as nails, Maybelle Murphy. At least, that's what everyone had thought. Apparently, they'd been wrong.

Maybelle and Devlin had never married, but Ash didn't fault them for that. Hell, the West was wide open and free. They weren't the first couple to set up housekeeping without the blessing of a preacher or the law, and he was sure they wouldn't be the last. At least they hadn't been hypocritical about it. And the love between them had been as plain as the nose on Frank Dunwiddy's face.

Since Dev's death, Maybelle had slipped a cog, though, and it made Ash sad. She'd been a real pistol, Maybelle. Poor Vernice had her hands full these days, tending to the crotchety old woman's needs and catering to her whims. Maybelle Murphy had never been an easy woman. She was sort of like her granddaughter in that respect.

Ash waved at Vernice, who waved back. She looked as if she might bust with happiness. He hoped Miss Georgina Witherspoon wouldn't be a terrible disappointment to her.

"Oh, my, is that my aunt?"

At least the newcomer sounded as if she were glad to meet her aunt. Although it went against the grain, Ash allowed her to score a point for it. "Yes. That's your aunt, Miss Vernice Murphy."

"Oh, my!"

Vernice couldn't stand it any longer, and rushed across the porch, down the steps, and into the yard, where she made a beeline for her niece. For her part, Miss Witherspoon didn't even wait for Ash to help her, but bounded down from the buggy as if on springs.

Ash watched, perplexed. He wouldn't have given her credit for so much energy and family feeling. He'd thought her to be as shallow as Phoebe.

She probably was, underneath. He watched the two women meet in the middle of the yard and embrace, crying and laughing, and generally behaving like a couple of women. He grinned, tugged at his hat, scratched his head, and surveyed the Murphy place.

Devlin and Maybelle had made a nice life for themselves out here, all right. It was a shame Dev had to go like that. He hadn't been one to work real hard at any known profession, but he'd kept the house and grounds up nicely, giving the house and barn a fresh coat of whitewash every year or two, and keeping the fences mended.

He and Maybelle had raised vegetables and cows, horses, and pigs, and kept a sheep or two. They'd never seemed to want for much, and Maybelle never seemed to mind that Dev took a drop or two every now and then.

Dev had been about the most entertaining fellow Ash had ever met, too. He guessed it was true what folks said about Irishmen: They might not like to work very much, and they might be a little too fond of their drink, but they could sure spin a yarn. Ash used to come out and help around the farm sometimes just so he could listen to Dev talk.

The two women finally quit hugging. Both were wiping their eyes. Ash had just finished unloading Miss Witherspoon's bags when Vernice rushed toward him.

"Oh, Mr. Barrett, thank you so much for delivering our beautiful Georgina to us! We're so very grateful—you must come inside—we have spice cake and dandelion wine—you know how mother loves to—and it was so nice—and you must be thirsty—before you go back to town."

Ash chuckled. Miss Vernice always got fluttered when she was excited. "Thanks, Miss Vernice. Don't mind if I do. How's Miss Maybelle today?"

Vernice's smile faded. Ash was sorry to see it go and felt guilty that it had been his inquiry, however kindly meant, that had vanquished it. Vernice began to wring her hands.

"I suppose she's as well as can be expected. She's in such a temper, though. I really don't see how I could have—it's so difficult—I mean—well . . ." Vernice's confession petered out.

Ash patted her hand. "It'll be all right, Miss Vernice. Now that you've got some help around the place, it'll probably be easier for you to handle things." He didn't believe a word of it. He guessed the lie was plain in his voice, because Miss Witherspoon frowned at him.

"Indeed," she said in a tone of ice. "I aim to be a *huge* help to my dear aunt and my grandmother." She seemed to forget her anger with him as she glanced around. Her face took on an expression that even by Ash's cynical standards could only be called radiant. "Oh, Aunt Vernice, I'm so *happy* to be here! I dreamed of coming and didn't think my parents would let me."

"I didn't think they would either, dear. I feared they wouldn't, and I didn't know what I was going to do. I mean— not that I didn't—but now that you're here . . ." She didn't finish, but hugged Georgina again instead.

Ash thought it was sweet, the way the two of them seemed to take to each other right off. He didn't expect it to last. As soon as Miss Georgina Witherspoon discovered how rugged life was out here in the territory where there were no amenities to speak of, she'd give up and go back to New York. Then poor Vernice would be left with the whole burden of caring for Maybelle again, and it would probably be worse because her hopes would have been crushed by her good-for-nothing niece. He disliked Miss Georgina Witherspoon for breaking her aunt's heart that way. He thought it was dead mean of her.

The place still looked good. Dev hadn't been dead long enough for it to go to rack and ruin. Ash hoped it wouldn't. He tried to help the two ladies as much as he could, and he knew other fellows in Picacho Wells did, too, but the farm really needed a permanent caretaker. There was nothing he could do about that, he supposed. He hefted the two bags and followed Vernice and Miss Witherspoon up the porch steps.

Maybelle's huge orange tabby cat, Oscar, tromped out onto the porch and eyed the visitors malevolently. That damned cat caused more problems for Ash than all the bank robbers in the territory. Maybelle worshipped the thing, but the Murphys' closest neighbor, Penelope Jones, was always complaining about it. Mrs. Jones kept telling Ash that there must be something criminal in its behavior. Ash had not yet convinced her that cats couldn't break laws and, therefore, couldn't be arrested. He had to admit, however, that Oscar did seem to go out of his way to trample Mrs. Jones's plants, kill her chickens, scratch up her seedlings, and chase her dog.

He skirted Oscar, holding one of Georgina's bags between the cat and his legs as he went past. Georgina, who hadn't been warned about the cat, said, "Oh, what a sweet kitty," and held out her hand—to pet it, Ash presumed. She got a slash on her wrist for her effort, and Oscar arched his back and snarled at her.

Ash expected her to shriek. Instead, she drew herself up straight, blinked in astonishment at the cat, lifted her wounded wrist to her mouth, and laughed.

"I guess I'll know better than to take you for granted from now on, won't I?"

Ash goggled at her.

Oscar hissed again. Georgina laughed once more and shook her head. "What a tough old cat you are, to be sure. You fit right in here."

Ash could hardly believe his eyes and ears.

Vernice said, "Oh, my dear, I'm so sorry. I should have cautioned you—that is, someone should have—it's a shame that cat—I mean . . ." Vernice gulped air. "That's your grandmother's favorite pet, and she won't hear a word against him. But he's an awful, vicious thing. I keep wishing a coyote would eat him, but so far none has."

Oscar hissed at Vernice this time.

"A coyote?" Georgina breathed the word reverently, as if she considered coyotes akin to angels.

Ash, figuring such a reaction typical of a city girl, snorted. "No coyote'd dare get within ten yards of that animal, Miss Vernice. You know that."

Vernice giggled and blushed. Ash grinned. He always had this effect on poor old Vernice. She was a sweetheart, but way past any hope of matrimony. Ash felt sorry for her on that account.

Ash pressed the latch of the front door and pushed it open, then stood aside to allow the two ladies to enter ahead of him. Dammit, he had manners, even if he wasn't from New York City.

He noticed that Miss Witherspoon grabbed Vernice's hand and held it tight. Vernice looked as if she might flutter up to the ceiling, she was so full of joy and trepidation.

"Mother," Vernice said, her voice quivering with emotion. "Mother, look who's come to visit us all the way from New York City."

Miss Witherspoon grabbed a hankie out of her pocket, quickly wiped her eyes, and said in a voice every bit as emotional as Vernice's, "Grandmother? Grandmother Murphy? It's so good to be able to meet you at last."

Ash stepped into the house and closed the door behind him, depositing the two bags next to the door. Then he stood back to watch the touching scene.

Sunlight poured into the parlor of the Murphy place, making

it look fresh and clean and pretty. Someone—Ash presumed it was Vernice—had set bowls of flowers around. There were lavender and white cosmos on a table next to the chair Dev used to sit in, and roses on the parlor table. Maybelle Murphy sat in a wheelchair—she'd broken her ankle at Dev's funeral and had been laid up since—a scowl on her face.

"So you're Evelyn's child, are you?" Her voice grated like a metal file, and she didn't sound at all pleased to see her only granddaughter for the first time.

Miss Witherspoon opened her mouth, then shut it again, not having anticipated this kind of greeting. "Er, yes. Yes, I'm Georgina."

"Georgina!" Maybelle Murphy spat the name out as she might spit out a bug she'd found in her oatmeal. "Stupid name for a girl, if you ask me. It's your father's conceit, that's what it is." She eyed Georgina up and down. "And look at you. Why, you look like a fashion plate out of one of those miserable, stupid female magazines."

Maybelle Murphy had eyes like those of a bird of prey. They were small and dark, and they glittered with predatory sharpness. Ash had never realized how much she looked like a hawk until today. And poor little Georgina Witherspoon had obviously stirred Maybelle's bird-of-prey instincts.

"I—I beg your pardon?"

Georgina's voice had gone exceedingly small. She was blinking furiously. If Ash didn't dislike her so much, he'd have felt sorry for her.

"Namby-pamby! That's what you are! That's what Evelyn was, too. Damned namby-pamby, prissy, feeble-minded society female who's no good for anything but breeding namby-pamby, prissy, feeble-minded society babies!"

"Grandmother!" Georgina was shocked. Ash didn't blame her.

"Don't you *grandmother* me, you ridiculous girl!" Maybelle Murphy reached into her lap, plucked up one of a pair of shoes lying there—Ash had no idea why—and heaved it at Georgina, who skipped to one side, thereby avoiding being hit. Agile little thing; Ash had to give her that.

"Oh, Grandmother!" Georgina looked as if she might burst into tears.

"Mother, stop it this instant. You know you don't mean any

of those awful things.'' Vernice was beside herself and definitely didn't know what to do with her unmanageable parent.

In spite of himself and his dislike of Georgina Witherspoon, Ash said, ''Stop cutting tricks, Miss Maybelle. You know you're only trying to create an impression.''

''Don't talk to *me* like that, you good-for-nothing galoot!''

''Oh, my goodness.''

Ash barely heard Georgina's horrified whisper. He was a bit peeved with Maybelle himself. After all, even if he didn't like Georgina Witherspoon, he didn't think she deserved this kind of abuse—at least not yet.

In an attempt to buck her up, he said, loud enough for Maybelle to hear, ''Don't pay any attention to her, Miss Witherspoon. She's only being ornery to upset you. Besides, the whole town knows Maybelle Murphy is several bricks short of a load.''

Georgina's big, cornflower-blue eyes, bright with tears of astonishment and worry—a powerful combination—blinked at Ash this time. His heart executed a backflip.

''You damned scoundrel! Don't you be calling *me* crazy! You don't know what the devil you're talking about!'' Maybelle Murphy heaved her other shoe at Ash, who sidestepped almost as nimbly as Georgina had.

Ash laughed.

Vernice uttered a little squeak of affliction.

Georgina only pressed the palm of her scratched hand to her cheek and stared with horror at her grandmother. She looked about ready to sink through the floor.

''It's all right, dear. Mother behaved very badly to you, and it was monstrous of her to do so, but please try to understand. She's been haunted by that awful man's ghost ever since he died.''

''Haunted by his ghost?'' What exactly was that supposed to mean?

''Yes.'' Vernice sighed. ''She claims his spirit has been hanging around the house since the day of his funeral. It aggravates her terribly.''

Georgina stared at Vernice, not at all reassured by this explanation of her grandmother's rude behavior. ''Er, I beg your pardon?'' Perhaps she'd misunderstood.

They were in the middle of snapping green beans for supper. Georgina had never snapped a bean in her life before now. In New York her parents had a whole house full of servants to perform these everyday tasks.

She wasn't distressed by the prospect of physical work. Rather, she was elated by it. After all, her goal was to fit in and become a useful member of the western contingent of her family. If that entailed snapping beans and cooking, so be it. Georgina wasn't sure, but she suspected a true western woman's chores probably included a good deal more than snapping beans. She looked forward to whatever this new life offered her.

At the moment, however, she was still attempting to come to terms with her grandmother who, although she hated to admit it, did seem to be somewhat unbalanced. Actually— Georgina gulped and tried not to exhibit her uneasiness— Vernice, standing here talking to her about ghosts as if they were as much a part of life as dressing gowns and slippers, didn't sound exactly rational, either. Georgina hoped to heaven the Murphy side of her family didn't contain a tainted strain.

"I know it sounds silly, but there it is," Vernice said in answer to Georgina's plea for clarification. "It's that Mr. O'Rourke. He died in February, you know, and Mother hasn't been the same since. It's because he's taken to haunting her, and she's very crotchety about it."

"Oh." Georgina tried to think of something intelligent to say and failed. She concentrated on snapping beans and hoped Vernice would not take her silence amiss. She also scanned the kitchen for possible weapons. She trusted the lunatic bloodline that seemed to run rampant in her family didn't include violence with anything more deadly than shoes.

Good. The knife was closer to her than to Vernice. If Vernice made a move to grab it, Georgina believed her reflexes would be quicker than her aunt's.

Vernice lowered her voice when she continued. "I hope your mother and father filled you in on the family history, Georgina. I know it's shocking, and if things hadn't come to such a pass, I'm sure they'd never have distressed you with it, but I suppose you need to know now." She shook her head sorrowfully.

Georgina nodded, embarrassed. "Yes. Mother and Father told me all about it before I came out here."

She'd been powerfully jolted, too, that day two months ago when her parents had sat her down in the parlor and bared their souls, her mother in tears. It had been dreadful to hear her mother, her face muffled in her soggy handkerchief, say that Georgina's father had married her mother in spite of her abysmal family background. Georgina had been touched when her father had patted her mother's knee and said that, however ignoble her kin, he'd married her because he loved her, and he'd never once regretted it.

Until now.

How many other families contained black sheep like Grandmother Murphy? Georgina wondered. Of course, since no properly brought-up person ever discussed such things as skeletons in closets and lunatics in territories, there was no way of knowing for certain. Still, Georgina suspected not very many mothers ran away from their families as Maybelle Murphy had done. She'd had the decency to wait until her children were grown up and Evelyn was happily married, but it was still a scandalous thing to have done.

And then to have lived in sin with a man after she'd absconded from New York . . . Well, Georgina would never, in her wildest imaginings, have suspected such a thing happening in her own family. She'd always been told that Grandmother Murphy had moved to New Mexico Territory after her husband died. But she hadn't. Not by a far sight. She'd left him. Bolted. Taken it on the lam. Moved out. Run away from home, as it were.

Georgina had always enjoyed her grandmother's letters from the territory. As they were peppered with references to rattlesnakes, horned toads, tarantulas, saloons, cowboys, bandits, Indians, and tobacco spit, perhaps Georgina should have suspected something amiss with Maybelle. But she hadn't. How could she have? Her own *grandmother*, for heaven's sake.

Vernice tutted. "It was a pure scandal, I fear. Even out here, where life is much too loose to begin with, it was considered shocking that they never married."

"Have you lived with her ever since she moved to the territory?" Georgina had never wondered before, but she did now. Perhaps Maybelle hadn't abandoned her family entirely.

Perhaps she'd—Vernice burst her bubble of hope at once.

"Oh, no. I only moved out here ten years ago. For my health." She patted her chest. "It's the dry air. It does one such good if one has a tendency toward lung complaints."

"Yes. I've heard as much."

"Mother didn't want me to come." Vernice's lips pinched together. "I didn't know why until I got off the train."

"Mercy."

"Oh, she was nice enough to me once I was here and there was no getting away from it. I was the first member of the family who really knew what was going on—about Mr. O'Rourke, I mean. She swore me to secrecy, but news leaked out. It has a habit of doing that." Vernice sighed forlornly.

"My goodness."

Georgina had to screw up her courage to ask something she'd been too timid to ask her parents. But Vernice was so kind and seemed willing to unburden herself. She blurted it out at last. "Why didn't they ever marry?"

"I don't know, dear." Vernice shook her head and looked very sad. "I know Mr. O'Rourke asked her once or twice, but Mother never accepted his proposals."

Such a scenario didn't sound right to Georgina, who had always assumed women wanted and needed to be married if they expected to get anywhere in life. What else could a woman do, after all? It's not as if there were worlds open to women on their own. And, according to popular logic, women didn't possess the mental faculties of men and, therefore, couldn't be relied upon to take care of themselves.

Georgina had never felt the need to question popular logic. Not that she had ever been or wanted to be on her own, but, well, she didn't understand her grandmother's refusal to accept the hand of a man with whom she lived, anyway. "But why didn't she? I mean, they must have"—she shrugged, not quite knowing what to say—"cared for each other."

"Oh, yes. But when they first moved out here, you know, your grandfather Murphy was still alive. Mother said she considered—" Vernice broke off suddenly and turned bright red. "Oh, dear."

Fascinated by these confidences, Georgina urged her on. "She said she considered what?"

"Oh, it's too shocking to say—I really shouldn't—it's not

to be spoken of—I mean, I shouldn't—and to a young, un-married lady,'' Vernice stuttered, her voice muffled by cha-grin.

''Nonsense.'' Georgina did her best to sound bracing and worldly. She was dying to hear the worst. ''I need to know, Aunt Vernice. How else will I be able to help?'' That didn't make sense even to her, but she hoped Vernice was too agi-tated to notice.

Evidently she was. Vernice took a deep breath. ''She told him she considered fornication less of a sin than divorce,'' she blurted out quickly, as if she couldn't get the words out fast enough.

''Oh.'' Actually, that made sense to Georgina. In a way. After all, Maybelle was an Irish Catholic. Georgina's mother had been a Catholic until she'd married George Witherspoon. She'd then turned to the Episcopal Church, the church in which Georgina had been reared.

Catholics weren't even allowed to obtain divorces, were they? Wouldn't they be excommunicated if they divorced? Georgina knew very little about the church of her grand-mother, but she understood not wanting to be banished from it.

''But what about after Grandfather Murphy died? Why didn't she marry Mr. O'Rourke then?''

''I don't know, dear. She's always been as stubborn as a mule. I suppose he didn't ask her in the correct tone of voice or something.'' Vernice put a hand on Georgina's sleeve and spoke confidingly. ''Your grandmother is a very strong-willed woman, dear. She has awfully peculiar ideas about some things, as well.''

''Yes. She must.''

The two women snapped beans in silence. Georgina's brow furrowed as she ruminated over all the things she'd seen and heard since Vernice's letter had arrived in New York City a little over two months ago.

After some time, she said, ''But about that ghost. Er, does Grandmother honestly believe it exists?''

''Goodness, yes. Why, he's a perfect pest.''

''Oh.'' That seemed to settle the matter, at least for the time being. Since Georgina didn't believe in ghosts, it still left open the question of lunacy. She guessed she'd simply have to wait and watch.

If things got too outrageous, she supposed she could always go home again, but she didn't want to. What was there for her in New York, after all? The same stuffy society she'd been born into twenty-three years ago. The same parties. The same people.

Henry Spurling. Georgina's nose wrinkled in distaste.

Now why, she wondered, should the thought of Henry make her feel sick to her stomach? She didn't understand it, but she aimed to hang around Picacho Wells until she figured it all out.

"Vernice, don't you and that silly girl have supper ready yet?"

Maybelle Murphy's voice grated like a rasp. Georgina and Vernice exchanged a glance. Vernice looked chagrined. Georgina, her heart filled with sudden affection and sympathy for this aunt of hers who was clearly faltering under the heavy burdens of her life, grinned at her. After blinking for a moment, Vernice grinned back.

Georgina whispered, "Don't let her upset you, Aunt Vernice. We're in this together now. You have an ally at last." She even managed a wink.

She called out to her grandmother, "Supper will be ready in a little while. Aunt Vernice and I are doing our best."

"Humph. Your best doesn't seem to be any too good."

"Then you'll have to put up with it until you can get around on your own." Georgina kept her tone light to rob the words of any sting. After all, crazy or not, obstreperous or not, Maybelle Murphy was her grandmother and, as such, if for no other reason—and Georgina couldn't think of one offhand—she deserved Georgina's respect.

"Humph. You're a sassy bit of goods, aren't you?" Maybelle didn't sound at all distressed by Georgina's sassiness. In fact, Georgina thought she detected a note of approval in the querulous old voice.

"I certainly am," Georgina agreed cheerfully.

Vernice giggled. "Oh, I'm *so* glad you're here, Georgina!"

"So am I."

She meant it, too. With, perhaps, one or two qualifications.

Chapter Three

Ash Barrett told himself the only reason he was riding out to the Murphy place was to check on Vernice Murphy. The poor woman had her hands full, what with that crazy mother to contend with and the added responsibility of a worthless city girl to take care of. Getting in the way. Whining and complaining. Demanding things.

The fact that the worthless city girl had shiny, wheat-colored hair, bright blue eyes, and skin like a porcelain rose didn't mean a thing. Nor did her shapely body. Hell, those were only trappings. Ash knew good and well a female's appearance didn't count for a hill of beans in the overall scheme of things.

In fact, pretty trappings generally meant there was something rotten at the core. Hadn't Phoebe demonstrated that fact to him years ago, beyond the shadow of any doubt? Yes, she had, and Ash didn't intend to forget it.

Besides, Georgina Witherspoon's nose was too small, her ears stuck out too far, and she wasn't tall enough for him. She wasn't perfect. Not at all.

Ash didn't like it that her imperfections failed to overpower her other attributes. Nor did he like it that he felt the tiniest— only the very slightest—smidgen of a proprietary interest in her. He tried reasoning away his interest as merely the result of his being the one sent to meet her train. If someone else had done it, Ash wouldn't be thinking about her at all this morning. He wouldn't have to. But he was the sheriff of Picacho Wells, after all. He reckoned it was his duty to look out for folks. Especially folks who couldn't look after themselves, and Georgina Witherspoon fit that bill to a T.

Anyhow, all that was beside the point. Ash had met pretty females before. Females no longer had the power to affect him in any way whatsoever. When he had certain needs, as all men did, the girls at the Turquoise Bracelet Saloon filled them admirably. He didn't want or need a woman of his own. He'd made that mistake once. In fact, the notion of marriage made him shudder as he guided Shiloh, his saddle horse, down the road from his home to the Murphy place.

Ash lived a little ways outside of town, on a small ranch which he operated when his duties as sheriff let him, which was most of the time. Picacho Wells wasn't a hotbed of nefarious activity. Yesterday's bank robbery had been a weird anomaly. Ash chalked it up to the full moon. All sorts of strange things happened during a full moon.

In fact, he realized, the full moon undoubtedly accounted for the marginal, almost minuscule, bit of interest he felt in Georgina Witherspoon.

The day was just about as perfect as spring days got in these parts. The wind was blowing, of course. The wind always blew. But it was almost gentle this morning. In the afternoon, around four o'clock, it would probably whip up into a frenzy.

The plains didn't look as dry and brown as they generally did because it had rained a week ago—a torrential downpour that had flooded many of the buildings in Picacho Wells. Spring floods were only natural and normal, however, and nobody much cared. They just shoveled out the mud and went on with their lives. Floods were as much a part of life out here as droughts were. Odd country, this. Ash loved it.

Originally from Galveston, Texas, he appreciated the lack of humidity in these parts. When it rained, it rained, but the moisture didn't stick around in the air to glue a man's shirt to his back and smother him when he tried to breathe.

Not that Ash didn't appreciate Galveston. That's where his money was, in his uncle's cotton brokerage business, and it was multiplying like bunny rabbits. Ash was, by anyone's estimation, a solidly wealthy man today. He supposed he could have retired, but he didn't want to. Hell, he was only thirty-three. Nobody retired at thirty-three. And what would he do if he couldn't be sheriff? Sit home all day and count his money? That wasn't his idea of a fulfilling life. Besides, he loved his job.

The plains were level and bare in these parts, covered by scrub grass and creosote bushes. There were a few rises here and there, but not many. Mostly the landscape was flat.

Folks had been planting trees in the area for a couple of decades, though, and civilization was taking a tenuous hold on the land. As he neared the Murphy place, Ash noted with approval the rows of fruit trees Devlin and Maybelle had planted. There were plums, peaches, and apricots coming into season now, and in the fall there would be plenty of apples and pears. Maybelle's peach preserves were the talk of the Picacho Wells Fall Fair. This autumn's fair would be the fifth annual. Picacho Wells was indeed growing by leaps and bounds. By God, there were upwards of a thousand people living in and around it now.

Ash smiled as he rode. Maybelle was probably sitting in that wheelchair of hers, slicing fruit for preserves and scolding Vernice, right this minute. He wondered if she'd managed to rope Miss Witherspoon into helping her. He doubted it. Hell, the girl would probably cut off a finger if she were made to handle a knife.

Pecan trees lined the drive of the Murphy place from the gate to the yard. That was another thing, Ash thought with another smile—anticipatory this time, and with a rumble in his belly—Miss Maybelle's pecan pies were about the tastiest he'd ever eaten. He hoped she'd make a bunch of them come fall. He'd buy as many as she wanted to sell him.

He almost fell from his horse when the porch of the Murphy house came into view through the pecan branches and he caught sight of Georgina Witherspoon. She sat on the porch and sweat beaded her forehead. Ash couldn't believe his eyes. He even rubbed them to make sure he wasn't seeing things.

No, by God, he wasn't. There she was, thumping away at the butter churn as if she'd done such chores all her life. Ash reined in Shiloh behind a bushy pecan tree loaded with fuzzy catkins, and watched.

He was certainly wrong about one thing. She hadn't churned

butter before. He ought to have known better. He grinned, pleased that his initial impression of her as a no-account city girl was right after all. She was useless. Laughable. As out of place here as a flower in a pigpen.

Folding his hands over his saddle horn, he watched, intrigued, as Miss Witherspoon tried to make herself useful. He counted. Thirty-seven nominally vigorous thumps of the dasher. A pause to wipe sweat from her brow. Twenty-one somewhat less vigorous thumps. A pause to turn the dasher to feel if the butter had come. Doubt. Another pause to lift the lid and peer inside. Disappointment. A huge sigh. Twenty-nine energetic thumps. Pause to catch breath. Seventeen more thumps. Pause.

She turned to look at the door of the house. "Aunt Vernice?"

"Yes, dear."

"Um, how long does it usually take for the cream to turn into butter?"

Ash grinned. She wasn't whining about it; he'd give her that much.

"Several minutes, dear. I know it's difficult work. Would you like me to take over for you? You can help your grandmother slice peaches."

Ash heard a cackle from inside the house, and a series of unintelligible words uttered in a scathing, rasping tone. Evidently Maybelle expected Georgina to accept Vernice's offer. She and Ash obviously shared the same opinion of Miss Witherspoon.

Georgina's spine stiffened. A look of defiance crossed her face. Her chin lifted. She resumed churning butter with a vengeance. "Oh, no. I'll keep going. I know I'll get the hang of this with time."

Vernice appeared at the front door, wiping her hands on a towel. "Are you sure, dear? I know you aren't used to doing these kinds of things. Unfortunately, we have to do our own chores out here. Even if we could afford them, there aren't enough spare people to do the work that servants do back in New York. I do miss that about New York." Vernice sounded wistful.

"Of course, you don't have servants." Georgina, on the other hand, sounded firm and resolute and even cheerful, if slightly breathless. "It's only us pampered city people who have servants."

She laughed, a light, happy, self-deprecating laugh that entered Ash's ears and slithered around in his body until he was warm all over. Vernice laughed with her. Vernice's laugh didn't do a thing to him; it only sounded like a laugh. Ash didn't like these symptoms; they made him uneasy. He tore his mind away from contemplating his reaction to various women's laughs and watched some more.

The churning didn't abate. By God, she was going to do it. Ash felt a lick of appreciation. Her arms must be about falling out of their sockets by this time. Churning butter wasn't something one could do in one's sleep. It took strength, endurance, and energy. And callused hands. Ash looked closely when Georgina released the dasher with her right hand—she kept churning with her left, albeit more slowly—and eyed her palm. Blisters. Ash would bet money on it.

That was enough for him. His compassionate impulses, usually reserved for people he respected, smacked him in the conscience, and he rode Shiloh out from behind the pecan tree and up to the porch. Georgina heard him and looked up from her churning—surprised, Ash presumed, that anyone should be calling on the Murphys this morning. When she realized who the visitor was, she frowned, although she didn't stop churning.

"Need some help, Miss Witherspoon?" He tried very hard to sound polite, but he knew he'd phrased his question wrong as soon as she narrowed her eyes.

"I should say not. I'm perfectly capable of churning butter, thank you very much."

Her attitude irritated him. Hell, he was trying to be nice, was all. He swung himself out of the saddle. "That so? And exactly how many crocks of butter have you churned in your life, anyway?"

A pause. A frown. "Not that it's any of your business—this is the first." Grudging. Her admission came out about as grudging as any Ash had ever heard and, as an elected sheriff in a wild territory, he'd heard plenty of them.

"You're going to tear the hell out of your hands."

"Thank you for your concern." She spoke through her gnashing teeth. "I can do my own work."

"You won't be good for anything if you get blisters all over your hands."

"I have some lanolin cream in the house. If I get blisters, I shall doctor them myself."

"*If* you get blisters?" Ash couldn't stand it. He knew her hands were already blistered. The notion of her tender skin being damaged did funny things to his innards. He didn't like it, but he wasn't going to fight it. He yanked off his gloves and stuffed them into his waistband. "Here. Give me that dasher."

"I will not!" She hunched over the butter churn as if she were a child protecting a beloved toy.

"Don't be foolish, Miss Witherspoon. If you're trying to be a help to your aunt, you won't do it by injuring yourself."

"Don't you dare call me foolish! Churning butter is a chore any true western woman should be able to do, and I'm going to do it."

Any true western woman? What in the name of gracious was she talking about? Ash marched up the steps and went over to her. "Don't be stupid. Give me that dasher."

"I won't."

"You will."

"I *won't*!"

"Dad-blast it, Miss Witherspoon—"

They were both startled into jumps when the front door swung open suddenly and Vernice rushed out. She was agitated, and Georgina hopped up from her churning stool, thus accomplishing what Ash had been trying to bully her into doing.

Georgina paled and held out a hand to her aunt. "Oh, Aunt Vernice, what is it?"

"Chickens!" Vernice's voice held a note of honest consternation.

Ash understood.

Georgina plainly didn't. "Chickens?" She gazed at her aunt as if she suspected she were as loony as her grandmother.

Ash grabbed the stool before she could regain her composure. "Chickens got out," he explained. "They're probably in the vegetable garden."

"Yes!" Vernice cried. "Yes, they're out there pecking at the bush beans this very minute!"

She raced down the porch steps. Georgina, unsure of herself in this calamity, stared after her. Then she glanced at Ash and glowered down at him. Too bad. He wasn't going to give up either the stool or the dasher to satisfy her misplaced notions of what a western woman should be able to do—whatever in hell that meant.

He glowered back at her. "You'd better help your aunt, Miss Witherspoon. Otherwise, you won't have any beans to preserve for winter."

"Oh." She blinked at him for a moment, as if she thought he might be trying to fool her in order to usurp her butter-churning assignment. Then she turned, held up a hand to shade her eyes, saw Vernice in the garden, noticed the chickens pecking away, and rushed down the porch steps to help rescue the beans.

Ash shook his head. This should be a show. If she couldn't even churn butter, he'd like to know what the hell she thought she could do to get a chicken away from a bean bush.

Georgina wasn't sure she should have relinquished the butter churn without more of a fight. Yet Aunt Vernice needed her. Blast that Ashley Barrett. If he hadn't come along, she could have helped her aunt and then finished making the butter.

As she ran toward the vegetable garden, she glanced at her hands. What a mess. Well, that was neither here nor there. She was going to conquer these new aspects of her life or die trying.

"Oh, help me get them, dear. Please! They're going to make such a mess of things."

"Of course," Georgina said, feeling game. She could catch a chicken. She knew she could. She made a swipe for one and it danced away, clucking up a storm. Blast. She didn't know chickens could move so fast. She reached for it again and got it without dislodging more than a few feathers. Her feeling of satisfaction lasted long enough for her to carry the chicken away from the garden and put it down. It headed right back to the bean bushes. Fiddlesticks.

"You have to put them to sleep, dear," Vernice told her. "Then they'll stay put while you gather the rest of them."

"Put them to sleep?" Georgina hadn't felt this ignorant since she was in grade school.

"Yes. Here, I'll show you."

Georgina watched, fascinated, as Vernice stalked a Rhode Island Red hen—Georgina knew it was a Rhode Island red because Vernice had shown her the differences between the buff orpingtons, Rhode Island reds, and white leghorns. She swept it up, quickly tucked its head under its wing, held it out in front of her and then, very slowly, circled her arms. Good heavens, did that put a chicken to sleep?

Evidently it did. Either that, or the circling motion made it so sick to its stomach it couldn't move. Whatever sensation prevailed in its chickenish body, when Vernice set it down outside the garden, it stayed there, its head tucked beneath its wing, and gave every indication of being asleep.

"My goodness." Georgina was terribly impressed.

Eager to practice this new and unusual skill, she tiptoed up on a buff orpington pecking like mad at a bean plant. "Oh, no, you don't," she muttered, and swooped. The chicken gave a big cluck as she lifted it, and pecked at her wrist. The sharp, pointy beak hurt, but Georgina remained undaunted. Doing her best to imitate her aunt, she tried to jam the chicken's head under its wing. It didn't want to go, so she forced it. She heard a snap. The chicken went limp.

"Oh, no!" She stared, horrified, at the dead chicken in her hands.

"That's all right, dear. We needed a chicken for dinner. In fact, I'll kill another one right now, and then we won't have to do it later."

And with that, Vernice yanked a white leghorn up by its head, gave it one swift swing, and broke its neck. Georgina swallowed. Mercy sakes, but life on a farm could be a violent affair without half trying, couldn't it? She'd had no idea.

She laid her dead chicken down next to the one Vernice had killed, and went back to stalking the rest of the bean peckers. It wasn't long before she had the hang of it. What you needed to do was be soft and gentle with them. Until it came to breaking their necks on purpose, of course. Georgina shivered, and despised herself for it.

After the last chicken had been put to sleep, she and Vernice carried them back to the chicken coop, as easy as you please. Georgina felt an odd sensation of victory. It might not be much, but by gracious, she'd been of assistance. She'd conquered the pecking chicken—and, what's more, she'd learned two new skills. She could now put a chicken to sleep, either temporarily or forever.

"Oh, I see what happened." Vernice's glum voice interrupted Georgina's thoughts. Her aunt was standing there, her hands on her hips, contemplating the screened-in chicken house.

"You do?" Georgina didn't see a single thing amiss, which figured. All right, so learning to be a true western woman took time.

"Indeed. It looks as though we had a chicken thief last night."

"My goodness." This sounded serious. She wondered if chicken thievery was a misdemeanor crime or if it was considered a felony out here where chickens mattered so much. Sort of like horse theft. "How can you tell?"

"There's a hole in the fence." Vernice pointed.

"Oh, yes. I see it." Georgina was surprised she hadn't noticed the spot where the chicken wire was scrunched up around a big hole earlier. She chalked up her lack of perception to her city upbringing, and renewed her vow to learn the ways of the West.

"I suspect a coyote." Vernice frowned at the hole in the fence.

"You mean a coyote made that hole?" Coyotes didn't have hands, did they? How could a coyote make a hole like that?

"They're devilish creatures, coyotes. Completely awful pests."

"Oh."

"I'll fix that fence for you, Miss Vernice."

Georgina whirled around when the deep, drawly voice came at her back. Ashley Barrett stood there, gazing at the hole, his hands stuffed into his back pockets. He didn't seem as tall this morning. Georgina wondered what that meant. Nothing good, she was sure.

She sniffed. "I'll get back to churning the butter." She turned to walk back to the porch.

"No need." Ash sounded smug.

Georgina frowned at him. "Why not?"

"It's all finished."

Drat the man. It couldn't have taken him more than a minute

or two to finish the job she'd ruined her hands over. Georgina sniffed again. "I'll take the butter into Grandmother then," she said, and left Vernice and Ash Barrett in the chicken coop. Which is exactly where he belonged.

The butter crock was as heavy as lead. Georgina hefted it and staggered to the door, only to realize she should have propped the door open first. Compressing her lips, she told herself not to be discouraged. She'd get the hang of this. It only took time, patience, and practice. She set the churn down with a grunt and a clunk.

"Here, let me do that for you."

It was Ash Barrett, who must have flown from the chicken house to the porch. "I thought you were mending the fence." It wasn't gracious, but Georgina didn't feel any too gracious at the moment. She was exhausted, out of breath, her arms ached, her hands were blistered, and she disliked this man.

He smirked at her. "Got to get some tools from inside the house."

"Oh." Because she didn't want him to know how much he disconcerted her, Georgina ground out a testy, "Thank you."

He picked up the butter churn as if it weighed no more than a bit of fluff. "My pleasure." He gave her a smile she knew was meant to annoy her.

It succeeded. Georgina pushed the door open and stood aside, wishing she could kick Mr. High-and-Mighty Ashley Barrett in his extremely well-shaped rear end as he passed.

She also wished she hadn't noticed his rear end. But honestly, how could she help but notice? Gentlemen in New York never wore their trousers tight like that. Georgina did not condone the wearing of such trousers. They were immodest and distracting.

On the other hand, as she'd had cause to note before, Ashley Barrett was no gentleman. She felt minimally better after she'd cleared up that point in her head.

She heard her grandmother's grating cackle before she reached the kitchen.

"Ha! Did that granddaughter of mine give up and make you finish churning the butter, Ash?"

Then she laughed, sounding exactly like Georgina expected a dozen witches might sound if they were all cackling together. Georgina, who had been taught as a very young girl that it was impolite to flounce, flounced into the kitchen and glowered at her grandmother. "I did not give up!"

Ash set the churn down on the big kitchen table and turned to grin at her. Maybelle looked up from her peaches. She grinned as well. Georgina felt silly. "Well, I didn't. I left off churning butter to help Aunt Vernice get the chickens out of the garden."

"That's true, Miss Maybelle. She didn't give up. Not without a fight." He removed his hat, plucked a bandanna out of his back pocket, and wiped his brow.

Georgina was pleased to see this evidence of his humanity. The butter churn clearly did not weigh as little as he'd led her to believe, the deceitful wretch.

Thank goodness. That meant Georgina wasn't as weak as she'd feared she was.

"And I only killed one of the chickens by accident in the process."

Ash Barrett stared at her. A grim sense of satisfaction filled Georgina. He hadn't expected her to admit to the homicide, had he? He'd been planning to tell her grandmother himself, and watch Georgina squirm. Well, he'd learn how wrong he was about her.

She continued, with vigor, "Which was perfectly all right, as we were going to kill two chickens for supper anyway. And Aunt Vernice taught me the proper way to wring a chicken's neck." She refused to allow her internal shudder to show, and was proud of herself.

The sheriff nodded slowly. "That's the truth, Miss Maybelle. She was putting those chickens to sleep as if she'd been doing it all her life after the first couple."

Triumph surged in Georgina's breast. She turned around and headed for the pump at the sink so he wouldn't see it.

"I'm glad the girl has some backbone to her." Maybelle's small black bird-of-prey eyes glittered. "I didn't expect it."

Georgina tried not to resent her. "I aim to be of help to you and Aunt Vernice, Grandmother."

Ash knew it was unreasonable, but he felt a touch of pride in Miss Prissy Witherspoon. Her voice held a whole lot of spirit, considering it was her own grandmother who was treating her like rubbish. Maybe he'd underestimated her. Probably not.

"And I *won't*," Georgina continued, "be intimidated by *you*." As she passed, she poked Maybelle in the upper arm with a blistered finger, astonishing Ash, who wouldn't have pegged her for possessing such humor, persistence, or pluck in so trying a situation.

The old lady cackled again, as if she were pleased with her granddaughter's spunk.

"And now I have to wash my hands and get some lanolin on my blisters. There's lots of work yet to do, and I'm going to do my share." She shot a mean look at Ash. "No matter what *some* people might want to believe of me."

Maybelle Murphy chortled again.

He had to hand it to her. As strange as it seemed—and it seemed exceedingly strange—Miss Georgina Witherspoon, from New York City, was winning Maybelle over to her side.

The sheriff stayed for supper. After he mended the chicken-house fence, he fixed a board on the porch that had started to sag; poured kerosene on a nest of yellow jackets, and set fire to it in order to get rid of the pests; shored up the pigpen where the pigs had loosened a couple of nails by butting against it; and fashioned a screen door out of some old chicken wire and lumber that Devlin had left in the barn.

It had been a productive day, and supper was delicious. Fried chicken, biscuits, and peach pie. Miss Georgina Witherspoon rolled out the crust herself, and it wasn't very tough at all. She said with a laugh that she'd get the hang of piecrusts one of these days, and Ash actually believed her, even though he didn't want to.

In fact, he was impressed. He rode home after dark, his way lit by the full moon, his belly full of good food, and his ideas about city girls having suffered a severe setback.

Georgina's hands hurt so much she could scarcely braid her hair for bed. They were blistered beyond repair, although the lanolin ointment Vernice had given her seemed to help some. She tied clean rags around them so the lanolin wouldn't get on the sheets and into her hair and make everything all greasy.

After she got her hair braided—into one braid tonight, as she couldn't bear to fuss with it long enough to make two—she sat on the edge of her bed, sighed deeply, and took stock of her day. She was purely exhausted, but she'd comported herself with good sense and fortitude, which was something she could be proud of.

"It's a hard life," she muttered at the candle flickering in its holder on the bedside table. Accustomed as she was to living with electric lights in her parents' New York home, having to rely on candles for light was a new and interesting experience for her. She hoped she wouldn't spill wax or set anything on fire.

Wondering if she had energy enough to pull back the quilt and crawl under the covers, she murmured, "I'm not really surprised to find that hardship has turned Grandmother Murphy into a mean old crone."

"Ah, child, she's not a mean old crone. Not a bit of it."

Georgina gasped and jumped up from her bed. A man! There was a man in her room!

Ashley Barrett. She knew it was he, even though it didn't sound like him. He was using a ruse, disguising his voice. The bounder! The cad! The filthy, disgusting reprobate! Georgina snatched up her hairbrush and wielded it like a bat, darting her gaze around the room in a frenzy of discomposure.

"Go away!" She squinted into the dark corners of her room and didn't see a thing. Where could he be hiding? Oh, *why* hadn't electricity come to the territory yet?

Under the bed! Quick as a wink, Georgina fell to her knees, every muscle in her body protesting, and pulled up the counterpane. It was dark as a pit under there.

Nothing was there, not even a dust ball. She jumped to her feet again and looked around wildly. "Where are you? Who are you?"

"Child, child, 'tis only me, Devlin O'Rourke, come to meet you. You're a pretty thing, you are. The spit of your darlin' grandmother when she was a girl, except you've not got her wild red Irish hair."

Georgina's mouth fell open. She sank onto her bed and stared, appalled, as a medium-sized, elderly, extremely handsome, gray-haired man with a bushy gray mustache materialized in front of her eyes.

Chapter Four

Not ten minutes later, Georgina was kneeling on her aunt's bedroom floor, weeping into Vernice's lap while Vernice stroked her hair and made soothing noises.

"It's all right, Georgina. Truly, it is. There's nothing amiss."

"Nothing *amiss*?" Georgina lifted her head and stared at her aunt's placid face, wobbly now through the film of Georgina's tears. "But I saw a *ghost*!"

"Of course you did, dear. It's all right."

"Oh, Aunt Vernice, I know you're trying to be kind, but it's too awful! I saw a *ghost*! Ghosts don't exist! I must be crazy! Just like Grandmother! Oh, whatever will my poor, poor parents say? What will they *do*?" She buried her face in Vernice's bathrobe again. "To think I came all this way to be of help to you, and no sooner do I get here than I succumb to the family curse, too. Oh, oh, oh!"

Vernice tutted. "Now, now, Georgina. You're just a bit overwrought. Mr. O'Rourke is like that. He had no right to spring himself on you so suddenly."

Georgina jerked her head up again. Vernice didn't sound at all the way Georgina thought a proper aunt should sound when learning of her only niece's incipient lunacy. She wiped the back of her hand—her scratched hand—across her cheek. The salt stung the wound, and Georgina frowned at it. Good Lord. Mad grandmothers, mad cats, and now a mad her. Maybe there was something in the water. "What—what do you mean?"

"You're not crazy, dear. I know it's disconcerting at first, but there's nothing innately insane about seeing Mr. O'Rourke. My goodness gracious, I see him all the time, and *I'm* certainly not a lunatic."

Georgina sprang to her feet. Oh, no, Aunt Vernice was crazy, too! She'd suspected it when Vernice had first chatted with her about the ghost in such an ordinary way. Georgina wasn't sure she could bear it. "You—you mean you see him, too?"

"Of course I do." Vernice laughed gaily. "It's very annoying, but there you go. At first I believed Mother was mad, just as you did. Then, after I met Mr. O'Rourke's ghost, I understood that she's merely angry with him for haunting her the way he's been doing. It's disconcerting, always having a ghost popping up at inopportune times."

"Oh." Georgina backed away from Vernice. Thus far, Vernice didn't seem to possess her grandmother's violent tendencies, but Georgina didn't aim to take any chances. Crazy people could be unpredictable. At least, she'd always *read* that they could be.

Oh, Lord, did that mean *she* was going to be unpredictable? Was *she*, Georgina Marie Witherspoon, going to start throwing shoes at people? The notion was too much for her. She collapsed into Vernice's rocking chair with a low moan and covered her face with her hands, shaking her head and wishing she'd never boarded that train at Grand Central Station. It had seemed like such a good idea at the time. An adventure and all that.

Some kind of an adventure this was. Seeing ghosts. Going crazy. "Oh, dear heavens."

"Don't carry on so, dear; although I do know how you feel. I felt the same way the first time I saw him. I nearly fainted dead away. He's a terrible fellow to go about frightening gently bred females the way he does."

"*Well, I certainly don't mean to frighten anyone,*" a lilting Irish-accented voice said.

Georgina gasped and jerked forward in the rocking chair, almost toppling it over on its runners.

"Mr. O'Rourke." Vernice's voice was more severe than Georgina had thus far heard it. "Do you see what you've done to our dear Georgina here? You had no business appearing to her without warning and terrifying her this way."

Georgina groaned. There he was. All five feet, eight inches of him: handsome, mustachioed, gray-haired, dapper—and transparent. She shut her eyes, but felt even more uncomfortable not being able to see him than she did when she had been, so she opened them and groaned again. "I don't believe in you."

"Fine, but you'd better get used to me, dearie, because I don't intend to go away until your grandmother comes to her senses. This was my home for twenty-five years, love, and I can't abandon it until I know your grandmother is over being mad at me. I can't go to my eternal rest while she bears me a grudge."

Georgina didn't understand and she was too overwhelmed to ask for enlightenment.

Vernice evidently did understand and didn't need enlightenment. "We've been through this before, Mr. O'Rourke. I have no influence over my mother. You know that. I never have had any influence over her. No one has. She's an independent woman, always has been, always will be, and there's no way our dear Georgina or I can alter her feelings about you an iota. You have no cause to haunt Georgina or me. Your quarrel is with Mother, and you should keep it there."

"Tut, the lass could help me if she wanted to."

Vernice shook her head. "Nonsense. Mother's angry with you for dying, and for doing so without clearing up matters with her."

"What matters? Exactly what matters need to be cleared up?"

Devlin sounded as frustrated as if he'd been a living man. Georgina considered this a bad sign, both because she was hearing a ghost, and because she'd always assumed before now that one's problems vanished when one's life was extinguished.

Good heavens, she was behaving as if she actually believed this was happening.

She shook her head, hard, and blinked at the two of them. It was difficult to get away from it: There they were, a real human being and a product of her fevered imagination, chatting together as if they both truly existed. She whispered, "Go away," hoping in that way to dissipate the image of Devlin O'Rourke, but her words did no good. Rather, they drew his attention away from Vernice and to her. She wished she'd kept her big mouth shut.

"I don't aim to go away, child, until that grandmother of yours comes to her senses," the figment of her imagination said, as if he were actually responding to her words, which he couldn't possibly be, because he didn't exist. Georgina wished she'd wake up soon. This was the worst nightmare she'd ever had.

"It's like this, dearie," the figment said, coming—wafting, actually—closer to Georgina. She drew back in the rocking chair and wished it didn't have rockers; she felt awfully precarious.

"Your grandmother and I loved each other for years and years. We lived together like man and wife for more years than she was married to that miserable old coot, Frederick Murphy."

"Miserable old coot? Grandfather?" Georgina couldn't believe her ears. Why, Grandfather Murphy had been a wonderful man and a pillar of society, hadn't he? She didn't actually remember him, since he'd died when she was barely two, but she'd heard only good things about him.

"Aye. Your grandfather." Devlin O'Rourke shook his ghostly head, creating a blur that made Georgina blink and shake her own head. *"He was a stinker, Frederick. As stuffy as a Christmas goose, he was. No sort of fellow for a free-spirited darling like my Maybelle to have married. But her family forced her into it, you see. She and I wanted to marry way back then, but they wouldn't let us. They thought I was a wastrel."*

"Oh." Georgina stared at him, almost wanting him to be real. This conversation was so interesting. "And you weren't? A wastrel, I mean."

Devlin snorted. It was a rather explosive snort, and it made Georgina give a start. *"A wastrel? I should say not. Why, I'm as good an Irish lad as ever was."*

Which, according to all the tales Georgina had heard about

the Irish, didn't necessarily negate his standing as a wastrel. She didn't mention it.

"As good a lying, good-for-nothing bastard as ever was, you mean!"

Georgina uttered a sharp scream and stood up so fast the chair skidded back, bumped into the wall, and commenced rocking wildly. When she whirled around to see from whence that strident declaration had come, she saw her grandmother, leaning heavily on a cane, standing in Vernice's doorway. She was also scowling for all she was worth at Devlin O'Rourke.

"Grandmother Murphy!" Georgina's voice had been rattled into a whisper.

"Yes, I'm Grandmother Murphy," Maybelle said, her voice hard as rocks. "*Murphy* is the right word. I'm *not* Grandmother O'Rourke, and never have been."

"'Tisn't my fault," cried Devlin. "'Tis your own stubbornness that kept you a Murphy instead of an O'Rourke, Maybelle, and you know it!"

"I *don't* know it!" And with that, Maybelle snatched a pretty ceramic pomander from the dressing table at her side and flung it at Devlin O'Rourke.

"No!" Vernice, who had been silent during the past few minutes, leaped from her bed and made a wild grab for the pomander. "Don't break that!"

The pomander flew right through Devlin O'Rourke's transparent body and hit the wall with a loud bang before it fell to the floor. Vernice scrambled for it as it rolled under the bed, picked it up, eyed it with concern, sighed with relief, and hugged it to her meager bosom. "That was a gift from my father, and I'll thank you to treat it with respect!"

"Your father!" If Maybelle could sound any more contemptuous, Georgina hoped never to hear her. "That fussy old fiddlestick!"

"Don't you dare say such things about him!" Vernice cried. "He was my father, whatever you think of him! At least he didn't run out on his children!"

Shocked by this show of defiance in the aunt whom she'd begun to consider rather shy and retiring, Georgina pressed a hand to her cheek and sank back into the rocking chair. She hated listening to heated disputes. Her parents had always argued behind closed doors, and for the first time Georgina re-

alized how right they'd been to do so. It was upsetting to hear
people rip into each other the way Grandmother Murphy,
Vernice, and Mr. O'Rourke were doing.

"I didn't run out on you!" Maybelle glowered at Vernice
for a moment before honesty got the better of her, and her
gaze slid sideways. "At least I waited until you were grown
up and on your own before I took off," she amended, not
quite as defiantly.

"That may be, but you still have no right to disparage my
father," Vernice said stoutly. "He might not have been intem-
perate enough to suit *your* unbridled passions, and *you* might
have considered him too straight-laced, but he was a kind,
patient, and generous man. Plus, he wasn't plagued by wan-
derlust, the way *some* people were."

Maybelle shrugged. "Oh, very well. I'll give him that. He
was nice enough."

Vernice sniffed. "And he was stable."

"I'll say he was." It didn't sound to Georgina as if her
grandmother considered her late husband's stability to be anything in his favor.

Devlin snorted. Vernice turned on him with a vengeance.
"Don't you dare say another thing, Mr. O'Rourke. You just
keep your mouth shut. *You* aren't my father! *You* aren't even
my *step*father! You have no right to disparage him. No right
at all. My mother never married you because—because—because—I don't know why, but she didn't. So there!" Vernice
flounced over to the dresser, placed the pomander back on its
doily with reverence, and scowled at her mother and her
mother's dead lover's ghost.

"I wanted her to marry me," Devlin grumbled. *"The good
Lord knows, I asked her often enough."*

"Ha! You silver-tongued devil, you! You never once asked
me and meant it. I know it, and you know it. I wasn't about
to marry a man for whom marriage to me would be, at best,
a perfunctory duty!"

"It would not!" Devlin's mustache bristled with indignation.

"It would, too!" Maybelle shouted, bristling in her own
right.

"Oh, no, you don't." Vernice, stormed over to the door and
took her mother's arm. "You're not going to have another

argument in my bedroom. I need my sleep, and I won't have you flinging my personal belongings around. If you want to fling something, use your own things. And if you want to carry this argument on in your own room, please have the decency not to shout at each other. Georgina and I would actually like to get some sleep tonight.''

Maybelle didn't bother to answer, from which Georgina deduced that she didn't much care what Georgina thought of them all. Oh, dear. This was so upsetting.

"I don't want to fight." Devlin sounded miserable. *"What I want is your mother to stop being angry with me."*

"Ha! You'll have yourself a damned long wait if that's what you want." Maybelle didn't sound at all miserable. She sounded hot enough to catch fire. She also sounded as though she, unlike her daughter and granddaughter, relished a good fight.

"Come along, Mother. I'll help you back to your room. You shouldn't be trying to walk on that ankle."

"Oh, bother my ankle!" Maybelle sounded extremely peevish.

Georgina watched as Vernice helped her through the door. She still sat in the rocking chair, her hands folded in her lap, because she was too overwhelmed to move. Then she recalled Mr. O'Rourke and, hoping against hope that he'd left the room with her grandmother, she slowly turned her head to look where he'd been. Where he still was, rather.

Botheration. Georgina sighed, discouraged.

Devlin eyed her, looking gloomy. *"You've not lost your mind, child. I'm a ghost, and you're seeing me, but I won't hurt you. I expect 'tis disconcerting to encounter your first ghost, but it's your grandmother's fault, not mine."*

Georgina cleared her throat and decided there was no way around it. Perhaps if she spoke to the thing, it would go away. "Is that so?"

"Aye, indeed it is. She won't admit that she loves me, y'see, child, and it's like to drive me wild, here on t'other side. I can't go to my peace without her vow to rest me heart on."

"Er—why not?" If a vow would make him disappear, it might be worth talking to her grandmother about him. If Georgina begged, perhaps Maybelle would give the man a vow of love if only to get rid of him.

"Y'see, dearie, t'would not be heaven unless I knew she'd be joinin' me there when her own time came."

"Oh." Georgina thought about that. The more she thought, the more perplexed she became. And irked. This sounded like a silly argument to her. "What I don't understand—among other things—is how matters should have come to such a pass between the two of you in the first place. I mean, you lived together for twenty-five years, didn't you? I should think that would be plenty long enough for two people to iron out these little difficulties. It sounds like poor planning to me."

Devlin snorted, something he seemed to do quite often, and of which Georgina did not approve. Snorting was common. On the other hand, ghosts weren't. Oh, dear. She pressed a hand to her forehead and wondered if she was becoming feverish.

"You don't know your grandmother, dearie. She likes things done her way. You heard her." Devlin pointed at the door. *"You heard for yourself. You heard her claim I didn't mean it when I asked her to marry me. Now, I ask you, would a man ask a woman to marry him if he didn't mean it?"*

Never having thought about the matter, Georgina couldn't come up with a definitive answer on the spur of the moment. She shook her head and hoped that would suffice.

Devlin watched her for a second, much to her discomposure, then shook his own head. *"Ah, child, you'll never understand. You're too far removed from it all. You're not even Irish any longer."*

He spoke as if not being Irish was worse than having consumption. Georgina didn't know whether to be amused or annoyed. Since she was about as far from laughter as she'd ever been in her life, and about as upset, she opted for annoyance. Surging from the rocking chair, she slammed her hands on her hips and glared at Devlin.

"If you and grandmother are examples of how the Irish behave, I'm glad I'm not! I don't even believe in you, for heaven's sake, I'm not about to sit here while you belittle me."

"Aye, child, I'm not belittlin'—"

Georgina, who had never said a disrespectful word to an older person in her entire life, shouted at him. "I don't care *what* you're doing. You get out of my aunt's room right this minute, whatever or whoever you are! Aunt Vernice doesn't want you here, and neither do I.'' She lifted her right hand and pointed at the door. Her finger didn't even tremble, and she was proud of herself.

With his head bowed and shaking mournfully back and forth, Devlin O'Rourke floated his way to the door. It was queer, being able to see furniture through him. Georgina also found it unsettling, the way his feet didn't quite seem to touch the floor, giving him an odd, wafting gait. On the other hand, he was a figment. She'd never encountered a figment before, so she guessed nothing one of them did should be considered outlandish, since they didn't exist.

Vernice came through the door just as Devlin was exiting, and Georgina stared, agog, as Vernice walked right through him, then stopped and shivered. She looked exasperated as she rubbed her hands up and down her arms.

''Sorry,'' muttered Devlin.

Vernice frowned at him and returned no response. He wafted off down the hall toward Maybelle's door. Vernice let out an aggravated huff. ''I do wish that man would stop popping up where he isn't wanted. And if he *has* to show up, I wish he'd stay in one place and not move about so that I don't walk through him when I least expect it. His essence is freezing cold.''

''It is?''

''It is.'' Vernice stopped rubbing her arms and gazed at Georgina. ''I'm sorry, dear. If I'd known about Mr. O'Rourke's ghost before I wrote to your parents, I probably wouldn't have been so concerned about Mother.''

''You wouldn't?'' Georgina would never be impolite enough to argue with her aunt, but she couldn't see offhand why a ghost should be less of a problem to Vernice than a mad mother.

''Oh, dear, no.'' Vernice walked to her bed, picked up a quilted comforter, and wrapped it around her shoulders. ''Once I realized that Mother wasn't crazy, but only being haunted by that man's ghost, I stopped being so worried about her.''

''Oh.'' That would put a new slant on things, Georgina guessed.

Vernice sank down onto her bed and gazed up at Georgina, her expression guilty. ''I suppose I should have written that you no longer needed to come out here, dear, but I so wanted to meet you. I hope you aren't angry with me.''

''Angry with you? I should say not!'' Georgina plopped herself down on the bed next to Vernice, put her arms around her, and gave her a big hug. She felt suddenly tender toward this dear, maiden aunt who was struggling valiantly against all odds—extremely strange odds, at that—to take care of a mother who didn't want to be taken care of. ''I'm glad I came. I've been wanting an adventure for my whole life.''

Out of nowhere, the absurdity of her situation struck her, and she giggled. ''And if meeting Grandmother Murphy and the ghost of Devlin O'Rourke isn't an adventure, I'd like to know what is.''

Vernice laughed, too, and hugged Georgina back. ''I'm so glad you're able to look at these things in the light of an adventure, Georgina. I'm afraid my sister Evelyn, your dear mother, would faint dead away if she knew what was going on out here.''

Georgina sighed. ''I'm afraid you're right. She almost had a spasm when she had to tell me about Grandmother and Mr. O'Rourke.''

''I'm sure it must have been dreadful for her.'' Vernice stood up, refolded the comforter, and laid it back at the foot of her bed. She was very precise about everything. Georgina admired that quality in her. There was nothing the least bit slapdash about Aunt Vernice.

''Actually, I'd never even thought about it,'' Georgina said after another moment of contemplation. ''I suppose I was too young when Grandfather Murphy died to make anything of the fact that Grandmother didn't live with him. It never even occurred to me to wonder why she should be writing to us from the territory while he lived right there in New York. I was only a little over two when he died, and I really don't remember him at all. I imagine that accounts for it.''

Vernice sighed. ''I suppose so. It was a most unpleasant episode, I can tell you. I was only twenty-three—your age—when Mother left home. Thank heavens Evelyn was already married. She's so sensitive. I lived with your uncle Clarence until I decided to move to the territory to help Mother.''

''It must have been a shock to you.''

''Not really.'' Vernice pinched her lips up so that she appeared considerably puritanical. ''I had an inkling as to what was going on. I thought I might have some influence on Mother. As if such a thing were possible.''

"Yes. I can see that Grandmother is not a woman to be easily influenced.'' Georgina smiled at the notion of anyone or anything influencing Maybelle Murphy.

"You can say that again.''

Georgina stood and cleared her throat. "Er, so . . . well . . .'' She began fingering the fringes on a nearby lampshade as she tried to work up the courage to ask her next question. "I mean . . . well . . .'' She sucked in a deep breath. "Does Devlin O'Rourke's ghost really exist, Aunt Vernice?'' She turned and faced her aunt, ready for the worst. "Does he really? Or are we all lunatics? I understand insanity runs in families. If we're crazy, I think it would be best to face the matter squarely and not try to cover it up or pretend the problem doesn't exist.''

Vernice smiled tenderly at Georgina. "Oh, my dear, of course we're not crazy. I admit there are strange quirks and odd starts in the family—one needs to look no farther than my mother to prove that—but wildness and irresponsibility are a far cry from lunacy. Besides, we're not *all* wild and irresponsible. Why, just look at you. Or me, for that matter.''

Narrowing her eyes and furrowing her brow, Georgina thought about it. She tried to be objective; she didn't want to sugarcoat any lunatic tendencies. She believed such things ought to be faced resolutely and realistically. If the entire Murphy-Witherspoon family had to be locked up in an insane asylum, at least they might be locked up together if they handled the matter properly.

After a few moments of thought, her eyes opened again and her brow unfurrowed. Vernice was right. No matter which angle Georgina looked at the problem from, it didn't add up to insanity. They all functioned too well for that. If they were crazy, they wouldn't be able to get through their normal, everyday activities without someone noticing, would they? And no one had ever cast the slightest aspersion on a Murphy's or a Witherspoon's soundness of mind until now—and it was a Witherspoon doing the casting.

She was still too unsettled to give up the insanity theory altogether, but Georgina did begin to feel the tiniest fragment of relief. "You may be right, Aunt Vernice.''

"Of course, I'm right. You'll realize it soon, Georgina.''

"It's still very difficult to come to terms with having a ghost in the family."

"It is indeed. Especially that one. Although, it's true, he isn't actually a member of the family. Not even by marriage." Vernice sounded grim, then let out a heavy sigh. "I've found the task becomes easier when I pray a lot."

Georgina nodded. She could see the sense in that. One needed to confide one's problems in someone, and God wouldn't have one locked up as a danger to society if one went to him with tales about ghosts and hauntings and so forth. Another, less perfect, person might not show the same tolerance.

"Sunday is only a few days away. Since your grandmother can't get around very well yet, she hasn't been attending church services with me, but I'd be very happy if you'd ride into town with me. I'm in the choir." Vernice blushed charmingly. "I fear we aren't the best choir in the world, but it does lift one's spirits to sing praises to our Lord. We'd be very happy if you'd like to sing with us, dear."

"What a wonderful idea." Georgina was genuinely pleased. "I used to sing in the choir at home—in Grace Church."

Grace Church, a gorgeous structure testifying to the general wealth of New York's Episcopalian community, had been almost a second home to Georgina. She'd taken piano lessons from the organist, sung soprano in the choir, and played piano for Christmas and Easter concerts there. She loved music and perceived Vernice's offer as a wonderful opportunity to lift her spirits.

Georgina's outlook was bright a few days later when she and Vernice set out for the little adobe church in Picacho Wells. Her mood didn't even suffer too much of a setback when they met Ashley Barrett on their way.

"So, you've finagled your niece into going to church with you, eh?"

Ash tipped his hat and winked at Vernice. Georgina was shocked. She considered winking at ladies a practice only indulged in by extremely unrefined rowdies. And the man was supposed to be the upholder of law and order! Well . . . Georgina just didn't know, that was all there was to it.

Vernice didn't seem to mind. In fact, she blushed and giggled. Georgina was sorry to learn that her aunt was susceptible to the charms of a handsome man, particularly since a pretty face was all he was.

"Yes indeed, Sheriff. Georgina is a wonderful musician. Why, she sings and plays and has a lovely voice."

"Does she?" Ash's jovial expression turned sour when he glanced at Georgina. She lifted her chin and stared back, defiant. Let the brute think whatever he wanted to think. Georgina wasn't about to let herself be daunted by *him*.

"Oh, my, yes. In fact, I've asked her to join our choir."

Ash's eyebrows lifted, and he sort of half grinned, as if he knew something about the choir Georgina didn't. Incensed by his attitude, she snapped, "Yes. I'll be very happy to sing in the choir, Mr. Barrett."

"You will, will you?"

The rat! He sounded so smug and superior, Georgina wished she could hit him.

"And she has the clearest, sweetest soprano voice you've ever heard," Vernice declared, although how she knew Georgina sang well was a mystery, since Georgina hadn't sung a note since she'd arrived in the territory.

The sheriff didn't seem to find a discussion of Georgina's musical accomplishments very interesting. He changed the subject and directed a question at Georgina. "How are your hands?"

She frowned at him, peeved that he should have brought up her encounter with the butter churn. "They're fine. Thank you." She added the *thank you* because she knew she should. She really didn't want to thank him for anything, no matter whether it was proper or not.

"Better go easy on 'em for a while. Don't want them to get infected." He swung his horse around and began to trot Shiloh alongside the Murphy buggy.

Vernice was driving, although Georgina now regretted not taking the reins herself. She was a wonderful driver, and she'd have loved to show this awful man how adept she was at some things. The fact that she'd not driven today because her hands were blistered galled her.

"I do so appreciate your helpful advice, Sheriff." Georgina might have chipped the words from a block of ice and flung them at him. She hoped he'd freeze to death on them.

He grinned at her, as if he knew his show of concern and proffered advice irritated her. "Yeah, you'll probably need a lot of advice from folks, since you're not used to the work we have to do out here."

"Oh, yes. But she's so clever, Sheriff." Vernice obviously didn't notice the hostile undercurrents that seemed so glaring to Georgina. She sighed happily. "We're going to Betsy Bailey's house on Thursday for the ladies' quilting society."

"That's useful." Ash eyed Georgina slanty-eyed, as if he couldn't feature her with a needle and thread in her hands unless, perhaps, she had to mend a torn silken ruffle because it was her maid's day off.

Georgina gritted her teeth. She wished she could snatch the buggy whip from its holder and slash the sheriff to bloody strips with it. She'd never been subject to violent urges before, and this one surprised, and rather dismayed her. She tried to force a sweet smile and almost succeeded.

"Quilting is a very useful occupation," she ground out. "And we've begun braiding scraps for rugs, as well."

"Yeah, I suppose you'd need to do that. We don't have any fancy carpet manufacturers out here like they do back East."

If he threw one more reference to her New York roots in her face, Georgina feared she might just scream. Since she'd die before she gave him the satisfaction of knowing he was getting to her, she sugared her smile up a notch and decided she'd outmaneuver him. "Indeed. No electricity, no indoor plumbing, no gas heating. It's not what I'm used to, and yet I'm loving every minute of it."

"Are you now."

Georgina was pleased to hear the trace of vexation in his tone.

"Oh, my, yes. Why, I've not only met my dear grandmother and aunt, but I'm learning all about the West. It's quite an adventure for me, I can tell you."

"It must be." His voice had gone vinegary.

"In fact," Georgina said in a burst of sudden inspiration, "I think I might just stay here forever."

"Oh, Georgina! That would be simply wonderful!" Vernice looked happy enough to burst.

The sheriff did not.

Chapter Five

The choir really stank. Ash tried not to grimace as it warbled its way through "Sweet Hour of Prayer." The only female choir member under seventy in the whole outfit was Frank Dunwiddy's wife, Beatrice, and she couldn't carry a note in a bucket. The rest of the old dears had voices that might have been all right forty or fifty years ago. Now they wobbled and screeched all over the place.

Oh, if one wanted to get particular—and as much as it pained him to admit it, Ash supposed Payton Pierce, Picacho Wells's sole banker, had an all-right voice, if you liked squeaky tenors. Ash didn't.

Payton Pierce was the only man in the choir, and the old biddies loved him. Ash had a feeling that was the reason Pierce had joined the choir in the first place: because he liked to be fawned over, even if the fawners were all 110 years old. That, and because Pierce liked people to think he was an honorable Christian fellow. As if a banker could be. Ash struggled to contain a snort of disgust. He wasn't an admirer of bankers, and he wasn't an admirer of Payton Pierce in particular.

Ash thought Picacho Wells's faithful should be grateful to Mrs. Dunwiddy's mother, who'd shipped a piano to the territory from New Hampshire. The Dunwiddys didn't have room in their house for the instrument, so they'd let the church borrow it. The minister's wife, Sally Voorhees, played the thing so the parishioners—what few there were of them—could pick out the hymn's tune if they listened hard enough. They'd never get it if they listened to the choir.

Ash wondered what Miss Georgina Witherspoon thought of the choir she'd so rashly agreed to join. He sneaked a peek at her, hoping to find her grimacing in repugnance. She wasn't. He did not despair. There'd be plenty of time to upset her later if she managed to remain sanguine through the choir. Since he'd known his presence would annoy her, he'd sat next to her in the congregation.

Not that there was much of a congregation. There were maybe seventy-five or eighty people who attended this church regularly. The rest of the town either went to the Catholic church, or adjured church altogether. Ash usually considered himself one of the latter. Today, however, he'd come to church. Not because he had hoped to see Miss Witherspoon. Hell, no. In fact, he'd been thinking lately that his presence at a church service on Sunday morning might act as an example to the citizens.

Picacho Wells's citizens, for the most part, didn't really need an example from him. They were a peaceful lot, mainly, and Picacho Wells itself was a peaceful place, considering it sat smack in the middle of the roughest part of a rough territory.

The town had sprung up sort of spontaneously around a little Mexican settlement in the last twenty years. It was, however, far from huge. Most of its newer citizens, until recently, hadn't attended church at all. Folks from the East had started moving in only a few years ago, and only because New Mexico Territory had come to be known as good cattle country. Picacho Wells was one of the several small villages catering to the cattle industry in the area, but virtually all of the ranchers were men. It had been Ash's observation that men weren't as likely to crave churches as women.

Females, as a recognizable portion of the population, were a relatively recent phenomenon. Ash could recall a time when there had been almost no women living in Picacho Wells. That was back in the bad old days, he reckoned, although he remembered them with a certain fond nostalgia. What women there were had possessed no morals to speak of, and there wasn't a man living in Picacho Wells then who would have dreamed of going to church on a Sunday morning.

For one thing, their hangovers wouldn't have let them. For another, there hadn't been any churches. Even the Catholics—and most of them spoke only Spanish—had to go all the way to Roswell if they wanted to worship, and that was a good twenty miles off.

Not any longer. About ten years ago, the local ranchers began pining for civilization and had started to find themselves wives. Even Ash, who had been a soldier fighting in the Indian War at the time, had finally succumbed to the lure of a permanent female body in his bed.

Unfortunately, he'd met Phoebe at the time his urges were at their peak, and eight years ago he'd leaped of his own free will into the inferno that had been his marriage. If Phoebe hadn't succumbed to a bout of influenza in the third year of it, Ash would be married still. The very notion made him feel sick to his stomach. He put a hand over his belly and let out a soft moan.

He shouldn't have done that. Miss Georgina Witherspoon had seen him do it, and she turned in her seat to glare at him. He grinned back, as pleasant as you please, hoping in that way to aggravate her. He was happy to note he succeeded. She pinched her pretty mouth all up and turned her head away from him again. She was sure fun to rile. Smelled good, too. He wished he hadn't noticed that.

Hoping to get a bigger rise out of her, he leaned over and whispered in her ear, "Not exactly the kind of choir you're used to in New York, I'll warrant." She smelled even sweeter up close. Ash breathed her fragrance in deeply, and tried to place it. Some kind of flower, he thought.

She jerked away from him as if she suspected him of carrying the plague. While Ash had been trying to annoy her, he hadn't expected her to react so violently to his nearness, and he realized he didn't like it. She hissed, "Please, Mr. Barrett! If you must speak to me, do so after the service is over."

"Right." Nettled, Ash settled back into his pew. The pews had been shipped in from a church in Amarillo that hadn't needed them after their sanctuary had been renovated. The churchgoing citizens of Picacho Wells were happy to get other people's leftovers.

Because he was so sore at Miss Georgina Witherspoon and her hoity-toity attitude, Ash stuck to her like a burr on a beagle after the service ended. He politely stood aside to let her go ahead of him up the aisle, and then took her arm—very gently and much to her displeasure—when she walked out the door.

"Unhand me!" she whispered.

He whispered back, his own whisper as grating as hers, "I'm going to introduce you to the preacher, for God's sake."

"Oh." She didn't appear reconciled, but she stopped trying to yank her arm away from him.

Because he was peeved with her, he tugged her a little too hard, making her skip to keep up with him. She didn't say a word. Proud little baggage, Miss Witherspoon. Her attitude both tickled and aggravated Ash.

The Reverend Mr. Voorhees turned as Ash and Georgina approached. He smiled the smile of preachers the world over. Ash had never yet met a preacher who didn't try to appear sincere and holy on Sunday morning, no matter what devilry he got up to the rest of the week. Actually, Voorhees was all right. Ash hadn't even heard a whisper of anything improper in his behavior.

"Miss Witherspoon, allow me to introduce you to the minister of our church, Reverend Mr. Voorhees." He put on his smoothest, most dignified and sherifflike expression, and smiled chivalrously at Georgina.

She smiled sweetly back at him, then turned and held a little gloved hand in the direction of Voorhees. Ash frowned, not sure why he should be vexed that she hadn't taken his bait.

"How do you do, Reverend Mr. Voorhees?"

"Very well, thank you. And how are you, Miss Witherspoon? Your aunt, Miss Murphy, has been telling us all about you."

"She has?" Georgina didn't seem awfully happy to hear it.

Ash smirked and said, "She probably didn't mention the butter, Miss Witherspoon. Or the dead chicken."

She gave him a look that would have killed him, or at least done him serious injury, if looks could do that to people. "My aunt, Mr. Barrett, is a wonderful person and only speaks well of others. I fear she's probably given Reverend Mr. Voorhees an exaggerated notion of my virtues and neglected altogether to tell him of my many failures."

Reverend Voorhees smiled a ministerial, self-satisfied smile. "My goodness, yes, Miss Witherspoon. Why to hear Miss Vernice talk, she looks upon you in light of her salvation." He let out a rich, unctuous chuckle to show that he didn't really mean it.

Georgina smiled back. Actually, it was more like a simper. Ash gawked at her. He didn't like the woman much, but he'd never seen her simper before. Hell, until now, he hadn't known she had a simper in her. She was faking it; he knew it. Before he could pounce and turn her simper into a tantrum, Frank Dunwiddy walked up to them.

"Howdy, Ash. Don't gen'ly see you in church of a Sunday morning."

Confound it, why did Frank have to show up now and expose him as the Sunday-morning shirker that he was? Ash frowned at his deputy to let him know he didn't appreciate his comment. Frank paid no attention to his frown, which was normal behavior on Frank's part.

Georgina turned, saw Frank, took note of his wife Beatrice and the seven little Dunwiddys, and blinked furiously. Ash knew how she felt. Meeting the Dunwiddys for the first time did that to people. Frank was all nose. Beatrice was all ears. Their children, every one of them, had inherited both exaggerated characteristics, and they'd every one been passed over for a chin. It was as if God had decided to fashion a joke for Himself. They were good people, though, the Dunwiddys. And they weren't ugly, taken individually. Together, they were a sight.

Reverend Voorhees introduced Georgina to the Dunwiddys. She made a valiant recovery of her wits and Ash was disappointed to see her behave as if she were truly glad to meet the unusual-looking family. "It's so nice to make your acquaintance, Mrs. Dunwiddy. Aunt Vernice has told me you're the best quilter in Picacho Wells. Your daughters are very lucky to have you as a guide."

Beatrice blushed. Ash clamped his lips together to hold in a savage curse. Dad-blast it, that was the one thing the snit could have said that would have endeared her to Beatrice forever. She hadn't yet behaved like a spoiled city girl, even though he knew good and well she was one. It was extremely irksome behavior on her part and Ash was becoming incredibly irritated with the whole situation.

"Oh, Georgina, there you are! I wanted to talk—oh, I see you've met—dear me, I hurried so—I didn't want you to—let me introduce you to—oh, I have to catch my breath."

Ash gave Vernice Murphy one of his more polished bows. "Good morning, Miss Vernice. How are you today?"

Vernice skidded to a halt in front of the Dunwiddys, slapped a hand over her heart, and panted. She was really kind of cute when she got into one of her dithers. "Oh, my!"

Georgina smiled at her aunt. "This is such a pleasant little church, Aunt Vernice. I'm so glad you invited me to attend services with you and to join the choir."

A huge smile spread over Vernice's face and she calmed down at once. Beatrice Dunwiddy looked as if somebody had just told her that her children were beautiful. The Reverend Mr. Voorhees preened. Ash uttered another silent curse. He very nearly slipped up and let it hit the air when he noticed Payton Pierce, appearing bankerly and dignified and smiling like the snake-oil salesman he was, walking up to the group.

"I see you didn't exaggerate your niece's charms, Miss Vernice." The banker gave a practiced bow.

Pierce's voice always reminded Ash of a gear that had recently been squirted with oil. It slithered and it flowed. Add to that the fact that Pierce was blamed near as tall as Ash himself, a good five years younger, good-looking, and a banker, and Ash could happily have shot the man if he hadn't sworn to uphold the law.

Miss Georgina Witherspoon's reaction to him was something to behold. Ash watched, disgusted. If she'd simpered for the preacher, she was all but falling over in a maidenly faint now.

"Oh, Georgina, I do so want you to meet Mr. Pierce. He's our banker here in Picacho Wells, and we're so pleased to have him singing in our choir. I wish we could get more men to sing with us." Vernice beamed at the two of them. Ash frowned, wondering if she'd been referring to him when she'd mentioned "more men."

Vernice didn't seem to notice. "Miss Georgina Witherspoon, allow me to introduce you to Mr. Payton Pierce. Mr. Pierce, my niece, Miss Witherspoon."

Georgina held out that delicate hand of hers, this time to Pierce. Ash remembered holding her hand, and he didn't like the notion of Pierce holding it now. He told himself to stop being stupid. Pierce bent and deposited a chaste kiss on Georgina's fingers, and Ash's hands bunched up into fists.

"How do you do, Mr. Pierce? Did I understand my aunt to say you're a banker? My father is a banker in New York City. It's so good to meet you."

So her old man was a banker, was he? Ash discovered he wasn't surprised. Disgusted, maybe, but not surprised. Ever since a banker in Galveston had made off with a lot of his money, Ash hadn't cared for bankers.

"Miss Witherspoon, this is a delight. I am charmed."

He kept hold of her hand for so long that Ash cleared his throat. Blast the man, what was wrong with him? For that matter, what was wrong with her? Was she so taken with Pierce that she'd forgotten Ash even existed?

Georgina seemed not to notice that Payton was holding her hand for an inordinately long time. She spoke to Pierce as if he were the only person in the world. "It's so nice to see a man in the choir, Mr. Pierce. It is a shame more men don't join church choirs. I suppose not many of them can sing." Ash guessed she knew he was there after all, because she turned her head deliberately and gave him a superior smirk. Not as subtle as her aunt, the little baggage. "Or perhaps they aren't moved to celebrate our Lord in song. Too few gentlemen are, I believe."

She placed special emphasis on the word *gentlemen*. Ash seethed.

Frank Dunwiddy let out a series of "haw-haw-haws." Until this morning, Ash had always enjoyed Frank's laugh. It was rich, genuine, and it invited folks to join him in laughter, which was, to Ash's mind, a good deal better than inviting them to do all sorts of other things he could think of. This morning, he wanted to shove Frank's laugh down his throat.

"If you're a-talkin' about Ash here," Frank said, slapping Ash hard on the back, "it's a miracle he even come to church today. He ain't a church-goin' gent, most Sundays. I 'spect his attendance this here Sunday might have somethin' to do with the company."

Ash glowered at Frank, who grinned back at him, knowing

full well exactly what he had done. Ash considered this base rebellion on Frank's part.

Vernice giggled. Pierce smiled his prissy smile and looked superior. Voorhees nodded genially.

Georgina pretended not to notice the sideways compliment Frank had paid her. "That doesn't surprise me at all, Mr. Dunwiddy. The sheriff doesn't seem like the churchgoing type. I suppose he generally has other work to do. Chasing villains and so forth." Butter wouldn't melt in Miss Georgina Witherspoon's mouth.

"I'm as much of a churchgoer as most of the men in Picacho Wells," Ash muttered. He wished he'd kept his mouth shut when he saw a look of triumph cross Georgina's face. It was so quick, if he hadn't been looking at her, he'd have missed it.

Blast it, she'd deliberately goaded him, the little shrew. Well, she wouldn't get away with it. He'd get even with her if it took him all week.

"Please allow me to see you two ladies home."

Ash was so mad and so involved in imagining ways to get even with Georgina that he almost missed Pierce's suggestion. He snapped to attention. "I rode to town with them this morning, Pierce. I reckon I can see them home again." As soon as he'd spoken, he wished he hadn't. It wasn't the words so much as the tone in which he'd spoken them. Blamed if he hadn't sounded jealous.

"In that case, I'd say you've done your part, Sheriff. Please allow me to relieve you of the duty on the way back to the Murphy farm. It will be a pleasure to see your grandmother again, as well, Miss Witherspoon."

She got out a thank you before Ash spoke again. "Nuts, Pierce. I live out that way. It's right on my way. It's no bother at all for me to see them home."

"But you mustn't be selfish, Sheriff." Pierce gave one of his prim, slithery laughs. Ash couldn't imagine why folks trusted him with their money.

In the end, both men saw the ladies home.

Georgina was feeling pretty good about church, her aunt, herself, Picacho Wells, and life in general. She believed she'd succeeded admirably in thwarting Sheriff Ashley Barrett's underhanded attempts to show her up as a good-for-nothing city girl.

She almost wished she hadn't been so successful when dust from Mr. Barrett's and Mr. Pierce's horses fluffed up on both sides of the buggy and made her sneeze. On the other hand, dust was only one more aspect of the territory that she aimed to conquer. Or at least learn to live with.

"Don't you think so, Georgina?"

Georgina realized Vernice had turned to look at her as if she expected an answer to some question or other. Blast. Georgina wished she'd been paying attention.

"I beg your pardon, Aunt Vernice?" She gave her aunt a gracious smile so Vernice wouldn't think she was deliberately ignoring her.

"I asked if you didn't think Mr. Pierce is a handsome man, dear."

Georgina had been so caught up in reliving her encounter with Ash Barrett outside the church that Vernice's question caught her by surprise. "Handsome? Er . . ." In truth, she hadn't thought about Mr. Pierce in terms of handsomeness. She hadn't thought about Mr. Pierce at all, really. She'd only used him as a way to dig at the sheriff.

She turned in her seat and looked at him now. He smiled at her, and she smiled back. When she turned around again, she said, "I suppose he is handsome." He reminded her of Henry Spurling, actually, but she guessed Henry was handsome. In a way. If you cared for that smooth-faced, thin, pallid, city-dwelling type.

Because she couldn't seem to help herself, she turned the other way and glanced at Ash Barrett. He gave her a ferocious frown in return, and she whipped her head back around, piqued with herself for looking. For one thing, she didn't want the sheriff to think she was interested in him. For another thing, she was annoyed to discover that she found him infinitely more appealing than Payton Pierce. Or Henry Spurling for that matter.

"Yes," she said at last, lying through her teeth. "Mr. Pierce is a very handsome man."

Vernice sighed happily. "Yes, all the ladies in town think so. Why, he's a topic of conversation at all the quilting bees."

She giggled like a schoolgirl. "I believe he's taken a fancy to you, dear."

Georgina stared at her, not having considered females in Picacho Wells as the types who would giggle over men. Perhaps they weren't so different from their eastern sisters after all. Well, except that they had to work a good deal harder. Her blistered hands took that opportunity to throb, as if to remind her of the latter point.

It was fairly appalling to think she'd taken Pierce's fancy, though. Except that it might irritate the sheriff to know a man—and the local banker, at that—appreciated her. Georgina grinned to herself, glad she'd thought of the latter point. It made any possible interest Pierce had in her much more tolerable.

"Of course, many of the ladies prefer the sheriff."

Georgina stopped herself from gaping at her aunt, because she knew gaping was an unladylike, undignified thing to do. "Do they? You astonish me."

Vernice shot her a surprised glance, and Georgina wished she'd not sounded so sarcastic.

"Why, Georgina, don't you think he's a handsome man? I certainly do. And Mother does, too." Her voice dropped in volume, even though there was no way either of the men could possibly hear her over the rumble of the wheels and the clatter of the three horses' hooves. "In fact, she doesn't care much for Mr. Pierce."

"Oh? Why not?"

"She says he's oily." Vernice gave Georgina a diffident smile. "You know what Mother's like."

"Hmm. Yes, she does seem to be a woman of strong opinions." Unfortunately, Georgina could see her point in this instance. She wished she couldn't. She peeked again at Payton Pierce, and sighed. Grandmother was right—he did look oily.

They arrived at the Murphy place shortly thereafter, and Georgina was spared further thoughts. She was not, however, spared further comparisons of their two accompanying protectors.

She tried not to show it, but she was discomposed when she realized the two men who had seen her and her aunt home from church planned to stay for supper. In fact, she was hard-pressed to keep from snapping at her grandmother, who had invited them.

"Why, thank you very much, Mrs. Murphy," Payton Pierce said, his smile looking to Georgina every bit as oily as his voice sounded.

"Thanks, Miss Maybelle. Don't mind if I do," said Ash, whose voice wasn't oily at all. In fact, Georgina liked his voice, drat it.

Maybelle cackled like a hen. Georgina got the feeling Maybelle knew Ash Barrett's presence bothered her. She also got the feeling Maybelle enjoyed watching people who disliked each other trying to be polite.

Her grandmother, Georgina concluded grumpily, might not be crazy, but she could be a very disagreeable woman without even trying.

As Georgina helped Vernice get supper ready, she kept glancing over her shoulder, wondering if Devlin was going to show up. If he did while the sheriff and the banker were present, she wasn't sure what she'd do. Of course, she'd attempt with every fiber of her being not to indicate by so much as a flutter of an eyelash that she was seeing a ghost. But the phenomenon of Devlin O'Rourke was so unsettling, how would she be able to maintain her composure?

All she needed, of course, was to give Ash Barrett a reason to consider her crazy. He already thought she was inferior and useless. If he deemed her a lunatic, as well, Georgina wasn't sure she could bear it.

Not, of course, that she gave a fig what Ash Barrett thought of her. He was an awful, dreadful, brutish fellow, and not worth her time. Still and all, it would be galling to know he thought she was crazy.

Vernice had put a pot of stew on the stove before they'd set out for church. Now she and Georgina were making dumplings. Georgina had never made a dumpling in her life. Doubtfully, she eyed the one she'd just patted into shape.

"My dumpling doesn't look anything like one of yours, Aunt Vernice."

"Nonsense, dear. It doesn't really matter what the dough looks like before you drop it in the pot. Dumplings always expand."

"They expand?" In heaven's name, how did they do that?

"Oh, my, yes. Why, they'll grow and grow until they cover the whole top of the pot. They'll soak up the gravy and taste delicious."

"Oh. I didn't know that."

Back home in New York, only the poor ate dumplings. Besides, a kitchen was as new, different, and incomprehensible to Georgina as a jailhouse would have been. She wished her mother had taught her at least some kitchen skills when she was a child. But that was impossible since her mother didn't cook, either. Bother. Sometimes being rich wasn't all it was cracked up to be.

Vernice gave a complacent laugh. Georgina was glad somebody around here was complacent. She could hear the men and her grandmother on the front porch. It sounded to her as if all three of them were taking verbal potshots at each other, couching them in polite terms and tones. She'd never heard anything like it. And they were laughing all the while. She didn't understand western sensibilities and wondered if she ever would.

Don't be silly, she chided herself. After all, she'd only been here a few days. One couldn't learn everything there was to know about a place in only a few days. No one could. She wasn't slow. Was she?

"Why don't you wash the dough off your hands, Georgina, and go out and ask the gentlemen if they'd like another glass of wine?"

"All right." Georgina wondered if her aunt was trying to get rid of her, but she didn't ask. She felt discouraged this afternoon.

Nevertheless, she found a tray, set the decanter of her aunt's homemade dandelion wine—and how did one make wine from dandelions, anyway?—on a tray, and carried it outside. Someone must have said something awfully funny, because they were all laughing. Her grandmother slapped her knee and had to wipe her eyes, she was cackling so hard.

They didn't hear her at the door. Georgina heard them, though, and stopped as if she'd been shot.

"And then the chicken's neck snapped, like that." Ash snapped his fingers, making a very loud noise. "And the bird was dead. I've never seen anything like it."

Grandmother Murphy's chortle sounded like a chorus of rusty hinges. Even Payton Pierce, who Vernice believed rather fancied Georgina, laughed softly.

"It's a good thing Miss Vernice was thinking fast. She told her it was all right that she'd killed the chicken because she'd been going to have chicken for dinner anyway."

Maybelle cackled harder.

"Then Miss Vernice picked up another chicken and wrung its neck on purpose. I thought Miss Witherspoon was going to lose her breakfast."

Maybelle whooped and Pierce's formerly strained chuckle became a belly laugh.

"You should have seen her face!"

"Hee, hee, hee," chortled Maybelle gleefully.

"And then I had to finish the churning for her because her hands had blisters the size of baseballs."

"Har, har, har." Payton Pierce's eyes had started to water from so much gusty laughter, and he had to snatch his pristine white handkerchief from his coat pocket.

"It was the funniest thing I've ever seen in my life." Ash was laughing so hard, he had to clutch his stomach. Georgina charged out onto the porch and slammed the tray down on the table next to him with a loud crash, and he jerked around. "Whoops. Didn't know you were there, Miss Witherspoon."

"Yes, I can see that." She smiled at him, lifted the wine decanter and pulled out the stopper. "Aunt Vernice asked me to bring you some more wine."

"Why, thank you very much." Ash gave her a wide, beautiful smile and held out his glass.

She ignored his glass, raised the decanter higher, and poured the wine out over his head.

Georgina had the satisfaction of knowing her joke achieved a bigger laugh than his had.

Chapter
Six

Ash's hair was still wet when he rode home from the Murphy farm after supper. And the wine stains would never come out of his shirt and trousers, which were, at present, hanging on the Murphy clothesline after having been hastily laundered under the backyard pump.

At this moment, Ash was clad in a pair of Devlin's old trousers and one of his shirts, both of which were too small for him. Dev had been a good five inches shorter than him and Ash knew he looked like a fool in the smaller man's clothes.

Damn the woman. He'd practically drowned himself at the pump out back after she'd poured the wine on him. It's a blamed good thing the weather was warm or he might have caught his death, and then he could have arrested her for manslaughter. Except that he'd have been dead. Ash growled savagely into the afternoon sunlight.

She wouldn't get away with it.

All the way home, Ash plotted revenge.

"That was a mean trick to pull on the sheriff, dearie."

Georgina had been lying in bed, her blistered hands cupping her head, staring at the ceiling, and savoring her victory over Ash Barrett, when the ghostly voice brought her pleasant

71

thoughts to a brutal end. She groaned and shut her eyes. "Oh, no. Not *you* again."

"Aye, it's me again. Devlin O'Rourke, at your service."

She opened her eyes and squinted at him. "The only service you can perform for me is to go away and leave me alone." Georgina felt no need to modify her curt tone for the ghost's sake. While it was true he was older than she, it was also true he'd invited himself into her bedroom, and his behavior was not only impolite, but quite shocking.

"Ah, child, you sound like your grandmother."

"I wish you'd go haunt her and leave me alone. I don't want you in my room. I'm a young, unmarried female, and your presence in my room is scandalous."

"Pisht." Devlin sounded disgusted. *"Now you sound like that prim maiden aunt of yours."*

"Aunt Vernice is a lovely lady," Georgina said, defending her aunt with vigor. "Unlike some people I could mention, she takes her responsibilities to her family seriously. And she behaves with courtesy and propriety. If you consider that prim, so be it."

She wondered if there were some way to exorcise a ghost from a particular room in a particular house. She really didn't think she'd mind Devlin O'Rourke hanging about if only he didn't do it in her room.

Good Lord, what was she thinking? Pressing a hand to her forehead, Georgina wondered if she might be ill. Could fever account for seeing ghosts? If it could, she guessed the whole western branch of the family had the same fever. What a depressing thought. She muttered, "Go away," and closed her eyes again.

"I'm not goin' away, child, and you're not crazy. For the love of Mike, dearie, haven't you come to terms with me by this time?"

"No."

Devlin clucked, reminding Georgina of one of the hens out back.

She tried again. "Go away. Please. I'm tired. I need my rest."

"Ah, child, I've come to you for help."

"I don't want to help you."

"But you're the only one who can."

"Fiddlesticks."

" *'Tis not fiddlesticks I'm needing, child, it's your grand-mother to speak gently to me.''*

"If you bother her the way you bother me, I don't blame her for not speaking gently to you."

"I don't bother her." Devlin's voice rose.

Georgina sighed. She didn't want to argue with a ghost. She didn't want to argue with anybody—well, except perhaps Ash-ley Barrett. And she didn't really want to argue with him, either. She wanted to pour another bottle of wine over his head. In spite of her annoyance with Mr. O'Rourke, she smiled. That truly had been a brilliant stroke on her part. She'd never realized how invigorating a good fight could be until she'd met the sheriff of Picacho Wells.

"Listen to me, Georgina, lass. Your grandmother likes you. If you'd speak to her for me, I'm sure she'll listen to reason.''

"This is ridiculous!" Georgina, feeling very cranky, swung her legs over the side of the bed and sat up.

There he was, sitting on the stool in front of her dressing table, looking downcast and miserable. In Georgina's opinion, he ought to feel downcast and miserable. Imagine, bothering her in the middle of the night this way. She tried not to be disconcerted that his essence didn't cast a reflection in the mirror. "If I promise to talk to Grandmother, will you go away and leave me alone?"

"Yes,'' he said despondently. *"If you promise me.''*

"Very well. I promise." She scowled at him to let him know she was promising only to get rid of him and, while she intended to keep her promise because she was a lady and an honorable human being, she didn't want to do it.

He remained seated, staring at her, looking unconvinced. Georgina got mad.

"I'm going to speak to Grandmother on your behalf, Mr. O'Rourke! Now get out of here and leave me alone. I would actually like to go to sleep. I'm tired. I've had a trying day, and I have to get up early to milk the cow."

She passed a hand across her eyes. They felt like they'd been glued together and pried open again, and she knew they wouldn't feel any better tomorrow morning when she arose at the crack of dawn to milk Bossy, the cow. Georgina truly didn't mind doing the chores required to keep the farm going, but she wished she could start them later in the day. The hours of farm life were apt to kill her.

"Vernice has taught you how to milk a cow, has she?"

Georgina opened her eyes and glared at the ghost. "You needn't sound so skeptical. Yes, she has taught me how to milk a cow." So she wasn't very good at it yet; she'd get better with practice. Vernice had told her so.

Devlin rose from the vanity stool. Thank God. He chuckled softly as he hovered just above the floor. *"All right, dearie, I'll let you get your beauty rest. And I aim to watch you milk Bossy in the mornin', too. I'll believe it when I see it."*

Georgina didn't respond to his threat or to his doubt, but she did understand why Grandmother Murphy felt impelled from time to time to throw things at him.

A pleasant and unfamiliar sensation of anticipation accompanied Ash to the Murphy farm the morning after his wine bath in order to return the clothes he'd borrowed and to pick up his own. He wasn't sure why he felt the way he did, although he knew it had nothing to do with the idea of seeing Miss Sassy Witherspoon again, because he didn't want to see her. Not only that, but he hadn't figured out how to get even with her yet. And even if he had figured out a good one, he wouldn't be feeling this delicious sense of expectation about it.

No. The anticipatory feeling he currently enjoyed was because of—it was because of—it was because of—pie! That's what it was. Of course it was. It was the pie.

Ash sighed, happy to have that puzzle cleared up. Hell, there had been a whole lot of Miss Vernice's dried-apple pie left over after supper last evening. She'd surely offer Ash a slice of it this morning. A hunk of apple pie and a slab of cheese and a cup of coffee was a breakfast any man would look forward to. Especially since the two Murphy ladies hadn't let Miss Witherspoon anywhere near the crust, so it wasn't tough at all. That piecrust had been as tender and flaky as . . . Well, it had been tender and flaky, at any rate, and the pie had been delicious. His mouth had started watering by the time he guided his horse between the two rows of pecan trees lining the way to the Murphy farm.

He rode Shiloh up to the house, dismounted, wrapped the reins over the porch rail, and headed for the barn, thinking he'd find Miss Vernice there, milking. He had decided that he should try and avoid Georgina until he had figured out a proper way to wreak his revenge. When he saw Georgina sitting on the milking stool, industriously trying to get milk from Bossy's teats, he almost fell over. "Good God, what the hell are you doing to that poor cow?"

She sat up straight, startled, a teat in her hand, and managed to squirt milk on Oscar, who'd been watching her with his tail switching back and forth as if he were waiting for an opportune moment to leap onto her back and scratch her to death. The cat yowled and sprang up onto a bale of hay where he arched his back and hissed at Georgina for several seconds before he sat down and began licking the milk from his fur.

Georgina gave Ash a severe frown. "Oh, it's *you*." From the tone of her voice, Ash might have been a skunk or a tarantula or a rattlesnake or some other loathsome beast. "What does it look like I'm doing?"

He frowned back, nettled by her attitude. "It's hard to tell, but it looks like you might be trying to make yourself useful." He used his most scornful tone, hoping in that way to irritate her. Not that she wasn't already irritated.

"I'm not *trying* to be helpful, Mr. Barrett. I *am* being helpful. If you don't believe me, ask Aunt Vernice."

"Hmm. You aren't going to be of much help if you keep jerking that teat. You're going to hurt the cow."

Her face flamed. Ash guessed she wasn't used to men using words like "teat" in front of her. Some kind of farmhand she was.

"Nonsense. I was doing fine until *you* showed up."

He decided to give up the argument for the time being. "Whatever. I came over to get my clothes. Where's Miss Vernice?"

She sniffed and turned back to Bossy's udder. "Your clothes are in the kitchen. Aunt Vernice ironed them after they dried. I think you ought to thank her."

"I already thanked her, Miss Witherspoon. And I think *you* should apologize for putting her to the trouble of having to do extra work."

She had the grace to look guilty. She seemed pale now that her blush had faded. Ash didn't like to see her looking pale, although he couldn't have said why. Some uncomfortable urge seemed to propel him to ask, "You feeling all right this morning?"

"Of course I'm feeling all right." She glanced up and skewered him with another one of her ferocious frowns.

Feisty little thing. Ash's insides grinned, even though he would have died before he'd have shown her how much her attitude tickled him. Without another word, he turned and strode toward the barn door.

Actually, Georgina wasn't all right. She'd been carrying on a verbal sparring match with Devlin ever since she'd come out to the barn to milk Bossy, and she didn't appreciate Ash bothering her as well. She pulled Bossy's teat, being careful not to squeeze it too hard. She'd done that the first couple of times she'd tried to do the milking, and Bossy had protested violently.

Devlin chuckled. *"You see, child, he's a good man. He's concerned about your health."*

"He is not," Georgina muttered, glad at least one of her adversaries seemed to be leaving. She was disgusted when she realized Ash had heard her speak. He stopped walking and turned around.

"Beg your pardon?"

Georgina frowned at him. She wished he didn't look so blasted handsome, standing there in the barn door with the morning sunlight at his back, outlining his muscled form in that outrageous way. Drat the sun, anyway. He looked so big and solid and strong.

Henry Spurling certainly didn't look like that. Henry looked as if a puff of wind might knock him over. So did Payton Pierce, for that matter. It galled her that the most appealing-looking man she'd ever met had to be this one, Sheriff Ash Barrett, whom she couldn't stand and who couldn't stand her.

"I didn't say anything," she lied grumpily.

"Y'did so, child. D'ye think the man's deaf?"

"Oh, shut up and go away," Georgina growled. She was shocked at herself. She'd never uttered such a vulgar phrase before in her life. Good gracious, these territorial men certainly brought out the worst in her.

"I'm going away, blast it, Miss High-and-Mighty Witherspoon," Ash said, sounding offended.

Oh, dear. She hadn't meant to speak to Devlin in Ash's

presence. Obviously, the sheriff couldn't see the ghost. This is exactly what she'd feared. Although it annoyed her to have to apologize to the man, she said, "I beg your pardon, Mr. Barrett. I wasn't speaking to you."

"No?" His dark eyebrows rose insolently. "You were telling the cow to shut up and go away?"

"Of course I wasn't talking to the cow!" Blast the man. He was the most impolite fellow she'd ever met. Imagine him taking her to task for talking to herself. Well, for talking to a ghost, rather—but he couldn't see the ghost. Oh, dear.

At any rate, if he'd been a gentleman, he would have ignored Georgina's lapse in manners. But Ashley Barrett, as she'd already had cause to notice more than once, was not a gentleman.

"Oh, I see," said Ash, sarcastic as all get-out. "You're talking to the cat you nearly drowned in milk."

"The lad's got a point there, darlin'." Devlin laughed again.

"I was not!" What with Devlin on one side and Ash on the other, Georgina felt beleaguered. "Will you please just go away?" She wasn't sure if her comment was directed at the ghost or the man, but she'd be pleased if either one did as she asked.

Fiddlesticks. Now Mr. Barrett looked angry. He stomped over to her. His presence made the cow jittery. Georgina didn't know why the ghost's presence didn't bother the stupid animal.

"I don't know what your problem is, lady, but—"

"Don't call me *lady*!"

Ash's mouth flattened out into a thin line. "All right. I don't know what your problem is, *woman*, but I don't like people dumping wine on me, and then being rude to me for no reason."

Georgina's head snapped up from her milk pail. Her mouth fell open for a second before anger made it slam shut. When she opened it again, she all but screamed, "No *reason*? Why, you miserable bully! You were laughing at me! You were sitting on that porch, telling my grandmother and that slimy man all sorts of horrid things about me!"

"They were the truth, damn it. I didn't make up any of it."

"That's not the point!"

Having been bred from the cradle to be a lady, Georgina was not accustomed to yelling at people. The fact that she was now screeching at Ash was a sign of her extreme agitation.

"The hell it's not!"

"The lad's right, lass."

"Don't you dare *lass* me!"

She was so furious, she didn't realize she'd just screeched at the ghost instead of Ash until she saw the puzzled expression on the sheriff's face. Bother! If it were possible to kill a dead man, Georgina might happily have killed Devlin O'Rourke. She decided to try to ignore him instead.

"The point is, you're no gentleman!"

"Oh, yeah? And just why exactly is that?"

"It's mean and unkind to laugh at someone, Mr. Barrett, or didn't anyone ever teach you manners? And manners make the man! *That's* the point!"

"The point is you don't belong here!" Ash was leaning toward her now, bellowing.

Georgina was so furious, she hardly knew what to do with herself. She jumped up from the milking stool. "I do too belong here! Just because I was born in New York City doesn't mean I can't learn how to live on a farm. Lots of people from New York move to the western territories!"

"Yeah? Well, they belong here. You don't!"

"That's not so! *Blast* you! You're not being fair!"

"You're a damned city girl, and you ought to go back to the city with your fancy airs and graces, dad-blast it!"

"What? How dare you! You make me furious!"

"Yeah? Well, you make me mad, too!"

"I can't stand it!" And with that, Georgina swooped down, picked up the milk bucket, and sloshed the warm fresh milk all over Ash Barrett.

Georgina was still thinking about the rippling muscles on Ash Barrett's naked arms and the short, curly hairs on his naked chest on Thursday morning when she drove the buggy to Betsy Bailey's house for the ladies' quilting society meeting. Vernice sat complacently next to her. Vernice had no idea of the tribulation under which Georgina had been operating since the milking incident.

She'd tried everything she could think of to stop remembering the way Ash's upper torso had looked, but so far she'd been unsuccessful. She'd even recited Bible verses and poetry aloud but such paltry methods hadn't worked. Georgina was trying to think of something more powerful to erase the image. A shotgun, perhaps.

Good gracious, but the man had muscles. Georgina fanned her face, which always seemed to get warm when she thought about the sheriff's naked chest.

It was her own fault. If she hadn't dumped milk on him, he wouldn't have had to remove his shirt and wash himself off under the pump. Grandmother Murphy hadn't helped any, either. Georgina remembered the scene vividly.

"I swear, child, I do believe you have some Murphy blood in you after all." Maybelle hadn't stopped laughing since Georgina and Ash had entered the house, Ash dripping from his bath at the outside pump.

Georgina had not been amused. "Of course I'm a Murphy."

Her voice had been as sour as the milk in the barn would have been by this time if Oscar hadn't licked it all up.

"She's got Murphy blood in her, all right," Ash had grumped. "She's a damned mad woman, too."

"What do you mean, *too*, you wicked man?" Maybelle had laughed some more.

Georgina had been about as far from laughter as she'd ever been. "Yes, Mr. Barrett, what do you mean, *too*? Are you implying that my grandmother and my aunt are crazy?"

He'd only muttered something unintelligible under his breath.

"She just tried to drown you so's she could look at your muscles, Ash. You know how we females are." Maybelle had so amused herself with that comment that she'd cackled for a good five minutes afterwards.

Georgina had been offended by her grandmother's comment. She'd also been furious. "That's not so! He was being horrid to me, and I couldn't help myself."

"Ha! A likely story. She's a red-blooded girl after all, Ash. A red-blooded girl."

Maybelle had winked at them both. Georgina had been shocked that her grandmother had such a lascivious wink— and at her age, too.

"Leave me alone." The sheriff, evidently feeling outnumbered by Murphys at the moment, had unbuttoned his shirt and tugged it off.

That's when Georgina had succumbed to lust. She'd never been so victimized before, and she was still surprised at herself and her reaction to Ashley Barrett's muscles and chest hair and so forth. She'd always believed herself to be above such nonsense. It was disheartening to discover how wrong she'd been.

Bother.

"Is everything all right, dear? You look a little downcast today."

Georgina, who was at least gratified that her hands were now well enough to enable her to drive the buggy, glanced at her aunt. Poor Vernice appeared very concerned, and Georgina felt guilty.

"I'm only a little tired, Aunt Vernice. That wretched Mr. O'Rourke has been plaguing me at night, pleading with me to talk to Grandmother."

Vernice tutted sympathetically. "I know what you're going through, dear. I'm awfully sorry. I wish I knew how to get rid of him."

Feeling put-upon and crabby, Georgina spoke her mind. "The only way to get rid of him is to convince Grandmother to confess her love for him. He claims he'll go away if he knows she'll join him when her turn comes to pass on."

Vernice sighed. "She'll never do it."

Georgina was way past the sighing stage. She huffed angrily. "Not any time soon, she won't. They're both as stubborn as mules, and it's we who suffer as a result."

"So true. So true."

"And now Mr. O'Rourke is sulking, and so is Grandmother, and they're both even more difficult when they're sulking than they are normally—and they're normally impossible."

"It's a sad state of affairs." Vernice shook her head and sighed again.

The morning was fine—the wind was hardly blowing at all—but Georgina wasn't in the mood to appreciate pleasant weather. She scowled as the buggy approached the main thoroughfare of Picacho Wells. Betsy Bailey and her family lived at the other end of town. If Georgina saw Ash Barrett this morning, she felt strongly inclined to run him over with the buggy. She'd never do it, because he wasn't worth getting herself arrested for, but the notion kept her pleasantly occupied for several minutes.

She caught sight of Ash only seconds before she saw Payton Pierce. She'd already figured out that the sheriff didn't care for the banker, so she decided to put on a show of friendly camaraderie with Pierce. She didn't like the banker much, but if she treated him well she might thereby rile Ash, and the effort would be worth it on that account.

Fortunately, Pierce saw the Murphy buggy and waved, smiling broadly, so it was natural for Georgina to pull the horse to a halt beside him. She gave him one of her best, most flirtatious smiles. "Good morning, Mr. Pierce."

He removed his hat with a flourish and bowed. "Good morning, Miss Witherspoon. Miss Murphy." It seemed to Georgina that it was an effort for him to remove his gaze from Georgina long enough for him to acknowledge Vernice's presence in the buggy. "Where are you lovely ladies off to this morning?"

Out of the corner of her eye, Georgina saw Ash Barrett— who had been striding down the boardwalk—stop, turn, and frown at them. Good. She kicked her smile up a notch and offered it to Pierce. "We're headed to Mrs. Bailey's house, Mr. Pierce. Today is quilting society day."

"Why, that sounds like a fine, productive occupation on such a beautiful summer day."

He gazed up at her, reminding her of Bossy the cow after she'd been milked and was feeling happy and contented. Ash, on the other hand—she could still see him out of the corner of her eye—looked like he'd just eaten something that disagreed with him. He veered from his path and began stomping toward the buggy. Georgina felt a surge of triumph.

"What are you doing out on such a beautiful day, Mr. Pierce? I should think you'd be in the bank counting your money." She gave one of the trilling laughs she'd been accustomed to using at parties back home in New York. It sounded out of place here in Picacho Wells, but she didn't care.

He laughed, too. His laugh sounded almost as silly as hers. "Ah, even bankers are men, Miss Witherspoon. We enjoy a brisk walk on a warm summer day."

"How nice." Now what was she supposed to say?

Pierce took the responsibility from her shoulders. "Er, Miss Witherspoon, Reverend Voorhees tells me that there will be a dance at the church on the Saturday evening after next. It would be an honor and a privilege to escort you to the festivities."

Before Georgina could come up with an appropriate answer, Vernice clasped her hands to her bosom and cried, "Oh, isn't that the sweetest thing? Why, how kind of you—isn't that the nicest—oh, Georgina, you *must* thank Mr. Pierce for his kind—such an amiable thing to—"

"Thank you, Mr. Pierce," Georgina said, interrupting her poor aunt's incoherent ecstasies. "A dance at the church sounds lovely."

Pierce bowed. "Of course, I shall escort your aunt and grandmother, too, Miss Witherspoon."

Vernice gushed out an, "Oh, how thoughtful!"

Georgina smiled at him, this time honestly gratified. At least the man didn't seem to have ulterior motives or wicked designs upon her person, which was a good thing since Georgina had recently decided she preferred muscular men to skinny ones. "Indeed. How very kind of you, Mr. Pierce." .

Ash had arrived at the buggy. He ripped the hat from his head and frowned at Georgina. It looked as if it took a good deal of effort for him to turn his frown into a smile for Vernice. "Morning, Miss Vernice. Quilting day, is it?"

"Oh, my, yes, Mr. Barrett. It's such a lovely—why, it's warm as toast—quilting is such a worthwhile—so amusing, too—don't you know, when we all get—it's much nicer to have company." Vernice ran out of breath and beamed at Ash very much as she'd beamed at Payton Pierce. Georgina took that as a bad sign, because it meant Vernice liked both men. "And Mr. Pierce has just asked our dear Georgina to the dance on Saturday night. Isn't that a considerate thing to do, Mr. Barrett?"

Georgina gritted her teeth. Vernice was talking of her as if she were a charity case, and Georgina didn't appreciate it—especially in front of Ash Barrett.

"Did he now? Slick worker for a banker, isn't he?" Ash's smile for Vernice vanished when he looked at Georgina. He didn't spare a peek at Pierce. "Miss Witherspoon." Georgina imagined that he'd have used the same tone of voice to tell a villain he was under arrest.

She gave him the sappiest smile in her repertoire, hoping to unsettle him. "Good morning, Sheriff Barrett. Did you ever get the milk out of your trousers?"

For a second she thought he might holler at her or slap the horse's rump to make him bolt, but he didn't. His lips flattened out, though, and he looked angry enough to commit mayhem. Georgina was delighted.

"Yes, thank you, Miss Witherspoon."

"I'm so glad." She lifted the reins, preparatory to starting the horse moving again. Ignoring Ash, she said, "Good day, Mr. Pierce. It was so nice to see you again. I look forward to the dance the Saturday after next." She elected not to mention Vernice's delight at the prospect. Let the sheriff think Pierce was escorting her alone to the dance.

Pierce bowed and smiled like a moonstruck schoolboy. "Good day to *you*, Miss Witherspoon. Miss Murphy."

Georgina heard Ash Barrett snort as she drove off down the road, and felt better than she had earlier in the day. She was so elated that her sense of satisfaction was only slightly diminished when she drove past the Turquoise Bracelet Saloon, and a ruffianly fellow who was leaning against the building leered at her. She merely lifted her chin and drove on, secure in the knowledge that nothing untoward ever happened in Picacho Wells. At least not in the daytime. Well, except for the occasional bank robbery.

She stopped thinking of villainies when they arrived at Betsy Bailey's house. She was eager to learn how to quilt. Her proficiency in frontier skills was growing by leaps and bounds.

Chapter Seven

Payton Pierce plopped his fancy derby hat back onto his slicked-down hair and smiled a superior smile at Ash. Ash wanted to pop him one. Damned banker thought he'd stolen a march on Ash, didn't he? Well, he hadn't. Ash wouldn't have asked Georgina Witherspoon to the church dance if she was the last female on the face of the earth.

"It doesn't look to me as if Miss Witherspoon likes you much, Sheriff."

"Yeah? Well, I don't like her, either." It was childish. Ash wished he hadn't said it when Pierce smirked.

"I'm happy to say that she seems to find my own company welcome."

"Good for you." Ash stamped off, grumpier than he could remember being since he was married to Phoebe.

His mood hadn't improved much by the time the church dance rolled around two weeks later. He'd intended to ask one of the other single ladies in Picacho Wells to attend the dance with him, but he hadn't worked up the enthusiasm. So he went alone.

Such behavior wasn't unusual. The dances at the church weren't romantic affairs. They were social get-togethers where people were as apt to sit around drinking cider and swapping farming tips as dance. It was mainly the youngsters who danced. Youngsters and courting couples.

Ash swigged down a gulp of cider and wished he hadn't thought about that last part. He'd seen Payton Pierce arrive with Georgina and the Murphy ladies about a half-hour earlier, but he hadn't gone over to say howdy yet. Hell, he wasn't about to give Miss New York City Witherspoon the idea that he was interested in her.

Except maybe to argue with. She was kind of fun to rile. Even if she did fight dirty. He grinned, despite himself.

Unfortunately, Georgina Witherspoon looked good enough to eat tonight. She was wearing one of her fancy New York dresses, Ash guessed, because he'd never seen a female out here wear anything quite like it. It was kind of purplish—maybe the color was lavender; Ash wasn't up-to-date on ladies' fashions—and it was made from some shiny, crisp fabric. Taffeta? Hell, he had no idea. And it had short, lacy sleeves that came down to about her elbow, with short sleeves of the same lavender taffeta capping the lace.

There was some of the same shiny fabric bunched across her bosom with a little bit of lace down the front. Ash would like to have a peek down there just to make sure her bosom was decently covered. He didn't notice any of her partners leering down her front, so he guessed it was. Good thing, too. He had a feeling if anything could provoke a disturbance, it would be Georgina Witherspoon's bosom. There was also some fancy beadwork on the front of her skirt, and she held a fan made of some kind of lacy stuff that was about the same color as her dress.

She looked good. Damned good.

He'd like to think she was trying to lord it over her new acquaintances in the territory, but he couldn't believe it. When she wasn't being attacked by men asking her to dance, she was chatting amiably with the other ladies in town. And none of them looked to Ash as if they were being catty, either. Maybe they liked her. He glowered at her, thinking she must be some blamed good kind of actress if she'd hoodwinked everybody in town but him into thinking she wasn't a stuck-up, snobby city girl.

She was a good dancer, too. So far she hadn't missed a

dance. No sooner did the fiddles quit playing one tune than men lined up beside her to ask her for the next dance. Ash disapproved mightily as he watched her whirl around the church basement.

She'd danced the first reel with Pierce and then taken a spin around the room with Frank Dunwiddy, who was a fair dancer in spite of his nose. Ash decided to ignore her for a little while longer. He walked up to the Murphy ladies, who were sitting on the sidelines chatting with some other maiden ladies and matrons.

He bowed in front of Vernice. "May I have the next dance, Miss Vernice? I understand Sam's going to strike up a waltz next."

"Oh, Mr. Barrett!" Vernice tittered.

Maybelle Murphy pursed her lips into a moue of distaste. "No need to simper, Vernice. Tell the man yes or no." She took a swig of whatever was in her cup. Ash suspected it was something stronger than cider.

"Mother!" Vernice cast an annoyed glance at Maybelle, then looked up at Ash again.

Ash grinned at Maybelle. "It's a good thing your ankle's still got you laid up, or I'd make you dance with me, Miss Maybelle."

Maybelle snorted. "A likely story."

"I do so love to dance, Mr. Barrett. So does Mother, although she won't admit it."

Maybelle snorted again.

Vernice's eyes were shining like stars, and Ash was glad he'd asked her to dance before he asked Georgina. Oh, he'd dance with Georgina eventually, but he aimed to wait until the chit knew he didn't care one way or the other and that he was only asking her to be polite.

"Thank you, Sheriff. I'd be very happy to dance with you." She got up, blushing, and walked to the floor with Ash.

He had the satisfaction of seeing Georgina glance at the two of them and frown before she looked up at her partner, a tall, good-looking cowboy named Pete Fanslowe, and smile. She sugared her smile for Pete in order to annoy Ash; Ash could tell. Well, to hell with her.

•   •   •

The party had been in full swing for an hour and a half before the sheriff finally asked Georgina to dance. Her feet were sore, she was perspiring, her hair had come undone in spots—and the first time she had an opportunity to sit down and rest for a moment, the blasted man asked her to dance. If there was one person in the universe whom Georgina didn't feel like sweating in front of, it was Ash Barrett. The wretch.

Fanning herself furiously, she frowned up at him. "I'm resting at the moment, Mr. Barrett."

He grinned down at her. "Mind if I join you?"

Before she could think of a snappy retort that would send him on his way with a flea in his ear, he'd snagged a chair and dragged it up beside hers. "It looks as if I have no choice," she snarled as soon as he was seated beside her.

"True enough, but look. I brought you some lemonade."

She sniffed. "Mr. Pierce just left to fetch me a glass of lemonade." Thirst compelled her to add, "However, I appreciate your courtesy." She took the glass and forced herself not to gulp it down. She was so dry, she wished she had another three or four glasses to follow this one up with.

"Feel better?"

Georgina eyed Ash to see if he was being sarcastic or if he was actually asking after her welfare. She decided she'd play it safe unless he forced her into doing something drastic. Fortunately, since her glass was empty, she couldn't douse him with lemonade even if he got her mad enough to do so. "Yes, thank you."

She patted her hair, took out a hairpin, tucked up a loose tress, and stabbed the pin back in. She wished there was a ladies' withdrawing room around here. But there wasn't. A frontier church-basement dance was certainly nothing like the grand balls she used to attend back home in New York City.

Neither Georgina nor her parents had ever aspired to be numbered among Mrs. Vanderbilt's famous four hundred, but they did belong to a very respectable echelon of society. In other words, she'd never danced in a church basement sprinkled with sawdust and with fellows who were farmers and cowboys providing the music.

"Are you enjoying the dance?"

Georgina eyed Ash suspiciously. He sounded gracious, so she figured he was up to something. "Yes, thank you."

"Good. I don't suppose it's anything like the parties you attended in New York City."

She weighed his statement, trying in various ways to make something out of it. He didn't sound disparaging, but she didn't trust him. "No, it's not."

"We have a good time, though, even if it isn't fancy."

"Indeed. It's a very lively gathering."

That was the truth. In fact, as Georgina glanced around the room, it seemed to her as if these westerners were having a better time than she and her friends generally did back home in New York. She decided it was because folks in the territory had fewer opportunities to socialize than people in more settled parts of the country; therefore, when they got together, they genuinely had fun and didn't try to look bored and dissatisfied.

Ennui was quite popular in New York these days. For the first time Georgina felt the stirrings of contempt for her acquaintances in New York City. If they had to work like these people did in order to sustain life, they wouldn't have time for their airs of boredom and languor.

Good God, she sounded like Ash Barrett. Georgina was horrified. She glanced quickly at Ash, hoping her thoughts weren't detectable on her face. He was watching the dancers. Thank heaven. The last thing she needed was for him to know she agreed with him, especially after all the grief he had put her through.

Bonnie Bailey, Betsy's oldest daughter, danced by in the arms of her fiancé, Percival Walters. Bonnie waved gaily, and Georgina waved back, feeling warm and happy all of a sudden. These people were so nice to her. She'd feared that they might hate her because she had more fashionable clothes than they had and so forth, but they'd all welcomed her with open arms. In fact, a few of the younger ladies in Picacho Wells had talked her into getting together with them so that they could teach her how to sew and she, in turn, could tell them about the latest fashions from New York and Paris.

Actually, no one in the whole of Picacho Wells appeared to dislike her, Georgina realized. Except, for Ash Barrett, of course, who seemed determined to loathe her for no reason at all, other than that she came from New York City.

"Bonnie Bailey looks happy tonight," Ash observed.

Again Georgina eyed him, wondering what contemptuous meaning lay hidden in his comment. She couldn't come up with one, so she gave him a cautious, "Yes. She does."

"Wonder why."

She squinted at him, not trusting him an inch, then decided she couldn't get into too much trouble by telling the truth, so she did. "Mr. Walters has asked her to marry him. Bonnie is very happy about it, since they've been keeping company for some time. Evidently he had been waiting until his business was well established before he felt comfortable in proposing to her."

Oh, dear. She was saying too much. Surely the evil Mr. Barrett would be able to twist her words into something horrid. She braced herself.

"Honest?"

Georgina turned in her chair and scrutinized Ash's face. He'd sounded candidly interested, and now he looked it. She opted for a short, "Yes."

"Well, I'll be. I wondered when he'd work up the nerve to ask her."

Feeling a bit peeved by his comment, which she considered a slight, Georgina said, "I don't believe *nerve* had anything to do with it. He knew it was his responsibility to be able to support a wife before he took one." There. Let him rip *that* up if he dared. Personally, Georgina admired Mr. Walters for his consideration. And his restraint. She understood some young men weren't so thoughtful. Take Ash Barrett, for instance. . . .

"Right. Responsibility." Ash sounded the faintest bit sarcastic but Georgina decided not to quibble with him.

"At any rate," he continued, "everyone looks to be having a good time."

That didn't seem to call for a response, so Georgina didn't give one. Where was that wretched Mr. Pierce with her lemonade? She was getting nervous sitting here with the sheriff. She was positive he was going to say something outrageous, then she'd get mad and lose her temper, and they'd have a big argument, and as a result she'd do something unladylike in front of the whole town. She'd never had any trouble controlling her temper before she met *him*. She tried to take another sip of her lemonade and was annoyed to rediscover that her glass was empty.

"What's the matter with your fingers?"

Georgina looked at her fingers. There was nothing wrong with them that she could see. She squinted at him. She knew he was up to something. "Nothing."

"Like hell." Ash reached over and took the hand not holding the glass. Georgina felt a charge like electricity go through her at his touch. Blast the man!

"They've got little wounds all over them." He sounded accusing. "What happened?"

She yanked her hand back. "Those are only needle pricks, from the quilting society. I'm learning how to quilt, and since the fabric is thick, I sometimes prick my fingers." She sounded as defensive as she felt. If he laughed at her for trying to learn to quilt, she just might have to throw her empty glass at him.

"Ah." He nodded and didn't sound sarcastic. "I see."

She said nothing.

Perhaps he wasn't going to be nasty about her trying to learn to quilt. She didn't dare let her guard down yet, but she wasn't about to invite rebuff by speaking.

After a moment or two, Ash said, "Here comes your Sir Galahad."

Her Sir Galahad? Georgina squinted at Ash, wondering what he was talking about and why he was sounding as sour as month-old milk. Then she saw Payton Pierce, skirting the dancers, heading for her with two glasses of lemonade in his hands. One of them, she presumed, was for him. She hoped Pierce wouldn't offer it to the sheriff because then he'd have to go back and get another one for himself, and she'd be alone with Ash again, waiting for him to strike. Conversing with him was like socializing with a cobra.

Thank God Pierce didn't do anything so foolish as offer the sheriff one of the glasses. He did give Ash an unfriendly look, then he smiled at Georgina. "Here you are, Miss Witherspoon. Sorry it took so long. They had to refill the bowl."

She smiled one of her best, most gracious smiles and decided to bat her eyelashes flirtatiously, hoping to aggravate the sheriff. "Thank you so much, Mr. Pierce."

"I already gave her some lemonade, Pierce." Ash's voice was hard and cold.

Georgina snapped, "Yes, but I do appreciate Mr. Pierce's thoughtfulness. Very much."

Ash said, "Humph."

Pierce said, "Would you care to go outside to cool off for a moment, Miss Witherspoon? It's awfully crowded and warm in here." He cast a murderous scowl at the sheriff. Ash humphed again.

Relief! Thank heaven. Georgina arose abruptly. "Thank you so much, Mr. Pierce. I should love to go outside to cool off."

She snapped her fan open and fanned herself furiously to prove it, looked down at Ash, and gave him one of her most superior expressions. She hoped he'd choke on it. "Thank you ever so much for the lemonade, Mr. Barrett." Then she turned, took Payton Pierce's arm, and walked away without a backward glance.

They visited the cloak rack first so Georgina could fetch her lightweight wrap. Mr. Pierce said he didn't want her to catch a chill, which she thought was sweet. When he helped her on with it, his hands seemed to linger on her shoulders a trifle longer than was necessary, but she chalked that up to his being a solicitous host.

The night air was cool, but not cold, and there was no wind to speak of, which was a mercy. Georgina had forgotten about her hair, and she didn't fancy it getting blown to smithereens just because she wanted to escape from Ash Barrett.

"My goodness, Mr. Pierce, but the stars look so close out here. Back home in the city, one can hardly see the stars for all the other lights."

"Come over here, and you'll be able to see the stars better."

Georgina allowed him to take her hand so that he could lead her around the building.

"Watch your step. It's very dark out here."

"It certainly is." Was he leading her to the churchyard? Yes, he was. Well, this was interesting. Georgina had never had a man show her a churchyard before. Not that he could really show her this one, since the night was pitch black. She bumped her dancing slipper against a headstone and stifled an ungenteel epithet.

"Here," Pierce said. "Now you can have an unrestricted view of the heavens."

Georgina shot a suspicious glance at Pierce, wondering what

he was up to. She supposed the view was unrestricted—but the view had never been obstructed to begin with. For goodness sake, there weren't any tall buildings to speak of. Or many trees, unless you went out of town to a farm or something.

However, the last thing she wanted was to fight with Pierce and hence, she decided not to point out the obvious. She had done quiet enough of that lately with Ash. "Yes. The sky looks ever so much larger out here in the territory than it does back home, where there are huge buildings blocking it everywhere one looks."

"Are you enjoying your visit to Picacho Wells, Miss Witherspoon?"

Without even stopping to consider his question, Georgina said, "Oh, my, yes." She loved Picacho Wells, in fact.

"I imagine it's not as noisy here as it is in the big city, either."

"No, it certainly isn't." She laughed with genuine amusement.

She'd never experienced silence as an entity before she visited her grandmother. But silence was as much a part of life out here as creosote bushes and coyotes. Georgina could easily imagine going mad with the silence if left alone for too long. She didn't say so because she didn't want her opinion to get back to Ash and be used against her somehow. But it was true. Some of the ranches in the area were as much as fifty or a hundred miles away from any sort of community. Why, anything could happen and nobody would ever know. This was a dangerous, beautiful, and wonderful place, and she adored it.

Pierce sighed loudly, interrupting Georgina's reverie. "Here, Miss Witherspoon. Let me show you something else."

Something else? In a graveyard? Oh well, who was she to refuse an adventure? Georgina allowed herself to be led to a largish monument that gleamed under the starshine. "It's, uh, very, uh . . . nice," she said, at a complete loss for something to say. For the life of her, Georgina could not understand why Pierce was showing her the enormous gravestone.

"That's mine."

She stared at the monument, then turned and stared at Payton Pierce. Unfortunately she was unable to read his expression as his face was hidden by the darkness. "Yours?" Whatever was the man talking about?

"Yes. I believed it would be prudent to arrange for my final resting place. I believe in thinking ahead."

"Ah. I see." He could call it prudence if he wanted to. Georgina thought it was morbid.

"Yes. I believe a man has to accept his responsibilities and act in a dependable and trustworthy manner."

"That's a wise philosophy, Mr. Pierce."

"Do you think so?"

Did she think so? Why in gracious did he think she'd said it? "I certainly do."

"The sky is beautiful tonight, isn't it, Miss Witherspoon?"

His voice had an taken on an odd texture, as if he had lowered it and was trying to sound seductive. Oh, fiddlesticks, he wasn't going to try to kiss her, was he? Georgina refrained from saying something biting. "Yes, it certainly is."

"Almost as beautiful as you are, Georgina."

Georgina? How dare he! She hadn't given him leave to call her Georgina! She held her temper and her tongue, but backed away from him all the same. While Georgina didn't mistrust bankers the way some people did—after all, her father was a banker, and he was imminently trustworthy and respectable— still and all, she did not trust Pierce. She said, "Thank you," in a tone she hoped was repressive.

Pierce failed to take her hint and instead, reached out and grabbed her arm. "Georgina!" His voice was deep, and it throbbed. Georgina considered this a very bad sign.

"Please let me go, Mr. Pierce. Your fingers are too tight on my arm."

She pulled. He pulled. She frowned into the darkness.

"Georgina, you're so lovely." He clamped his free hand on her other arm.

"If you please, Mr. Pierce. Release my arms. You're crush-ing my lace."

"Call me Payton."

"No, thank you."

He hauled her against his chest and tried to kiss her, but she turned her face away. He got her ear.

"You're so lovely." His voice had deepened to the point that he was nearly growling at her.

She yanked on her arms, trying to escape his pythonesque embrace. "Thank you. Unhand me, if you please. And don't call me Georgina."

"But—"

"No! Let me go!"

"But I'm overcome with admiration for you."

Through gritted teeth, Georgina said, "If you admire me so much, do as I request!"

"But my passion for you is so—Ow!"

Her slippers weren't designed for kicking, but Georgina put a lot of force behind the one she aimed at his shin and hoped it would hurt like the dickens. She stabbed him in the stomach with her folded fan next.

He said, "Grmph!" and dropped her arms to crumple forward and clutch his stomach. Georgina felt triumphant. She aimed another whack on his head with her fan. Since her toes hurt from the first kick, she decided not to kick him again unless it proved necessary.

He said, "Ow!"

"What the hell are you doing to Miss Witherspoon, Pierce?"

Ash appeared at that moment holding up a lantern, glaring at Pierce with such intensity that Georgina drew away from him. She shook her head, thinking that she didn't need this.

"He's not doing anything to me," she said, irked. Not any longer, he wasn't. He was too busy bending over and clutching his stomach with one hand and holding his head with the other. Georgina didn't say so, but she was pleased to see her handiwork. She'd done all right, especially for a female.

While Georgina had never considered herself revolutionary in any way, and had never even thought about fighting for women's rights, living in the territory had evidently shoved her in that direction. Not for the first time, she resented Ash Barrett butting in and telling her what to do. She wanted to take care of Payton Pierce herself and didn't care to receive any help.

"What *had* he been doing?"

"That's none of your business, Mr. Barrett." She was very angry with both of these men, Pierce for trying to take advantage of her, and the sheriff for thinking she couldn't see to her own welfare

Ash loomed from behind the glow of the lantern like an avenging angel. Or an avenging desperado. Something bent upon vengeance anyway. Georgina sighed, exasperated. "Nothing is the matter, Mr. Barrett. We went outside to take the air."

"I don't believe it."

By the light of the moon and the stars and the lantern, Georgina managed to glimpse Ash set the lantern down on a tombstone and grab Payton Pierce by the collar of his formal evening coat. Pierce let out with a squeal that didn't sound even faintly masculine. Then Ash slammed Pierce's jaw with his fist, and Pierce went sailing over backward and landed on the base of his own monument.

Georgina thought his landing place rather appropriate, but she didn't approve of men beating up on other men, particularly when the other man had no muscles and couldn't defend himself. "Stop it this instant, Mr. Barrett!"

"Confound it, he was mauling you!"

"He was not!"

"Noooooooo!" said Pierce.

Ash grabbed the front of Pierce's coat this time and dragged him off of the monument. "You bastard. No one treats a lady like that in my town."

His town? For heaven's sake. Georgina was not amused. "Stop yelling, Mr. Barrett. If you'll let the poor fellow catch his breath . . ."

She might as well have saved hers, because Ash wasn't listening. Instead of doing as she'd asked, he punched Pierce again, hard, on the jaw. Georgina heard an awful crunching sound and a bellow of pain, although she wasn't sure which man had bellowed.

The sheriff began shaking his hand as if he'd hurt himself, and poor Mr. Pierce crumpled up on the ground. Ash reached down to grab his fallen foe again, and Georgina decided things had gotten completely out of control.

"Stop it!" she shrieked at Ash.

"Dammit, I won't have him pawing you!"

"I can take care of myself!"

"The hell you can! You're a woman, for God's sake!"

Ash had reached his arm back, fist bunched, preparing, Georgina presumed, to strike Pierce on the jaw again. She grabbed Ash's arm in both of her hands and leaped forward with all of her weight behind the movement.

His arm dropped under the weight of her body, and he hollered, "Hey! What the hell are you doing?"

"Preventing you from committing murder!"

He shook her off as if she weighed no more than a feather. "I'm not murdering him! I'm teaching him a lesson!"

"Noooooooo," cried Pierce once more.

"Stop it this second, you brute!"

"I'm not a brute!" Ash leaned over to grab a piece of Pierce's clothing and yank him to his feet.

Georgina kicked the back of Ash's knee, and his leg folded up. He was barely able to stop himself from falling on top of Pierce. "Hey!"

She belted him then with her own fist, on his back, and followed up with a crack from her fan.

"Ow! What the hell are you doing?"

"Stopping you from hurting that poor man!"

"That poor man?" Ash stared at her, confounded.

"Yes!" she screamed.

"What are you yelling at *me* for? You ought to thank me for rescuing you!"

"I didn't need to be rescued! Not by you or anyone else! And I certainly don't recall ever asking you for your help!"

"The hell you didn't!"

As much as she'd always expected to be taken care of by men, Georgina was at present in no mood to appreciate the sheriff's chivalry. She was furious. First Pierce had managed to get her alone outside—because she was trying to escape from the sheriff—and now Ash was trying to kill him for getting her alone outside.

In that moment, Georgina finally understood what the suffragists were talking about, what they were fighting for. In that moment, in fact, she became a positive revolutionary. She considered all men worse than fools and *knew*, beyond the shadow of a doubt, that women would do a much better job of running the world than idiot men.

She folded her hands into fists and went at Ash again, this time aiming for his chest, since that's what she could reach.

He blinked down at her as if she were a raving lunatic, which made her even madder than she already was.

"You drive me *crazy*!"

He grabbed her wrists. "I drive *you* crazy?"

"Yes!"

"What the hell do you think you do to me?"

"Don't you dare use profanity at me, you horrible, ghastly *man*!" She managed to wrench one of her wrists free from his grip, although it hurt to do so, and used it to punch him in the stomach.

"Ooof! Confound it, that hurt!"

"Good! I'm *glad* it hurt, you vicious fiend! You're supposed to be the sheriff here! You're supposed to uphold the law! You're not supposed to go around beating up on weaklings!"

"Weaklings?" It was a gasp, and it came from Pierce, who had managed to struggle to his feet, although he still swayed some.

"Yes!" Georgina, beyond diplomacy, turned her head to glare at him. "You stay out of this! This is all your fault!"

"But—"

Ash muttered, "Oh, shut up, Pierce." He had managed to get Georgina's loose wrist under control again, and he held her at arm's length, trying to dodge the kicks she was aiming at his shins.

"But . . ." Pierce tugged his suit coat down and bent to dust off his trousers. He looked troubled. His expression exasperated Georgina.

"Oh, go away, you fool! If you weren't such a sneaky, conniving thing, this never would have happened to begin with."

"Sneaky? Me? Conniving?"

"Get the hell out of here, Pierce, before I turn this woman loose and she attacks you again."

"I'm not going to attack him, you monster! You're the one who tried to kill him! *I'm* not trying to kill anybody!"

"You could have fooled me," Ash grumbled.

Georgina registered the fact that Payton Pierce had begun backing away from the two of them. She was glad to see him go, because she was nowhere close to being done screaming at Ash, and she didn't fancy having an audience.

"*Any*body could fool you!" she cried in response. "You're the biggest numskull I've ever met in my life. You're mean and awful and say terrible things to people! And about them!"

"This is stupid."

"It is not!" She got him a good one on the shin, and he tried to turn her around so her feet were heading in the opposite direction from his own personal limbs, but had no luck.

"You're just mad because I caught you in the graveyard being mauled by the banker."

"I wasn't being mauled!"

"Looked like it to me."

"Rubbish! I was defending myself from untoward advances, until *you* came along!"

"What's the difference between untoward advances and being mauled?"

"There's a *world* of difference! A *universe*!"

"Oh, for God's sake."

Georgina was just beginning to feel good about how she was faring in this war of words she was waging with Ash Barrett when he pulled the lowest stunt of their entire relationship thus far.

He hauled her to his chest, pinned her arms at her back, and kissed her.

Chapter Eight

Lord, Lord, what had he done?

Ash, whose base base male instincts responded instantly to the closeness of Georgina's body, maintained sufficient mental resources to ask the question of himself before his masculine needs overwhelmed his common sense, and caution flew out the window.

She fit into his embrace as if she'd been made for it. She was soft as eiderdown. And she smelled so sweet. And the way she melted against him was about as delectable as anything he'd ever experienced.

Her little fists battered against his back for about three seconds, then she sighed, her lips relaxed beneath his tender assault, and she started kissing him back. Her hands unclenched, and she began running them up and down his back, feeling his body, probing, as if she wanted to feel every inch of him. He knew exactly how she felt, because he felt the same way about her.

Blast it, Ash wished respectable ladies didn't have to wear so much whalebone. He wanted to feel her body against his—every precious inch of it. Not just a thigh here and a breast there. He wanted to feel the whole, gorgeous package. Naked.

He outlined her lips with his tongue, and then trailed kisses down her chin to her throat, where he pressed his tongue against the base and felt her pulse pounding against the delicate skin. She wanted him, Ash thought to himself. Sweet Lord have mercy, she wanted him as much as he wanted her.

"Oh, my." The words were tiny, and they came out in a breathy whisper that did something strange to Ash's senses. Not that they weren't addled already.

"Oh, my," she whispered again.

"Mine," he growled, and even he didn't know if he was deliberately misunderstanding her little exclamations or stating his own desire. "Mine."

She whimpered. Her hands had begun traveling up and down his arms now, pressing his biceps, his forearms, sliding back up to his shoulders. He finished feasting on her throat and moved his lips lower. All evening he'd been fascinated by her ball gown and the way it had that swath of fabric gathered over her bosom. He wanted to rip the gathers away and then rip away the material underneath, and see for himself what treasures all that material and boning hid. He wanted to see her naked breasts and to suckle at them; to feel her nipples pebble under his tongue's assault. To nip them, and listen to her moan her hunger into his ear.

She moaned, all right, but it wasn't into his ear. She bent her head and kissed the side of his neck while her fingers played in his hair. This time he moaned.

His moan seemed to galvanize her into activity. Suddenly Ash felt her fingers trembling over his shirt buttons. He'd noticed before that she was an agile little thing. Now she had his shirt unbuttoned in a couple of seconds, and her hands were splayed against his chest, her fingernails digging into him. Ash wasn't sure how much more of this he could take standing up.

Hell's bells, they were in the graveyard. What the hell kind of spell had she put on him to make him act so crazy.

"Oh, Ash," Georgina whispered. His name sounded like honey on her lips. "Oh, Ash."

"Georgina," he growled, and his hand slid beneath the gathers on her bodice. It was a tight fit, but he nearly burst from his britches when he felt the soft flesh of her breast. She was built like something from an adolescent boy's fantasy. Lush. She was so very lush. And soft. And her nipples were hard already. He groaned and pressed his lips to the very slight bulge of cleavage that spilled over the confines of her ball gown. Damn all these stupid clothes.

This was too sweet. Too wonderful. He kissed her lips again, getting lots of help from her. In fact, she sucked his lower lip, almost sending him over the edge. He ground his arousal against her thigh and reached down to lift her skirt. She uttered a soft scream against his lips. Good. He hoped she'd scream when she reached her climax. He aimed to work at it.

It took him a good deal of maneuvering, but he finally managed to reach beneath her drawers to the soft, supple flesh of her buttocks. He squeezed gently, and growled with lust. This was hell. It was heaven. If he couldn't take her soon, he knew he'd die.

"Oh, my." This *oh, my* was different from her first few. This one was gruff and deep and throbbed with desire. She wanted him. Ash could tell. She wanted him as no other woman had ever wanted him. Georgina Witherspoon was no Phoebe, who'd faked passion. This was genuine. It was glorious. It was—

Ash released Georgina and leaped away from her as if she'd suddenly turned into a werewolf. Or a vampire.

Or a wife.

Hell! If he continued as he'd begun, he'd be a married man tomorrow. He stared at her, aghast. She stared back, her beautiful lips parted and wet from his kisses. She looked befuddled and a little startled. She blinked. He swore.

"Dammit."

He was so hard he ached. He wanted her so much he could taste it. She wanted him, too; she was looking at him as if she wanted to eat him for breakfast—a prospect that made Ash shut his eyes and whimper with unfulfilled agony. What he wouldn't give to spread her legs and kneel between them, to taste her and to let her taste him, and to . . .

And he'd better stop thinking like that right this minute.

"Oh, God." He raked a hand through his hair. He couldn't get his vocal chords to work right, so he swore again. "Dammit."

He desperately wanted to bury himself in her moist softness, to pump in and out until the world went away and ecstasy engulfed the both of them. He wanted to make love to her night and day and for the rest of his life. He wanted to stay in bed with her for a week and a half—even then, he didn't think he'd have had enough of her.

And if he did, he'd prove himself to be the biggest ass in the world.

Twice.

She held out a hand that trembled. Her eyes were huge with wonder, disappointment, and perplexity. Thank God she didn't look as if she intended to start bawling any time soon. As much as he hated to admit it, he guessed she had a right to cry.

"Ash?" Her voice was low and uncertain.

All right. He had to pull himself together. He might never recover his composure completely—he knew good and well that after this every single time he so much as thought about Georgina Witherspoon he'd get hard—but he had to try to regain some sense of decency. He was the sheriff, for God's sake. He couldn't go around seducing respectable virgins. Hell, seducing virgins got men married. He'd shoot himself before he made that mistake again.

She repeated, "Ash?" Her voice sounded a little stronger.

He cleared his throat. What was he supposed to say? "Er, um, I . . ." Dammit.

"Sheriff?"

Her voice was definitely stronger now. She dropped her hand to her side and lifted her chin. Her hair was a mess. Crap. Had he done that? He guessed he had. Aw, hell.

She straightened the gathers at her bosom. Ash couldn't watch. It had been such a pleasure unstraightening them that he wished he'd been able to undo more. She tugged at her skirt, and the wrinkles fell away. Had he untied her drawers' strings? He thought he remembered doing so, but wasn't sure.

As soon as she sidestepped behind one of the headstones and began maneuvering under her skirt, he guessed he had. He cleared his throat again. He had to say something. Anything. And soon.

"Er, Miss Witherspoon—"

"Miss Witherspoon?"

Uh-oh. Her voice had changed again. It didn't sound as it had seconds earlier. It sounded cold now. Hard. He guessed maybe it was a little late to be calling her "Miss Witherspoon.'' Generally by the time a man got to undressing a female, they were on a first-name basis. Aw, hell.

''Ah, Georgina, I—I, ah, well, I guess I got a little carried away there.''

''A little carried away?''

She had her voice under complete control now. Ash was sorry to hear it. How had she recovered so fast? He was still about as confused and frustrated as a randy sixteen-year-old.

''I'd say you might have gotten a little carried away.'' She marched out from behind the headstone. Her eyes had scrunched up into slits. Angry, mean-looking slits. She twitched the crisp material of her oversleeves down so that it covered the lacy stuff underneath, then reached up to feel her hair.

Ash felt guilty. And helpless. And really, really stupid. ''Er, do you need any help?''

''No, thank you.'' Now she sounded polite. Icily polite. The kind of polite people used to show other people how much they hated them. ''I do believe I would rather slit my throat than accept help from you at this moment.''

Crap. Ash shut his eyes and prayed for inspiration—or maybe a bolt of lightning—to strike him. He'd really botched it this time.

''Er, Miss Witherspoon, we should talk about this.'' He really didn't want to talk about it, especially not with her. Nevertheless, Ash had never shirked a responsibility in his life, and he didn't intend to start now.

''No, thank you.'' More frigid politeness. ''I don't care to talk about anything with you.''

Feeling abused and misunderstood, Ash tried again. ''Now, listen here, Georgina. I'm, sorry if I got a little, ah, enthusiastic—''

''A little enthusiastic?''

She had been stabbing pins into her hair the way Ash suspected she'd like to be stabbing pins into him. She was doing a pretty good job of getting her hair under control, even in the dark and with no mirror handy. Ash was impressed. Her hair looked much better now. Less ravished. Thank God, thank God. Maybe nobody would know what they had been doing out in the churchyard.

"I'd say you did, indeed, get a little enthusiastic."

He frowned. "Well, I wasn't the only one." Shoot, now he was whining. He cleared his throat again. "I mean—well—I mean, we're both adults, Miss Witherspoon."

"Yes, I suppose we are, Mr. Barrett."

His name sounded like a chunk of ice when she said it like that. He sighed deeply. He'd enjoyed hearing "Ash" from her lips. He wondered if he ever would again.

That was no way to think. Confound it, what the hell was the matter with him?

"Ah, are you all right?" That was a nice thing to ask, wasn't it? He was supposed to be concerned about her welfare. After all, he'd very nearly taken her maidenhood.

God, what a thought.

He shut his eyes for a moment and thanked the good Lord he'd come to his senses in time. If he hadn't, he'd have to marry the woman, and then his life wouldn't have been worth living. Ash hoped if he kept that thought in mind, he'd survive the frustration of the evening.

"I'm fine, thank you, Mr. Barrett."

Ash heaved a huge sigh. This really wasn't fair. "Listen, Miss Witherspoon. I'm sorry I . . ." He was sorry he what? Kissed her. Like hell he was. He was sorry he hadn't gone all the way with her, is what he was sorry for. Confound it, this wasn't fair. "I'm sorry I kissed you." There. So what if it was a lie?

"Are you?"

Shoot, if she got any colder, she'd freeze solid. And so would he. Well, there was no help for it. Ash lied some more. "Yes. I'm very sorry. It wasn't a fitting thing to do, and I apologize for my actions." There. She would let him off the hook now. He'd just issued her a very polite apology, hadn't he?

"It was a beastly thing to do, actually."

Evidently it hadn't been quite polite enough. Ash began to feel the slightest bit put-upon.

Beastly, was he? He wasn't sure he could tolerate much more of this. "All right, it was beastly," he ground out. "I'm sorry. There. I've apologized. All right? What do you want me to do? Shoot myself?"

"Well, I have some other ideas but that would be a good start."

He ripped his hat from his head and slapped it against his leg. Confound it, she wasn't fighting fair. Not that she ever had. He should expect dirty tactics from her by this time. "Well, I'm not going to shoot myself, blast it. I'm *very* sorry. Isn't that enough?"

He could hardly believe it when Georgina began to walk toward him. Really, it was more like a stalk. Ash backed up a couple of steps until he caught himself doing it and told himself not to be so stupid again. Hell, once an ass was enough for any man in a single night. He desperately hoped she wasn't carrying a derringer up her sleeve.

She poked her finger at his chest. Hard.

"Ow." He rubbed the spot she'd poked.

"You," she said in the coldest, hardest, meanest voice he'd ever heard from anyone, "are the biggest scoundrel I've ever met in my entire life. You're a cad. You're a beast. You're a brute and a lecher and a rogue and a lout."

Criminy, he wasn't that bad, was he? He didn't get to ask, because she continued.

"You're worse than evil, because you were elected to protect and serve the people of Picacho Wells. You weren't elected to seduce maiden ladies."

"Now wait a minute—"

"You weren't elected to beat up bankers."

"Beat up bankers? Dammit, I was trying to help—"

She poked him again, and he shut up. "You weren't elected to lift ladies' dresses and feel their intimate areas."

Good God, had she really said that? Miss Georgina Witherspoon, proper New York City lady? Ash gaped at her.

"You weren't elected to undress respectable females in the churchyard and try to have your wicked way with them."

"Have my wicked way with—"

"You weren't elected to ruin upstanding, principled women."

"Now, just a minute here, Georgina."

"Don't you dare call me Georgina!"

Her screech hurt Ash's ears. He grumbled, "Miss Witherspoon."

"That's better." She nodded once sharply. "You're a low

man, Mr. Barrett. You're a snake. A rat. A skunk. You're worse than despicable. You take advantage of helpless females—''

''Helpless?'' Like hell she was helpless. She was about as helpless as a coiled rattler.

''*Helpless* females whom you are supposed to be protecting.''

''Hey, wait a minute here. You were the one who said you didn't need rescuing.''

''I *didn't* need rescuing! Not from that idiotic banker. He's about as dangerous as a dandelion puff. But *you*! Ooooooh, *you're* another matter altogether, aren't you?''

''Am I?'' Ash was lost now. He didn't know what in blazes she was talking about, and he was pretty sure he didn't really want to know. Unfortunately, he had a feeling he was going to find out anyway.

''You are. You use the power of your office to frighten defenseless women into submission.''

''The hell I do! You're about as defenseless as a tarantula.''

''Don't you dare compare me to a spider!''

''Well, you sure as the devil weren't frightened. Not of me.''

''You're quibbling, and you know it. You're a wicked, horrid man, and I never want to see you again as long as I live!''

She whirled around, crossed her arms over her breasts—her heaving, soft, supple, gorgeous—oh, Lord. Ash wished he were dead. He said, ''That's fine with me,'' and wished he meant it.

''Good. Now go away.''

''All right.'' He didn't move. He couldn't just leave her this way. Could he? No, he couldn't. Not in the state she was in. Not in the state he was in. Hell's bells, he hated this.

''I don't hear you moving.'' She ground the words out between teeth that were clenched up as tight as her fists had been.

''Now, wait a minute, Miss Witherspoon. I don't like leaving you out here in the dark—''

''Then leave the lantern with me.''

''Listen, I don't want to go away until I know you're all right. Are you sure—''

''I'm sure.''

Hellfire. He wasn't going to win this one. Not by a far sight.

Ash sighed again, heavily and dolefully, and turned around. It took him a long time to get out of the churchyard because he kept looking over his shoulder at Georgina, whose back he could barely discern even with the help of the lantern light.

He didn't want to leave her there alone, all by herself. Without his arms around her. Not that she wasn't able to take care of herself. She'd proved that a couple of times already tonight, more's the pity.

He was almost to the church before he realized that his chest was cold and that his shirttails were flapping behind him in the breeze. He stopped behind a tethered horse, buttoned up, stuffed his shirt into his trousers, adjusted his belt, wished his erection would go away, walked around outside the church until it did, and returned to the dance.

He didn't see Payton Pierce anywhere. Good. He might be inclined to arrest the bastard for indecent groping of a city girl in the cemetery. If that was a law. Ash didn't know or care. Besides, if he arrested Pierce on that charge, he'd have to take himself to jail as well.

Dammit.

He stomped over to the punch bowl and glared at the lemonade sloshing inside of it.

"Need something a little stronger than lemonade, sheriff?"

That voice. Ash scowled and looked over to where it had come from. Sure enough, there was Maybelle, grinning at him as if she knew exactly where he'd been and exactly what he'd been doing. On the other hand, she was holding up a flask, and he really, really did need something stronger than lemonade at the moment.

He said, "Yes," and marched over to Maybelle, who cackled when she handed over her flask.

Ash tipped it to his lips, took a huge gulp, and almost gagged. "What the hell's in this thing?"

Maybelle was laughing so hard she could hardly answer him. "That's sarsaparilla, sheriff. Cleans the palate. However, I do have me some rye in this other flask here."

He handed the sarsaparilla flask back to Maybelle and resisted the urge to whap her one upside the head. She was an old lady, and he was the sheriff, and the sheriff couldn't go around whapping old ladies, no matter how much they deserved it. He grabbed the other flask from her hand and this time sniffed it first before he took a careful sip.

Ah, this was better. It was rye, all right. Good rye. He took two healthy swallows before he handed the flask back to Maybelle.

"Feel better now?"

No. He didn't feel better. But because he'd cut out his tongue before he confessed to this old coot what he and Georgina had been doing amid the headstones, he simply said, "Yes. Thanks."

"Heh, heh, heh. That damned banker came in here a little while ago looking like somebody'd punched him a couple of good ones. His formal coat was all dusty, the sleeve was ripped, and his jaw was already puffing up. I told him he'd best get some raw beef on his jaw and eye if he didn't want to scare customers away from the bank come Monday morning."

"Is that so?" Ash squinted down at the old lady. She looked like a cat who'd just caught a whole bush full of canaries and was now torturing them—and having a damn good time doing it. Because he was so aggravated by the whole situation, he snatched the flask away from Maybelle again and took two more healthy glugs.

Maybelle watched him, her little bird-of-prey eyes twinkling up a storm. "Yes, indeedy. I told him he was going to terrify folks when he sings in the church choir tomorrow."

"You did, did you?"

"Sure did. I told him he didn't look much like a respectable Christian banker with that shiner of his." Maybelle tapped her chin with a gnarled forefinger. "Now I wonder who could have punched him like that."

"Yes. I wonder."

"And why anybody would want to."

Furious, Ash grabbed the flask again and drained it. "I have no idea."

Maybelle went off into a rusty peal of witchy laughter. Ash wished the flask had contained more rye. He wanted to get drunk.

"Oh, look," Maybelle cried, sounding pleased. "There's Georgina. Maybe she knows how Mr. Pierce could have sustained such an injury after walking outside with her."

The crafty old woman was squinting up at Ash like the devil

himself. Confound it, was she wise to all his secrets? He scowled at the door and saw Georgina standing there, looking serene and unruffled and infinitely ravishable. He stifled a groan, which was a good thing because Maybelle's sharp glance was darting between him and Georgina as if she were a hawk and they were a pair of fat, juicy mice.

"Yeah," he said. "Maybe she can tell you."

As for him, he was going to go to the Turquoise Bracelet Saloon and drink for a while. And maybe chat with one of the girls there. He might even do more than chat. He was so upset and bothered at the moment, he didn't know what he wanted to do, but he sure as blazed didn't aim to stick around the church basement and watch Georgina Witherspoon dance with other men all night long.

Maybelle's cackle followed him out the door along with the the rasping strains of "Turkey in the Straw." He felt like killing something.

"I never want to see him again as long as I live." Georgina spoke through tightly clenched teeth. She wasn't sure her jaw would ever loosen again.

The Murphy-Witherspoon ladies had to rent a buggy from Tooley's Livery because no one could find Payton Pierce when the time came for them to go home after the dance was over. Georgina had rejected the notion of leaving immediately after her sojourn in the graveyard because she'd not give Ash, the despicable lout, the satisfaction of knowing his lustful, improper advances had driven her away.

Then she could have screamed when she didn't see Ash again for the rest of the dance. How could she lord her serenity over him if he wasn't there to resent it?

Blast the man! He was the most intolerable, horrid, beastly, ghastly, awful person she'd ever met in her life. She refused to think about how she'd felt when he kissed her.

Anyway, she also wouldn't have allowed Payton Pierce to take her home even if he'd been found. She'd rather have walked the seven miles to the Murphy place than share a buggy with *him*, the slimely toad.

Georgina wondered why she didn't consider Payton Pierce's advances lustful and improper but only annoying, whereas she considered the sheriff's not merely lustful and improper, but entirely too close to stunning. She decided it was because Pierce was merely ridiculous.

Ash, on the other hand, could be downright dangerous. *Blast* the man.

"Won't be able to work that one out, girl," Maybelle said, grinning up a storm. "Town's too small. Got to see folks whether you want to or not. There's no avoiding 'em. Especially the sheriff."

"Gr-r-r-r-r," said Georgina.

"My goodness," tittered Vernice. "I never would have imagined Mr. Barrett doing anything untoward. He's always been such an upstanding gentleman."

"Gentleman? Ha!"

Vernice let that one slide. "But I do wonder what happened to Mr. Pierce. He went outside with you looking perfectly respectable, and came back a few minutes later looking as if he'd been in a fight."

"He *had* been in a fight. He tried to kiss me, and I hit him."

Maybelle went off into a loud and raucous string of guffaws.

Vernice said, "Merciful heavens." She didn't sound particularly shocked.

"He's a ridiculous excuse for a man," Georgina said. "A worm."

"My goodness." Vernice was gazing at her curiously. "But Georgina, if he tried to kiss you, it must mean he favors you."

"Favors me? That miserable pip-squeak?"

Taken aback by Georgina's assessment of Pierce, Vernice blinked once or twice, then ventured timidly, "You don't care for Mr. Pierce, dear?"

Georgina frowned grimly into the blackness in front of her. Driving in the territory at night wasn't anything akin to driving in New York City at night. For one thing, her parents would have had a conniption if Georgina had gone out at night without several chaperones and someone to drive her wherever she was going. For another, out here there were no street urchins begging for money. In addition, as she drove the Murphy buggy to the Murphy farm, there was no loud music blaring from dance halls, no streetlamps, and no other traffic.

Not only that, but there wasn't a speck of light anywhere except the moon, a few stars, and the bouncy light afforded by the single carriage lantern swinging from a hook at the side of the buggy. That one measly lantern didn't cast enough illumination for a prairie dog to see a snake by. Fortunately, the horse didn't seem to be able to go fast enough to hurt himself, so Georgina wasn't worried. Besides, she was too angry to be worried.

"Mr. Pierce is all right, I suppose," she muttered grudgingly.

"Oh." Vernice sounded puzzled. "But you didn't care for him kissing you?"

"I should say I didn't!"

"Oh." Vernice sat back, evidently unable to think of another question.

Maybelle didn't suffer from her daughter's lack of imagination. "I'll warrant that silly banker's got a kiss like a wet noodle. Not like Ash Barrett's kiss, eh?"

She poked Georgina in the ribs with her pointy elbow, which hurt. Georgina also didn't appreciate her inference. "Whatever *do* you mean, Grandmother?"

"I'll wager good money that Ash Barrett kisses like a man. A man who knows what to do with a woman." She chortled wickedly.

Georgina decided she was glad, after all, for the darkness. If Maybelle could see how hot a blush she blushed, she'd never live it down. She said, "Certainly not!" Then she said, "I mean, how should I know?" Then frustrated and irked, she said, "I don't want to talk about it."

"But you never want to see him again." Maybelle cackled some more.

Georgina thought her grandmother had an entirely too-wicked cackle, and she couldn't understand how her own dear mother, Evelyn Witherspoon, every inch a lady, had survived a childhood with Maybelle Murphy. Perhaps Evelyn was a changeling. On the other hand, Vernice seemed fairly normal and sedate. Perhaps it was Grandmother Murphy who was the changeling.

For pity's sake, she was losing her mind. "I prefer to let the matter drop," she said in a tight voice.

Maybelle laughed some more.

Vernice murmured, "I'm afraid I don't understand, dear," and subsided into silence.

Georgina understood. And she'd never been so humiliated

in her entire life. Not only had she succumbed to the lures of a practiced seducer, but she'd then been totally, absolutely, and unconditionally rejected by him.

She hoped Ash Barrett would die a long, miserable, agonizing death. Perhaps he could be stung to death by wasps. Or nibbled to death by red ants. Something painful. Something that would last long enough for him to regret the evil way he'd treated her. Something that would make him pay for rejecting her. Leprosy. Consumption. Scalping. That was a good one. Too bad scalping had ended in eighteen seventy-six. She growled again.

Georgina was not accustomed to being rejected. While it was true she wasn't the most beautiful female in the world— and while it was also true she'd never gone out of her way to entice men, a practice she considered demeaning—she still had a healthy respect for herself and an appreciation of her assets, both as a woman and as a person.

Never, not once, had a man thrust her away as Ash Barrett had done tonight. As if she were of no more import to him than a piece of dust. As if she were some loathsome and disgusting vermin.

And after she'd all but raped him. It was too humiliating. Too mortifying. It was simply too gruesome to think about, yet Georgina couldn't think of anything else.

The fiend. The cad. The beast.

She'd pay him back. Somehow. Some way. She'd pay him back or die trying. Even if it meant playing up to that idiot Payton Pierce, she'd pay Ash Barrett back for treating her as if she were of no more worth than an old shoe, suitable only for discarding.

Suddenly—and for the first time in days—Georgina thought about Henry Spurling. Good heavens, she'd forgotten all about poor Henry. Yet they were supposed to be almost engaged. Sort of. After a fashion. Was she being disloyal to Henry?

Bother. She glared into the blackness of the surrounding desert, wishing life could be simple for once. She'd come out here longing for adventure, but tonight she felt as though she might have experienced one adventure too many.

Well, contemplating disloyalty could wait. Henry Spurling could wait. He was in New York anyway and couldn't see what transpired here in the territory. If Georgina had to flirt a little, Henry would never hear about it.

She felt better.

Besides, Henry was as big a poop as Payton Pierce. They deserved each other.

Evidently, Maybelle had filled Devlin O'Rourke in on what had transpired at the dance, because he materialized in Georgina's room as she prepared for bed.

"You've got it all wrong, child."

If there was anything Georgina didn't need at the moment, it was an argument with Devlin O'Rourke. She turned and gave him her most furious frown. "Leave me alone! Get out of here! Go haunt my grandmother!"

"Ah, dearie, you're being silly. It's not Pierce you want to be flirtin' with, child, it's Ash. Pierce is the biggest bore in Picacho Wells."

Georgina could well believe it, but she wouldn't admit it to a soul—or even to a ghost. "Go away." She was brushing her hair violently, wishing she could be dragging the sharp boar bristles of her hairbrush across sensitive portions of Ashley Barrett's body. If there were any sensitive portions of his body. She doubted it.

"Now, now, dearie. You're only being stubborn. Ash Barrett's a big, strong, red-blooded fellow. If he stepped over the line tonight at the dance, it's only because he thinks you're a lovely young thing. And he's right. He probably couldn't control his reaction to your beauty."

"I don't want to talk about it." Her jaw ached from clenching her teeth so tightly for so long.

"Ah, Georgie, you're as pigheaded as your grandmother." Devlin sounded glum.

"Don't call me Georgie!" She hated that nickname almost as much as she hated Ashley Barrett. "And don't call me pigheaded either!"

"You're being foolish."

"I am not."

"Sure, and you are. You're just mad because Ash made you feel like a woman for the first time in your life. You ought to be thanking the lad."

It was too much. Georgina rose from her vanity bench and

turned to face the specter. She knew good and well heaving a hairbrush at a ghost wouldn't do her any good in the long run, but she did have the pleasure of hearing the brush smash against the wall after it sailed through Devlin O'Rourke's ghostly essence. And she took great satisfaction from the look of transparent shock on his transparent face.

She went to bed that night wondering if the territory made all females into raving lunatics, or only those associated with the Murphy clan.

Chapter Nine

Georgina took special care with her toilette on Sunday morning. She didn't know if she'd see either Ash or Payton in church, but she aimed to put on a good show if she did. She wasn't going to let either one of those evil men know that they'd unsettled her. At all. In any way.

This Sunday, Maybelle was going to accompany her and Vernice to town. She claimed that if she was well enough to go to a dance, she ought to be well enough to attend church.

Personally, Georgina didn't know how Maybelle Murphy dared enter the portals of a church for fear of being blasted by a bolt from heaven as the result of desecrating the Lord's sanctuary.

"You're looking spiffy this morning," Maybelle said around a mouthful of sausage as they all sat around the table eating breakfast.

"Thank you." Georgina took a bite of sausage, too, and wondered if she'd ever be able to make sausage that tasted this good. Until she visited her aunt and grandmother, she'd never considered what went into creating sausages. She'd never had a reason to. In her mind, sausage had simply come from the kitchen, cooked and ready for eating. No one in the Witherspoon family ever had to *make* the stuff.

But Vernice had made these sausages—which Georgina had

to admit were much better than any she'd eaten in New York—out of a hog the Murphy ladies had raised and butchered themselves. The notion of slaughtering a hog didn't appeal to Georgina much. If she could slaughter something else—a sheriff, perhaps—she might have looked upon the prospect of sausage-making with greater pleasure.

On the other hand, she supposed sausage-making was a frontier art and, therefore, something she ought to learn. She sighed, wondering if she'd ever get the hang of this territorial life.

"I'm looking forward to hearing the choir now that you're in it, Georgina. No one else there can sing worth spit."

Now there, to Georgina's mind, was an expression that left nothing to the imagination and, therefore, ought to be used sparingly, if at all. She wrinkled her nose. "They're singing to the glory of God, Grandmother. I don't suppose the good Lord cares if they have splendid voices or not."

"I suppose He doesn't." Maybelle didn't sound as if she appreciated the good Lord's complacence in this instance.

"You could sing with us, Mother. You have a very pretty voice." Vernice smiled lovingly at her mother.

Georgina had to hand it to Vernice. Nothing kept her spirits down for long—not even a grouchy mother or a disturbing ghost.

"Aye, that she does."

Speaking of ghosts . . . Georgina looked up from buttering a biscuit and frowned at Devlin O'Rourke, who had just materialized and was currently hovering over the breakfast table.

She sighed bitterly. She used to scoff at people who claimed to believe in ghosts. She used to think it was silly to hold seances and to pretend to commune, through spirit boards and fortune tellers, with departed relatives. She only wished her former beliefs had been true. Real ghosts were a large pain in an anatomical area Georgina was too much of a lady to mention, even to herself.

"Maybelle and me," Dev went on in a dreamy voice, *"we used to sing together all the time."*

"Humph," said Maybelle, sounding as disagreeable as she looked.

"Darlin', why won't you tell me what I need to hear from your sweet lips? I'd be goin' away if you did, and you'd never

be bothered by my spirit again. All I need is some assurance from you."

"Go away," said Maybelle, unmoved. "You're a lying, black-hearted, worthless deserter."

"Black-hearted? Deserter? Sure, and it wasn't my idea to die when I did!" Dev slapped a hand to his chest.

Georgina glanced away quickly. It was disconcerting to see his hand slide through his body that way. She concentrated on her biscuit. She'd prepared the biscuits this morning and, while they couldn't be said to be precisely light and fluffy, at least they weren't hard as little cannonballs, as her first couple of batches had been. She was getting better at this life. She hoped her self-esteem would be boosted with the knowledge, but this morning it didn't seem to want to be boosted. It merely sat there, deflated and gloomy, and didn't move. Bother. She was tired out from the dance, that was the matter with her.

"Pisht, Maybelle, darlin'. If you'd only admit that you love me, I'll leave you all in peace. Admit it. You know it's true. You've loved me for years."

Maybelle hurled a biscuit at him. Naturally, his body wasn't solid enough to stop the progress of a flying biscuit, so it hit the wall behind him and broke into a million pieces. Georgina glowered at the mess and almost wished her biscuit-making skills hadn't improved quite so much. At least when she made little cannonballs, they wouldn't break apart like that.

She heaved another sigh and murmured, "Grandmother," in an aggrieved tone that she knew would have no effect whatever on Maybelle.

She was right.

"I'll be damned if I'll tell you I love you, you miserable scoundrel!"

And another thing Georgina despaired of was ever getting her grandmother to cease cursing. It was a highly unladylike habit, and Georgina had been shocked the first few times she'd heard her. She'd never heard a female swear before. It was very upsetting.

She chewed her biscuit and tried to ignore the quarrelsome couple at the breakfast table. She supposed she should get up and clean the mess from the smashed biscuit, but she'd learned shortly after her arrival that it wasn't worth cleaning anything while Devlin O'Rourke and Maybelle Murphy remained in a room together. After Devlin dematerialized, she'd see to the cleaning up.

"Please, Mother." Vernice sounded hopeless. Georgina knew exactly how she felt. "Whatever will Georgina think of us if you continue to swear like that?"

"She ought to know me by this time. She's been here damned near a month."

Vernice sighed this time. Georgina merely chewed doggedly, hoping Mr. O'Rourke wouldn't accompany them to church. Not only would the biscuit crumbs on the floor attract ants and mice if they didn't have time to sweep them up, but singing in the choir in close proximity to Payton—if he showed up—would be a difficult enough task. If every time she looked into the congregation and saw not merely Ash—if he showed up—but her grandmother's dead lover's ghost as well, Georgina wasn't sure she could refrain from running, screaming, from the sanctuary.

This whole situation was terribly stressful. And here she'd believed she'd be dealing only with a madwoman when she set out from New York. Ha! Insanity would have been a jolly vacation compared to this. She buttered another biscuit.

"But why won't you declare your love?"

Wonderful. Georgina frowned up at the ghost, disgusted. He had started whining. She did not approve. She possessed too much pride to whine, and she believed others should as well. "Behave yourself," she snapped. "Grandmother won't be impressed if you act like a mewling infant."

"Oh, my." Vernice stared at Georgina, aghast.

Georgina was a little aghast herself. She'd never spoken to an older person in such a disrespectful tone of voice. Still a body should only be expected to take so much. She said so.

"I'm tired of having you bothering me all the time, Mr. O'Rourke. There's nothing *I* can do to sway my grandmother. You ought to know her well enough by this time to know that no one can influence her if she doesn't want to be. I don't understand why you persist in haunting Aunt Vernice and me. It's Grandmother whom you need to sway, not us. We'd give anything if she'd say whatever you want her to say so you'd disappear." She bit savagely into her biscuit.

"Has he been showing up in your bedroom at night?"

Georgina eyed Maybelle, not sure she liked the gleam in her little black eyes. "Yes. Why?"

"Why, you lecherous old goat!" Maybelle hurled a coffee cup at the ghost this time. It shattered with an earsplitting crash, and shards of china flew all over the room.

"Mother!" Vernice shrieked, starting up from the table.

Georgina, more practical than her aunt, made a quick sweep of her arms, thus gathering the rest of the breakables into a heap in front of her. She leaned over so that Maybelle couldn't get at another one without a struggle. She said, "Stop it!" not with any hope it would help but out of habit.

Devlin shot up and hovered against the ceiling. *"It's not what you're thinking!"*

"The devil it's not! I know good and well the only reason you're going to Georgina's room at night is so you can see her undress, you rascal!"

"Good Lord." Georgina looked up from the pile of crockery she'd been guarding. "You don't mean it."

"Like hell I don't!" Maybelle jumped up from the table, remarkably spryly, considering she was old and had sustained a broken ankle not many months before. "He's a lying, cheating reprobate, and I'll never, *never* tell him that I love him. Because I don't!"

"But love!"

"Don't you *but love* me, you swine!" Maybelle shook her fist at Devlin. "You never loved me! Why should I say I love you?"

Georgina, too dejected to offer any further objections to this argument, merely shook her head and sighed again. Vernice, who had already fetched the broom to sweep up biscuit crumbs, now began to ply the broom on the crockery shards.

"You're wrong, Maybelle! You're one hundred percent wrong about me, and I'll haunt you until the day you die to prove it."

Georgina shut her eyes and wondered if she were evil for wishing her grandmother would die soon and solve all of their problems.

Probably. She was very discouraged.

Ash's eyes ached. So did his head. His mouth felt as if someone had stuffed cotton wadding into it—after he'd wiped the bottoms of his boots with the cotton.

He hated drinking. Although, it must be admitted, his hangover had at least ousted Georgina Witherspoon from first priority in his mental processes this morning.

When he'd been fighting Indians, he and the other soldiers had learned one or two tricks from the enemy. Ash used one of them this morning in an attempt to cure his aching head. Willow-bark tea. Worked swell for headaches, even if it did taste like something the cat had coughed up.

Hell. When had his life taken this turn, anyway? How had he let one lone female succeed in banishing several years of calm and peace in his life? It wasn't fair. After he'd quit the army and Phoebe had finally quit him, he'd thought the only thing he'd ever crave again in the world was peace and quiet. He'd thought he'd found it here in Picacho Wells.

Ash wrinkled his nose, held his breath, and swallowed the tea. He managed to keep it down with an effort.

He'd left home when he was sixteen, seeking adventure. Since both the Mexican and the Civil War were long over, he'd joined the army of the West in hopes of fighting Indians. He'd found adventure, all right. And plenty of Indians. And fights. He'd seen enough bloodshed and grisly death to last a lifetime. He'd also seen more famine, despair, illness, and grief than he'd realized existed on earth. He'd believed, in fact, that during the Indian war he'd seen the worst life had to offer a man.

And then he'd married Phoebe.

He shook his head slowly, wondering how one relatively small woman could have affected him so painfully. He'd loved her so much. When he'd realized she was nothing but a tart in fancy clothes, it had broken his heart. Nearly killed him. He'd been such a fool for that woman.

"Dammit, she's dead." He spoke fiercely, hoping in that way to jar the unhappy memories of his marriage out of his aching head.

Unfortunately, it didn't work. They all came swarming back: Phoebe in her wedding gown, looking more beautiful than any woman had a right to look. Lord, he'd been proud— and so happy. His eyes watered, and he wiped at them, telling himself it was the hangover making them drip.

Then the other images came: Phoebe whining at him because she didn't want to live in the territory. Phoebe telling him how much she hated him; how she'd only married him for his money; how she wanted to stay in Galveston where there was some fancy society and other men—men who made her feel pretty and wanted.

His heart ached in time with his head, and he took another couple of swigs of willow-bark tea. The stuff was foul.

What had really hurt—hurt more than anything—was when she said she'd rather die than bear his child. She'd refused to go to bed with him after the first week or so. Didn't want to ruin her figure, she said. Told him he could go rut with whores if he had to, but she wasn't going to.

At least she'd had the grace to die before she'd ruined his life completely, although at times he wasn't really sure that she hadn't. And he'd still loved her at the end. He didn't know why. A man's fantasies died hard, he reckoned, although hanging on to one about Phoebe being anything but a sucking leech seemed nonsensical.

And now, as much as he hated to admit it, he was in danger of falling for another fancy city woman. The idea made his stomach, which had almost settled down, churn feverishly. He fought his nausea and drank some more tea.

"Dammit, she's not Phoebe." He told himself that because he couldn't stand feeling like a fool twice in one lifetime. "She makes butter. Well, she tries to make butter. She more or less milks a cow. She almost quilts. She even cooks, after a fashion. She at least attempts to do things Phoebe wouldn't have been caught dead doing, and she even seems to like trying to do them. Besides, she has the only good voice in the choir."

That didn't work, either. He still felt like hell.

That was neither here nor there. Ash Barrett would be roasted on a spit before he'd let Miss Too-Good-for-this-World Witherspoon know she'd gotten to him with her fancy airs, sweet smell, and low-cut ball gown. He'd go to church today if he had to crawl there.

He glanced in his shaving mirror and wished he didn't look so green. Aw, hell.

Ash still didn't feel human when he mounted Shiloh and headed to the church, his head aching in time to the rhythm of Shiloh's gait.

• • •

"What the devil are you looking at?"

Georgina had been driving the Murphy wagon down Picacho Wells's main street, preparing herself to enter the church and face her doom—that is to say, preparing to face Ash and Payton. Her grandmother's sharp voice startled her. She turned her head to see to whom Maybelle had addressed her pungent remark.

She frowned when she caught sight of the same ruffian who'd stared at her so rudely the other day staring at her lecherously again today. He lounged against the wall of the Turquoise Bracelet Saloon and didn't so much as bat an eye at Maybelle's question. He only continued to leer at Georgina, who lifted her chin and pretended to ignore him.

"Damned jackanapes," Maybelle muttered. "If he says a word to you, Georgina, shoot him."

Georgina eyed her grandmother. "I don't have a gun, Grandmother."

"No *gun*?" Maybelle stared at Georgina as if she'd just told her she had no head. "How in the name of glory do you expect to survive out here if you don't have a gun, girl?"

"*I* don't have a gun, Mother," Vernice pointed out. "I'm surviving quite well."

Maybelle snorted. "Hell, Vernice, you're too old to inspire any man to ravish you. You don't need a gun."

That was mean, and Georgina didn't appreciate it. She said, "Don't be nasty!" in a reproving tone.

Maybelle reacted as was normal for her. She ignored both the words and the tone. "I'm going to teach you how to use a derringer, Georgina, and you're going to buy yourself one. Tomorrow. I'll come to town with you and help you get a good one from the dry goods store."

Feeling unequipped to argue this morning, Georgina only said, "Fine," and hoped her grandmother would shut up. She did. Thank heavens.

After she tied the horse under a tree and fetched her Bible, she took a deep breath, said a brief prayer, and headed for church. She was holding her head so high she nearly tripped on the stairs leading to the sanctuary. Her grandmother cackled, and Georgina felt silly.

She saw Payton as soon as she and Vernice walked into the choir room to put on their robes. He seemed to be hiding

behind several other choir members, although she couldn't be
sure. Georgina felt a good deal of contempt for him if he was
trying to avoid her. The idiot. Not only was he too tall to hide
behind a bunch of women, but it was undignified and cowardly
for him to want to do so. She'd bet money that Ash—the
abhorrent wretch—wouldn't try to hide from her.

She wasn't going to hide, either. She didn't aim to allow an
indiscretion to daunt her. She had too much pride for that. She
wasn't going to let Payton or Ash think she was ashamed of
herself. The fiends. Smiling for all she was worth, she walked
right over to the banker. He blinked at her and looked terrified.
She greeted the women who had been talking to him, and then
took the bull by the horns. Or the chicken by the feathers.
Whatever.

"My goodness, Mr. Pierce, what a terrible bruise you
have." She gave him her friendliest, most open and honest
and sympathetic smile.

He seemed to shrink a little. "Er, yes. I—ah—had an accident."

Georgina tutted appropriately. "I'm so sorry to hear it."

"Yes, ah, thank you." He swallowed, then cleared his
throat, then blurted out, "Miss Witherspoon, may I talk to you
for a moment? Only a small moment?"

For pity's sake, now what? Georgina really didn't want to
be alone with the man. Not that she couldn't defend herself
against any puny assault he might manage to launch, derringer
or no derringer, but she didn't much want to have to. On the
other hand, what could happen to her in church on a Sunday
morning?

She smiled graciously. "Of course, Mr. Pierce."

"Thank you." He sounded almost inhumanly humble.
Georgina's contempt for him swelled.

They walked outside and paused at the gate to the churchyard, a locale Georgina considered rather ironic, although she
didn't say so. "Yes, Mr. Pierce? You wished to speak to me?"

He cleared his throat again and fidgeted. Thunderation, the
man was nervous. "Yes, Miss Witherspoon, I—ah—I wanted
to tell you how dreadfully sorry I am about my conduct yesterday evening. I stepped over the bounds of polite behavior,
and I apologize. I don't know if you will ever be able to

forgive me, but I would consider it noble of you if you would at least consider it.''

Hmm. Georgina pondered her options. She actually hadn't intended to punish the man—after all, she didn't fear Payton Pierce in the slightest. On the other hand, perhaps it might be wise to withhold total forgiveness for a little while. Make the worm squirm, as it were.

Then again, she could probably use Pierce. Ash didn't like him and perhaps if Georgina pretended to be fond of the banker, it would aggravate the sheriff.

No. That was too conniving. Georgina didn't play games like that. She'd seen other young ladies use coy tricks of that nature in New York and had always deplored their dishonesty. She didn't intend to sink to their level. She opted, therefore, to tell Pierce the truth.

"I forgive you fully and freely, Mr. Pierce. Let's try to forget all about the incident.'' To show him she meant it, she held out her hand for him to shake.

Pierce eyed her hand for a moment as if he wanted to make sure she really meant to shake his hand and not slap his face with it. His nerves appeared to have been soothed when he finally took her hand in a limp clasp and shook it. "Thank you very much, Miss Witherspoon.''

"Think nothing of it, Mr. Pierce.''

He kept her hand in his. Drat the man, what was the matter with him? Georgina frowned slightly.

"Miss Witherspoon . . .''

"Yes?'' She tugged on her hand, and he released it. Good thing, too. She might have had to hit him, and it would be nowhere near as satisfying to wallop Payton Pierce as it was to dump liquids on Ash Barrett.

"Er, I know I disgusted you last evening with my deplorable conduct, but I hope I haven't ruined myself irremediably in your eyes.''

"Heaven's no, Mr. Pierce.'' What *was* the man talking about?

Whatever he thought they were talking about, he appeared comforted by her answer. "I'm so glad. Then, ah, well, do you think I might still hope?''

For what? Georgina didn't know, so she figured she had nothing to lose. "Of course, Mr. Pierce.'' She gave him a sweet smile to let him know she meant it, even though she wasn't sure she did since she didn't know what he wanted to hope—

Oh, good Lord. Suddenly, Georgina realized what it was he wanted to hope for. "Er, that is, well . . ."

Fiddlesticks! What could she say now? Again, she opted to tell the truth, surprised at having found honesty the best policy twice already today—and it was still morning. On the other hand, it was Sunday. Perhaps the sanctity of the day had something to do with it.

"What I mean is, well, there is a gentleman named Henry Spurling in New York . . ." She let the sentence trail off, hoping Payton Pierce was smart enough to figure out the end of it on his own.

He was. His face fell. "Oh. You mean you're already promised?"

"Not exactly. There's been, ah, an understanding—of sorts—between us for several years now." She dipped her chin and tried to appear dainty and demure. She never used to have any trouble appearing dainty and demure. Perhaps she was getting more into this rugged territorial life than she'd given herself credit for.

"I see." Pierce sounded morose. He brightened slightly and said, "But nothing is fixed irrevocably between you?"

"No. Not exactly. But our parents have desired the match for a long time now."

He grabbed her hand again. Georgina frowned at him.

"What about your desires, my dear Miss Witherspoon? You must consider your own feelings in a matter of such great import."

She pulled her hand out of his grip. "Yes. I am considering my own feelings. Thank you for your concern." She made her voice the tiniest bit colder to warn him against trying to snatch her hand again.

"Of course. But—but—but if you haven't yet given your word, then I may hope?"

There he was again, back to hoping. Georgina was really tired of this conversation. "You may do as you see fit, Mr. Pierce. Now I believe we should get back inside the church. The Reverend Voorhees is ringing the bell." As if to prove she wasn't lying, the bell in the church steeple gonged.

"Yes, of course." Pierce looked anything but satisfied.

Well, that was his problem and he'd have to learn to live with it. Georgina wasn't going to give him a promise she didn't intend to keep—or even hint at one. She wasn't that sort of woman. She smiled at him to let him know that she didn't hate him, even if she'd rather die than let him kiss her again.

With fair grace, he bowed and crooked his elbow. Georgina placed her hand on his arm, and they walked to the church's backdoor together. She was happy when she saw that Ash looking none too healthy this fine summer morning, had seen them at the churchyard gate and had stopped to stare. His expression was more than merely sour. It was really quite murderous. She was glad of it. Pretending to ignore Ash, she warmed her smile up a few degrees for Pierce. She hoped Ash would choke to death on his bile.

"It was kind of you to apologize to me, Mr. Pierce. I fear you did rather startle me last night."

She shouldn't have said that, because the man blushed. After sliding another glance at Ash, she decided maybe it wasn't a bad thing after all. The sheriff looked ready to commit foul deeds and mayhem.

Georgina was pleased with herself when she joined the choir, filed in with them as they took their places in front of the congregation, and began to sing "Christ, Whose Glory Fills the Skies." Ash sat right next to Maybelle, looking about as stormy as a New York City sky in February.

"I don't *want* the sheriff to teach me how to shoot your blasted derringer." Georgina glared at her grandmother, who glared back at her.

"Too bad. He's coming to dinner today. He said he'd teach you how to aim and shoot my derringer, and that's what he's going to do."

Horsefeathers. Georgina's feeling of triumph had come to a crashing halt shortly after services had ended and she'd started to drive them all back home. They hadn't been in the wagon for more than ten minutes before Maybelle had sprung the news of Ash's impending visit. Georgina was not at all happy about it.

For one thing, she didn't trust him with a gun in his hand

and herself present. For another, she didn't trust herself with
a gun in her hand and him present.

Add to that the flutters in her stomach that always showed
up when he did, and Georgina knew she was in for an unpleasant afternoon.

Ash wasn't thrilled with the prospect of teaching Miss Cozy-
Up-to-Rich-Bankers Witherspoon how to shoot a gun. Even a
derringer.

On the other hand, he couldn't have refused Maybelle's in-
vitation to do so if his life had depended on it. He chalked up
his lack of resistance to his hangover, and cursed himself for
drinking so much. He refused to acknowledge the slight—the
very slight—tingle of anticipation in his innards at the notion
of sparring with Georgina again.

He'd managed to suppress his unruly tingle and was in an
unmitigated foul mood when he rode Shiloh down the path
through the pecan trees to the Murphy ranch. At least his head
had stopped aching. If they served anything more exciting than
boiled chicken for dinner, though, he might not survive.

Luck was with him, at least regarding the food. Vernice had
fricasseed a couple of chickens, and the Murphy ladies served
them up with dumplings, carrots, and potatoes. Ash managed
to survive the meal, and even eat a piece of spice cake for
dessert.

"Would you care for more coffee, Sheriff?" Vernice was
smiling at him as if he were the most wonderful human being
in the universe. Ash appreciated Vernice a lot that afternoon.
Every time he glanced at Georgina, she looked as if she were
hoping he'd turn around so she could stab him in the back
with the carving knife.

"Thank you, Miss Vernice. This was a delicious meal."

Miss Vernice's niece, needless to say, hadn't spoken a word
to him all during the meal, except for a few stiff "thank yous"
and an "I beg your pardon." She wasn't being rude. She just
wasn't very friendly. Well, he wasn't friendly with her, either.

In spite of the state of his health, her proximity disturbed
him in a way that had nothing to do with his hangover. Confound it, what was the matter with him, anyway? He should
be able to resist an attractive member of the opposite sex with
no trouble at all—especially a worthless city girl. That's what

Phoebe had been, and he'd learned the hard way what worthless city girls were like.

With Georgina so close and all, he refused to acknowledge her attempts to overcome her city roots and to fit in here in the territory. Since she was within touching distance, he didn't want to like her at all, much less respect her. Hell, if he began respecting her, there was no telling where his lust would lead him, but he expected it would be somewhere perilously close to disaster. He'd been down that road once, by accident. He wasn't about to head down it again on purpose.

From the way she glowered at him, he guessed he wouldn't have too much trouble resisting her. Even if his own base, lustful nature overpowered him, she didn't look like she wanted to be kissed let alone touched by him at all.

Ash sighed heavily. Shoot, he didn't want to do this.

He forced himself to smile at Georgina. Politely. He was going to be polite if it killed him. "Would you care to go out back by the barn and practice shooting, Miss Witherspoon?"

By the way she eyed him—cold and hard and hateful—he guessed she wouldn't care to do any such thing.

"Yes, thank you, Mr. Barrett." Chipped from stone, is what those words were. And she threw them at his head as if it were the enemy and they were weapons.

Ash sighed again. "Fine. Let's take your grandmother's derringer, then, and get started. The ability to shoot a gun is one a lady often needs out here."

"Yes. Grandmother Murphy told me as much. She said a derringer is a fine weapon to use on a man who tries to get too forward in his attentions." Now she was trying to bludgeon him with her words.

Ash wished he'd stop thinking such things. Hell's bells, he wasn't a fanciful man. These images must be another byproduct of his hangover. He'd never get drunk again as long as he lived, no matter how many Georgina Witherspoons he fondled and then couldn't take to bed—perish the thought.

"Fine. Let's go."

She ripped off her apron, slapped it over the back of a chair, snatched a shawl from a hook by the backdoor, and stomped outside. Ash stomped after her then had to turn around, stomp back inside, and take the derringer from Maybelle's hand. Her wicked cackle followed him back outside again.

Chapter Ten

"No, dammit, don't close your eyes!"

"Stop swearing at me!"

If Ash Barrett touched her again, Georgina wasn't sure she could bear up under the strain of it. Every time he stood behind her and put his arms around her to guide her aim, she wanted to drop the blasted gun, turn into his embrace, and kiss him silly.

This was awful. Her temper had frayed to such a degree that she was about to lose it entirely and begin screaming.

"I'll stop swearing at you when you stop closing your eyes when you pull the trigger. How the hell can you aim if you close your eyes every time you shoot?"

"If someone's close enough for this gun to work on him, I won't have to aim!"

"Dammit, that's not the point!"

"Stop swearing at me!"

"Dammit!"

Ash let his arms drop from her shoulders—thank God—and stormed away from her. When he got as far as the cottonwood tree beside the barn, he slammed his fist against it, dislodging a shower of fluffy white cotton, and turned around to glare at her. "What the hell kind of logic is that?"

She sniffed and lifted her chin. She'd been lifting her chin a good deal today. "It's perfectly good logic."

"It is not. It's stupid. Just because the thing's called a belly-gun doesn't mean it isn't useful if you're standing a few feet away from someone."

"Oh?" Georgina had a feeling she was being ridiculous about this whole gun thing, but her nerves were in tatters, and she couldn't seem to help herself. "Then why do they call it a belly-gun?"

"Because it's good close up, too." If he gnashed his teeth any harder, they'd begin to shave down.

He went on, "You can keep from getting into a desperate situation in the first place if you use the threat of a shot in the gut to hold a man off."

Loath to admit that Ash was, in fact, right in this situation, Georgina tossed her head and muttered out "I suppose so."

"You suppose so." Ash lifted a hand and passed it over his face, as if he were trying to smooth out the lines of frustration.

Georgina felt a teeny-weeny pinch of repentance for being such a poor student. But if he had to teach her how to shoot a gun, why in the name of mercy did he have to put his arms around her to do it? It was too distracting to have his arms around her. She liked the sensation altogether more than she should. When he had his arms around her, she felt safe. Protected. Warm and comfortable. She wanted to curl up in his arms and cuddle there forever while he touched her body the way he had yesterday evening at the dance.

Good heavens, this would never do. She sucked in a lungful of air and let it out in a gust. "I beg your pardon, Mr. Barrett. I shall try to keep my eyes open and aim properly."

He stared at her, his eyebrows drawn down into a ferocious frown. "You mean it?"

She resented his asking and almost told him so. Knowing she'd only start another argument if she did, she took another deep breath, let it out slowly, and said, "Yes."

He stood there, glowering at her, for another several seconds. Then he nodded once curtly and walked back to her. "All right. Turn around and look at the target."

Georgina turned and eyed the board with a big black bull's-eye that her grandmother had nailed to a nearby pecan tree. So far, Georgina hadn't hit it once. She was glad the chickens lived several yards away on the other side of the barn.

Although she'd braced herself to feel Ash's arms go around her again, the touch of them shocked her. She hoped he wouldn't notice the gooseflesh rising on her arm. Or the shiver she wasn't quite able to suppress.

"You cold?"

Drat! His voice, warm and rich and hinting of dark, sensual pleasures, thrilled her. She said, "Not at all," in as indifferent a tone as she could manage.

"You shivered a little."

"Oh. Did I?"

"Yes. You sure you're not cold?"

His hands had been lightly gripping her wrists, showing her the proper way to hold the gun. Now his right hand slid up her arm, and his left drew her arm to her waist, where he held it loosely.

"No. I'm—ah—not cold. Not at all."

"Good. I thought you might be. There's a little breeze to-day."

Ash made his own little breeze against her neck with his warm breath, and Georgina nearly swooned. She kept herself upright only through a great effort of will. "Is there?" Her voice was all air. Good heavens, what did that mean?

"Yes. A very slight breeze. Very small. Nothing to worry about."

"Ah. Good."

Sweet Lord in heaven, the man was nuzzling her neck! She was going to faint. She was going to scream. She was going to die right here and now. They'd find her this evening when she didn't come in for supper, and she'd be cold on the ground.

Ash's lips touched her bare skin, and she revised her death scene. She wouldn't be cold at all. She'd be a pile of ashes. Probably still smoldering.

His hand tightened at her waist, and he drew her back a pace, until her spine was smack against his chest. He was so big. Georgina had never felt awfully small before, but now she did. She felt like a delicate, fragile sweetmeat being served up for the delectation of this big, alarming, sheltering, over-whelming male. The sensation was new to her, and exquisite. She sighed with pleasure.

"I think you're getting the hang of it now." His voice was a low rumble that Georgina felt in every nerve of her body.

"Am I?"

"Sure. You just need to point and squeeze." He demonstrated the squeezing part, very smoothly, with his left arm at her waist.

"Oh. I see." She dropped the derringer. It fell with a soft plop to the grass at her feet.

"There you go again, Miss Witherspoon, not paying attention. You dropped the weapon." His right hand traveled down to her wrist, and his fingers first covered and then slid between hers.

"Mercy, how clumsy of me." She turned her hand over in his.

"Yes. Clumsy."

Oh, dear. This wasn't right. How could she learn to shoot a gun this way? "Perhaps I should try again."

"Sure. Good idea."

He lifted her right arm and, with his fingers still twined with hers, pointed at the target. He pulled her back against him again, and she felt the bulge in his trousers. Very delicately, she pressed her hips against it and rubbed. His soft growl in her ear sounded almost desperate.

So she did it again. "Is that what I'm supposed to do?" she whispered.

"Yes. That's exactly what you're supposed to do."

"Good." Her eyes had slid shut several seconds before. Now she let her head fall back until it rested against his shoulder. He nuzzled her ear. He was so tall and broad, and it felt so luxurious to let him hold her like this. Georgina had never experienced anything quite like it. When his hand slid up her bodice to her breast, she moaned softly.

She knew she shouldn't be moaning and allowing the man to hold her in this perfectly delicious—no, no. Indelicate. That's what it was—in this perfectly indelicate manner. Georgina said, "Oh, my."

"Does that feel good?" His voice was so soft she barely heard it, but she felt it clear down to her toes, which curled in her shoes.

"Is—is that the way to hold a gun?"

"Yes. You have to be very gentle." He demonstrated by very gently lifting his other hand to her bosom and then by very gently squeezing her breast.

Georgina knew she was going to die any second now. What a lovely way to go. "Gentle," she murmured. "Gentle."

"Very gentle." He tenderly twitched a nipple between his thumb and forefinger.

"Oh," whispered Georgina. "How nice."

"Very nice," he agreed, his breath warm on her neck. "Very, very nice."

Her own hands had been idle during the last few seconds. Now she lifted them and clutched his shoulders. She couldn't reach anything else, what with him holding her back to his front the way he was doing. His shoulders were very large. And very hard. Almost as large and as hard as his arousal against her hips. She murmured, "Gentle," and rotated her hips.

He growled—very gently—in her ear. Georgina was delighted, so she did it once more to see if it would happen again. It did. The insistent tickle of pressure and ecstasy became a throbbing pulse between her thighs. Georgina wished she could do something about it. It needed attention. Desperately. So, since there seemed nothing to impede her, she turned in Ash's arms until the juncture of her thighs pressed against the bulge between his legs.

There. That was it. Just what the doctor ordered.

Ash growled again.

Georgina rubbed her point of need against his bulge. Oh, yes. That felt wonderful. It was almost—but not quite—relief.

His arms went around her, and all of a sudden Georgina found herself being squeezed—not gently at all—against his body.

"Confound it," he growled. "This isn't fair." He kissed her savagely.

No, she guessed it wasn't fair. They couldn't keep doing this out in the open this way. They really ought to go somewhere private to practice these things. Her supply of breath was occupied in kissing Ash, so she didn't say so.

"This is driving me insane," he ground out against her lips.

Since he followed the declaration up with a swoop of his tongue, Georgina was spared an answer. She did, however, respond to his tongue's invasion appropriately. Merciful heavens, she'd had no idea people did things like this. How totally appalling. How totally wonderful. She moaned, hoping in that way to get her point across.

She was startled when Ash fumbled for her hand and drew it between them. When he pressed her palm against his erect sex, which she could feel outlined against his twill trousers, she gasped.

"That's what you do to me, blast it," he muttered. "Do you feel that?"

How could she not feel it? She nodded, suspecting her vocabulary was inadequate for the situation.

"It's got to stop."

She knew what to say about that. "Yes." There. She wished she meant it.

"Every time I see you, this happens to me."

Did it really? How thrilling—er—dreadful. "Oh."

"Oh? Is that all you can say?"

Actually, yes. It was all she could say.

"You're about to drive me crazy, Georgina. You're from New York City, for God's sake, and I'm a sheriff in New Mexico Territory."

That was self-evident, so Georgina didn't consider that it called for a response.

"This is crazy."

It was crazy, all right. Georgina was so fascinated with Ash's present state of intense arousal that she squeezed his erection with her hand. He groaned. She squeezed again, then rubbed her hand over it, trying to discern its exact shape and size. She'd been so sheltered in her lifetime. It seemed a pity now. If she'd, say, grown up on a farm, she'd probably know all about these things. "I have so much to learn."

He groaned louder.

"This is all so new to me."

It seemed to take a monumental effort for Ash to grab her hand and draw it away from his crotch. "You're going to learn more than you want to any second now if you keep doing that." He stepped back, holding Georgina away from him, and looked down into her eyes.

She didn't understand why he wasn't still holding her, though. She frowned. "But—"

"No. You do funny things to me, Miss Witherspoon. I react strongly to them."

Her reaction to him was pretty strong, too. Thankfully, although her brain was befuddled, Georgina sensed this would not be the right time to announce that. Instead, she said, "Oh?"

"Oh? Is that all you can say?"

Since it was, she nodded. She didn't understand when Ash closed his eyes and seemed to be praying. What a strange man he was.

"How's the lesson coming along?"

Her grandmother's fiendish voice ripped through the still summer air like a gunshot. Ash jumped a foot. So did Georgina. Ash's hands fell away from her shoulders in a heartbeat. Georgina whirled around and saw Maybelle Murphy, cackling up a storm, limping toward them, stabbing at the ground with her cane as if it were a lance and the dirt an enemy.

Without stopping to think, Georgina swooped down and plucked the derringer off the grass. She turned, lifted her arm, squinted at the bull's-eye, and fired. She heard Ash mutter a crisp "Blast" at her back, and she blinked.

"Merciful heavens," she said, flabbergasted. "I hit the bull's-eye."

Maybelle had joined them. "You're a good teacher, Ash Barrett." She slapped him on the back, and he took a startled step forward. "A damned good teacher."

Ash's gaze traveled from Maybelle to Georgina to the bull's-eye and back again. Georgina's gaze traveled from her grandmother's wicked smile to Ash's crotch. She lifted her head again immediately. "Yes," she said, hoping to distract them all. "He's a very good teacher."

Ash left shortly thereafter. Georgina, along with Vernice and Maybelle, waved at him from the front porch.

"I wonder why he doesn't turn around and wave back," Vernice said, clearly puzzled.

"Probably Georgina can tell us," Maybelle said, obviously delighted.

Georgina kept her mouth shut.

Georgina didn't see Ash Barrett for almost an entire week. She told herself she was glad of it. When she gathered eggs on Monday morning, she caught herself glancing out over the endless, barren plains, trying to catch sight of dust in the distance that might signify a visitor. *Not* Ash, of course, because she didn't want to see *him*. But somebody.

No visitors came to call.

When, later that afternoon, she, Vernice, and Maybelle went to town to purchase a derringer for Georgina's use, Georgina discovered herself eyeing all the buildings closely and wondering where the sheriff might be. She didn't see him anywhere, which seemed strange. After all, wasn't he supposed to be keeping the peace in Picacho Wells? That was his job, wasn't it? Didn't he have to keep an eye on things?

Whatever his job was supposed to be, he was nowhere in sight. Georgina told herself she wasn't disappointed, although she couldn't account for a certain heaviness in her chest that lasted for the rest of the day.

When she churned butter on Tuesday, she recalled the first time she'd churned butter and discovered herself sighing and wishing . . . Actually, she wasn't sure what she wished for, but she was sure it had nothing to do with the sheriff.

On Wednesday when she and Vernice went to town to do some shopping before they attended choir rehearsal, she again failed to spot Sheriff Ash Barrett anywhere. In her estimation, this prolonged absence indicated a clear dereliction of duty on his part, and Georgina wondered why the citizens of Picacho Wells tolerated such slothful behavior from their sheriff. Her intensely crabby mood wasn't improved during choir rehearsal, when Payton Pierce gazed moony-eyed at her the entire time.

Her grandmother hadn't helped her overall mood, when she chose to give Georgina some choice advice about her appearance.

"You're looking peaky, girl. What you need is some good, hot, old-fashioned loving. You've got to cozy up to Ash Barrett some more. I'll bet anything that man knows how to turn a girl into a woman, and I'll bet even more that she'd enjoy every minute of it." Then she'd cackled knowingly.

Vernice had cried, "Mother!"

Georgina had first had to repress a strong impulse to throw something at her grandmother. And then she had to repress an even stronger urge to agree with Maybelle.

She'd lain awake for nights now, thinking about how Ash had touched her. He'd kindled all of her feminine impulses, reactions, and sensations. They were feelings she hadn't known she possessed until Ash Barrett had made her aware of them, the beast. Now she was frustrated all the time, had an awful time sleeping, and was forever squirming when no one could see her.

"You've got to get that man to make love to you, Georgina. You can do it yourself, of course, but it's nicer with a man."

"*Mother!*"

Maybelle had huffed indignantly at Vernice. "Prude."

Georgina had blinked at her grandmother and wondered what she was talking about. She could do it herself? Do what herself? Bother. She wished she wasn't so innocent. She didn't ask, and, as a result, her frustration grew in proportion as the week progressed.

On Thursday morning, Vernice woke up with a sniffle.

"But you go on to the quilting society, Georgina. There's no need—you're doing so well—I don't want to be a nuisance—and the ladies do so love—you can bring me all the news—it's such a bother to have a summer cold—but you go on. Please, dear. Anyway, you have to take the paisley calico to Betsy Bailey for me, because I promised her I'd bring it." She sneezed violently.

"Of course I'll go to the quilting society, Aunt Vernice." Georgina hadn't considered not going, truth be told. She never gave in to ill health herself, and was pleased that her aunt didn't expect to be pampered. After all, it was only a little sniffle.

Georgina knew her eagerness to go to town had nothing to do with the possibility of seeing Ash Barrett again—mainly because Ash Barrett seemed to have skipped town, the rat. "And I'll be happy to take Betsy your paisley calico. Oh, it's very pretty, isn't it? Is it from a skirt?"

"No. It was a dressing gown Devlin used to wear."

"Oh." Goodness, the fellow had been flamboyant, hadn't he? Still was, for that matter. He'd about driven her mad the past several nights, pestering her about Ash Barrett. It seemed that as soon as she recovered from an indecent suggestion proffered by Maybelle, she received a barrage of unsolicited relationship advice from Devlin O'Rourke. For some unknown reason Devlin seemed to think that Ash was the perfect match for her. Georgina had had just about enough of the whole affair.

Georgina spent a lot of time wishing there was some way to get rid of the bothersome ghost. Unfortunately Maybelle continued to refuse to tell him she loved him. Impossible people, both of them.

"The paisley will look quite nice in a quilt."

"It'll look a far sight better in a quilt than it ever did on Devlin O'Rourke," Maybelle said, then snorted.

Georgina sighed.

Devlin O'Rourke, who had been dangling overhead and staring with great longing at Maybelle, said, *"Sure, and you don't mean it, Maybelle. I was a handsome lad, I was."*

"You haven't been a *lad* for twenty years and more, you ridiculous man."

Georgina and Vernice exchanged a glance. Knowing by this time that the argument might go on for hours, Georgina took the piece of paisley cloth from Vernice and kissed her cheek, whispering, "Good luck," into her ear.

Vernice smiled gratefully and gave Georgina a hug. "I'm so glad you came out here to us, dear. Life is so much more pleasant with you around."

That was about the nicest thing anyone had ever said to her. Even though she was a little late in leaving the house and would be late to the quilting society meeting, Georgina was in an almost-sunny mood when she got into the buggy's driver's seat, encouraged the horse, and set out for town. In spite of her grandmother and Devlin O'Rourke. And Ash Barrett, whom she couldn't seem to forget no matter how hard she tried.

"It's only glands," she muttered, frowning against the bright territorial sunlight. Georgina had been to school. She knew about glands. They got people into trouble all the time, glands did.

But she was no innocent schoolgirl who could be swayed by her glands into indecent actions by a practiced and wicked seducer. She knew better. She had standards. Principles. Strong backbone and moral fiber.

Good heavens, she sounded like an advertisement for Quaker Oats. Did they have Quaker Oats out here? Now there was something to contemplate. Georgina managed to consider Quaker Oats for a good three seconds before her treacherous mind turned once more to the problem of Ash Barrett.

"He's such a *fiendish* man," she told the horse, who didn't seem to care. "He's sneaky. He creeps up on me until I don't know what I'm doing, and then he pounces. It's so difficult to keep track of him."

She knew she was lying. She was falling into an infatuation with him, was the problem, and she knew it. What she needed to do was think about her home and family. Henry Spurling. She'd think about Henry Spurling.

Henry lasted even fewer seconds than Quaker Oats had, which Georgina considered a telling—and unfortunate—sign. Henry was so *boring*. Ash Barrett wasn't boring. Far from it. Which was also unfortunate.

But the day was lovely—there was hardly any wind at all— and the sun was shining, and Georgina was looking forward to the ladies' quilting society. She enjoyed chatting with the other ladies and learning all the latest gossip. Anticipation, therefore, shortly made her mood bounce back from its Ash-induced funk.

She was about a mile from Picacho Wells when she saw a lone rider heading toward her. For a second she thought it was Ash, and her heart swooped crazily.

It wasn't long before she realized her mistake. Whoever that was riding toward her, his posture was nothing like the sheriff's. Ash rode as if he'd been born on a horse. He rode easily. Beautifully, even. Georgina knew men in New York who would kill to have the expertise on a horse that seemed to be second nature to the sheriff of Picacho Wells. She sighed dreamily, then realized her thoughts had drifted back to Ash again. Drat!

In the meantime, the man had ridden close enough for Georgina, who had sharp vision, to discern his features. They were hard and mean, and he had little squinty eyes and a poorly shaven face. A spurt of alarm went through her. Dear heaven, it was the leerer. It was the same insolent man who had lounged against the saloon and ogled her as she drove past. The one with the big gun on his hip and the air of somebody who didn't care about the law or honest citizens or much of anything else but his own pleasure.

He was undoubtedly only on his way somewhere. He wouldn't bother her. He was merely passing through the area. There was no reason for her to be afraid of him.

She didn't believe it.

Pulling her horse to a halt in order to better evaluate the situation, Georgina tried to get her heart to stop thundering. She would not show this fellow any fear. Trying to appear unconcerned, she glanced to her right and her left, and wished with all her heart that she'd arrived in Picacho Wells already. As much as she appreciated the emptiness of this unspoiled countryside, she had to admit that meeting strangers on a New York City street, with hundreds of other people around, didn't dismay her as much as meeting that man in this place.

This was all she needed. She'd spent the entire week in a state of almost unendurable stress, and who does she run into on her way to town? Could it have been Ash Barrett, the cause of her anxious state? Heavenly days, no.

Why should *he*, who'd sworn to uphold law and order, patrol the area to ensure that delicately reared females were not molested by smirking evildoers? Georgina huffed. Ash Barrett was only the *sheriff* in Picacho Wells. There was no reason *he* should bestir himself to make sure women weren't persecuted by leering beasts like this horrid man, who was leering at her again today.

Oh, Lord, oh, Lord, oh, Lord, what was she going to do? She couldn't try to outrun him. For one thing, he actually might not have any evil intentions and she'd feel stupid if she ran away from an innocent man. For another, she'd never get away with it. Her buggy and horse could never outrun a lone rider on horseback.

She felt in her pocket for her derringer, and was relieved to find it there, small, slick, and lethal. Perhaps her grandmother wasn't so crazy after all.

For insurance's sake, she plucked the buggy whip out of its holder. She'd known how to use one since she was a girl, and, quite frankly, she was a little more confident of her ability to inflict damage with the whip than with her derringer. She hoped she'd be able to demonstrate her skill on the approaching villain. If he was a villain. Oh, dear, this was so confusing. Georgina tried to pray, but her nerves were crackling, and she didn't have much luck.

Georgina realized that perhaps her plan of stopping to collect her thoughts might not have been the best; the man was coming toward her even faster now and she was just sitting there, waiting for him. She shook her head, disgusted with herself. She clicked to the horse, and the buggy started rolling again, toward town. Where in the name of mercy *was* anybody? Every now and then she encountered people on the way to Picacho Wells. Why couldn't she encounter somebody today? Somebody besides that man, of course.

Her heart, which had been hammering in spite of her efforts to steady it, sank like a rock as the man rode even closer. His leer for her today appeared much more deadly, and infinitely more triumphant, than any of the other leers he'd thrown at her. It boded ill. She knew it.

Good heavens, he was huge. Georgina knew that if it came to a struggle, she wouldn't stand a chance. She laid the buggy whip across her lap and reached into her pocket for her derringer as he drew up next to her buggy.

"Well, hello there, miss." His voice sounded as if it had been ruined by tobacco and strong drink, and Georgina shuddered when she heard it. He had a terrible face; terrible because it held not a trace of human kindness. He reached out and grabbed the horse's bridle, thereby making the animal, a placid creature who preferred stillness to activity anyway, stop moving.

Her throat constricted and her ears rang as the blood in her veins pumped wildly, but she gazed at him without wavering. "Please release my horse, sir." She'd never seen a more ruthless-looking individual, even as illustrated in the *New York Times*.

"Please release my horse, sir," he repeated in an affected, high-pitched simper. Then, in the low, gravely voice that was his naturally, he said, "Hell, lady, I'll release your horse. Then I'll take over the drivin' for you. How'd you like that?"

"I wouldn't like it at all," Georgina said stiffly. "I have business in town. Now go away." To emphasize her statement, she pointed her derringer at him.

A flicker of annoyance crossed his face when he saw the gun. "Hell, lady, what do you think you're going to do with that peashooter?"

She'd been hoping to frighten him with it, actually. Before she had a chance to say so, or to pull the trigger, he jerked the horse's bridle, making the buggy shimmy and Georgina lose her balance. His hand came down, hard, on her arm, and the derringer fell from her grip. She gasped in terror and pain.

"That wasn't a nice thing to do, lady. I think I ought to teach you some manners." And with that, and with an evil smile that made Georgina's insides shrivel up, the rogue drew a long-barreled Colt from a side holster, and aimed it straight at her.

Chapter
Eleven

Confound it, where was she? Ash drew the curtain back from his office window and glared into the sunshine-speckled street outside. She and Miss Vernice were supposed to come to town on Thursdays at elevenish to participate in the ladies' quilting society. All the other ladies were already here. Where were they?

He'd managed to avoid being seen by Georgina all week long, and it was about to kill him. He wanted to see her so badly he ached, but he wouldn't admit it to a soul—particularly not his own. He'd been hiding out in his office all morning, most of the time standing and looking out the window. Looking for her.

Lord, he was an ass. It was a warm day, and he was all but stifling in the office because he didn't want her to see him today, either. But she was late, and he was worried.

Hell, she was a woman. Women were always late. Look at Phoebe, for the love of God.

But Georgina had never been late to one of her silly meetings since she'd come to Picacho Wells.

She'd never been late to choir practice, either. Blast Payton Pierce to pieces. As if on cue, Pierce emerged from the bank and stood on the boardwalk, alternately looking up the street

143

and eyeing his big silver pocket watch. He was waiting for her, too, damn his eyes.

But Pierce had already seen her once this week. Hell, they'd sung together at choir rehearsal, if you could call what the choir did singing, for an hour or more last night. Greedy bastard. Ash hadn't seen her once all week, except to peek at from behind his curtained window. It was his turn today.

He snorted derisively. What was he thinking? His turn? He was losing his mind.

But she wasn't coming. Where in the name of holy hell was she? For crying out loud, anything could happen to a body out here. This wasn't New York City, for the love of Christ. This was the New Mexico Territory. There were all sorts of things out there on the plains. Cougars. Buffaloes. Bad men. Coyotes. Flash floods. Lightning strikes. Hell, even a prairie-dog hole could cripple a horse, and then whoever was depending on the horse could cook under the hot sun or die of thirst or . . . Aw, hell.

Ash's nerves were all but jumping out of his skin when he saw a lone rider heading out of town. He frowned. That was a bad man, and Ash knew it. He'd even sent a telegraph wire to the authorities in Santa Fe, describing him and asking if he was wanted for anything. He hadn't received an answer yet, but he anticipated his suspicions would be confirmed once it came.

His kind was not uncommon in the territory, although Ash did his best to keep them out of his town. They were a hardened lot who were eager to take whatever they wanted, regardless of the consequences. If the rogue kept riding in that direction he'd run into Georgina, and Ash wouldn't put it past him to try to assault her. His blood ran cold.

"She'd better have that blasted derringer with her." He muttered, trying to ignore the worry that was quickly overtaking him. His stomach churned with worry. His nerves skipped. His skin crawled. His spine tingled.

A derringer wouldn't do her a hill of beans worth of good against that outlaw's Colt, and Ash knew it. He also knew that if he rode after the man and intercepted him, there was a good chance the bastard would start a gunfight. The last thing Ash wanted was for Georgina to be hit by a stray bullet. Plus, the man hadn't done anything wrong—yet.

On the other hand, he wasn't about to quibble over details if Georgina's life was in danger. His jurisdiction as sheriff didn't cover arresting men because they had looked at Georgina lecherously in the past. Hell, if that were possible, Ash would have arrested Pierce a long time ago. He *had* to know that she was safe. He hurried outside and unhitched Shiloh from the rail in front of the sheriff's office.

"Where are you going, Sheriff?"

Ash looked up, scowling. That voice. That thin, squeaky tenor voice. Payton Pierce. Ash wanted to ask why the hell Pierce cared where he was going, but he didn't. It was Ash's responsibility to protect all the citizens of Picacho Wells, even the bankers. "Just going out for a ride, you know, to look things over."

"Miss Georgina should have arrived for her quilting society meeting before this time."

Ash wanted to shout at Pierce and ask him if he thought Ash didn't know that already. He told himself to calm down. Pierce had as much right to worry about Georgina Witherspoon as Ash did, damn him. "Yes," he said, trying not to growl. "I know."

"Are you going to look for her?"

What the hell business was it of his? Ash controlled himself and didn't ask, which he considered rather noble under the circumstances. He ground out a brief, "Yes," and mounted Shiloh.

With a little flutter of his hands, Pierce hesitated for a moment. Then he blurted out, "I'm going with you."

Like hell he was. Ash didn't say so. Instead, he nudged Shiloh around and kicked him into a gallop. He couldn't see the villain any longer, and he wasn't about to wait until Pierce got himself organized.

Dear God, he hoped Georgina was all right. Georgina *had* to be all right. He prayed hard as he rode out of town.

What on earth good was a teensy little derringer against a huge gun like that, anyway? Georgina felt her terror take a swerve into anger. If only Ash Barrett had taught her how to shoot a *real* gun, she might be able to help herself in this situation. But no. A derringer was a *lady's* weapon.

A lot of good that did her now. If a so-called lady isn't

accompanied by a gentleman whose aim in life is to protect
her, she'd be better off with a bigger gun. Bitterness ate into
her stomach as she considered her options and came up with
none. Wonderful. After this horrible man used her as she suspected he wanted to, he'd probably kill her. Then wouldn't
Ash be glad? She knew she was being unfair to Ash, but she'd
have been less than human if she'd been able to be fair right
then.

"Don't worry, child. I'll help you."

Georgina jumped a foot and jerked her head around, staring
blankly toward the voice. Devlin O'Rourke! It was Dev!
Thank God, thank God. Maybe he could help her. Since she'd
become accustomed to speaking to the ghost as if he were a
real person, she missed the puzzled look on her captor's face.
With a thrill in her heart, she cried, "Oh, my! What are you
doing here?"

Her enemy said, "I'm talkin' to you, lady."

Why was that beast talking to her as if he couldn't see Dev?
Georgina recalled with a start that Dev could appear to whom-
ever he pleased, and evidently he hadn't pleased to be seen by
the gunman. That might be a good thing. Or it might not.
Whatever it was, she felt somewhat more brave now that she
knew she wasn't entirely alone. She frowned at the man with
the gun. "I wasn't speaking to you."

*"Keep your spirits up, lass. We'll take care of this crea-
ture."*

Dev spoke bracingly, which irked Georgina. She didn't need
moral support. She needed to be rescued. "What can you do?"

The brute with the gun said, "I can do any damned thing I
want to do, and don't think I can't."

His words, and the tone with which he spoke them, went a
long way toward vanquishing Georgina's trepidation. She de-
tested impertinent people. "*Will* you be still? Your constant
interruptions are very rude."

"Who the hell are you talkin' to, lady? What are you, some
kind of loon?"

Georgina's temper snapped entirely. She'd had enough of
people calling her a lunatic because she was being driven wild
by monstrous circumstances and an incredibly annoying ghost.
"No, I am *not* a loon, you devil! And don't call me *lady* in
that impudent manner!"

He laughed wickedly. The man had the audacity to *laugh* at her! Outraged, Georgina instinctively moved her hand toward the buggy whip, but the click of the Colt's hammer being drawn back stayed her. Blast! Whatever could she do now? Fling the ghost at him? It was an appealing thought, but she couldn't very well get a firm grip on Devlin O'Rourke.

"You and me, we're gonna have us some fun." The man winked suggestively.

Georgina, pushed by circumstances and two very irritating men, understood exactly what he meant. She was almost too mad to be frightened. She wouldn't panic. She *wouldn't*.

"I sincerely doubt it." Her voice was as sour as lemon juice.

He laughed at her again, a laugh that once more made her long for a bigger gun.

Ash held a firm appreciation for the perils of travel in southeastern New Mexico Territory. The terrain was rough, and even the most experienced cowboys found it difficult to navigate. Today, however, he pushed Shiloh harder than was usual for him because he was in such a state of anxiety.

When he heard a horse behind him, looked, and beheld Payton Pierce on his fine-boned gray—a showy horse unsuitable, in Ash's opinion, for the rigors of the West—he pressed Shiloh even harder.

"Sorry, boy, but I don't want that stupid banker riding with us." He was sure Shiloh would understand and approve of his desire in this instance, since Shiloh, a fine, sturdy piece of horseflesh, made a mockery of Pierce's gray.

"Wait up!"

Pierce's shrill tenor voice made Ash wince. He hunched over and pretended he hadn't heard. He kicked Shiloh gently and sped up a bit more.

Ash Barrett, sheriff of Picacho Wells, wasn't about to deputize Payton Pierce to hunt bad men with him. And he wasn't going to allow an unofficially deputized citizen to act as a deputized one, either. Anyway, he'd already decided he was going to rescue Georgina Witherspoon by himself or die trying.

• • •

"Put that buggy whip back where it belongs and get down off that buggy. Now." The scoundrel made a gesture with his gun hand, and eyed her with a wicked gleam.

Georgina carefully slid the buggy whip—and a whole lot of good *that* had done her—into its holder and considered her situation. The derringer was out of the question—it was also on the floor. The buggy whip was also out of the question. Piffle. What was she supposed to do now? Throw Aunt Vernice's paisley calico at him?

"Do what the man says, child."

Although she appreciated Dev's attempt at help in this perilous circumstances, she wished he'd go back to the Murphy place and haunt her grandmother. His comments disconcerted her and interfered with her thought processes during what might well be a life-or-death confrontation.

Oh, dear Lord. It *was* a life-or-death confrontation, wasn't it? For a second, fright almost overwhelmed her, but she crushed it beneath her anger. She was up to this. She was up to anything, blast it! She *had* to think of something. If she didn't, that awful man would force himself on her, and she'd sooner die—although that option didn't appeal to her, either.

Furious that so many things were beyond her control, she snapped at Dev, "Why should I?"

"Because I told you to." The man with the gun sounded peeved.

His peevishness was nothing compared to Georgina's. "I wasn't talking to you!" She pressed a hand to her forehead, wishing she could think clearly. But how could she? With a gunman in front of her and a ghost behind her, she was completely distracted.

Dev said, *"Because I don't want him to shoot you before I can think of some way to thwart him."*

"But I don't want you to do anything." That's all Georgina needed, she thought dismally, was to have the ghost of Devlin O'Rourke do something that would get her killed. As if she wasn't in enough peril already.

"Pisht, Georgina, you're turning out to be stubborn as your grandmother." Even Dev sounded peevish now.

The outlaw scowled at her. "That's too bad, lady. I'm the one with the gun, and you're going to do what I say."

Irked by Dev's assessment of her, she cried, "I am not!,"

not realizing that the gunman thought she was shouting at him.

"You are, too. Even if you don't have red hair." Dev shouted back. The noise made Georgina's nerves jangle like Christmas bells.

The gunman, clearly frustrated with the situation, growled, "You are, too. If you don't believe me, I'll give you a demonstration."

He fired a shot into the ground beside the buggy. Startled, the horse shuffled sideways, and Georgina had to calm him down before she could turn her attention to her tormenter. "Will you stop that? There's no need to frighten my horse!"

"Get the hell down from that buggy," he commanded. "Now."

"For God's sake, do as he says, child!" Dev's voice shook, as if he were afraid. Wonderful. If even the ghost, who was already dead, was afraid of this beastly gunman, what could *she* do?

Georgina didn't think any of this was fair. Since, however, she hadn't yet come up with a plan to rescue herself, and since she was feeling besieged from all sides, she grumbled, "Oh, very well," and climbed down from the buggy. She pretended to stumble as she did and as she crawled up off the floor, she grabbed the derringer and shoved it into her pocket.

The damned banker's horse was faster than he looked. Ash still hadn't managed to shake Payton Pierce. He guessed he'd just have to put up with an onlooker, then, because he wasn't going to stop and try to reason with the fool man.

When he heard a gunshot not far off, the blood seemed to freeze in his veins. He swore fiercely and kicked Shiloh into a ground-swallowing gallop.

"Be careful, boy. Don't fall, whatever you do."

His brain chanted *Georgina, Georgina, Georgina,* as he rode. He'd have given anything he owned—hell, he'd have stolen something and used that—to have her safely in Picacho Wells just then.

Shiloh evidently shared his rider's concern. He managed to avoid all the gopher and prairie-dog holes in his way as he tore across the plains.

Even over the clatter of Shiloh's hooves, Ash heard Pierce's gray.

• • •

"That's better," the man with the gun said. He was smirking again.

"I sincerely doubt it." Georgina wanted to cross her arms over her stomach to hold her anxiety inside, but she wouldn't give him the satisfaction. Sweet heaven, what was she going to do?

"For the love of Christ, child, don't make the man mad."

Blast the interfering ghost! Georgina was upset enough without him interrupting. She snapped, "He must already be mad, or he wouldn't be doing such things."

She still might be able to use the derringer, so she discreetly fluffed her skirt to make sure the folds of her dress didn't block the pocket containing the gun. If worse came to worst, she'd wait until he had her pinned down and shoot him in the belly. Dear Lord, what a time to find out why they called them belly-guns!

The outlaw walked over to her, sauntering in a way Georgina considered both ill-bred and portentous. She wished he wasn't so big. "You sure are a hellcat, ain't you, lady?"

She drew herself up. She would *not* show him any fear. "No, I am not. And you, sir, are no gentleman."

Dev appeared overhead, fluttering transparently. *"Be careful, girl. Try not to antagonize him."*

She ground her teeth together and told herself not to scream. "He's already antagonized."

"Oh, so I'm not a gentleman, eh? And I'm antagonized, am I?"

Dev fluttered harder. *"For the love of God, Georgina. If he shoots you, your grandmother will never agree to spend eternity with me."*

Georgina, beside herself, cried, "Is that all you can think about in this situation? Yourself? I can't *believe* this!"

"What the hell are you talking about now? I think you're crazy, lady."

"I'm not crazy!"

"Georgina! Calm yourself this minute. I have a plan." Dev's voice sounded firm.

Georgina tried to calm down. As much as she hated to admit it, she knew the ghost was right. If she aggravated this wretch too much, he'd probably shoot her even before he raped her.

She took a deep breath, hoping it would help. It didn't, but she muttered, "All right." Because she couldn't help it, she ground out, "This isn't fair."

The gunman eyed her suspiciously. "You're nuts, lady."

"*I am not!*" Oh, dear, she hadn't meant to screech. Now she'd made him angry.

He walked over to her and she braced herself. He didn't hit her, thank God, but he looked meaner than ever. "Get the hell over there."

He grabbed her arm and flung her at the buggy. She stumbled, but managed to gain her balance before she fell. She held a protest in check.

"Nuts or not, I aim to enjoy myself before I leave this town for good, believe me."

Georgina's heart sped up and seemed to lodge itself somewhere in her throat. This was going to be the ultimate test of her strength of spirit and intelligence. She'd either ward him off or die trying.

She shut her eyes tightly and opened them again. She wouldn't panic. She wouldn't show this man that she was afraid of him, no matter how terrified she was. Instead she glowered at him to let him know that, while he might have the larger gun, he was the lesser human being.

Sweet God in heaven, that was her buggy. Ash's heart fell sickeningly as he reined Shiloh in. And that was the man he'd followed out of town. He'd been right about the bastard.

Ash frowned furiously at Pierce, who pulled his horse up next to Shiloh. "What's going on?" Pierce's tenor squeaked so badly, Ash would have snorted in derision if he hadn't been so worried about Georgina.

"Look for yourself," he ground out. "But keep your damned voice down."

"There's no need to swear, Sheriff."

"God dammit," muttered Ash, which he figured pretty much told Pierce what he thought of his observation.

Pierce shaded his eyes and squinted into the distance. "Good God, that man is accosting Miss Witherspoon!"

"Yes, dammit."

Pierce scowled at Ash, who scowled back. The banker apparently decided to take Ash to task for his language later. "What are we going to do?"

"*You're* not going to do anything. *I'm* going to save her, but I have to think of a plan first. If we just ride up on him, he's liable to shoot first and ask questions later."

"I don't care what you say. I'm going to help you save her."

"Curse it, you're not the sheriff of Picacho Wells. I am."

"I don't care who you are. I'm going to help rescue Miss Witherspoon."

"I haven't deputized you, Pierce. You stay out of it."

"I will not."

"Confound it, stop being stupid. You're not fit to be rescuing ladies from outlaws."

"I'm as fit as you are."

Ash turned in his saddle so as to look Pierce square in the face. "Hogwash! I've been in the Indian army and I'm a duly authorized sheriff. You're a damned banker!"

"I may be a banker, but I also know how to shoot a gun!" Pierce turned, too, and glared straight at Ash.

Ash supposed he was trying to look fierce, but to Ash he looked merely petulant. "I'm not going to argue with you about it. You stay right here, Pierce."

"I will not."

Ash rolled his eyes and wondered if he'd get in trouble for laying the chowderheaded banker out cold.

Dev said, *"What I'm going to do is appear to this man and scare him, Georgina. Then, when he's off guard, you get out your derringer and shoot him."*

Nervously fingering her skirt, wondering exactly when she should reach for the derringer, Georgina asked, "What if he isn't scared?"

"I'm not scared, lady, and don't you think it." The gunman gestured with his gun for her to move to the back of the buggy.

Georgina pressed a hand to her cheek and wished her brain would stop jumping and skipping about. She was so scared, she was getting light-headed. And things only seemed to keep getting worse.

"He'll be scared." Dev gave Georgina a little ghostly peck on the cheek, for encouragement she presumed. She didn't

need encouragement, she needed Ash to come save her, blast
it. *"Remember how scared you were when I first appeared to
you."*

"Yes," Georgina said grimly. "I remember."

Her tormentor glowered at her. "What the hell are you talking about now? What do you remember?"

"I'm not talking to you!"

"Dammit, lady, how come you keep saying you're not talking to me, when I'm the only one around here?"

"You are not." She was going to faint. No, she wasn't. She
couldn't faint. If she fainted, he'd have won. Lord, she wished
this was over.

"I'm going to distract him now, Georgina. Be prepared."
Dev appeared directly above the villain.

She said through her teeth, "I'm prepared."

"Oh, really?" The outlaw reached for his belt buckle and
unfastened it. "So am I, lady. In fact, I'm gonna lift up your
skirt and have me some fun. What do you think about that?"

Georgina's heart gave a terrified spasm, but she squared her
shoulders and glared at him. "I think you're disgusting."

"Whoooooooooooo!" cried Devlin O'Rourke suddenly.
"Booooooo!"

Georgina let out about a bushel of air she'd been holding
when the gunman gave a start of horror and spun around. She
had to give Dev credit. He scared the bejeebers out of her
adversary when he materialized suddenly to one side of him,
waving his arms like a demented scarecrow. Somehow or other
he'd made his hair stand on end, too, so he really did look
quite ghostly, even if it was full daylight.

The scoundrel uttered a loud scream and fired a wild shot
at the ghost. "What the hell are you?" He shot again, crazily.

Georgina realized that Dev had carefully chosen the location
of his materialization. If he'd appeared directly in front of the
ghastly man, the villain might have shot through him and hit
Georgina by accident. As it was, his bullets were flying off
into the desert, harming nothing and no one. She grabbed the
derringer out of her pocket. *Finally*, she might have a chance
to use it.

"I am the ghost of all your victims," Dev said in a ghoulish
voice. Then he whooed and booed again, and again the outlaw
shot at him, turning white with panic.

Georgina, although badly frightened, had been keeping careful count. That was four shots so far, including the one he'd already fired into the ground. According to Grandmother Murphy, gentlemen often left one chamber open to avoid shooting themselves in the foot and so forth when they were in their cups. Since this man was obviously no gentleman, Georgina decided she'd better not depend on an open chamber. She shouted, "Scare him again, Mr. O'Rourke!"

The gunman whirled around and fired a shot in Georgina's direction. She shrieked and ducked instinctively.

Dev shouted, *"Be careful, Georgina! His gun might not be empty!"*

Terrified and more angry than she'd ever been in her entire life, Georgina fired a shot at the outlaw. He screamed again. She hoped it was because her bullet had found its mark.

"Georgina! Georgina! What the hell are you doing?"

That voice! Georgina whirled around, her derringer pointed. Good Lord! It was Ash and Mr. Pierce. She couldn't remember ever being so happy to see anyone.

"Whoooooooooooo!" Dev cried desperately. Georgina realized he was trying to keep her tormenter occupied so he couldn't shoot either of the men who had finally showed up. *"Booooooo! Whoooooooooooo!"*

"Aaaaaaaargh!" cried the gunman. He shot at Dev one more time and then again, on an empty chamber. Then he screamed once more, and threw the gun at the ghost.

It was the chance Georgina had been waiting for. Ignoring Ash Barrett and Payton Pierce, she walked right straight up to the villain and shot him in the thigh.

He screamed again and collapsed onto the desert, clutching his leg and writhing in the dirt.

"A good place for you," Georgina said, satisfied with her handiwork. Then she sought out Dev, who was still fluttering over the bandit. "Thank you," she said with a grateful smile. He tipped his ghostly hat at her.

"You're welcome," said Ash Barrett.

Georgina turned to him and sucked in a breath of hot air. She was just about to tell him exactly how "grateful" she felt toward him when she remembered that Dev could only be seen if he chose to be. She doubted that Dev was about to show himself to Ash and thus decided to grit her teeth and keep her mouth shut. Ash would probably think she was crazy, too, if she kept talking to someone he couldn't see. It galled her to see him take all the credit but she figured it was better than him thinking she was a lunatic.

Georgina's tight rein on her temper collapsed as soon as the Sheriff resumed speaking. "Thank God we got here in time!" Ash declared. "Are you hurt, Miss Witherspoon?"

Fueled by her leftover terror, her anger flared. This was the last straw. It was bad enough that the sheriff of Picacho Wells had taken his precious sweet time in getting here, but now he actually expected her to *thank* him for finally showing up.

"In time?" she asked incredulously. "You got here in *time*? In time for what, pray tell? What did either of *you* do to save me?"

"Help me," the outlaw sobbed from the dirt. "Help me! She's crazy! She tried to kill me!"

Georgina grimaced at him. "Honestly! Some people are too ridiculous to live. He was going to do awful, lewd things to me, Sheriff, and now he's whining because I shot him, which is nothing compared to what he planned to do to me! Arrest him at once!"

She realized that Ash was staring at her in a half-puzzled, half-delighted way. Her heart executed an excited leap. She lifted her chin proudly. She could take care of herself, by gum, and Ash wouldn't be able to deny it any longer.

Payton grabbed her arm. She turned and frowned at him. "Release my arm if you please, Mr. Pierce. I've had enough of being manhandled today."

The gunman moaned again and Georgina gave him a swift kick to shut him up. She didn't care if he was in pain. Not after what he'd planned to do to her.

Ash slipped his gun into his waistband. Mr. Pierce, Georgina noted acidly, hadn't bothered to arm himself before he dashed to her rescue. How he had planned to save her from an armed bandit without a weapon, she had no idea, and she really didn't care enough to ask. "And now, if you will all excuse me, I must be on my way to the ladies' quilting society. Sheriff, I will stop by the jail to press charges once the meeting ends."

Ash's grin made her heart thump like a woodpecker.

"You're really something, you know that, Miss Wither-spoon?"

She felt her cheeks get hot and turned to climb back into the buggy. "I shall take that as a compliment, Sheriff."

"Good. Because it was meant as one."

"Thank you."

Good heavens, if she didn't get out of the line of Ash's gaze pretty soon, she was going to fling herself into his arms and beg him to have his way with her. With some difficulty, she settled herself on the buggy seat, clicked at her horse, and started on her way to town.

Georgina smiled as she drove off. While she hoped nothing like this would ever happen again, she was pleased to know that she could protect herself if it did.

"That was a close call, darlin'."

She nearly jumped out of the buggy when Dev suddenly materialized beside her. She'd forgotten all about him. "Thank you very much for helping me, Mr. O'Rourke."

"You're welcome."

Georgina didn't really mind Dev sitting next to her, even though his aura was very chilly. Actually, what with all the nonsense that had gone on in the sunshine back there, the coolness of Devlin's essence felt rather refreshing. "I have to admit I was worried there for a minute or two." And if that wasn't an understatement, she'd never uttered one. She amended, "I was *quite* worried." Scared to death was more like it.

"You should have been. That there's a bad man."

"Yes, I noticed that quality in him."

"But the sheriff, now. Well, child, that man's fallin' head over ears for you."

Georgina's astonishment was unfeigned. "What? What did you say?"

"Pisht, girl, there's no need to holler."

"I beg your pardon. But I do believe you're mistaken on that score, Mr. O'Rourke. Mr. Barrett and I don't care for each other at all."

She was not encouraged when Dev went off into a gale of laughter.

Chapter
Twelve

When she arrived home later that afternoon, Georgina had already decided to approach Maybelle and try to get her to talk to Dev, at least. She figured that, as long as Devlin had performed heroically, there was no point in wasting it. If she could convince Maybelle that her dead lover was a hero and a savior of innocent maidens' virtues, perhaps Maybelle would finally admit that she loved him and he'd go away. Georgina used to be fairly adept at wheedling her parents; perhaps her grandmother would also prove to be susceptable to a good wheedle.

As she approached Maybelle Murphy, who looked to be as cantankerous and unwheedleable as ever, she began to doubt her plan. However, she wasn't going to give up without a fight and so she resolved to add a little drama to spice up the story some. Couldn't hurt, and Georgina had noticed that Maybelle seemed to enjoy drama.

"You know, Grandmother," Georgina said as she approached her, trying to appear casual, "if it wasn't for Mr. O'Rourke, I might well be lying dead in the desert right now."

Vernice dropped a small pot she'd been carrying to the stove and slapped her hands to her cheeks. "Merciful heavens! Whatever—good gracious, Georgina, what—whatever is the—how could such a thing—"

"What the devil are you talking about?" Maybelle, never one to beat around the bush, glared first at Vernice and then at Georgina.

"I mean that I was accosted outside of Picacho Wells today by a vicious gunman who wished to do me harm."

"Good Lord in heaven!" Vernice paled and staggered backward. Georgina almost wished she'd been slightly less dramatic, if only for her poor aunt's sake.

"Fortunately, Mr. O'Rourke saved me." He'd helped, at any rate, and Georgina didn't aim to be proud with her grandmother. She'd save her pride for Ash Barrett. She'd as soon Maybelle consider her dead lover a hero as Georgina a heroine. Maybe then they would all be able to sleep through a whole night.

"You're joshing!" Maybelle sounded scornful.

"I am not!" Georgina began to feel the least bit disgruntled. "The horrible man planned to do evil things to me, and then shoot me!" At least, she presumed that had been his intention. She was positive about the evil things part.

"Well, I'll be jigged." Maybelle's expression held respect. About time, too. "What happened?"

"Oh, Georgina! I knew I should have gone—it was so stupid of me—just because I have a little cold—oh, I'm so sorry!"

Feeling guilty, Georgina took time to hug her aunt before continuing with her story. "It's not your fault, Aunt Vernice. That awful man might have hurt you if you'd been with me."

"Ha! I thought you said Dev rescued you. Do you mean to say you think he'd let Vernice get shot, and not you?" Maybelle snorted contemptuously. "I wouldn't be surprised, at that."

Irked, Georgina snapped, "I do not mean to say any such thing! I'm sure Mr. O'Rourke would have saved Vernice, too!"

"The girl's right, Maybelle."

Oh, wonderful. Georgina frowned at Devlin O'Rourke. She'd hoped to soften her grandmother's heart toward him, but she didn't trust him not to ruin everything. She gestured for him to go away, but he paid her no mind, which didn't surprise her.

Hoping to preclude any unhelpful interruptions from the

ghost, Georgina hurried to say, "I know very well that Mr. O'Rourke saved me from a fate worse than death today, and words can't convey how very much I appreciate it."

"Goodness gracious sakes alive!" Vernice sank into a chair and pressed a hand over her heart.

Maybelle snorted. "A fate worse than death, my hind leg. It would do you good to have a good roll in the hay, Georgina. Only not with an outlaw." She grinned evilly at her granddaughter. "Ash Barrett would be a good choice."

"Aye, your grandmother's probably right about that, girl."

Vernice cried, "Mother!" in a stifled voice.

Georgina scowled for a moment at her grandmother and Dev, decided she couldn't win this one, and retired from the lists. Drat the contentious old couple, anyway.

After his ill-fated attempt to save Georgina Witherspoon from rape and plunder, Ash tried like the devil to avoid running into her. He discovered, as she had, that it was impossible to avoid others when one lived in a community as small as Picacho Wells. He did, however, fight tooth and nail when Sally Voorhees asked him to sing in a trio with Georgina and Payton for a special end-of-summer service the minister was planning.

Not only did Ash not want do anything at all, ever, for as long as he lived, in conjunction with Payton Pierce, but if he had to stand next to Georgina for however long it took to sing a song, he wasn't sure he would be able to account for his actions. Nearness to her brought out something primitive in him, and he was pretty sure the churchgoers of Picacho Wells would consider it obscene.

"Shoot, I can't sing, Sally," he said, in a voice closely resembling a whimper.

"Nonsense, Ash. You have a lovely baritone voice. I remember it from when you and Phoebe used to attend services."

Ash's stomach cramped at the mere mention of Phoebe's name. Lord, Lord, he remembered those days. She used to go to church because she could dress up and flaunt her finery in front of the other ladies in town.

She also used to say that she couldn't bear staying in that awful house alone with Ash for one minute longer. And, she invariably continued, explaining that even if the folks in Picacho Wells were simpletons and rubes, they could talk. Unlike Ash who, she claimed, remained silent in order to torment her.

That wasn't the reason for his reticence, of course. He had clammed up because every time he tried to sweet-talk Phoebe out of her dismals, she went off into a tantrum.

He'd learned shortly after the marriage rites had been spoken that he couldn't win. He grimaced, remembering, then shook off the mood.

"Besides," he said to Sally, "I have to work."

"Nonsense. Even sheriffs get Sundays off, Ash Barrett, and you know it."

He did know it, but he resented her bringing it up when it had been such a handy excuse. "Well, Sally, you never know. If something comes up, I'll have to attend to it. You know that's the truth. That's what the city government pays me for."

"Oh, don't be so obstinant, Ash! Nothing will come up that needs the sheriff's attention on a Sunday morning. Nothing ever happens."

She was pretty much right about that, drat it. Nevertheless, Ash continued to fight. "Wait just a minute there. Miss Witherspoon had an encounter with an outlaw only the other day."

"That wasn't on a Sunday. It was on a Thursday. And it didn't happen in town."

She sounded so reasonable. Ash begrudged her since she seemed to be determined to rope him into this singing thing. "It could have been a Sunday and in town, curse it! Crooks don't necessarily respect the Sabbath the way the rest of us do, you know."

Sally tutted at him. "Miss Witherspoon is well able to take care of herself, as you ought to know by now."

Yes, he knew it. He frowned at Sally because he still didn't want to admit that a fancy-dancy city girl didn't need a man to help her survive in the big, ugly world. He continued to balk. "Maybe. But not everyone is as lucky as she is."

"It wasn't luck that saved her, and you know it. Anyhow, this has nothing to do with outlaws kidnapping ladies. This has to do with your singing in a trio for the special summer service. We *need* you, Ash."

"There's got to be someone else in town who can sing baritone, blast it." He was finding it difficult not to use a bunch of "damns" and "hells," and realized his vocabulary hadn't improved any since he'd left Galveston when he was sixteen.

"You're being deliberately obtuse, Ash. You know as well as I do that the only other man in town who can sing a note is Frank Dunwiddy, and he has to watch all those children while his wife sings in the choir."

"Can't she watch the kids for a few minutes?"

Sally shook her head. "No. She deserves one morning's rest from those children, Ash Barrett, and if you don't believe it, you try taking care of seven children twenty-four hours a day, seven days a week."

Shoot. Put that way, Ash had to admit poor Mrs. Dunwiddy probably did deserve a break on Sunday mornings. He wished he wasn't such a fair-minded man. It would save him a lot of grief.

Sally continued her assult. "Just because you choose not to use your voice for the Lord's good, doesn't mean you *shouldn't*. After all, one ought to use the gifts one is given. Don't you think so?"

She smiled at him so sweetly that Ash, who had been prepared to bellow out another refusal, couldn't. He hemmed and he hawed and hawed and hemmed, but Sally won in the end.

"Miss Witherspoon created the harmonies, Ash. She wrote them herself. She's a very talented lady."

"Yeah," said Ash. "I'm sure she is." Dammit.

Sally Voorhees laughed at him.

It transpired, therefore, that on the first Wednesday in August, Ash found himself participating in choir practice. What's worse, he found himself standing with Georgina and Pierce in front of the choir as Sally Voorhees played the introduction to "Come, Christians, Join to Sing" on the piano.

Georgina stood between him and Pierce which was, to Ash's mind, a good thing or his impulse to commit mayhem might have overcome him, to Pierce's detriment. She was the one handling the melody. He and Pierce were supposed to chime in with the harmony in the chorus.

Since Georgina only came up a little farther than his shoulder, Ash had a good view over the top of her head of Pierce. He'd as soon not. But there was no help for it. He frowned at Pierce, who frowned back.

"Come, Christians, join to sing," Georgina began in her clear, beautiful soprano voice.

"Alleluia! Amen," sang Ash and Pierce.

Georgina glanced up at Ash. She looked startled. Ash glowered down at her. Confound it, he might have been roped into singing this stupid song, but he'd be hanged if he'd let Pierce out-sing him.

"Loud praise to Christ our king," sang Georgina.

"Alleluia! Amen," sang Ash and Pierce again, even louder than before.

This time Georgina glanced up at Pierce, who stared out into the empty sanctuary, attempting to appear holy. At least that's what it looked like to Ash, who had already loathed the man on principle, and who had started piling up specifics against him in recent weeks. Ever since Georgina had come to town, as a matter of fact.

"Let all, with heart and voice, before his throne rejoice; praise is his gracious choice," Georgina sang, her own voice reverberating gorgeously through the church.

"Alleluia! Amen," shouted Ash and Pierce.

Georgina clapped her hands over her ears, then raised an arm to signal Sally to stop playing.

As soon as the music ceased, Ash heard titters and muffled laughs from the choir. He turned around and scowled at the dozen or so old ladies sitting there. They all tried to look innocent, but he knew better. He felt pretty foolish, although he wasn't about to let it show. Pierce, he noticed, was trying to look innocent, too. The snake.

Georgina cleared her throat. "Perhaps we should begin again, gentlemen." She placed special emphasis on *gentlemen.* "I don't believe you need to sing quite so loudly. The sanctuary is small, and there are only the three of us." She shared a sugary smile between Ash and Pierce. Ash wanted to punch Pierce in the jaw for receiving so lovely a smile from her.

This was terrible. If he didn't get himself under control pretty soon, there was no telling what might happen. He vowed to spend at least an hour tonight after he got home in remembering every lousy minute of his marriage to Phoebe. If that didn't cure him, maybe he should just put a bullet in his head and get it over with.

"I believe," said Payton Pierce in a superior squeak, "that

Mr. Barrett should soften his voice some. He's much too loud.''

"Me?'' Ash's attention sprang instantly from Phoebe and bullets to the brain and fixed on Payton Pierce. "*Me?* You're the one who was hollering.''

"I was not hollering, Mr. Barrett.'' Pierce put on his most gallingly noble expression.

"Sounded like it to me,'' Ash grumbled.

"Er, gentlemen, I believe you could both soften your voices some and the hymn would sound the better for it. It's such a pretty hymn. We don't want to overpower it.'' Georgina smiled at them again. "All right?''

Ash didn't like it that she was treating him the same as she was treating Pierce. Pierce wasn't anything special. Pierce was a banker, for God's sake. He was a pallid shadow of a man compared to Ash. Pierce hadn't ever done anything interesting in his whole life. He hadn't fought Indians. He hadn't ever gone up against bad men in the territory. He hadn't been elected sheriff by a whole town. Hell, he hadn't been elected to anything by anybody.

"All right, Sheriff?''

Ash realized Georgina had been speaking. He frowned at her. She seemed taken aback for a second, and then she frowned, too. Ash recognized that frown of hers. It cheered him up some.

"Sure,'' he said. "That's fine.'' He wished he knew what she'd said that he'd agreed with.

"Fine,'' said Georgina, her tone clipped. "Then let's try the song again.'' She nodded to Sally Voorhees, who played the introduction once more.

"Come, Christians, join to sing.''

Ash and Pierce squinted at each other over Georgina's head. Ash really, really, really didn't want to be doing this.

"Alleluia! Amen!'' He didn't bellow this time. Neither did Pierce. Ash felt deflated somehow.

Then Georgina smiled at him, and he felt better all of a sudden.

"Loud praise to Christ our king.''

"Alleluia! Amen!''

They finished the whole first verse without a fight breaking out. Ash decided maybe singing in church wasn't too asinine an occupation for a grown man to participate in after all. At least it earned him another smile from Georgina, which almost made it worthwhile.

Then she smiled at Pierce, and Ash's mood soured again. Well, he guessed he could stand it. It might hurt, but he could stand it.

Georgina started the second verse. "Come, lift your hearts on high."

"Alleluia! Amen!"

"Let praises fill the sky."

"Alleluia! Amen!"

Silence.

Ash glanced at Georgina. Her mouth was open, but nothing was coming out. She looked shocked.

Without thinking, Ash pulled his gun out of his waistband. "What is it?" His voice was as crisp as autumn leaves.

After another several seconds of silence, during which Ash looked wildly around the sanctuary for whatever invading desperadoes were lurking there, he heard Georgina whisper, "Henry?"

Henry? Who the hell was Henry? What the devil was she talking about?

Then he saw him. At the door of the church there stood a man. A skinny, pasty-faced, sickly-looking man. He had a fancy suit on, a fancy hat in his hand, fancy shoes on his feet, and a sappy smile on his face.

Georgina said in a slightly stronger voice, "Henry? Is that really you?"

Ash looked from Georgina to the putative Henry to Payton. He looked as troubled as Ash felt.

Confound it, what was going on here?

"Hello, Georgina," the sap at the door said. His voice was even thinner than Pierce's. "I considered writing, but thought it would be more fun to surprise you."

Georgina whispered, "Good Lord." She sounded surprised, all right, and not particularly happy.

Ash considered shooting whoever this Henry fellow was, decided it was probably a bad idea, and stuffed his gun back into his waistband. He did it reluctantly. This looked like bad news to him.

As for Georgina, she was not at all pleased to see Henry

Spurling standing in the door of the one lone church in Picacho Wells, New Mexico Territory. In fact, she was hard-pressed to keep from stamping her foot and demanding to know what he thought he was doing, chasing after her in this absurd way. She had a feeling such a question asked in such a way would be improper and impolite, so she didn't ask it. She did, however, force a smile to her lips.

"Good heavens, Henry, this is such a shock."

With some effort, she managed to step down from the small raised platform upon which the choir sang and walk in a dignified manner to the door, holding her hand out for Henry to shake, and trying to appear glad to see him. It took her no time at all to realize she wasn't glad at all; rather, she wished Henry would fall through a hole in the earth and vanish from her sight forever.

That wasn't fair of her. It wasn't Henry's fault he was Henry Spurling and not Ash Barrett.

No, no, no! That's not what she meant. What she meant was that it wasn't his fault she held only tepid affection for Henry.

The blithering fool! Why had he come all this way in order to spoil her visit to the territory? Georgina felt very put out, but she tried not to show it. She tried even harder when Henry took her hand and kissed it. Pooh. His kiss was as watery as his eyes. She didn't want his lips anywhere near her.

He didn't release her hand and, since he was Henry and he probably thought she was going to marry him, she didn't snatch it out of his grip. She even managed to maintain her smile.

"I'm over my sore throat and croup now, Georgina."

"Yes, Henry, I see that."

"So I thought I'd come out here and find out how you're faring in your mission of mercy." He gave her one of the smiles which he considered knowing, and which Georgina had always considered ludicrous.

"My mission of mercy?" She knew what he meant. He meant he believed her to be honorable and magnanimous for coming all the way out here to help her aunt in nursing her insane grandmother. Georgina knew she was being unreasonable when she experienced a strong urge to bust Henry in the jaw.

He lowered his voice. "You know. Your—you know."

"Yes, Henry," she said, her voice as sweet and syrupy as molasses. "I know."

"It was an awful burden you assumed, Georgina." He made his voice even softer. He sounded like a hoarse mouse when he did that. Georgina figured he was trying to sound loving and compelling. Maybe even seductive, perish the thought.

"It's not been bad at all, actually." She tried to sustain her friendly attitude. She wanted to punch him and then shoot him with her new derringer.

"But this place, Georgina!" Henry looked around, an unpleasant expression on his face. "How can you abide living in such a—a rugged, ugly place. You, who are used to the best of everything and who cherish beauty and theater and opera and so forth. It makes me want to weep for you, my dear, brave girl."

His dear, brave girl? Good heavens. "Nonsense, Henry." She made her voice brisk and lied like a rug. "I haven't experienced a single second of unpleasantness since I arrived." She continued, no longer lying, "I adore living here. I may just remain, in fact."

Henry's head whipped around and he goggled at her. Good. Let him goggle, the imbecile. She smiled.

"You mean to say you *like* living here?"

"I love it."

"My goodness."

Georgina doubted that Henry could appear any more amazed than he did just then. He gazed around the sanctuary once more, and Georgina did likewise.

Oh, Georgina allowed that the accommodations were sort of rough in Picacho Wells. The citizens here hadn't had a couple hundred years to perfect their living conditions as those in New York had, for heaven's sake. Things would improve in time. Georgina thought it was awfully stuffy of Henry to hold their lack of sophisticated trappings against them.

"I think it's quite remarkable that the town has managed to become so settled in so very few years. Why, imagine, Henry, only twelve or fifteen years ago, the place wasn't even here."

Henry frowned. "I wonder if the world was better off twelve or fifteen years ago."

Before Georgina could take Henry to task for his snobbish attitude, or stomp on his shoe and hurt him, footsteps, loud and echoey, sounded from behind her. She knew to whom they belonged, because every time she heard them her heart sped up.

She turned around, and her smile for Henry turned upside down as she took note of Ash's expression. He looked like he wanted to shoot Henry, too, the beast. If anyone was going to shoot Henry Spurling it would be her, not Ash. What had poor Henry ever done to him? Whereas only seconds earlier, Georgina had wanted to send Henry to perdition, she was now unaccountably assailed by an impulse to protect him.

She said, "Sheriff Barrett," and gave him a formal nod.

Ash looked like he was holding himself back from committing havoc only with difficulty. "Who's that?" He ground the words out from between clamped teeth.

Georgina thinned her gaze to tell him to behave himself. She turned and took Henry's hand, hoping in that way to soothe Henry's nerves, which had never been awfully good, and also to annoy Ash Barrett. She was gratified to see that her ploy unquestionably achieved both aims.

"Henry, please allow me to introduce you to the sheriff of Picacho Wells, Mr. Ashley Barrett. Mr. Barrett, this is a friend of mine from New York City, Mr. Henry Spurling."

"A friend?" Henry sounded hurt. Georgina was sorry about that, but she wasn't about to introduce him as anything warmer or more intimate than a friend. She had a lot of thinking to do about that particular matter.

"Yes, Henry, you're one of my oldest and dearest friends." Georgina gave him a glittering smile of warning, which made poor Henry jump slightly and appear taken aback. Hmm. How interesting. Perhaps she'd learned a few new and useful social skills, as well as some new and useful frontier skills, since she'd come to the territory.

"Er, yes," he said. "Yes, Miss Witherspoon and I have known each other for years."

He held out his hand for Ash to shake. Georgina thought it was peculiar that Ash seemed to find it difficult to take the newcomer's hand and shake it civilly. He looked rather as if he'd like to wring it off of Henry's arm. Which he could probably do, since he was so much bigger and stronger than poor Henry, who had always been a weakling.

Georgina told herself not to be catty.

"Where are you staying, Henry?"

"There's a hotel here in town. It's not much, but—"

"Ah, yes. The Picacho Wells Hotel." Georgina thought it wise, if not polite, to interrupt Henry's assessment of the local hotel, particularly with Ash Barrett standing nearby and in a touchy mood.

"It's certainly not like any hotel in New York City," Henry said, and laughed.

Georgina could have slapped him, "Of course it isn't. This is a young, vital, new country. It's not old and stuffy like New York."

Henry blinked at her. Georgina realized her tone had been a speck tart. She cleared her throat. "Yes, well, you must come to Grandmother's farm tomorrow and visit with us all."

He lifted his eyebrows at her suggestion. Shaking his hand as if it hurt—apparently Ash hadn't been able to resist squeezing it harder than was necessary—he said, "Is that wise? I mean, is it safe—er—I mean, is it prudent to visit?"

Georgina felt her lips tighten and made an effort to relax them. "Of course it's wise, Henry. Neither Grandmother nor Aunt Vernice have ever met you. They'd be thrilled."

Ash snorted softly at her back.

"They'd be *thrilled*," she repeated, "to meet you. And they're both lovely ladies."

Another snort, this one louder. Georgina turned her head and gave Ash a good glower to let him know what she thought of him. Or wished she thought of him, anyway. He glowered back, which seemed so typical, Georgina almost grinned.

Her almost-grin vanished as soon as it had begun. Oh, wonderful. Here came Payton. He looked as grouchy as the sheriff. She sighed before she could stop herself.

"And here is another gentleman who lives in the great, new territory, Henry. Please allow me to introduce you to Mr. Payton Pierce, Picacho Wells's banker. Mr. Pierce, this is my dear friend from New York, Mr. Henry Spurling."

Since Ash refused to step aside, Pierce had to jog around him in order to shake Henry's hand. Georgina thought Mr. Pierce and Henry resembled each other—not in physical appearance, perhaps, but in inner essentials. They were both as exciting as day-old biscuits.

"How do you do, Mr. Spurling?"

"Very well, thank you, Mr. Pierce."

"It's a pleasure to meet you."

"Likewise."

They sounded alike, too. Georgina stared at them, amazed. Fancy that. They might have changed places and no one would know the difference. And she'd all but agreed to marry Henry Spurling. What an appalling thought. Thank God she'd come to the territory before she'd thrown her life away on the mouse!

A sound from behind her made Georgina turn. She caught Ash's eye and knew without words that he'd guessed her thoughts. He even grinned. It was a devil of a grin, and it made Georgina blush and wish she could hit him. Or kiss him.

Oh, dear.

Chapter Thirteen

Henry Spurling rented a horse and buggy and drove out to the Murphy farm the day after his arrival in Picacho Wells. Georgina was surprised by her enormous sense of disappointment when she heard the buggy, looked outside, and saw Henry—instead of someone else whom she chose not to name—driving down the path through the twin rows of pecan trees.

Maybelle walked up to stand next to her. She squinted through the window, too. "Looks like you hooked yourself another banker, girl." She didn't sound at all approving.

Georgina sighed deeply. "Yes. He is a banker. He's in business with my father."

"Humph. That figures. Why do you favor those milk-and-water boys, Georgina? Hell, isn't there enough Irish in you that you can tell Ash is the man for you? You'd die of malaise in twenty minutes if you ever went to bed with Pierce or this pasty-faced banker fellow."

"Let's see this new lad of yours," came a voice from the ceiling.

Georgina sighed, looked up, and saw Devlin O'Rourke hanging there, as handsome and immaterial as ever. "He's not my lad," she muttered, knowing her protest would do no good.

"He don't look very promising, Georgina. Why don't you dump him and take up with Ash?"

"I am *not* attached to Mr. Spurling. And I don't want to *take up* with Ash, or anyone else, for that matter!"

"Pooh," scoffed Maybelle. "Evelyn wrote and said she was looking forward to the day she could call that simpleminded twit her son-in-law." She pointed out the window, where Henry seemed to be having a little trouble with his horse and buggy.

Georgina said, "He's not simpleminded," in a perfunctory tone. Then she sighed again and glanced out at Henry who was still having trouble with his horse. Henry had always preferred taking cabs or walking to dealing with horses, which he rather feared.

Oh, very well, Georgina thought. Perhaps he was a blockhead.

"Anyway, nothing has been settled between us." Feeling defensive and worried about what her grandmother might say and do to Henry, Georgina decided to anticipate his arrival. She left the window and went to the front door.

"Oh, Georgina, it's so thrilling to meet new people!" exclaimed Vernice who had moved to stand beside her.

Georgina smiled at her. Vernice always tried to offer the best interpretation of things, even for boring people like Henry. Georgina appreciated her for it, particularly in this instance. "Yes, I'm sure it must be exciting. In New York, of course, a body sees strangers every day."

"I remember it well." Vernice sounded nostalgic. "Out here, it's exhilarating when new people come to town."

"Yes, I can understand that. One very rarely sees strangers here." If she could remember to look upon Henry's visit in that light, Georgina guessed she could stand it. She'd lain awake for a long time last night, contemplating Henry, Picacho Wells, and her own life.

It didn't surprise her any when she came to the conclusion that she no longer had the slightest desire to marry Henry Spurling. Her feelings about marrying him had always been lukewarm; now they were positively negative. What had surprised her somewhat was that she realized she hadn't been lying to Henry when she spoke to him in church. She really did love living in Picacho Wells, and she honestly didn't want to leave the territory. She was having the time of her life here. The notion of going back to New York and resuming the insipid lifestyle to which she'd been accustomed literally made her stomach ache.

But what could she do if she remained here? She had no idea. She supposed her grandmother and Aunt Vernice would allow her to continue living with them—perhaps they'd even welcome her presence—but Georgina had always sort of anticipated setting up housekeeping on her own someday. Well, perhaps not exactly on her own.

Actually, she'd always expected to marry. She'd even sort of looked forward to marriage, since the married state afforded women more freedom than they had as young, unmarried ladies. Since, however, the only eligible men who'd ever expressed a desire to marry her were Henry and Payton, that idea no longer held much appeal.

If Ash were to ask her . . . But no. She couldn't think like that. They hated each other, didn't they?

It was all too confusing. She'd gone to sleep under the influence of her chaotic thoughts and thus, this morning she hadn't been surprised when she awoke with a brutal headache.

As she gazed at Henry, she wondered if he might not be the biggest headache of all. She figured it was a toss-up between him and Payton—she couldn't figure out who was worse.

Bother.

At any rate, Henry was here, and so was she, and she now had to deal with him. She opened the front door and prepared to do her duty.

"Lord, child," she heard at her back. *"The man looks more like a ghost than I do."*

"He's been ill," said Georgina, and rolled her eyes in exasperation as if the situation wasn't bad enough already. The addition of Dev and Maybelle's comments was liable to push her over the edge.

"Oh, the poor fellow," whispered the ever-compassionate Vernice.

"He looks like he needs a decent meal, too."

"He looks like he needs a kick in the butt to me."

Georgina and Vernice exchanged a glance after Maybelle's caustic comment, then faced their approaching guest. They both smiled at him, knowing their smiles would be the only hint of friendliness Henry was likely to receive inside the Murphy house.

• • •

Ash was sitting at his desk in the sheriff's office, brooding, and he couldn't help but hear her since she was standing on the boardwalk right outside his door. He jumped up from his desk, hated himself for it, and sat back down again. She was nothing—*nothing*—to him. Nothing. Not a thing. Nothing.

"And here we have the sheriff's office, Henry. You remember Mr. Barrett, one of the men you met yesterday? The one who sings baritone in our trio?"

"Ah, yes. He was the large, dark man, wasn't he?"

Ash had picked up a newspaper just arrived from Santa Fe, and was trying to pay attention to it rather than the conversation going on outside. Henry Spurling's voice penetrated his office and Ash's hands bunched up on the paper, wrinkling it into a tight little ball.

That voice.

That *description*. Large and dark? Him? He squinted at his door, wondering if he could go out there and punch the man in the nose.

No. Of course he couldn't. He passed a hand over his eyes, and wished he'd get over this odd impulse he had to seize other men away from Georgina and tear them into bloody strips.

"He is rather large," he heard Georgina say. "Do you think he's dark?"

"Perhaps it's only his glowering aspect that makes him appear dark," Henry conceded in what Ash guessed was supposed to be a humorous tone. It made him want to throw the wadded-up newspaper on the floor and jump up and down on it.

"Yes, that might be so."

Dammit, she didn't have to *agree* with the bastard! Ash couldn't stand it another second. Even though he didn't want to, he got up and went to go greet Georgina and her chowderheaded banker friend from New York City. He was practicing smiling as he walked to the door of the office, but wasn't sure he'd succeeded by the time he pushed it further open and went outside. From the start of alarm Henry Spurling gave, one would have thought Ash had shot a gun at his back. Which didn't sound like a half-bad idea.

He tipped his hat. "Morning, Miss Witherspoon. Good morning, Mr. Spurling."

Georgina smiled. Ash was sure she didn't mean her smile for him, and his already-bad mood worsened.

"Good morning, Mr. Barrett. I'm giving Henry the grand tour of Picacho Wells this morning."

"That ought to take ten minutes or so." Ash tried to sound civil.

Georgina laughed.

Henry looked superior. "Ten minutes might be five too many." He sounded superior, too.

Ash again experienced a strong urge to punch him. "Yeah. Picacho Wells isn't New York City."

Henry laughed as if Ash had said something funny. Ash discovered his hands were balling into fists, and made a conscious effort to relax them. He took comfort from watching Georgina roll her eyes, as if she found Henry as ridiculous as Ash did.

Payton Pierce's voice sailed across the road to them, perfecting Ash's day. He grimaced.

"Good morning, Miss Witherspoon," said Pierce. "Good morning, Mr. Spurling." He sounded friendly. Ash looked at him, saw at a glance that his tone of friendliness was all an act, and felt minimally better.

"Good morning," said Georgina. She sounded bored.

"Good morning," said Henry. He didn't, which showed how much he knew.

"Well, you two enjoy your grand tour." Ash turned and went back into the building, unable to cope with two rivals— that is to say, two bankers—in one morning. Their voices, like a thin, reedy duet, followed him.

Georgina watched the expressions of the three men in her life with interest. They didn't like each other; that much was obvious. Could they possibly consider each other rivals for her affections? She could almost believe it of Henry and Payton— but Ash? The notion confounded her.

He didn't even like her, did he? He gave no evidence of liking her at all. Well, except for that time in the graveyard. And that time he had tried to teach her how to shoot.

Her body tingled at the memories her thoughts evoked. Mercy sakes, was she turning into a wanton female like her grandmother? She pondered that possibility as Henry and Payton's voices chased each other in her head like mice on a wheel. A rusty, squeaky, irritating wheel.

Perhaps it wasn't only wanton women who felt these sensual passions. After all, would God have given females carnal reactions to certain men if He didn't want them to act upon them? In the proper confines, of course. Which meant marriage. Which brought Georgina back to Henry and Payton. Rather, Henry *or* Payton.

Bother. Why couldn't her body tingle at the thought of one of them? Why did it have to be Ash Barrett whose body she wanted to rub up against naked?

"Whatever is the matter, Georgina?"

She gave a start when she realized Henry had spoken to her. "What? I beg your pardon?" Oh, dear, she hoped her thoughts hadn't been discernible on her face.

"You looked as if you were lost in contemplation, darling."

"Darling? Georgina frowned at Henry, who was smiling down upon her as if she were a prized possession of his—a pedigreed Persian cat or a new walking stick or something. She didn't appreciate his proprietary air one little bit. She didn't appreciate the scowl on Payton's face, either. As if he had any right to resent another man calling her darling!

Not that she wanted Henry to call her darling. He'd only done it to prove a point to Pierce. And it wasn't even a valid point.

Fiddlesticks. Sometimes men were too much trouble for her to bother with.

Georgina chose to ignore Henry's question. What made him think he had access to her thoughts, anyway? "Are you ready to continue our tour of Picacho Wells?"

Henry eyed the dusty street doubtfully. "I suppose if we must. I'll be very happy when you return to New York City, Georgina. And I'm sure you will be, too."

"Miss Witherspoon seems to be enjoying her stay here." Pierce sounded both defensive and moderately irate.

Henry laughed. Georgina had never noticed before how self-satisfied and smug Henry's laugh could be. She grimaced before she could stop herself.

Henry smiled fondly at Georgina again. He tried to take her arm, but she stepped away from him, annoyed that he had been so forward to voice what she had already told him wasn't true. She had no desire to return to New York City, especially if it meant marrying Henry. Henry, however, was oblivious to her reaction and continued to prattle on. "Georgina has always been a good-natured girl, Mr. Pierce, and would never dream of disparaging the town where her grandmother and aunt live."

A loud "Ha!" issued from the sheriff's office.

Georgina turned her head and saw Ash, sitting on his chair, with his booted feet on his desk, looking out at the three of them through the open door. She lifted her chin and turned away from his frowning gaze. Neither Pierce nor Henry seemed to have noticed Ash's addendum to the conversation.

"She isn't one to complain," Henry went on in his self-assured way.

"I'm sure that's true," Pierce said, his voice thin and tight.

"Oh, I complain often enough when I feel there's reason to do so." Georgina, on the other hand, was feeling particularly feisty, and her voice asserted as much. "If I didn't like Picacho Wells, I'd say so."

"You're such a sweet thing," Henry purred.

"Yes, she's a lovely young woman," squeaked Pierce.

Georgina heard a contemptuous snort from the sheriff's office.

"Let's be on our way, Henry. It must be getting on towards noon, and you'll need to have a bite of luncheon. You mustn't skip any meals, you know, since you've been so gravely ill."

"You're right, of course. The doctor told me as much. You're so kind to look out for me."

Now he was condescending to her. Georgina, furious, added sweetly, "And then I believe you should lie down and take a nice long nap, Henry. I know your constitution always has been rather sickly."

Good. She'd annoyed him. Payton smirked and then adopted an expression of mock sympathy. "I'm so sorry to hear it, Mr. Spurling. My own constitution has always been remarkably robust. One needs to be healthy if one intends to conquer the territory, you know."

"How lucky for you," Georgina murmured. *And how unfortunate for the rest of us.*

"I don't intend to conquer the territory," said Henry, somewhat heatedly.

"Yes. That's a wise decision on your part, Spurling." Pierce oozed false sympathy.

"Anyway, I'm not sickly. At least, not anymore."

Henry's voice went up half an octave, and he'd put on his fussy face, the one Georgina remembered so well from New York. She shook her head, astonished that she could have once actually considered marrying him.

"You know, Mr. Pierce," Henry continued. "I would definitely be able to live here in the territory—I simply choose not to do so. This place is beneath a man of my social standing."

Oh, you wouldn't last a day out here and you know it, thought Georgina triumphantly. Henry was obviously peeved about her calling him sickly and about Pierce telling him that he basically wasn't strong enough to survive the territory, so now he was going to insist on explaining how he would never choose to live here anyway, as it was just too uncivilized and barbarian a place.

Conceited snob.

"And what exactly would you suggest we need to do to make Picacho Wells suitable to a man of your 'social standing,' Mr. Spurling?"

Payton was peeved. Georgina grinned inside. Perhaps these two weren't so boring after all. If they continued this cultivated arguing, they might even be entertaining. Of course, neither man would stoop to physical violence or even, probably, rude words. No. They were both too cosmopolitan for that sort of thing. They'd merely snipe at each other, couching their verbal barbs in polite phrasing.

"Well there are just so many things that would need to be done. For one thing, paved streets are definitely needed to hold down the dust, which you must admit is quite a problem." Henry cast another superior glance up the road. "The place is quaint, but I shouldn't think it's very attractive to the right kinds of people."

The right kinds of people? Georgina couldn't believe he'd said that.

On the other hand, she guessed she could. Had she ever been like that? The notion made her shudder inside.

"I don't believe that's so, Spurling, although I do agree we are in the beginning stages of town-building. This is a growing, vibrant community. The citizens of Picacho Wells, however, have better things to do with their money and time at the moment than pave the streets."

"Oh? My goodness, I should think that cleanliness, being next to godliness and so forth, should be a priority." Henry gave a supercilious laugh.

"This is a new community, Mr. Spurling. I'm sure you've never given much thought to the sorts of things folks need to do in order to create something, since you've always resided in New York. Your imagination and cunning have never been called into play, as New York City was established long ago." Now Pierce sounded supercilious.

Georgina was fascinated. She'd never expected to be entertained by these two stuffed fish, but she was as she listened to them, by their oh-so-polite arguing.

"I can assure you that I am as competent and imaginative as the next fellow when it comes to understanding the problems of creating and developing a new city or town."

"Is that so?"

"Yes."

"And in your vast experience, have you considered that before people require paved streets, they need water? Wells, Mr. Spurling. Wells are what the citizens of this community need."

"Water is important," Henry conceded. It sounded as if it cost him.

"Yes. Water is vital. My bank is lending money all the time to finance the digging of wells for use in the community. And windmills. You'll notice all the windmills." Pierce gestured to a row of windmills lined up behind the main business street of Picacho Wells.

"Yes, I did. Of course, without indoor plumbing and a water-storage and pumping system, one needs windmills, I suppose. When you get the water problem solved, then perhaps you can work on electricity and plumbing. Sanitation, Pierce. People find those things such conveniences, don't you know. And life is so much healthier with sanitation. Or perhaps you've never lived with electricity and plumbing?"

Now that, to Georgina's way of thinking, was quite a comeback. She might even be proud of Henry if he wasn't such a pompous prude.

"Sanitation in New York City doesn't seem to have done much for your own health, Mr. Spurling," Pierce commented, keeping his tone smooth and silky.

She managed to pull Henry away from the spat eventually, but not without a struggle. She was exhausted when she finally left him at the Picacho Wells Hotel and headed back to her grandmother's house. She wished she never had to set eyes on either Henry or Payton again.

As for Ash, well, Georgina just didn't know about him, that was all.

She was so weary from her morning with Henry Spurling that she took her own advice and lay down to take a nap after lunch.

She couldn't have been asleep for more than ten minutes when she heard a timid knock at her bedroom door. She sat up and rubbed her eyes, feeling guilty for succumbing to her fatigue.

"Yes?"

"It's Vernice, dear," came her aunt's voice. "Mr. Pierce has come to call on you."

"He has?" Georgina frowned. What in the world was Payton Pierce doing here in the middle of the day? Didn't he have a bank to run? "I'll be right there."

She quickly washed her face to wake up, tightened her corset laces, patted her hair into place, yanked her dress over her head, whacked it a couple of times to get the wrinkles out, and went reluctantly out to the parlor. Her grandmother was already there, glowering at the banker from the sofa. Devlin O'Rourke hovered above him—Pierce obviously couldn't see him—and looked as if he wanted to drop something on his head.

Vernice appeared to be happy. She was always happy to receive visitors. Georgina smiled. She was ever so fond of her sweet aunt.

"Look who's come to call, Georgina," Vernice called happily, pausing in the act of pouring tea into Pierce's teacup.

Georgina's eyes opened wide when she saw Devlin O'Rourke make a swoop for the cup. His intention, she was sure, was to push it aside, thereby making Vernice pour tea onto the table so that it would ultimately drip onto Pierce's well-polished shoes. While Georgina would love to have Dev dump tea all over Pierce, she wasn't about to let him upset Vernice. She cried, "No!" and Dev shot up to the ceiling again, obviously peeved that Georgina had stopped him.

He frowned down at her. *"Spoilsport."*

Payton Pierce blinked. "I beg your pardon?" He arose, as a properly brought-up young man should do when a lady enters a room, although he appeared both puzzled and alarmed.

Georgina didn't blame him. He couldn't see Dev and probably thought she'd hollered at him. He couldn't know that the ghost had planned to ruin his shoes. She forced herself to smile cordially. "I beg your pardon, Mr. Pierce. I sneezed."

"Oh."

Thank goodness for manners. If Ash were here, he'd have flat-out told her that her *no* hadn't sounded like a sneeze to him. Pierce was too namby-pamby—rather, he was too much of a gentleman—to say such a thing.

"God bless you," her guest said, rather perfunctorily.

"Bilgewater!" Maybelle poured brandy from a flask into her teacup and downed the liquid in one gulp. Pierce stared at her as if he'd never seen a woman do anything like that before.

With a sigh, Georgina guessed he probably never had. She hadn't, either, until she'd come to the territory. She sat on the sofa next to Vernice, thus making sure that Pierce had to sit on his own chair well away from her. "How kind of you to visit us today, Mr. Pierce. I should expect you to be in Picacho Wells, watching over our money." She smiled at him to let him think she was joshing, even though she wasn't.

He didn't smile back. He looked, in fact, deadly serious. Georgina didn't know what his expression foretold, but she wasn't optimistic.

"He's a banker," Maybelle said. "He doesn't care about anyone's money but his own."

"I'm sure that's not true, Mother." Vernice was used to her mother's disputatious personality, but she still always tried to blunt Maybelle's barbs. Georgina admired her aunt's tenaciousness.

"I'm sure Mrs. Murphy is only having her own little joke," Pierce said, sounding not sure at all.

"Yes," said Georgina. She hoped he'd leave soon. She'd

already wasted a whole morning on Henry. And she didn't relish wasting her afternoon on Payton. She had work to do around the farm. The notion of having real work to do cheered her oddly. She wished Ash were here to see her do it.

"May I speak to you for a moment, Miss Witherspoon?" Pierce appeared to be awfully nervous.

Georgina looked around, wondering what was preventing him from speaking to her right here and now. If he could see Devlin O'Rourke hovering overhead, she might have understood his reluctance, but . . . "Of course, Mr. Pierce. Feel free." She waved a hand in the air, giving him leave.

"Alone?"

Botheration. The last thing she wanted to do was waste any more time listening to whatever Payton Pierce had to say. Georgina feared it might be a marriage proposal, and she wasn't sure she could keep from exploding if it was.

Why couldn't an *interesting* man propose to her? Just once. Was that too much to ask?

Evidently it was.

She heaved a great sigh. "Certainly, Mr. Pierce. Would you care to come out on the front porch with me?"

Maybelle snorted. Georgina scowled at her.

"The boy's going to ask you to marry him, girl. Sock him in the jaw when he does."

Georgina looked up, noticed the belligerent cast to Devlin O'Rourke's features, and sighed again. She wanted to tell him to stay out of it, but if she spoke to a ghost whom Payton didn't see hovering above his head, he would think she was crazy. Feeling resigned and discouraged, she stood.

Payton Pierce arose, too. "Thank you, Miss Witherspoon." He turned and bowed graciously to Vernice and Maybelle.

Vernice fluttered like a butterfly.

Maybelle snorted again.

Georgina sat on a wicker porch chair with her hands folded demurely in her lap and watched as Payton nervously paced the porch. She could envision Ash pacing. Only he would look like a panther—sleek, dark, and deadly. Pierce just looked like a mouse about to be attacked by the family cat.

Whatever Pierce looked like, he was having trouble getting to the point. He hadn't said a word since they'd exited the house. Georgina, who was already bored with him, tried to urge him to get it over with, whatever it was.

"You wished to speak to me, Mr. Pierce?" She honeyed her voice to encourage him.

"Yes." He continued pacing.

Georgina sighed. "Perhaps if you sat down, you'd feel more comfortable?" She phrased her suggestion as a question in order to soothe his nerves, which appeared to be extremely ragged.

"Yes." Pierce stopped pacing and frowned at the chair set opposite to the one in which Georgina sat.

She'd already positioned the wicker table in between the chairs, just in case Pierce made a grab for her. After his fumbling in the graveyard, she didn't trust him. She gestured to the chair. "Please."

"Ahem." Pierce walked heavily to the chair and sat in it. Then he folded his hands and dropped them between his knees, looking pitiful. Georgina might have felt sorry for him if she had liked him better.

She smiled and gave him another, "Please."

"Miss Witherspoon. Georgina."

She frowned.

"Miss Witherspoon." Now he sounded desperate. "Miss Witherspoon, you told me once that I might still hope."

Oh, dear, it *was* going to be a proposal. Georgina stifled a groan. "Did I?"

"Yes." He stuck a finger inside his collar and ran it around his neck, as if he'd tied his tie too tightly and was trying to loosen it. "Yes, you did."

"Oh." She tried to think of something else to say, couldn't, and decided she wouldn't bother.

"And so I've been hoping."

"Oh."

Pierce licked his lips. "I know you told me once that nothing had been decided between you and Henry Spurling."

"Yes?"

"But now that he's come to visit Picacho Wells, I wondered if that might have changed."

"Umm."

He looked at her.

She looked back.

His expression intensified.

She sighed deeply. "No, Mr. Pierce. My intentions toward Henry Spurling have not undergone a change." She declined to say what they hadn't changed from.

"Oh." He frowned heavily. His frown gave him a peevish expression, which Georgina took note of. He wouldn't be a pleasant person with whom to live. She'd stake Granny Witherspoon's pearls on it if they weren't still in New York.

She didn't bother trying to respond to his *oh*.

"Well, then." His voice sounded firmer.

Georgina waited, but he said no more. She tilted her head, wondering if she was supposed to know what he was thinking by invoking transcendental energy and reading his mind.

"Well, then," he repeated, "I believe I have a right to know what his intentions are toward you."

She lifted her brows into two high arches and hoped they adequately displayed her disapproval at his assumption of rights. "Really."

As if he couldn't sit still a second longer, he popped up from his chair and resumed pacing. Now he looked to Georgina like an agitated squirrel. "Yes, I do."

"Then why don't you ask him?" She used her frostiest tone, hoping to shame him.

It didn't work. "I will. I intend to do exactly that."

"Hmm." Irked didn't half describe Georgina's condition. She wondered if she should just swear off men entirely, since they were all so silly.

He whirled around, making her start. "You see, Miss Witherspoon, I have a good deal of affection for you. I can't abide thinking that an unscrupulous city fellow from the East might be taking advantage of you."

"Unscrupulous? Henry?"

"Yes. I don't trust that man. He—he—he bears all the earmarks of a scoundrel."

"Henry? A scoundrel?" Good heavens, Georgina thought, the man was mad! "I can assure you, Mr. Pierce, Mr. Spurling wouldn't know how to be a scoundrel if he wanted to be one, which he doesn't. He is a man of the highest moral principles." He was so stuffy, in fact, that Georgina had occasionally wanted to stick him with a pin to see if he was full of cotton fluff, as she suspected.

A fierce flush invaded Pierce's cheeks. He looked like he might throw a tantrum any second. "It's kind of you to say so, Miss Witherspoon."

"Kind?" Georgina stood, feeling chillier by the second toward this ridiculous fellow. "I'm not being kind in the least, Mr. Pierce. I have known Mr. Spurling all my life, and I believe I know him rather better then you do. If he has any intentions toward me, they are strictly honorable, I can assure you."

He shook his head. "It's charitable of you to say so, Miss Witherspoon. I've come to expect such generosity of spirit in you. But you're too unworldly to understand the ways of men."

"Good heavens." She couldn't believe her ears.

"It's true, ma'am. I know it will come as a shock to you, but there are men in the world who prey on innocent females. They abuse a woman's purity. They're the vilest sorts of fellows, and they take advantage of women every day."

"Every day? My, they must be very busy fellows."

He gave her a small frown. "I'm not exaggerating, Miss Witherspoon."

"Of course not."

"There are terrible men out there, waiting for a likely female upon whom to pounce. They're conniving, unscrupulous men. Men with no morals and no principles."

"Henry's not one of them."

"No?" Pierce's brow was furrowed up so hard, he reminded Georgina of the wax image of Neanderthal man she'd seen in a museum once. "You're too young, too innocent, to know what evil men can get up to, Miss Witherspoon."

"Young? I am twenty-three years old, Mr. Pierce."

He'd opened his mouth, ready, Georgina was sure, to dispute any allegations she might be going to make, when her words penetrated the soup he called a brain. His mouth clanked shut and then opened again. "You are? Twenty-three? Really? I had no idea you were that old." He sounded vaguely appalled. Georgina was not amused.

"Yes," she said in her coldest voice. "I am twenty-three. An old maid to you, Mr. Pierce, evidently."

"What? Oh, no! No, indeed, Miss Witherspoon. You're far

from being an old maid! Why, you're remarkably well-preserved.''

Well-preserved? Georgina would like to preserve him. In a jar full of formaldehyde.

"But that's not the point," Pierce continued, oblivious to how insulting he was being.

"Oh? And exactly what *is* your point, Mr. Pierce. I presume you didn't come all this way only to tell me I'm past my prime."

"Good heavens, no. I came here to warn you about that fellow. To urge you to be on your guard so that he doesn't take advantage of you."

"I see. So this was an act of charity for you."

"I mean, you may not be—well, you aren't as young as I thought you were, but you're still naïve to the ways of the world. There are awful men out there, Miss Witherspoon. Men who prey upon young—or even not-so-young—girls—women, rather. Men who do unspeakable things. Men who . . ."

The notion of Henry trying to take sexual advantage of a respectable virgin was so inconceivable that Georgina laughed out loud. She doubted if Henry would know what to do with a female if she pranced naked in front of him.

Not like Ash, who'd know in an instant. Who might even strip her himself. A shiver rattled her.

Bother. Why had she thought of Ash yet again? Vexed, Georgina said, "Nonsense. You don't know Henry, and you don't know what you're talking about, Mr. Pierce. I shan't sit and listen to you assert any more slanders against him. Henry's a fine man." If by *fine* one meant upstanding, conventional, and moderately pompous. She didn't add that part.

"Oh, dear, now I've upset you." Pierce at least had the grace to sound contrite.

"Yes, you have." Georgina allowed herself to sound almost as angry as she felt.

"But, my dear Miss Witherspoon—"

The *dear* part finally pushed her over the edge. Georgina did something she'd never done in her entire adult life. She stamped her foot. "I am *not* your *dear anything*, Mr. Pierce. I'm not anyone's *dear*, and I'll thank you to remember that! I don't know if this was supposed to be some sort of awkward marriage proposal, or if you only came here to disparage an esteemed friend of mine, but you've failed on both counts.''

She paused to catch her breath. She knew her cheeks were flaming. So were his. Her anger had evidently caught him flat-footed and dumbfounded, the idiot.

''Now,'' she continued in a voice of steel, ''please leave my grandmother's house. I don't want to see you any longer today.''

''But—''

''No! Depart, if you please! Now!'' She pointed with a steady finger to his buggy.

He departed. His head was hanging, and he looked like a whipped dog, but he departed. Georgina watched him grimly, wishing she could hurry him on his way with a flatiron flung at his back. She'd never experienced violent emotions until she came to visit her grandmother, and wondered if her recent savage impulses were a precursor to insanity. She wouldn't be surprised.

She was more pleased than not when Oscar arched his back and hissed at Payton as he passed on the way to his buggy.

When Devlin applauded from the roof of the house and she looked up and saw him there, grinning like one of Satan's minions, her already unsteady mood deteriorated.

Chapter
Fourteen

Ash had awakened that morning feeling crabby, and had been getting grumpier and grumpier as his day progressed.

He laid the cause of his mood at Georgina Witherspoon's feet, and reviled himself for it. Blast the woman, what was the matter with him that she could affect him this way? He, who hadn't been affected by a female since Phoebe'd had the good sense to die?

He hadn't seen Georgina since yesterday, when she'd been showing that simpering boyfriend of hers from New York around town. Then, a little later in the day he'd seen Pierce— who obviously didn't have enough real work to do to keep him busy—haring out of town in the direction of the Murphy place.

Ash had hoped he'd fall off his horse and die a miserable death in the desert, but knew his hope remained unfulfilled when Pierce rode back into town a couple of hours later. At least the banker didn't look happy. Ash took small comfort from that.

What in the name of mercy did Georgina think she was doing, allowing herself to be courted by *two* worthless city fellows? And both of them bankers, too. Didn't she know herself better than that?

Hell, she was no weak-kneed, lily-livered, good-for-nothing city woman!

He almost fainted dead away when he realized what he'd just admitted to himself.

"Damn." He ran a hand through his hair and wished he could go back to bed and sleep for a decade or so.

Could his assessment of Georgina be correct?

Ash forced himself to sit down and take stock, logically and without his carnal instincts getting involved, of what he knew about Georgina Witherspoon.

When she'd first arrived in Picacho Wells, Ash had known without the slightest hint of a doubt that she was another Phoebe. She was pretty, silly, vain, and useless.

Then he'd come to know her.

"Damn." He hated it when his prejudices got knocked around by reality.

Oh, all right. So she wasn't useless. He guessed she wasn't silly, either. Vain? He couldn't say for sure, but it didn't look like it from here. All the other women in town liked her, and frontier females didn't cotton to conceited city girls.

Drat.

She was pretty, though. He tested that particular truth and decided he couldn't hold her prettiness against her.

Actually, he'd rather be holding it against himself. Bare-assed naked.

"Dammit, Barrett, stop thinking things like that!"

He shook his head hard and tried to dispel the image his vagrant thought had provoked. It didn't want to be dispelled, but Ash had some hard thinking to do, so he tried his best.

Because he was having a difficult time thinking in his chair, he went outside and walked down the boardwalk, his hands behind his back, his head lowered. It helped to clear his head when he could expend some energy in movement. He barely noticed the people he passed on his contemplative stroll. He nodded to a few of them when they managed to catch his attention, but his thought processes were focused on Miss Witherspoon.

It was galling to him that he was spending so much time thinking about a woman from New York City. He'd believed himself to be above such nonsensical pursuits. Hell, he was a

Texan. Texans had no love for New Yorkers. She was a damned Yankee, dammit!

He stopped dead in his tracks when he caught sight of Georgina, strolling by on the boardwalk across the street as if his thinking about her had conjured her up and plunked her down in the middle of town. *His* town. She was alone. Ash frowned and glanced around, trying to find Vernice, Maybelle, or even one of her idiotic banker friends. He didn't see any of them.

What the hell did she think she was doing, coming to town alone? Fury and protectiveness and something else Ash didn't want to speculate about arose in his breast. With a muttered curse, he tromped across the street, straight at Georgina.

"Miss Witherspoon!"

Georgina, who had been studying a display of ribbons in the window of Montgomery's Dry Goods Store, gave a start of alarm and whirled around. When she saw Ash, looking like a thundercloud about to burst and storm all over her, she straightened her spine, lifted her chin, and frowned at him. "Yes, Mr. Barrett?" She used her chilliest tone, hoping in that way to show him he couldn't talk to *her* like that.

Ash halted in front of her, still looking stormy. "Where are all your men friends today?"

"Where are all *what* men friends? What are you talking about?"

"That damned banker from New York, and Payton Pierce. What happened? They finally get tired of trailing around after you like a couple of hounds after a bitch in heat?"

Even from Ash Barrett, who had never treated her as a lady should be treated, this was more than Georgina cared to take. She stared at him, wondering if he'd lost what was left of his mind. She considered slapping his face, decided that's what he wanted her to do so he could call her names, and said instead, "What in the name of glory is the matter with you? How dare you speak to me that way?"

"This is stupid."

"It certainly is!"

She took a step, intending to walk around him and continue perusing hat ribbons. Drat the man. Of all the obstreperous, miserable, horrid, rude—"Ow!"

He'd grabbed her arm, right above the elbow, hard. "Just a minute. I'm not through with you."

She drew herself up to her full five feet, three inches and stared at him as she used to stare at rude university students in New York who thought it was funny to make lewd comments about passing ladies. "I'm sorry you feel that way, sir, as *I* am through with *you*!"

"Confound it, just listen to me for a minute, Georgina!"

"And when, pray, did I give you leave to call me 'Georgina'?"

"Curse it, you didn't."

Ash looked very aggravated. Georgina noted that he still hadn't released her arm. She pointedly eyed his hand where it clutched her.

"Listen, I have to talk to you, and I don't give a damn about the social niceties anymore."

"What exactly do you have to talk to me about?" Georgina shot back.

"About that man."

The way he'd said *man* made Georgina wonder to whom he could be referring. The villain she'd shot was still locked up, wasn't he? "What man? Isn't he still in jail?"

"In jail?" He looked ferocious. "He probably ought to be, but I don't suppose he is."

She shook her head, confused. "What *are* you talking about, Mr. Barrett?"

"Confound it, stop calling me Mr. Barrett!"

"Oh, this is too much! First you accost me on the street, bruising my arm and now you're telling me not to call you by your proper name! I do believe you've gone mad!"

"Yeah," he said. "Me too. Come here."

And with that, to Georgina's shock he grabbed her hand and pulled her between the dry goods store and the leather and saddle shop.

"Stop it! Stop it this minute! What are you trying to do to me?" Georgina squawked.

"Be quiet!"

"I *won't* be quiet!" she screamed back at Ash.

"Yes, you will."

He grabbed her arm again and hauled her to the clump of trees next to the graveyard, then stopped and released her arm.

"Now, I want to know exactly what kind of game you're playing, dammit." He stood in front of her, glowering, his fists planted firmly on his lean hips.

Georgina decided it would be better if she didn't think about his lean hips. She rubbed her arm, where she was sure he'd left bruises. "Don't you dare curse at me, you vicious brute. And I'm not playing any kind of game. Whatever are you talking about?"

"The game you're playing with those two bankers and me! That's what I'm talking about."

Georgina squinted at him, trying to understand what he was talking about. "I still don't know what you mean."

"*Dammit!*" He turned and slammed his fist into a tree. Georgina blinked, wishing she didn't care if he hurt himself or not. He turned and glared at her some more. "You know good and well that if you marry one of those idiots, you'll be miserable for as long as you live!"

Dumbfounded, Georgina could only repeat herself. "What? What are you talking about?"

"Stop asking me what I'm talking about!"

"But you're not making any sense! What idiots? Who's marrying whom?"

"You! You're going to marry that idiot Henry Spurling or that idiot Payton Pierce, and either one of them will ruin your life!"

"I'm going to do no such thing." She was really furious now, and stalked up to stand right in front of him. She shook her finger in his face. "And even if I had such plans, what right have *you* to comment on them?"

"I'm a *man*, dammit! I'm not one of those sissy pansies you fancy!"

"I don't fancy either one of them!"

"You told Pierce that Spurling was your fiancé!"

"How dare you gossip about me behind my back!"

"I don't gossip! I'm a man, dammit, and men don't gossip!"

"Fiddlesticks! They do, too. Anyway, what right have you to say whom I can and can't marry? What if Henry were to marry me? So what? You have nothing to say about it!"

"Confound it, you can't marry that bastard! Not if you expect to have a decent life."

"Oh, this is ridiculous." Georgina turned and started stalking back to the main part of town. She wasn't sure if she should be irate or befuddled or happy that Ash seemed to be taking an interest in her welfare—even if he wasn't awfully genteel about expressing his concern.

"It's not ridiculous!"

His shout made her wince. She kept walking.

"Dammit, don't walk away from me!"

He grabbed her again. This was getting very tiresome. Georgina turned and spoke with rigid courtesy. "I appreciate your concern for my welfare, Mr. Barrett, but I must repeat that you know nothing of my situation. Even if you did, you have no right to offer suggestions, much less make demands, or grab me in this ungentlemanly way."

He released her arm and ran a hand through his hair, dislodging his hat and mussing his hair. Georgina experienced a mad desire to smooth it back into place. He had such lovely, thick hair, and the sun made it glint silver and red and gold. She gave herself a hard mental shake and told herself to stick to the here and now.

"Listen, Miss Witherspoon," he said in a less aggressive tone. "I'm only concerned about your welfare."

Georgina said, "Humph. I'll just bet you are."

Ash sucked in a lungful of air and released it noisily. "I know, I know. You're right. I have no right to advise you."

"*Advise* me? It sounded to me as if you were issuing commandments, Mr. Barrett."

"Will you stop calling me *Mr. Barrett* in that superior tone of yours? You sound like a big-city snob when you do that."

"Do I?" If Georgina had ever been more confused, angry, and upset in her life, she couldn't remember when.

"Yes. Call me Ash. Please."

Unwilling to concede anything to him, she muttered, "I'll think about it."

He turned and walked to the same poor tree he'd hit before. This time he kicked the tree's trunk. Georgina didn't think the tree deserved such rough treatment and said so.

"Thunderation!" replied Ash. "You drive me crazy."

"You don't do much for my sanity, either, Mr.—Ash." *Mr. Ash.* Now there, to Georgina's way of thinking, was an almost appropriate name for him, the blistering fool.

"Listen, Georgina—"

She decided not to make an issue of the *Georgina* question.

Ash continued, "I know what I'm talking about. You'll be miserable if you marry one of those men."

"You know nothing whatever of the matter."

"I do so! I made that mistake once, and believe me, I know!"

She blinked, taken aback. "You're—you're *married*?" Good God. She pressed a hand to her heart, wondering why it should suddenly be aching so badly. What difference did it make to her if this awful man was married?

"No, I'm not married," he said crossly. "She died."

Relief flooded her, and she knew she was being not only irrational but unkind. "I'm very sorry for you."

"Don't be. The marriage was a huge mistake." This time it was he who shook his finger at her. "That's what I'm trying to tell you! Don't marry either of those bankers, because they'll make your life hell on earth."

Becoming more out of sorts with each passing second, Georgina asked sarcastically, "Oh? And whom do you suggest I marry instead?"

"Hell, I don't know." He turned around. Then he turned again, in the opposite direction. Then, just when Georgina thought he was going to keep going around in circles all day long, he turned once more and shouted. "*Me!* Confound it! I'm the one you should marry! You should marry *me!*"

She stared at him, her mouth open, unable to force words out of it even if she could have formulated them, which she couldn't. She stepped back. Then she stepped forward.

Then he marched up to her, grabbed her, and drew her to his chest so abruptly that she crashed smack into him, and he kissed her.

Oh, dear. This is exactly what she wished would happen when Henry or Payton kissed her, but it never did. It was only when she was in Ash's arms that her bones melted and her knees turned to water and her senses got knocked awry and an insistent tickle started deep within her and puddled between her thighs. She murmured something, intending it as a protest, but it didn't even sound like one to her. Oh, well.

"That's what you need," Ash growled into her mouth. "You'll never be happy with one of those sissy city fellows."

She murmured something else—she didn't know what it was supposed to be—but it came out as a little mew. Not like one of Oscar's mews, which were always angry and aggressive. No, this mew was more like one from her mother's cat, Buttercup, when she was being offered a delicious tidbit to eat.

Ash still held her to his body, but he'd stopped kissing her. She was very disappointed, especially when he glowered down at her, still looking angry. "Confound it, you can't marry those two men."

"I don't think the law allows a woman to marry more than one man at a time anyway."

"That's not what I meant, and you know it."

Tentatively, Georgina touched Ash's chest. She wished she could rip his shirt from his body and feast her eyes, hands, and mouth on his broad chest. But no. She could only finger his cotton shirt and wish. "What did you mean?"

"I mean you can't marry either one of them, because he'd make you miserable. Hell, I'll bet they're even fussy in bed."

She felt her cheeks burn. "I don't believe you should be speaking to me about such things, Mr. Barrett. It's most impolite."

"Mr. Barrett? God, I told you I can't stand you calling me that!"

And he kissed her again. This time Georgina anticipated it, and she kissed him back. Enthusiastically.

His hands began to wander after a very few seconds. Georgina was delighted.

"Confound it," he muttered. "This is insane. You don't even know what a man's touch is like. You'll never find out if you marry one of those damned bankers."

Georgina said, "Mmmmm."

"It's not fair."

Georgina said, "Hmmmm."

"You need to know what you'll be missing if you tie yourself to one of those fools."

Georgina said, "Aaah," because his hand had just covered a her breast and her nipple had pebbled instantly. His hand felt so good there that she wriggled into his touch.

He growled.

And with that, he picked her right up off the ground and

carried her to the back of the sheriff's office, where he had his buggy hitched up. He placed her in the buggy, jumped up to the driver's seat, and took off like a bat out of hell.

Surprised out of her sensuous stupor, Georgina shrieked, "Where are you taking me?" She slammed a hand to her hat because it felt like it was about to fly off of her head.

"Home!"

Home? He was taking her home? After kissing her to within an inch of her life? How—how terribly disappointing.

It wasn't fair. Georgina was being bounced around too hard to conduct a proper argument, but she stored her words up, and tried to form them into phrases of the most cutting variety. All of her hard work flew out of her brain, however, when, instead of driving the buggy straight down the road leading to the Murphy place, Ash made a wild turn to the right, and drove it down another road entirely. It was one Georgina had never traveled before.

She yelled, "Where are you taking me?" in words made ragged by bounces and jolts.

"I told you. I'm taking you home!"

Gracious sakes alive, what *did* the man mean? He must have gone crazy. Georgina could think of no other explanation for his bizarre behavior.

Suddenly he cut left down another road, this one much narrower. He hadn't driven the buggy very far when the path opened out into a meadow, in the middle of which rested a charming white house with a cunning porch decorated with a porch swing and several wicker chairs.

Fences and gates stood around the house, where Georgina saw—not too steadily because of the jostling of the buggy— horses, cows, and sheep grazing peacefully. How pretty it was here. Why, if she'd been given an opportunity to create an ideal place for herself, she didn't think she could have come up with anything better than this.

But where was she? She opened her mouth to scream her question at her abductor when she realized he was pulling the buggy up to the front porch.

"There," he said in a gruff voice. "We're here."

Georgina struggled to regroup her scattered thoughts. Then she tested her voice. "We're here?"

He jumped down from the driver's seat and came around to

her door, which he yanked open. "Home. We're home."

And with that, he grabbed her around the waist, tossed her over his shoulder, and stormed up the porch stairs with her. Georgina was thrilled. Now *this*, she thought, is the way seductions were supposed to be carried on. None of that tepid, bankerish balderdash. *This* was passion. *This* was excitement. It was also somewhat uncomfortable, but Georgina wasn't about to complain.

Even though she was more or less upside down, she took great interest in the insides of what to her had been a practically perfect house outside. It was perfect inside as well, thought Georgina, and wondered who had done all the decorating.

The front door had opened into a small entryway, which led directly into the parlor. Due to her situation, she hadn't seen much of the furniture but what she had, had seemed tasteful. She'd had a better view of the floors, which were hardwood and scattered here and there with rugs, which were very pretty, and looked as if they'd been made by some Indian tribe or other.

Oh, my, there was a bearskin in front of the fireplace. Georgina had always thought it would be charming to have a bearskin rug in front of a fireplace, although she couldn't think why, offhand. Dime novels and Theodore Roosevelt, she presumed.

Ash took her through a hallway, and she lost sight of the parlor. Hmm, there were pictures on the wall here. A man and a woman. The man looked vaguely like Ash, but the style of the tintype was that of earlier in the century. Perhaps these two people were his parents. Funny. Georgina had never thought about Ash having a family. Yet he'd been married. One simply never knew, did one?

He kicked open another door, and Georgina's heart began hammering in earnest. Good heavens, it was a bedroom! *His* bedroom! He set her gently onto a high four-poster bed. She was impressed. Most of the beds she'd seen thus far in Picacho Wells were tick-mattressed, makeshift sorts. Not this one. This one he must have imported from somewhere else.

She realized she was wasting her energy on trifles, and thought she'd better scream at him for a while instead. "What do you think you're doing?"

He stopped in the act of unbuttoning his shirt and stared at her. "What?"

She cleared her throat. "Do you intend to ravish me?" She was polite.

"Ravish you?" He seemed surprised by the question. In fact, it seemed to bring him up short. He looked at his hands, which clutched his shirt.

"Why else would you be removing your clothes?" It seemed a reasonable question to her.

He looked up again. There was an odd, blank look on his face. He muttered, "Good God."

He might have been carved from stone. Georgina almost wished she hadn't asked about his intentions, because she feared he might stop. She said, "If you do intend to ravish me, I believe you'd better get at it." She smiled, trying to make her smile a winning one. "Don't you think so?"

"Ah . . ." He swallowed.

Oh, dear, he wasn't going to stop now, was he? Georgina didn't suppose she'd ever have a better opportunity to experience rampant lust than right here, right now, with Ash. Ladies weren't even supposed to know what lust was, for heaven's sake. If he stopped to think about what he was doing, he'd probably discover some scruples. She decided she'd better take matters into her own hands, so to speak.

"I'm sorry I interrupted you." She reached for the buttons on her shirtwaist. She was glad she'd set aside her New York wardrobe for the simpler costumes prevalent in the Wild West, because it was much easier to slip out of a shirtwaist and skirt than a basque, overskirt, jacket, shirtwaist, and all the trimmings that went into New York fashion.

She saw him swallow again.

"Don't let me stop you," she murmured, hoping to encourage him. She slipped her shirtwaist off and got up onto her knees to unbutton the waist of her skirt.

Her ploy worked. With a savage growl, he ripped his shirt from his back, removed his boots, shoved his trousers down, and stood before her in his underwear. She was soon similarly arrayed, except she still had her shoes and stockings on. She lifted her shift to expose one black garter, and peered at him through half-closed eyes. "I don't suppose you'd care to help me."

Quick as a wink, he removed his underclothes and flung himself at her on the bed. Georgina had to dodge or be flattened.

Her dodge didn't work. He grabbed her and flattened her anyway, kissing her mercilessly. Oh, my, but this was thrilling!

He sat up again, suddenly, and brought her with him. "I'm going to show you what a *man* feels like, dammit."

He reached for her chemise straps as he spoke. Georgina helped him by shrugging them off. When his mouth closed over her bared breast, she almost died then and there. She'd thought that feeling his hands there was exciting. This was ten times more so.

"You're beautiful," he mumbled, moving his tongue playfully around her nipple.

She couldn't speak. With trembling fingers, she began unlacing her corset. She couldn't wait to get out of the wretched, confining thing. When it finally fell away, she sighed deeply.

Ash growled, grabbed the corset, and flung it across the room. Then he pushed her onto her back again and kissed her some more, using his tongue as she'd never known a tongue could be used.

Georgina had never felt more free. All she had left to get rid of were her petticoat and drawers. She fumbled for the petticoat tapes and untied them, wriggled out of it, then shoved off her drawers, and lay there, naked as the day she was born. Although, she had to admit, there was a good deal more to her now than there had been on the day she was born.

Ash sat up abruptly and stared down at her with hungry eyes. Georgina, never having been seen by a man in anything less than full battle gear before this moment, blushed so hotly she feared she might ignite. Instinctively, she crossed her arms over her breasts.

"No," Ash growled. He reached for her hands and gently thrust them aside.

Good heavens, this was so embarrassing. She wished he'd kiss her again. At least when he kissed her, his eyes were closed. Or hers were. Anyhow, when they kissed she didn't feel so exposed. She feared she wouldn't come up to his expectations, and the idea dealt a hard blow to her confidence.

"Stop staring at me," she commanded, trying to sound firm. Blast! Her voice trembled.

"No." He shook his head.

Georgina frowned. Trust Ash, the most recalcitrant man she'd ever met in her life, not to do the one simple thing she asked of him.

She tried again. "You're embarrassing me."

Again he shook his head. "You're the most beautiful woman I've ever seen, Georgina. You never need to be embarrassed."

"Oh." That put a different light on things. She still felt uncomfortable under his gaze, as if she were a side of beef on display in a butcher's shop.

He reached his hand out and, almost shyly, splayed it against her stomach. His hand was brown as a berry from the work he did outdoors in the territorial sun. It looked amazingly dark against her white, white skin—skin that had seldom been exposed at all, much less to daylight. She saw him lick his lips.

"You're—" His voice had gone hoarse, and he had to clear his throat. "You're very delicate."

"Am I?"

He nodded. "I—I don't want to hurt you."

Georgina frowned. This didn't sound good. If he stopped now, she'd die. She knew it. "I'm not that delicate," she declared stoutly.

"Yes, you are."

"I am not."

He joined her in a frown. "Yes, you are."

"Am not."

"Are too." He removed his hand from her stomach, leaving a cold spot.

Georgina was horrified when Ash pushed himself off of the bed. "I can't do this."

She sat up as if he'd slapped her. "You *what*?"

"I can't do it."

She could see for herself he was lying. Granted, she didn't know much about these things, but she couldn't imagine how his sex could get any stiffer. He was huge and hard and about as ready as he could possibly be, or she was a three-legged goat. "Yes, you can."

He shook his head. He looked to be shaking all over, actually. "No. No, I can't do it."

This was ridiculous. Georgina bounced up from the bed, too,

and strode over to her skirt, which was bunched up on the floor. She reached down and picked it up, her bare bottom pointed at Ash. He groaned again, and when she turned her head, she noted that he'd been staring at her naked bottom. The fool. She groped through the yards of fabric until she found her pocket. She reached into it and fished around for her derringer until she felt it. Then she pulled it out and aimed it straight at the most outstanding target on Ash's body.

"You will make love to me right this minute, Ashley Barrett, or I'll fix it so that you'll never make love to another woman again as long as you live."

Chapter Fifteen

Ash could hardly believe his ears and eyes. There stood Georgina Witherspoon, naked as a jay—a gloriously perfect jay—pointing her little gun at him and threatening to shoot him if he didn't make love to her. For a moment, he hesitated. Then he shook himself hard. He had dragged her here in a fit of temper like some Neanderthal. While he felt like a bastard for doing what he'd done, it certainly didn't look like Georgina was objecting to being in his bedroom. Dammit, she was threatening to shoot him if he didn't stay with her in his bedroom.

"Well, hell, I reckon I can't very well resist if you're going to threaten me with a gun."

"No. You'd better not." She thinned her gaze and looked about as belligerent as she could look, which wasn't very. "I mean it, Ash. You come here right now and finish what you started."

He grinned at her. "All right, Georgina. Don't get mad, now."

"I fear I'm already mad."

He got the feeling she didn't mean angry in this case. "Put the gun away, sweetheart. This will go smoother if you don't shoot me."

She squinted at him. "I'm not sure I trust you."

He gazed at her perfect body, her breasts as luscious as melons, their dusky nipples hard, her smooth white skin, her barely rounded belly, her flaring hips, the blond curls between her thighs that were only a little darker than the hair on her head, her perfectly delectable thighs and calves, and his erection gave an enormous throb.

"You can trust me." Lord, Lord, he could hardly believe this. She was all of his most lurid fantasies come to life. And she was threatening him with a gun if he didn't have sex with her.

"Do you mean it?"

"I mean it."

She eyed him slantwise, as if she still didn't trust him. Hell, all she had to do was look below his waist, and she'd believe him.

"Honest. If you don't believe me, look at this." He gestured at his turgid sex and had the satisfaction of seeing her eyes go wide and her cheeks blossom red.

"Yes, I already noticed that."

"Then you must know I'm telling the truth."

"Very well." She laid the derringer on the table beside the bed.

Ash licked his lips. He didn't like leaving the gun on the table, so close to her. He was almost positive that she was a virgin, and if she got mad when he hurt her, she might just reach for the blasted thing and blow him to kingdom come. "Get on the bed, Georgina. I'll join you there."

After the briefest of hesitations, during which he held his breath and feared she was going to change her mind, she did as he'd asked, and wriggled back so that she could rest against a pillow without taking her gaze from him. She looked perfect on his bed. She looked as if she belonged there.

This wasn't the same bed he'd had during his marriage. When Phoebe died, he gave that one away, and ordered this one from San Antonio. He couldn't bear the memories the old one had called up.

But this one was just right. Georgina looked like a pagan princess lying back against his pillows. He walked slowly to the bed. Fortunately, she closed her eyes when he knelt on the bed and kissed her, so she didn't notice when he snaked a hand out, quietly opened the night table's drawer, and shoved the derringer into it.

He felt much better when the gun was out of sight, but he decided he'd better go slowly and carefully from here on. If he scared her and she changed her mind, he might not survive the disappointment.

"I don't know what to do." Her voice was small and tentative.

"That's all right, honey. I do."

She swallowed. "Yes. You said you've been married."

He nodded and decided she didn't need to know that his experience came primarily from sources other than his marriage bed, which had been almost celibate thanks to Phoebe's selfishness and odd notions. "Just relax now. I'll take care of you."

She said, "You'd better," in a tone that led him to believe she meant it.

"I will," he promised.

He did his best. He tried with all the restraint he possessed to go slowly and carefully, and to make the experience as good for Georgina as he could. It was certainly good for him.

Except during his marriage Ash's sexual experiences had, until now, been carried out with women who knew what was what. Georgina didn't. Not only was she as innocent as a newborn babe, but she was delicate. No matter that she disagreed on that score; Ash knew better.

Her skin, for instance, was like satin, it was so soft, smooth, and silky.

Lord, she was gorgeous. Ash wasn't sure how long he could keep this up without bursting, but he aimed to give it a good try. He wanted to explore every inch of that magnificent body even if it killed him.

Georgina arced like a bow when his wandering tongue grazed over her breast. She had lovely breasts. Just big enough, and as firm as ripe peaches. And her nipples—well, her nipples were telling an interesting story, to Ash's way of thinking. They were pebbled up hard as anything. When he licked one, she moaned, deep and hungry. Then he took it gently in his teeth, and she groaned.

Ash almost burst at Georgina's reaction. He had long imagined what it would be like to make love to his sweet Georgina. And now he knew. She was the most responsive woman he'd ever lain with. He'd never be able to get to sleep again, because now he'd be thinking about this every night.

Georgina wasn't sure how long she could survive this amazing experience. Until today, she'd always assumed the marital act was carried out in darkened rooms, under the covers, quickly and briefly, sort of like executions.

But Ash's bedroom wasn't dark at all. Indeed, sunlight poured into the room through the windows and, if she opened her eyes, which seemed to want to stay closed, she could actually see what he was doing to her in the mirror of his dressing table. She supposed she should be feeling more scandalized with herself but everything just felt too delicious to worry about that now. All that mattered now was that she was here with Ash and he was making her body feel things she had never imagined possible.

That was her in the mirror making love to a perfectly spectacular male—and in her mind there was absolutely nothing scandalous or wrong with that.

This was the most exciting thing that had ever happened to her. She'd come two thousand miles to seek adventure and, by gum, she was finding it. In fact, she was finding more here than she ever had back in New York City, She knew beyond a doubt that intimate intercourse with Henry or Payton would never have been this exciting.

This was special. It was wonderful. And it was about to kill her.

Her hips moved against Ash's muscular leg. If he didn't start concentrating on the pressure between her thighs, Georgina might just have to take things into her own hands.

She had about given up when Ash finally addressed the throbbing need between her legs. His hand brushed the triangle of curls that protected her womanhood, and Georgina almost screamed, her desire was so great.

He lifted his mouth from her breast. "Are you all right?" His voice sounded ragged.

She couldn't use hers at all. She only nodded in response.

He said, "Good," and went back to feasting on her breast and probing the softness at the junction of her thighs.

Thank goodness. While Georgina appreciated his concern, she also had feared for a second that he was still harboring reservations and might abruptly decide to end this ecstasy.

He dipped a finger into her wetness, and her thoughts shattered like glass. Good heavens, was he supposed to be doing that? His finger moved, touching the nub of all her passions, and she decided not to try to second-guess him. He obviously knew exactly what he was doing.

She, on the other hand, didn't. The way his fingers were making magic on her caused her to lift her hips. Was she supposed to be doing that? Was it shocking of her?

A very few more strokes of Ash's fingers made Georgina's questions scatter like so much chaff in the wind. She'd never felt anything so wonderful in her life.

"That's the way," he murmured into her ear. "That's the way, sweetheart."

Good. She was glad he'd clarified things for her. The pressure was building and building until she wasn't sure she could stand it another second longer.

"Come on, sweetheart. Show me that you like it. That's the way."

His low, soothing voice distracted her for a second—and then her body exploded. With a small shriek, she convulsed under his touch.

"Beautiful. Oh, God, you're beautiful."

It took her a while to process the words he whispered as he watched her. She didn't have time to savor them, because as soon as he uttered them, he kissed her again, threw his leg over hers, and guided himself to her wet passage.

With a quick thrust, he entered her, and Georgina's ecstasy came to a sudden, jarring halt. She uttered a small yelp of pain. Her cry of hurt wasn't as loud as her cry of pleasure had been, but it stopped Ash cold and a look of concern replaced the desire that had been in his eyes.

"I know it hurts now but I promise it will never hurt again, sweetheart." He gazed down at Georgina with such tenderness that she almost melted.

Georgina realized that she was getting used to the feel of him inside her. The pain had faded and been replaced by a sensation of fullness—strange, but not altogether unpleasant. He moved a little and she stiffened, then relaxed again.

He ground out, "All right?" He sounded really quite concerned and also a bit desperate.

Georgina gasped out her pleasure, unable once again to form a coherent thought, let alone a full sentence.

He didn't say another word, but thrust deep inside her with a groan. Georgina lifted her hips instinctively moving her body in time with his. Ash kissed her hard and continued to bring Georgina to the crest of desire. She'd never felt so many emotions at once and she felt both thrilled and overwhelmed at one time.

Abandoning herself to the delight of being in so intimate a situation with him, she kissed Ash back. Perhaps her grandmother wasn't such a wanton, outrageous woman after all: For the first time since she had arrived, Georgina realized how much she respected her grandmother for following her heart and not paying attention to some nonsensical social structures.

The thought occurred to her that she loved Ash Barrett, but she was too wrapped up in the moment as well to think about the ramifications and consequences of that. She simply wanted to enjoy the experience and revel in the attention Ash was showing her body. For all she knew, she'd never have another adventure this wonderful in her whole life.

Ash's concentration seemed to be intense as he thrust into her over and over again. The pain was but a memory now, and Georgina felt the pressure of pleasure building again with each stroke until she was sure she'd die. And then her world exploded again in a convulsion of release. With a loud cry, Ash's release came too.

He collapsed onto her body like a spent rag and panted like a racehorse for several seconds before he slid to her side, wrapped his arms around her, and hugged her to his body as if he feared she was going to try to escape.

"You're wonderful," he gasped into her ear.

"Thank you." Since she had no experience in these matters, Georgina wasn't sure what she was supposed to say, if anything, but she decided it would only be fair to return the compliment, especially since she meant it. "So are you."

He hugged her again, pressing her so close to his chest that he drove the breath out of her. Georgina couldn't have cared less—she was so happy to be in his arms that he could have squeezed her to kingdom come and she wouldn't have given it a second thought. They lay wrapped in each other's arms for long enough that she dozed off. She woke with a start, and had no idea how long she'd been asleep, but it was long enough for Ash to have unwrapped her and rolled onto his back.

She was disappointed, wanting more than anything to still have his arms around her. She was even more disappointed when she glanced at him and saw him frowning at the ceiling. To her way of thinking, this occasion did not call for frowning.

"What's the matter, Ash?" She kept her voice gentle and sweet, unsure what the problem was exactly.

He glanced at her, and his frown softened slightly. She felt vaguely encouraged, although she knew better than to expect much of anything of an optimistic nature from Ash Barrett. He always seemed to find the cloud behind the silver lining— especially when he was dealing with her.

"Nothing's the matter." He turned on his side and began running a hand over her naked body.

Georgina was surprised to discover this bold action on his part didn't embarrass her at all. In fact, her body responded instantly to his touch. Sort of like a sulfur match. Or a fire-cracker. By Jupiter, she'd had no idea love-making could be so spectacular.

His petting her did not, however, answer her question. Something *was* the matter, and she aimed to get to the bottom of it. "Ash you don't look happy."

She was happy. Under the circumstances she considered it a bad sign that he didn't. After all, it was she who was no longer the virgin here, not he.

"I'm fine." He sighed, deeply and soulfully, although he continued to make magic on her body.

It was interesting, Georgina thought, to discover how very delicious a man's work-roughened hand could feel on her na-ked flesh. She had a notion not any man's hand would do, however. She yanked her attention from the small fires Ash was reigniting with his hand roaming her naked body and back to his downcast mood with some difficulty. "You're not look-ing fine."

Bother! He removed his hand from her stomach, turned onto his back again, and flung the back of his wrist over his eyes. Georgina didn't know why he couldn't stroke her and think at the same time. Surely he was a man of some intellect, even if it was disordered some of the time. He couldn't need all of his bodily functions to concentrate on one simple question, could he? She decided he was merely being selfish.

"I was just wondering how soon I could talk the preacher into marrying us."

For the second time that day, Georgina reacted to something Ash did suddenly and spontaneously—only this time, it didn't feel good. A shock jolted her from her head to her toes. She sat up and stared at him. Clearly, she must have misunderstood. "I beg your pardon?"

He opened his eyes and peered at her through his fingers. "We'll have to get married now." He didn't sound glad about it. Not one little bit.

A chill crept through Georgina's body which, only seconds before, had been warm as toast and tingly with newly discovered delights. Her grandmother and Devlin crept into her brain as ice invaded her veins.

If this is how that damned Irishman had proposed to Maybelle, Georgina no longer wondered at her grandmother's refusal to marry him.

"My, what an interesting proposal of marriage." The chill Georgina felt was nothing compared to the frost in her voice.

Ash's hand fell away from his eyes, and he turned his head. "What?" he said, as if her tone offended him. "What did I say? Hell, I asked you to marry me, didn't I?"

"Did you?" She flung her feet over the side of the bed.

He flung his feet over the other side. He still watched her. "Yes, I did. You heard me, didn't you?"

She had already stood and was stamping around the room, looking for items of clothing that had been flung thither and yon when his question made her stop short. She spun around, more furious than she could ever remember being. While he had made her incredibly angry before with his biting comments and insults, nothing could compare to this slight. "No, actually, I did not hear anything resembling a proposal, Mr. Ashley Barrett. What I heard sounded like the whining of a man who knows he's gone too far and now fears he'll have to pay for it." She saw her skirt and pounced on it, shaking it as she'd like to be shaking him.

"Confound it, that's not true!"

"It is, too." Georgina was feeling crabbier with every second that passed. Since she couldn't very well put on her skirt before she put on the rest of her underthings, she draped it over a chair and resumed looking. If she ever did this again, she aimed to be careful with her clothes since it was distracting to have to search for them while trying to conduct an argument.

"Listen, Georgina, we have to get married now. You know that as well as I do." He got up and began stomping around collecting fallen pieces of clothing as well. He found her chemise and handed it to her.

She snatched it out of his hands. "Thank you." She slipped it over her head and wriggled it down and around her body. "We absolutely do not have to get married now."

When she was through dealing with her chemise, she noticed Ash's eyes were fixed on her bosom and had gone hot again. So had the tool between his legs. She glared pointedly at him and then down to his erect member, her meaning clear. He turned around, apparently embarrassed.

"Yes, we do. For God's sake, we went to bed together. You're just being stubborn."

"I am not just being stubborn."

He threw her shirtwaist at her. She caught it in midair and jammed her arms into its sleeves.

"You are, too! Dammit, you drive me crazy!"

He'd driven her crazy, too, but she thought she'd better not mention it. Her body, however, remembered, and flushed. Oh, my, he had made her feel wonderfully, splendidly crazy.

That, however, was nothing to the purpose, and she didn't aim to allow herself to become distracted. This discussion was too important to her future happiness and well-being. "I'm sorry about your lack of sanity, Ash, but unless you can ask me to marry you in a tone that leads me to believe you actually want to do so, you're destined to remain a bachelor."

She thought that was a good line, and smiled as she recovered one of her stockings. Where the blasted garter had got itself off to was another matter. She surveyed the room, scowling, and pounced on the other stocking.

"I can't believe this."

"You'd better believe it, because it's true."

When she eyed a garter, picked it up, and sat on the straight-backed chair in front of the dressing table, Ash had resumed storming around the room, picking up his own clothes. He glared at her as he shoved a long, hairy leg into his trousers. He really had splendid legs. Long and strong and bulging with muscles, they'd felt quite exciting rubbing against her own legs. Georgina sighed, remembering, caught herself doing it, and with some difficulty returned her attention to her garter.

Ash still hadn't offered a retort, and when she looked up wondering why he was so quiet, he was watching her leg avidly. She lifted her chin and went searching for the other garter, trying like the devil to ignore his heated gaze.

He cleared his throat. "Listen, I'm sorry if I didn't sound very romantic when I proposed, Georgina. It's only that I've been married before, so it's not like—well, you know."

She sat again and squinted at him through eyelids gone narrow with rage and hurt. "No, I'm sorry. I don't know. I, for one, have never been married. However, I do recollect you telling me you'd been married before, and that it had been a ghastly mistake. And now you're telling me that you're willing to commit another ghastly mistake because you perceive that you have no alternative, although you really don't want to." She yanked on her stocking and tied the other garter.

"No! Confound it, that's not what I meant!"

Shaking with fury and on the verge of tears, Georgina rose from the chair and glanced around for her shoes. She didn't want to cry in front of this man and give him the satisfaction of knowing how much he had hurt her. "Isn't it?"

"No, it's not! I don't understand what your problem is, anyway. I asked you to marry me. Isn't that what you females want? You torture a man until he gives in to his lust, and then you've got him hooked. Well, you've hooked me. Isn't that enough for you?"

She walked right up to Ash and looked him straight in the eye—well, almost straight in the eye. She had to crane her neck back a ways since he was so much taller than she was. "I want you to understand something, Ash. I don't want there to be any mistake about it. Are you listening to me?"

"I don't see how I can avoid it," he muttered grumpily.

"Good. Then here it is. I wouldn't marry you if you were the last man on earth. I wouldn't marry you if you held a gun to my head. I wouldn't marry you if—"

All at once, Georgina thought about her derringer. She glanced at the night table and didn't see it. Immediately she knew Ash had done something underhanded with it. She glared back up at him. "Where's my gun, you fiend?"

"Fiend? Now I'm a fiend?"

Georgina wasn't sure, because she hadn't known him long, but she suspected he couldn't look more exasperated than he did just then. His attitude only fueled her anger. In a way, she was grateful, because she no longer felt the least little bit like crying. "Yes. You're a fiend. Now where's my gun?"

He huffed hard. "It's in the drawer. I'll get it."

She turned abruptly and headed for the night table. "Stay right there and finish dressing. *I'll* get my *own* gun."

"Confound it, I don't trust you with it."

She ran the last several steps to the night table in case he tried to beat her to it. "Well, now, isn't that just too bad, because I got here first."

She turned and pointed the derringer at him for long enough to relish the look of worry on his face. Then she stuck it into her skirt pocket. "Don't worry. I won't shoot you. Not that you don't deserve it."

"Why? Because I made love to you or because I asked you to marry me?"

She sat on the bed and thought about his question for a few moments before she answered. Fortunately, she masked her thought processes by making a show out of tugging on her shoes. When she was finished with the right shoe, she looked over at him. "What we did today bore no resemblance whatever to making love, Ash."

At least it didn't on his part. Georgina didn't want to think about it from her perspective for fear she'd start to cry and never be able to stop. "And if that was a question you asked me about the marriage part, I missed it entirely. It sounded like a statement or a command to me."

He rubbed a hand over his face. He was plainly as frustrated as all get-out. "Confound it, I'm sorry if I didn't ask you properly." He walked over and stood in front of her. "Will you please marry me? There. Is that better? Shall I get down on one knee? Is that what you want?"

She wished she hadn't put on her left shoe. She'd like to

batter him with it. Instead, she smiled sweetly up at him. "No, Ash. That's not better at all. It's worse. And no, it's not what I want." She jumped up from the bed, saw her hat in a corner, and dashed over to fetch it. As she tied the ribbons, she said, "Now, if you please, take me back to town. My horse and buggy are still there, and I want to go home."

"I'm not going to let you drive home alone. Not now. You're too upset to drive properly."

That might well be true, but Georgina would never admit it. "Drive me to town this minute, Ashley Barrett."

"No. What do you take me for, anyway? I'm not going to let you drive home alone."

"I'd rather not answer the part about what I take you for. And I'm perfectly capable of driving myself home alone."

"No. I'm taking you home."

She gaped at him. "Of all the high-handed men I've ever known in my life, you take the cake, do you know that? What, pray, is going to happen to my grandmother's buggy and horse if you take me home?"

"Go ahead. Call me all the names you want. I'm still taking you home. Then I'll go back to town and get Maybelle's buggy. Don't worry. I won't let anything happen to it." He shot her a furious scowl. "Or you, either."

Something had already happened to Georgina today. She'd made love to a man for the first time, fallen head over heels in love with the wretched fellow, and had her heart broken. But she'd die before she told him any of that.

"Fine," she said, her voice as hard as marbles. "Take me home."

"Fine," he said, his voice as hard as hers. "I will."

Neither one of them spoke a single syllable on the ride from Ash's place to the Murphy farm.

When he aimed the horse down the twin rows of pecans, he said in a voice that sounded like it hurt coming out, "You get on inside the house. I'll go back to town and fetch Maybelle's buggy."

Georgina didn't even argue with him. She merely nodded. She couldn't recall ever feeling as unhappy and hopeless as she felt just then.

Her defiant attitude lasted until she'd stormed to the house, stomped up the steps, wrenched the door open, and slammed it behind her. Then, when she saw Vernice and Maybelle's questioning glances from where they sat in the parlor, her composure collapsed like a burst balloon.

She ran to her grandmother, flung herself onto her knees, and burst into tears. Oscar, who had been preening himself on the back of Maybelle's chair, gave a yowl and leaped to the floor.

Maybelle and Vernice exchanged a concerned glance, then Maybelle began stroking Georgina's head softly. "It's all right, girl. You go ahead and tell Granny Murphy all about it. Then we can decide how best to kill Ash Barrett."

Georgina wouldn't have thought it possible before it happened, but, with her face still buried in the folds of her grandmother's skirt, she laughed.

Chapter
Sixteen

Ash couldn't believe it that Georgina's stony attitude hadn't softened one iota in the time it had taken them to travel from his home all the way back to the Murphy place. He'd sort of expected that she'd come to her senses before then, but no such luck. She wasn't inclined to give up a good anger once it took hold, he reckoned. In that regard, she was not unlike her grandmother, dammit.

He'd never seen anything like it. When he drew the buggy up to the porch, she didn't even wait until he could help her out, but bounded down on her own. Then she flounced away from him as if she'd never even been kissed, much less bedded, and he could only scratch his head and watch her go, his heart behaving in a manner he'd never experienced before.

His heart used to be a fairly reliable organ. Not today. Today it ached. It throbbed. It hurt like a son of a bitch. When Ash remembered the ecstasy he and Georgina had shared in his bedroom—before the prospect of marriage had driven all the happiness from his body—his undependable heart soared like a hawk. Then it took to aching again. Dammit, his heart never used to give him any trouble. Well, except for Phoebe, but that was a long time ago, and he was older and wiser now.

Pressing a hand to his wounded heart, he wondered if he had a touch of indigestion.

He drove back to his house in a black temper. There he collected Shiloh, returned to town, tied his horse to the back of the Murphy buggy, drove the buggy to the Murphy place, and sat there, stewing and wondering what he should do next.

Should he knock on the door and demand that Georgina marry him? Or should he quietly put the buggy in the barn, unharness the horse, brush him down, give him some grain, and leave?

After a few gloomy moments, Ash decided to do the latter. If anyone inside the place wanted to talk to him—or holler at him or shoot him—he'd be in the barn, and they could have at him with his blessing.

No one did. The place might have been deserted, except that there was smoke coming from the kitchen chimney. They were cooking. They were good cooks, the Murphy-Witherspoon crew. He sighed despondently and wished he hadn't remembered that aspect of domestic bliss. He faced the prospect of eating cold corn pone and fried bacon. The reality of his anticipated supper only deepened his already foul mood.

Georgina hated his guts. He'd suspected as much for quite a while, but there could be no doubt about it now. He'd ruined any possibility of a truce between them.

He'd blundered badly. Like a total fool, he'd bedded her and then not gushed out a pile of slop regarding love and devotion and all that related hogwash, the way he'd done with Phoebe. He shuddered, remembering what a jackass he'd made of himself with his wife. Phoebe'd taken every ounce of love he had given her, trampled all over it, and then thrown it back in his face, along with her sincere loathing.

Ash had never been so wrong about a person as he'd been with Phoebe. He wasn't about to make the same mistake a second time. His pride wouldn't let him.

Of course, Georgina wasn't Phoebe. He had to keep reminding himself of that. Hell, the first time Ash kissed Phoebe, she'd laughed coyly, as if she'd just won a prize, and he knew at that moment that she expected him to marry her.

Not Georgina. In spite of himself, Ash grinned. Damned if she hadn't gone to bed with him—and enjoyed herself, if he was any judge—and then refused his inelegant proposal of marriage. Ha! The woman had grit; he'd give her that.

His grin soured. What he'd done was, he'd probably driven

her right into the arms of one of her other suitors. One of those jackass bankers. What a horrible thought.

Ash allowed himself to contemplate what he'd feel like if he were to see Georgina married to another man. His insides curdled as if they'd been pickled in vinegar.

Georgina wailed, "I *won't* marry him! I *won't!*"

"You just drink this tea and tell me all about it, honey. Don't let what anyone else thinks make you do anything. Especially not something so important that it will affect the rest of your life. I did that and I not only hurt myself, but a whole lot of other people as well. I'll stand by you, no matter what you decide."

"We both will," Vernice said, her kindly voice as gentle and soothing as a summer breeze.

Georgina sniffled and wiped her eyes on her grandmother's apron. Since her knees had begun to ache, she pushed herself away from Maybelle and sat on the floor next to her chair. "Oh, Grandmother Murphy, I was so stupid."

"It's never stupid to love someone, sweetie," Maybelle said in the most affectionate tone Georgina had ever heard issue from her wrinkled lips.

Oscar hissed at her, which made her feel as if the world might not be totally askew. When she lifted her head and saw Vernice, smiling tenderly at her and pouring out another cup of tea for herself, Georgina started crying again.

"Oh, Aunt Vernice and Grandmother Murphy, you've been so wonderful to me. And this is how I've repaid your kindness! I'm so sorry!" Georgina buried her head in her hands.

"Fiddlesticks!" Vernice's voice was firm, which surprised Georgina. She was used to flutterings and palpitations from Vernice, not firmness. "You haven't done a single thing to us, Georgina. If you've hurt anyone, it's yourself, not us, but it's not your fault. You're upset, and that's too bad, but it's truly not your fault."

"Aye, child, dry your eyes. There's nothin' in this life worth crying those bitter tears over."

"As if *you'd* know anything about it," Maybelle said to her dead lover's ghost. "Get out of here. This is girl talk."

"Pisht, Maybelle. I'm fond of the girl."

"I don't care if you are, Devlin! You're a man and a rogue,

and you have no business here!'' Maybelle heaved a darning egg at him, and he vanished.

Vernice shook her head. ''It's so disconcerting to have that man hovering about. You never know when he'll pop up.''

''If he turns up again today in this room, I'll swat him like a fly.'' Maybelle returned her attention to Georgina.

''If you'd just tell the man what he wants to hear, Mother—''

''Never!''

Vernice, perceiving the steel in her mother's answer, sighed and sipped her tea.

''Pay Dev no mind, Georgina. He's a man and an idiot and can't possibly understand anything. So, tell your old grandmother what happened today that has you in such a fuss.''

''Oh, Grandmother!'' Georgina broke down in tears again, but this crying jag didn't last very long. After blowing her nose and sniffling and wiping her eyes, she told Maybelle and Vernice exactly what had transpired at Ash Barrett's house, leaving out the more salacious—and delicious—details. She expected Vernice to be shocked, but her aunt remained placidly darning stockings—she'd retrieved the darning egg—and only nodded sympathetically. During her confession, Georgina appreciated her territorial relatives more than she could ever express.

When she came at last to the end of her recitation, she realized she was still sitting on the floor, leaning against her grandmother's chair, and had started petting Oscar, who didn't even scratch her for it. In fact, he was purring. She'd never heard the beast purr until this minute.

She sniffled again. ''So I refused him. He didn't want to make the offer, you know.''

Maybelle sighed. ''I'm sure you're right. That first wife of his was a piece of work.''

Vernice tutted. ''I fear Mother is correct, Georgina. I'm not surprised that Mr. Barrett doesn't look upon marriage with favor. Phoebe was far from an ideal spouse for the poor man.'' She sounded sad about it.

''The poor man, my foot. He was an ass to marry her.'' After a good, derisive snort, Maybelle said, ''He's a damned fool, though, to compare our Georgina here with that worthless Phoebe of his.''

"Yes, that's so," Vernice agreed. "But you know what they say: Once burned, twice shy."

"Fiddlesticks. The man's an ass."

Georgina couldn't have said it better herself.

"You did the right thing, girl," Maybelle went on. "He needs to know that women are often better off without husbands. Marriage isn't the only worthwhile life for a female to pursue. Men! They're such fools."

"I believe Mother is right about that, too, dear. It's far better to remain a spinster than to marry the wrong man. I've seen such tragic things happen to women whose husbands aren't good providers or who are unfaithful and mean. Or drink to excess." She shook her head and looked somber.

"That's the truth," Maybelle said firmly. "And you must know, too, that a woman gives up damned near everything when she marries, so it's best not to marry at all unless you're absolutely sure about the man."

Vernice nodded her agreement. "I chose not to marry a man even though I cared for him, and I was right to reject him. He turned out to be a terrible drunkard."

"My goodness." Georgina had never heard this tale about her aunt's former life.

"Listen to her, Georgina. I remember it. Howard Phipps. He was a handsome devil, but he turned out to be a wastrel, and Vernice saw right through him when no one else did."

It was the first time Georgina had heard Maybelle say anything nice about her daughter. Georgina looked at the two of them, saw them smiling at each other, and realized how deeply the bond of love between them ran. She was touched.

She was also feeling better to a degree, although something else had begun to plague her. She cleared her throat. Oscar hissed at her. She stuck her tongue out at him and continued petting him. She could have sworn he grinned at her. "There's one thing, though . . ." She wasn't sure how to phrase her concern.

Maybelle took the matter out of her hands. "Don't worry about it, Georgina. If there's a baby, it will be perfectly welcome in this house."

"Oh!" cried Vernice, and clasped her hands to her bosom, darning egg and all, her face alight with happiness. "Wouldn't that be perfect? A precious little baby!"

Georgina blinked at her relatives, dumbfounded. "Er, you mean, you wouldn't mind if I had a . . ." She couldn't make herself say the word aloud. *Bastard* sounded so crude.

"Nonsense! Nothing would make us happier. Would it, Vernice?"

Vernice didn't really have to answer her mother's question, because her face told the story. She'd be ecstatic if Georgina were to have a baby, in or out of wedlock. Georgina felt her spirits rise slightly higher. Maybe her life wasn't over yet after all.

"And you never know," Vernice went on. "He may come around. I'm sure he loves you, dear. I've seen the symptoms before."

Georgina blinked at her, surprised. Ash loved her? Hmm. You'd never know it to judge by his marriage proposal—if one could call such a grudging command a proposal.

"Harrumph. Men! They're all alike. Don't have him unless he admits he loves you, girl. If you marry him before he declares what's in his heart, you'll have to live with doubt for the rest of your life, and you'll give him an excuse to ride roughshod over you and pretend he was coerced. If he admits he loves you, snap him up. Ash is a good man, but he's an idiot. They're all idiots." Maybelle's lips pinched together.

Georgina watched her grandmother and realized the old woman was right. Perhaps she hadn't been merely stubborn and silly by refusing to marry Devlin O'Rourke all those years. And perhaps she wasn't being merely stubborn and silly now by not giving in to his silver-tongued pleas. Perhaps she was wise to withhold a promise to the ghost until he did his part. By heaven, it all suddenly made sense to her.

"You're right, Grandmother. I do believe you're right."

"Damned straight, I'm right. Lord girl, men have all the rights already. The only thing we women have is control over our own bodies, and half the time people try to make us believe we don't even have that much. But we do. By God, don't give yours up until that man tells you exactly what he aims to do with it. You're a prize, Georgina, and don't ever let yourself believe otherwise."

Vernice nodded. "Wise words, dear. I believe my mother is absolutely correct in this instance."

Maybelle nodded, too, although her nod was much more

firm than that of her daughter. "I am right. Men have all the property, they have all the money, they have all the power. Hell, if you marry that dunce and it doesn't work out and you have children, he could even take *them* away from you if he wanted to. Not that most men want anything to do with their spawn. Idiots. They're all asses. They drop bastards all over the world as if children were no more important than dog droppings."

"Mother!"

Georgina was rather shocked at her grandmother's words, too. As much as she deplored Maybelle's plain speaking, however, she had to admit she'd spoken only the truth. Women got the blame for illegitimate children, but men were probably more at fault than women were. Men had even led women into lustful acts with false promises, and then assumed no responsibility for the consequences.

She definitely had formed a very low opinion of men since coming to the territory. "I'll be blasted if I'll have a man who feels he's been forced into marrying me."

"That's the ticket!" Maybelle beamed down at her.

Vernice nodded. "You're being very wise, Georgina. And if there should happen to be a sweet little baby, we'll rear it with all the love and devotion in the world. It won't miss a thing, dear."

That was unquestionably the nicest thing anyone could have said to Georgina right then, and she once again burst into tears under the influence of it. Oscar, disgusted, hissed once and stalked away, his tail switching.

"And don't go running to either of those banker fellows, either. They're even worse than Ash."

Through her tears, Georgina nodded. Although her words were watery, she said, "Don't worry, Grandmother. I wouldn't have either one of them on a platter."

"That's my girl."

The following day, Ash knew what he had to do, so he dressed in his best Sunday suit to do it. He saddled Shiloh and went to town first, just to make sure his sheriff services weren't needed. He knew he was only putting off the inevitable.

He was almost in front of his office when he ran into Payton Pierce. Pierce looked like he'd eaten something bitter. Ash tipped his hat, feeling not as ill-disposed toward the banker today as he usually did. Unhappiness did that to a fellow, he reckoned. Drew him closer to his fellow sufferers.

"Pierce," he said.

"Barrett," Pierce said back. He was making a beeline for his bank, his countenance as unhappy as Ash had ever seen it. Ash shrugged and opened his office door.

Pierce stopped right before he got to the bank door. "Are you going to be visiting Miss Witherspoon today, Mr. Barrett?"

Ash turned and frowned at the man, wondering what exactly he was up to. "I don't know. Why?"

The banker scowled and kicked a pebble off the boardwalk with some force. "I just wondered. She gave me my walking papers yesterday."

Ash's mouth fell open. He didn't know what to say.

"And that grandmother of hers . . . Well, if I ever met a more unpleasant woman in my life, I certainly don't remember when."

The expression on his face was as close to barbaric as it could probably get. Ash hadn't known he could look like that. He almost liked him for a second or two.

Pierce went on. "I suppose she's going to marry that Henry Spurling fellow from New York."

Ash gulped. "Really?" His heart gave the hardest spasm of its entire career.

"That must be it. Why else would she refuse me?"

Ash could think of at least 146 reasons for a beautiful, vivacious woman like Georgina Witherspoon to refuse to marry Pierce, but he didn't think it would be polite to enumerate them. He only shook his head.

"I think she's making a terrible mistake," Pierce said. "A terrible mistake. She'll find out one of these days, when she's stuck in New York and dreaming about life out here in the territory. I hope she chokes on her decision!" And with that pleasant thought, he opened the door to the bank, went inside, and slammed the door behind him.

Ash stared after him for several seconds, then went into his own office. Frank Dunwiddy was sleeping in his chair, his hat pulled down over his face, resting on his enormous nose. He pushed the hat back and yawned when Ash woke him up.

"You need me this morning, Frank?"

Frank eyed him up and down, unused to seeing Ash dressed up. No one was used to seeing Ash dressed up, as a matter of fact. Ash didn't explain his unusual mode of dress.

"Naw. Nothing's going on in town, I reckon."

Ash nodded. "Then I'll be gone for an hour or so. If you need me, I'll . . ." He'll what? Shoot, he didn't want to admit he was going out to the Murphy place to propose to Georgina properly. "I'll be back in a couple of hours." There. He didn't suppose the town would burn down in a couple of hours. And if it did, well, he'd find another job somewhere else.

"Fine. You go do what you have to do."

Frank grinned at Ash, who didn't appreciate it. He slammed out of his own office much as Pierce had slammed into his.

He rehearsed all sorts of proposal scenarios in his head as Shiloh carried him down the road toward the Murphy farm. His main concern was Georgina. Would she still be mad at him? Would she still refuse to marry him?

Naw. She'd have had a chance by now to think about things, and perceive that there was no alternative for them. They had to get married, whether Ash wanted to or not.

This morning, after having thought the matter over for most of the night, he wasn't altogether positive that marriage to Georgina would be as awful as he had originally believed. At least she wasn't prim and prissy, as Phoebe had been. And she'd probably enjoy the sexual aspects of married life. He got hard, remembering their encounter of the day before, and his mood improved slightly.

His fair mood crashed into a smoldering heap again when he rode out from between the pecan trees and into the Murphy yard. Hell's bells, was that Henry Spurling standing on the porch? Aw, hell. Ash pulled Shiloh to a stop and glared at the porch.

If it was Spurling, and Ash was fairly certain it was, he didn't look any too happy. He pulled Shiloh behind a pecan tree and watched the scene that was developing on the porch. Straining his ears, he could just make out the words being said.

"But Georgina, you can't mean it!" Spurling sounded flabbergasted.

"I do mean it, Henry. Now please go back to town. If you ask, I'm sure you can get a ticket back to New York soon."

Georgina, on the other hand, sounded relatively serene.

"But—but—but it was decided years ago!"

"Not by me, it wasn't."

"But surely you'll do what your parents want you to do, Georgina!"

"I'd be happy to do what my parents wanted me to do if I thought it would be the right thing for *me* to do. In this instance, I fear it would be a catastrophe."

"A catastrophe! But, Georgina—"

"Oh, Henry, please just go away! I'm tired of arguing with you. Why do men always want to argue so much?"

Poor old Henry looked as if he'd never been in such a pickle before. He grabbed his hat from his head and slapped it against his leg. "I can't believe this! You can't just send me away, as if I meant no more to you than—than—than a casual acquaintance!"

"Of course you're more than a casual acquaintance, Henry. We've known each other all of our lives. I've always considered you a friend—one of my very best friends, in fact."

"A friend! A *friend*? Well, I like that!" He turned and stormed to the other end of the porch, then stormed back again.

Ash rode Shiloh a little closer until he could clearly see Georgina standing in the doorway, looking unruffled and beautiful. Her being unruffled didn't seem right to him. She ought to be upset. Or angry. Or something. Hell, not only was she no longer a virgin, but there was a raving lunatic stamping around on her front porch.

"I believe friends are a very important aspect of a person's life, Henry. I should be happy if you were to consider me your friend." She smiled one of her sweet smiles at poor old Henry, who still looked fit to be tied.

"Friends! But we're going to be married!"

Georgina shook her head. "No, Henry. I'm sorry if you came all this way on that assumption. I shan't be marrying you."

Satisfaction flooded Ash. So, she'd rejected both bankers, had she? That must mean she was ready to accept his proposal and he wouldn't have to grovel or plead or argue or anything. Thank God. He didn't think he was up to fighting a battle with her again today.

Henry stormed back to the door and shook a finger in her

face. "Dash it, Georgina, you wait until your parents hear about this! They won't be pleased! They won't be pleased one bit! And *then* what will happen, hmm? Do you think they're going to allow you to waste yourself on some stupid *cowboy*?"

Blinking in time to the movement of his finger, Georgina frowned at Henry. "Whatever are you talking about, Henry? What cowboy? I don't believe I know any cowboys. Why should my parents care if I choose not to marry you? I'm sure they only hope for my happiness, and I wouldn't be happy married to you."

"Ha!" said Henry, still wagging his finger.

"And you wouldn't be happy married to me, either, so you see we're both better off this way."

Henry stared at her incredulously. His hand dropped to his side. "Better off? But—but—"

She shook her head. "No, Henry. I'm sorry if you're surprised about this, but honestly, you assumed too much. You should have asked me before you settled it in your mind that we were to be married."

"But—but . . ." Henry's voice petered out. It looked to Ash as if he was running out of steam. Under the circumstances, he didn't blame him.

Georgina adopted a compassionate expression. "I really am sorry you came all this way only to be disappointed, Henry. I wish you'd written me. I could have spared you the long trip to the territory."

Henry stared at her for a moment or two before he seemed to shake himself all over. He slammed his hat onto his head. "You haven't heard the last of this outrage, Georgina! I know very well that your parents aren't going to allow you to throw your life away in this vile place!"

"This vile place?" Georgina glanced at the countryside behind Henry as if she couldn't imagine what he was talking about. "My parents have nothing to say about it, actually."

"Nothing to *say* about it!" Henry goggled at her. "We'll just see about that! They aren't going to let you remain here. It's dangerous! It's wild! It's uncivilized!"

Ash frowned. He didn't appreciate old Henry's assessment of his home. Ash liked it here.

Georgina laughed softly. "Picacho Wells may have one or two wild characteristics, Henry—"

"One or two!" Obviously, Henry could scarcely credit those words coming from Georgina's lovely lips.

"But I love it here. This is a vital, vigorous, thriving community."

"Vital? Vigorous? Thriving? You're out of your mind, Georgina!"

She offered him another sweet smile. "Then you're well rid of me, aren't you?"

"No, I am *not* well rid of you! We'll just see about this." Henry turned and stormed down the porch steps. "You're going to marry me, Georgina Witherspoon, if it's the last thing you do!" And with that threat, and with a fierce shaking of his fist, Henry hauled himself up onto his horse—he wasn't much of a horseman, Ash noted with satisfaction—and rode away, bouncing in the saddle in what looked like a painful manner.

Georgina sighed once, shook her head again, and went back into the house.

Ash gulped. It was his turn now. Of course, he had an advantage over those two banker fellows, since he'd already given Georgina a taste of his kind of love. He went hard, remembering, and told himself to stop thinking and act. He had to do this, even if he didn't want to.

"Stop remembering your damned marriage, Barrett, or you'll never get this over with, and you know you have to do it," Ash muttered to himself.

That bucked him up some. He wasn't the kind of man who'd seduce a female and then abandon her. Not on his life. Not him. He was honorable. Hell, he was a Texan. Texans knew right from wrong. They didn't expect to play without paying.

Lordy, Ash wished he knew another Texan he could unburden himself on. He was pretty sure most men didn't fear marriage the same way he did. But that was probably due to the fact that they didn't know what hell marriage could be.

"Take it easy, Barrett. All marriages aren't as bad as yours was," he said out loud.

The truth of his simple reminder buoyed him. He even managed to dismount, drape Shiloh's reins over the porch railing, walk up the steps, and knock at the door without losing courage.

He didn't doubt that Georgina would accept him. Yesterday

she'd been in a tiff of some sort brought about by the shocking
nature of their sexual involvement and her own female emotions. Female emotions were always unreliable. Up and down.
Wobbly. Unstable.

Oh, Lord, what had he done?

Before he had a chance to turn and escape his fate, the door
opened and Ash found himself looking down into the beady
little eyes of Maybelle Murphy. Damn, he'd been hoping
Vernice would answer the door. Vernice wasn't as crazy as
Maybelle or Georgina. Besides, Vernice liked him. He wasn't
sure about the other two. He removed his hat.

"Morning, Miss Maybelle. How are you today?"

"What the hell are you doing here, Barrett?"

Ash felt his eyes widen at Maybelle's greeting, which hit
him like a whiplash. "I—er—I—"

Aw, dammit. She must know all about what had happened
yesterday. Ash stiffened his spine. He had an obligation as a
man and a Texan, and he aimed to fulfill it.

"I've come here today to ask for the hand of your granddaughter, Miss Georgina Witherspoon"—suddenly, he wondered what Georgina's middle name was. He probably should
know, if he was going to marry her—"in marriage."

"Oh, you did, did you?"

This didn't sound right to him. Maybelle ought to be thanking him for doing the right thing. Ash squinted down at her.
"Yeah. I did. I came here to ask Georgina to marry me."

"Well, you can go away again, because she's not going to
do it."

Maybelle stepped back in order to close the door in his face.
After the slightest of hesitations brought about by shock, Ash
slammed the flat of his hand against the door. "Wait a minute,
Maybelle. What do you mean, she's not going to marry me?"

"What I said, you stupid man. You got mud in your ears?
Now get your hand off the door so I can close the blamed
thing."

"But—but she has to marry me."

"I do not!" piped a voice from behind Maybelle. Ash
looked around her to see Georgina standing there, her fists on
her hips, looking ready to shoot him if he didn't get his hand
off the door.

"You heard her, Sheriff. She doesn't have to do anything if she doesn't want to," Maybelle said.

"But—but we—we—"

"You had a grand old tumble in the hay yesterday. Yes, Ash, I know all about it."

Ash couldn't recall the last time he'd blushed, but it had probably been more than twenty tears ago. He blushed now, though, hot as a firecracker, and felt foolish. Nevertheless, he knew where his duty lay. "Then you know we have to get married now, Miss Maybelle. We have to."

"Horse shit. If that's not the dumbest thing I've ever heard in all my born days, I don't know what is!"

"Maybelle," Ash said, getting peeved, "don't be silly. We committed a—a sin."

"Pshaw!"

"Dammit, most people think it is! It's customary for a couple to get married after they . . . do that."

"It's customary to get married *before* they do that, you skunk!"

She had him there. Ash grumbled, "All right. But we didn't wait, and now we have to get married for Georgina's sake."

Maybelle guffawed again. "Get out of here, Ash. You can go straight to hell."

"And don't stop for water on your way," added Georgina in a loud voice that didn't have a hint of flexibility in it.

And, since Ash made the mistake of scratching his head, thus removing his hand from the door, Maybelle slammed it in his face. He staggered backward several paces and stared at the door. It didn't open again.

Well, hell. Here he was, behaving in the time-honored manner prescribed for a gentleman under these circumstances, doing the right thing, performing his duty as a man and a Texan, and he gets the door slammed in his face. Ash scratched his head again, put his hat on, took it back off, stared at the door, and thought hard.

On the one hand, this let him off the hook. Hell, he supposed he could just march off, having offered to do the right thing and been rebuffed.

On the other hand, it didn't really let him off the hook at all. The fact still remained that he had taken Georgina Witherspoon's virginity. . . .

"Damn." He wished he wouldn't react like a randy bull every time he thought about Georgina naked. He told his body to calm down.

At any rate, he'd bedded her, and now he was prepared to pay the price for his folly. He hadn't even considered what he'd do if his proposal was rejected, because he hadn't imagined it would be. Shoot, what was he supposed to do now? He backed up another foot or two and leaned against the porch railing. He couldn't see inside the house because the curtains were drawn across the windows.

If it were any family in the world but the Murphy-Witherspoon clan, Ash could probably just go away and wait until they cooled off. But he didn't trust those two females to come to their senses. He wasn't sure they had any. But surely they'd see there was only one alternative in this circumstance.

Something occurred to Ash, and it made him straighten up as if he were a bowstring and somebody'd just pulled him taut.

Good God, what if she was with child? It only took once, and yesterday might have been it. It had not happened with Phoebe, but Georgina wasn't Phoebe. Besides, Georgina had enjoyed it, unlike Phoebe. Not, of course, that that made any difference. Still . . . Oh, Lord, he'd bet good money those two silly women hadn't thought about the possibility of a baby. He walked to the door and knocked again. He remembered his hat in time to remove it politely.

This time when Maybelle swung the door open, she carried a shotgun. Ash frowned at it. "You aren't going to need that, Miss Maybelle. For God's sake, what do you take me for?"

"A good-for-nothing scoundrel, a low-down toe-sucking rat, and a bastard son of a bitch."

"Sorry I asked." Miffed, Ash sucked in a big breath. "Anyway, I don't think you've considered all possible aspects of this situation, Miss Maybelle."

"Like hell."

She was being very difficult. Ash probably should have expected it. "Yeah? Well, did you think about what would happen if Georgina turns out to be with child? What then?"

"Then she'll have a baby, won't she? That's what generally happens in cases like that, isn't it?"

Ash stared at her, incredulous, for the first time feeling something akin to Henry Spurling. "But—but—"

"But what? Listen here, you snake in the grass. You just get out of here, or I'll blow a hole where it'll do some good."

Since she was aiming the shotgun at his crotch, Ash didn't have to ask where that was. He scowled, plopped his hat onto his head again, and walked down the porch steps. "You haven't heard the last of me, Miss Maybelle." Good God, he even sounded like old Henry. Well, he couldn't think about that now. "And you can tell that granddaughter of yours so, too!"

"She doesn't have to tell me anything!" sang a familiar voice from behind Maybelle. "I heard every word."

Frustrated almost beyond bearing, Ash hollered, "Confound it, I'm trying to do the right thing here, Georgina!"

"You can take your good intentions and go straight to the devil with them, Ashley Barrett!" Georgina hollered back.

She sounded awfully damned pleased with herself.

Ash was so upset, he didn't know what to do. He wasn't about to give up and ride away. Instead, he stormed up the road between the pecan trees on foot, cursing and muttering to himself. When he got to the end of the road, he turned around and stormed back the other way. Then he stormed out to the barn and hit the side of the barn with his fist three or four times, startling the resident horse and mule into a frenzy and the chickens into a flutter of clucks and feathers. He turned around, walked over to a big mulberry tree, hit it, hurt his fist, looked up into the sky, shook his fist at God, turned around, folded his arms across his chest, and slumped back against the mulberry trunk, deflated.

"Dammit," he muttered, wondering what to do now. He wouldn't give up and go away. There was too much at stake here. His honor, for instance. Not to mention Georgina. Lordy, she might still up and marry one of those idiotic bankers, and then where would that leave Ash? Alone. That's where it would leave him, which is exactly where he wanted to be.

He couldn't account for the ache in his chest every time he thought about facing the long future without Georgina to pester him.

"Don't give up the fight, boy, it's your life you'd be throwin' away if you give up on our Georgina."

Ash leaped away from the tree and glanced around wildly. That was Devlin O'Rourke's voice! He'd recognize it anywhere. God knows, he'd listened to it often enough over whiskey and yarns at the Murphy kitchen table.

Then he saw him. Devlin. Big as life. Only he was transparent. And he wasn't alive. Ash could see the tree right through his body.

He pressed a palm to his forehead. "Hell, I've lost my mind."

Chapter Seventeen

"You haven't lost your mind, boyo. But you're going about this thing all wrong."

Ash rubbed his eyes. Lordy, he never knew stress could mess up a man *this* badly. Hoping the apparition was an optical—and auditory—illusion, he walked away from it. If he pretended he didn't see it, it would probably disappear. Not that it was there to begin with. He suppressed a miserable groan and devoutly prayed his sanity would return soon.

"You can't get away from me, Ash," Dev said, following along right behind him. *"I'm here, and I've got a good deal to say to you."*

Wonderful. Just what he wanted to hear. Ash didn't turn around or acknowledge the ghost's presence in any way. It was an illusion. It would go away. He just had to keep pretending it wasn't there.

"Pisht, Ash, don't be a fool. You're making a big mistake. I know, because I made the same one, and I'm payin' for it. Every day of my death, I'm payin' for it. I don't want to see you go down the same road."

Dammit, the thing was chasing him! Ash gave up his dignity and started running toward Shiloh.

"It won't work, Ash!" Dev called. *"I can keep up with you*

and your horse and a dozen like you. I'm no longer confined by space and gravity like you are!''

''Hell.''

Realizing it was useless, not to mention unmanly, to run away from a figment, Ash stopped running and turned abruptly. It was clearly too abrupt for Dev, because his essence sailed right through Ash's stomach, creating a really odd sensation in his middle.

Ash covered his stomach with his arms and wished he could go back to bed and start his day over again. Better yet, he wished he could go back and start yesterday all over again. He'd try harder to resist the temptation of Georgina if he had to do it over. He harbored an unhappy suspicion that his resistance would crumble no matter how many chances he had at that particular temptation.

''What are you?''

''That's better. Come over here, boyo.'' Dev floated off toward a small stand of live oaks, beckoning to Ash as he went.

Ash hesitated for several seconds, his mind racing. Mainly, he supposed, he was hoping this manifestation of Dev would vanish. Ash knew it wasn't real. It couldn't be real. Dev was dead, for the love of God.

It didn't disappear. When it looked at him over its shoulder and shook its head as if it intended to float back and scold him some more, Ash decided to spare himself that misery, at least. He followed it. Slowly.

Dev smiled and settled himself on a low branch of the nearest oak tree. *''There. That's not so bad now, is it, lad?''*

Ash eyed the thing slantwise. If this wasn't so bad, he'd like to know what was. Offhand, he couldn't think how it could get much worse. ''What are you?'' he asked again, not really expecting an answer.

He got one anyway. *''I'm the ghost of Devlin O'Rourke, of course. I'm exactly what you see with your own two eyes. You might as well believe in me, boyo, because I'm not going anywhere until you see the light.''*

Now, there, in Ash's opinion, was a really frightening threat. And here he'd thought his day couldn't get any worse. ''Um, and exactly what light would that be?''

"The light of your sweet Georgina, is what light, you fool boy!" Dev laughed heartily.

Ash didn't. He continued staring at the ghost, wondering what he could do about getting rid of it. Nothing occurred to him. He said, "Sweet?" for the sake of saying something. *Sweet* wasn't the first adjective that occurred to him when he considered Georgina Witherspoon.

"You know she's sweet, boyo," said Dev, answering Ash's tone rather than his question. *"She's the sweetest thing on this earth for you, lad. Not for everyone, mind, but for you, she's the one."*

Another depressing thought. Ash eyed the ghost suspiciously. "And how would you know anything about it?" He felt like an ass, talking to a figment. Since the figment seemed to expect conversation, however, Ash guessed he'd better go along with the phenomenon until sanity returned, or they came to lock him up in a lunatic asylum, whichever came first.

"Because I know you, lad. And I know our Georgina. She's the one for you. No doubt about it."

"Hmm."

"Oh, I know all about your problem, lad. You're scared to death of the married life. Don't say as I blame you. But look at me!" Dev pointed at his chest.

Ash blinked when Dev's finger slid in his chest all the way up to the first knuckle. This was a very unsettling experience. He hoped it wouldn't last long. "Er," he said, "yes. I see you." He didn't mention that he fervently wished he didn't.

"Oh, aye, you see me. But you don't know what you're seein'."

He could say that again. Ash didn't tell him so, but merely nodded.

"The reason you see me, in fact, is because I made the same mistake you're making now. It's no fun being a ghost, let me tell you."

It wasn't any fun being visited by one, either. Ash just nodded again.

"And the reason I'm still hovering between this plane and the heavenly one is because of the mistake I made and that you're making now."

Ash cleared his throat. "And what mistake is that?"

"It's in not declarin' your love to the girl, boy! You love

her. Madly and passionately! But you won't admit it. Not even to yourself, you bullheaded idjit."

Dev was beginning to remind Ash of Maybelle, and he didn't appreciate it. He and Dev had always been friends, and now Dev was calling him names. "Now wait a blamed minute here, Dev—"

The ghost held up a hand to stop Ash's protest. *"You don't have to tell me, lad. I know all about it."*

That made one of them. "Yeah? Well, why don't you tell me, and then we'll both know."

"That's precisely what I aim to do, boyo. You just sit down there and listen to me." The ghost pointed to a spot behind Ash's back.

Ash looked around. Sure enough, there was a big rock close behind him, so he sat on it. "Go on."

"It's because of Phoebe, boy. That's your problem."

"You're telling me." If that was the big revelation, Ash wished Dev had spared them both the trouble.

"No, no, no," Dev said, sounding exasperated. *"It's your bad experience with Phoebe that's coloring your opinion of Georgina. You aren't seeing our Georgina right because your vision's filtered through layers of Phoebe."*

"Is it?"

"It is. And you'd know it if you'd stop being scared for a minute and actually think about how you're feelin'." Dev tapped his head, again losing half of his finger.

The effect was very disconcerting to someone who'd never encountered a ghost before. Ash grimaced and looked away.

"You think that because you loved Phoebe and she turned out to be a shrew, all women are like that. But they aren't, lad, and I'm here to tell you so."

Ash rose from his rock. "All right. Thanks, Dev. You've told me. Now I'll just go back home." He took a step in the direction of his horse hoping he'd be able to escape.

His hopes came to naught.

"Wait just a minute there, Ash. You're not going anywhere until I'm through with you, so you might as well resign yourself to it."

Great. Just what he wanted to hear. Ash sighed deeply and settled back down onto his rock. "All right. Go on."

"You made a mistake in marrying Phoebe, Ash. You know

it. Hell, everyone knows it. She wasn't cut out for life away from a big city."

A brilliant observation. Ash nodded again. "Go on."

"But, because Phoebe broke your heart and shattered your dreams, you've gotten into thinkin' all females are like she was."

"And you're trying to tell me they're not?" Ash's disbelief came through loud and clear.

"Exactly. Precisely. All you have to do is look at my own darlin' Maybelle if you don't believe me."

Ash squinted up at Dev, who still resided on an oak branch. "Maybelle?" When Dev nodded, Ash spent a moment comparing Phoebe with Maybelle. "You're right. So what? Georgina isn't like Maybelle, either." He might have added a *thank God*, but he wasn't sure what this figment could do to him if it got mad at him.

"She's more like Maybelle than she is like Phoebe. Which you'd see for yourself if you'd only get your head out of the sand and look."

"That's silly, Dev. She's a city girl, too. Hell, she's even more of a city girl than Phoebe was, if it comes to that. She's from New York City, for Chrissakes!"

"Pisht!" Dev waved New York City away as if it were a pesky gnat. *"It's not the girl in the city, lad, it's the city in the girl. Georgina's primed and ready to hack out a new life for herself in an untamed land. Phoebe wouldn't have been ready for anything but featherbeds and cushions if she'd been born in a log cabin in the wilderness."*

Ash mulled over Dev's comparison for a second. He wasn't ready to admit to anything, because the rest of his life was at stake if he came to the wrong conclusion. It occurred to him that, after yesterday, his whole life was at stake anyway, and despair swamped him for a second. He managed to shake it off, but it was an effort.

He decided to hedge. "Oh, yeah?" It wasn't much, but Ash, who'd known Dev for years, thought it was probably enough to set him going again. He was right. Ash couldn't recall a time when Dev had been at a loss for words.

"Pisht, lad, is that all you can say? Compare the two women yourself for a moment, if you will. For one thing, would Phoebe have come all the way out here, on her own, to help

an aunt she'd never even met care for a woman everyone assumed was crazy?''

The idea of Phoebe doing anything at all for another person was so absurd, Ash actually barked out a short, harsh laugh. "Hell, no."

"Point number one," Dev said in a voice full of satisfaction. *"Point number two, would your precious Phoebe ever have volunteered to cook a meal or make butter?''*

Ash pondered that one. Phoebe used to cook and make butter, but she'd never liked doing it. She'd had servants in Galveston, and wanted them in Picacho Wells, too. Never mind that there weren't any to be had or that, at the time, Ash couldn't have afforded servants if there were servants standing around on the street corners. Not that there had been any street corners in town at that time, anyway. "No."

"There's point number two. And then there's the matter of the quilting society. I don't recollect your precious Phoebe—"

"Confound it, she's not my precious Phoebe!"

"Ah, but she was once, lad, and that's the whole problem.''

"It is?" Ash didn't get it.

"Of course, it is. Think, boyo! If you hadn't loved the woman, and if she hadn't broken your heart into little bitty pieces, would you be balking now at taking the lovely Georgina as your bride? Not for a second, you wouldn't, and you'd know it if you'd stop being a coward and think!''

Ash scowled, disliking the coward part. He also didn't believe it, and he told Dev so.

The ghost shook his head as if he'd never encountered a more idiotic specimen of humankind in his life. Or his death, for that matter.

"You're being ridiculous, lad. You love the girl. Admit it.''

Ash's stomach seized up and he had to slap a hand over it. Lordy, this was awful. If the mere word "love" made him sick, what Dev wanted him to do was impossible.

Dev tutted. *"Jay-sus, boy, you're worse than I was.''*

"Oh?"

"I wouldn't tell Maybelle I loved her, and now she refuses to tell me she loves me. And so I'm hanging out here in this abominable limbo, not one thing and not another, not in heaven and not in hell, suspended between heaven and earth,

and for what? For a damnable lie! Because I did love her! I do love her! She was the light of my life and she's the hope of my death! I can't go to my eternal rest without knowing she'll be joining me there! For God's sake, man, don't make my mistake! Save yourself while there's time!''

Good God, the ghost was crying. Ash stared at him, unnerved. He'd seldom seen a man cry, let alone a ghost. And all this because of love? He snorted, thinking Dev, far from persuading Ash to declare his love—if he had any—for Georgina, was confirming his opinion of the exalted emotion. Love stank.

Dev wiped his transparent cheeks with his transparent fingers and eyed Ash, disgruntled. *''Oh, aye, I know what you're thinkin', boyo.''*

"You do?" Ash doubted it.

''Oh, aye, I do. You're thinkin' I'm a foolish old dead man who doesn't know what hell a female can create in a man's life. You're thinkin' I don't know what it's like to love a female beyond bearing and to have your love thrown back in your face as if it was garbage. You're thinking you'll never submit yourself to that kind of pain and humiliation again.''

Actually, that about summed it up. Ash hated to admit it, so he only grunted.

''But your mistake is in thinking that Georgina is Phoebe. It's the same mistake I made, thinkin' Maybelle was like Laurinda O'Dell. I wasn't about to give my heart into the keeping of another like Laurinda. Not me. Not Devlin O'Rourke. Fool! I was a damned fool! And so are you.''

Who in hell was Laurinda O'Dell? Ash deemed it prudent not to ask.

''Now, I knew your Phoebe, Ash Barrett, and I know Georgina Witherspoon. There never were two women as different as those two unless it was my Maybelle and Laurinda.''

"Is that so?"

''Yes. And you'd see it, too, if you'd open your eyes and look. But listen here, Ash. It's the love angle you've got to conquer. You've got to admit to yourself that you love the woman. And then you've got to admit it to her. Get down on your knees and beg the girl to marry you! Tell her you'll die if she doesn't. Tell her that if she doesn't take you, you might

as well put a bullet in your brain, because life won't be worth living. Tell her—''

Ash stared at the ghost, horrified. "Damned if I will!"

"Then you're an even bigger fool than I thought you were," cried Dev. *"And I already counted you the biggest fool in the territory. Think about it!"*

Ash was through thinking. This conversation was making him queasy. He got up and dusted off his hands. "Thanks for the chat, Dev. I've got to go now."

"No! Damn you, Ash Barrett, you stay right here and listen to me!"

"No. Blast it, Dev, I'm tired of this. Hell, I don't even believe in you!"

"No? Well then, believe in this!" And Devlin O'Rourke shot like an arrow from the oak branch, straight through Ash's shoulder.

Ash hollered in pain and astonishment.

About that time, Georgina, who had been feeling quite proud of her independent stand on the matter of Ash Barrett and his tepid proposal, pulled the parlor curtain aside a little ways to see if Shiloh still stood outside. She hadn't heard Ash ride off, and she was curious. She was even more curious when she saw Ash standing in the small stand of live oaks out by the barn.

"Good heavens, whatever is the matter with the man?"

"What man?" Vernice joined her at the window. "Oh, my goodness. Poor Mr. Barrett."

"What's going on?" Maybelle elbowed her way to the window. "Hmm. Drunk, most like."

"Drunk?" Georgina looked at Vernice, who shrugged. "He didn't seem intoxicated when he came to the door."

"No, he didn't," Vernice affirmed.

Maybelle snorted. "Men. Damned fools, all of them. You did the right thing, Georgina. Don't go out there and give in to him just because he's gone crazy."

"Oh, do you think he's gone crazy?" Vernice sounded concerned.

"Doesn't matter if he has. Don't let Georgina go out to him. He's not worth it."

Georgina pressed a hand to her cheek and wished she knew what to do. At present, Ash was flailing his arms in the air and leaping about as if he were being pursued by demons. Georgina felt some concern, since he appeared to be in pain. She hoped it wasn't her refusal to marry him that had sent him over the edge into madness.

She frowned and told herself not to be silly. He hadn't wanted to marry her in the first place. He'd only proposed out of some misguided masculine code of pride or ethics or some other idiotic thing.

As if she could read her mind, Maybelle said, "And don't go getting any fool ideas in your head that you're his cure, either. Make the man tell you he loves you and then make him propose properly. If you don't, you'll regret it all your life."

Georgina sighed. "I don't expect he ever will, Grandmother."

"Fiddlesticks. He will when he starts using his heart along with his head. Men! They think the two are disconnected."

"And they aren't?"

"Hell, no! They're all bound up together." Maybelle went back to the chair, where she'd been knitting a lap robe for Vernice.

"Hmm." Georgina and Vernice stared at the spectacle Ash was making of himself for another few moments. Then Georgina said, "Well, I don't suppose watching him dance around is getting the dinner cooked."

"No," agreed Vernice without much enthusiasm. "I don't suppose it is." She watched for another second and burst out, "Oh, but Mother, do you really think the poor man is all right?"

Maybelle snorted again. "He's as all right as he's ever been, which isn't saying much."

Georgina, bowing to her grandmother's superior knowledge of the masculine gender, let the curtain drop and returned to the kitchen where she'd been chopping onions. She worried about Ash, although she knew she probably shouldn't.

In the meantime, Ash was having a very bad time out there under the oak trees. Devlin O'Rourke, shouting at him the whole time, shot through and around him like so many freezing cold thrusts of a lance.

"Hey!" Ash bellowed. "Stop that! It hurts!"

"It'll hurt a damn sight worse if you don't unbend and tell

that woman how you feel about her!'' And with a *whoosh*, he shot through Ash's chest.

"Ow! Confound it, stop it!"

"I'm not going to stop it until you stop trying to get away from me!'' *Zoom*, he shot through Ash's other shoulder, making him spin around and clutch his arm.

"You're killing me!"

"Tosh! I couldn't kill you if I wanted to. I'm only teaching you a lesson. And it's a lesson you need!'' And with a *zip* Dev lanced through both of Ash's knees, sideways, making them buckle.

Ash collapsed, drew his knees to his chest, turned over, and tried to hide. It was no use. Dev only hovered above him for a second or two and then, with a *whump*, he rocketed through Ash's entire body—back, stomach, knees, the hands clutching them, and all. At last Ash gave up. He didn't want to do it, but he couldn't fight a ghost. He'd never realized until this minute that ghosts fought almost as dirty as did women.

"Truce!" he hollered. "Uncle! I give! I'll stay and hear you out!"

"That's better.'' Dev sounded out of breath, which made no sense, although he wasn't up to pursuing the matter.

Ash was not happy. It galled him to give in to a ghost, especially one who used means that Ash couldn't combat, in order to achieve his aims. He waited until Dev had settled himself back on the oak branch, then tried to rise. His body protested mightily.

"Dammit. What the hell did you do to me?"

"Merely a little ghostly persuasion, boyo. You'll be all right in a few minutes. Why don't you just lie back and relax whilst I try to knock some sense into your head.''

Perceiving no alternative, Ash rolled onto his back and tentatively flexed his limbs. Shoot, they felt like jelly. His arms flopped at his sides at last, although he felt no inclination to lift them. He hoped his strength would return eventually. In the meantime, he kept his knees bent because they didn't seem to want to straighten.

"Now,'' said the ghost, settling back into what looked like a damnably comfortable position to Ash, who could only squint into the oak branches from flat on his back. *"It's like this. You can try to fool yourself for years, lad, but it won't*

*wash. You love the girl. If you don't believe me or don't want
to admit it, think about how you'd feel if you were to see her
marry that pasty-faced banker fellow."*

"Which one?"

"What does it matter? Either one would do."

Ash grunted, the vision too appalling for him to consider
without feeling sick. "She wouldn't marry him. She already
told him so."

*"Oh? And what about next month? Will she still feel the
same way when she's got him declarin' his devotion to her
every five minutes? When you won't even admit to liking her,
much less needing her?"*

"Needing her?" God, what an awful thought.

*"Yes, you fool. Needing her. Like you need sunshine and
water and food. It's the same thing. It's the way I needed
Maybelle and wouldn't tell her. Now look at me."*

Ash did and wasn't comforted. Also, he was beginning to
feel more than a little abused and mistreated. At least he could
stretch his legs out now, so he did. He still couldn't stand up.
"Wait a minute here, Dev. If you're so all-fired in love with
love, why in blazes didn't you tell Maybelle so before now?"

*"I'm tellin' ya, lad! It's because I was as much of a damned
fool as you are!"*

"Blast it, why don't you tell her now? What's stopping
you?"

*"She is, dammit! She won't believe a word I say anymore,
because she's mad at me for dyin' before I told the truth. Now
she won't listen to me at all!"*

"That's stupid."

"Pisht!" Dev waved an arm in the air in a gesture of su-
preme frustration. *"You know it's stupid. And I know it's stupid. And I'd be surprised if Maybelle didn't know it was stupid,
but you're dealin' with Murphys here, lad."*

"Georgina's a Witherspoon," Ash pointed out reasonably.

*"Bunkum. She's a Murphy inside, and that's what counts.
There's no talking to a Murphy once they get their minds made
up. They're a stubborn lot, the Murphys, and there's no sway-
ing them unless they want to be swayed. Maybelle's so mad
at me, I don't know if I'll ever be able to rest in peace."*

Ash had a discouraging notion that Dev was right about the

innermost part of Georgina. The notion didn't make him happy at all. "Well, hell."

"You can well, hell for the rest of your life, and it won't change things. Tell me the truth. You love the girl, don't you."

Ash's stomach clenched. Then his teeth ground together. Then his head ached. Then his heart gave a hard, vicious spasm. He hated this. He hated it so much he almost choked on it.

Dev watched from his oak branch, his expression mild, but interested. *"Do you see how it is, lad? You were burned so badly by Phoebe that you daren't love another female. But it's too late. You already do. Might as well give up the struggle, boyo, because it's no use. I know."*

He sounded gloomy, which, for the first time in their brief acquaintance, made him fit Ash's prior perception of what a ghost should sound like.

Georgina was getting fidgety. "I don't like it, Aunt Vernice."

"What's that, dear?"

Georgina looked over to where Vernice sat, placidly crocheting. Dinner preparations were over, and the stew was bubbling on the stove. But every blasted time Georgina looked out of the parlor window, she saw Ash.

First he'd been behaving like a lunatic, waving his arms and flailing around as if he were trying to avoid being stung by a swarm of yellow jackets. A few minutes later when she peeked outside, he'd been lying flat on his back in the middle of the oak grove, talking to himself. This time when she glanced toward the stand of oaks, he'd managed to sit up and was leaning against a big oak trunk. He still appeared to be babbling to himself, though.

As much as she hated to admit it, even to herself, Georgina found herself worrying about him. After all, he *was* the only man who'd ever moved her to sin. And—she hated admitting this even more—she loved him.

Drat the luck! Of all the men in the world, why it had to be Ash, of all prickly people, with whom she'd fallen in love was the great mystery of her life. And unless things changed drastically, it was destined to remain a mystery. Piffle. Georgina felt very put-upon.

"Mr. Barrett," she said to Vernice. "He's sitting out there

under a tree, and it looks like he's talking to himself."

Maybelle, who still worked on the lap robe, snorted. "Hell, he's probably been attacked by Dev. You know how those two loved to talk when Dev was alive. Dev's probably out there telling Ash all about how awful women are. Ha!"

Georgina glanced over her shoulder at her grandmother, stricken by the wisdom that occasionally came from the old woman's lips. "I wondered about that possibility, Grandmother. But—well—wouldn't I be able to see Mr. O'Rourke if he was there?"

Maybelle looked up, her beady bird's eyes alive with mischief. "And how long did you live here before he showed himself to you, Georgina? The man's a devil as well as a ghost. If he doesn't want us to see him, we won't see him, blast his soul to perdition."

"Mother!" Vernice tutted.

Georgina was past being shocked by her grandmother's free use of profanity. "Oh. That's right, Grandmother, I forgot." She peeked out the window again. Ash was still there, sitting under the oak tree, and his lips still moved. He was gesturing now as well. "I wonder how he does that—appearing and not appearing and so forth."

"Humph," muttered Maybelle. "I don't care how he does it. I wish he'd stop."

Georgina heaved a sigh. "Perhaps they're discussing things out there and will come to some vast conclusions that will make all of our lives easier."

Vernice and Maybelle both looked up from their needlework, their faces twin pictures of incredulity. Georgina noticed them and laughed. "Oh, all right. That's too much to expect from a couple of men, I suppose."

"You *suppose*? Ha!" Maybelle snorted again and went back to her knitting. Vernice, always the demure one, only shook her head and smiled gently.

With another sigh, Georgina let the curtain drop. She didn't know what she wished for; whether she wanted Ash to stay there so she could keep an eye on him, or go away so she wasn't tormented by the sight of him. Every time she saw him, she longed for things she couldn't have. His love, for one thing. A life together, for another. And children. She'd love to have his children. She'd wager he'd be a good father. Strict, but loving.

Georgina shook her head to rid herself of those hopeless dreams and went back to the kitchen, where she was supposed to be stirring the rice pudding. She hadn't stirred it enough, and she had to scrape some burned junk from the sides of the pot, but she guessed that was all right. A little burn added flavor, according to her grandmother.

She laughed out loud when she realized how much she'd come to cherish her cantankerous grandmother.

Chapter Eighteen

"All right, dammit!" Ash cried, defeated. "I love her! Now will you leave me the hell alone?"

"No." Devlin O'Rourke crossed his arms over his chest and continued staring stubbornly at Ash.

With a huge sigh, Ash pushed himself to his feet. Thank God his body worked again. He'd begun to wonder if it would ever recover from Dev's energetic haunt. He groaned as he tested his limbs and they protested. "What am I supposed to do to get rid of you?"

"Tell the woman you love her and beg her to marry you. Get down on your knees if you have to, but tell her. Tell her you can't go on living without her. Tell her the truth, lad."

"It's not the truth that I won't go on living if she doesn't marry me," Ash muttered, feeling bitterly imposed upon.

Dev threw up his ghostly arms. *"Don't you have the least speck of Irish in your soul, Ash?"*

"No."

"Not even a hint of the poet?"

"I don't think so."

The ghost swooped down and landed directly in front of Ash, who leaped backward several paces. He wished Devlin wouldn't do that.

"Do you have to take every single word a body says literally?"

"You aren't what I'd call a body."

"Nit-picking. You're nit-picking, but what I'm telling you is the most important lesson you'll ever hear in your life, boyo. If you don't learn it now, it'll probably be too late."

After heaving a gigantic sigh, Ash mumbled, "Go on." He guessed there was no way out of it now.

"Tell the woman you love her. Because it's the truth, even if you wouldn't literally die if she won't have you. The fact is, you love her as you were never able to love Phoebe, because Phoebe wasn't who you thought she was."

"And Georgina is?"

"Yes! Use your eyes and brain, Ash! She'll never let you down the way Phoebe did, because she's not projecting a false front."

Ash could vouch for that part. Her front was her own, every succulent inch of it. He wished he could revisit it, in fact. He sighed again, wishing this was over and Georgina was his, and he didn't have to go through all of this hogwash.

"And here's another truth. If Georgina condescends to marry you, she'll be your best earthly companion and solid life's mate for the rest of her life. She won't shrink from a bit of work or balk at the notion of exercise in bed."

Ash had already noticed that, as well. He wished he hadn't. The reaction he experienced every time he thought about what he and Georgina had done yesterday was about to kill him.

"So go on, Ash. Beg her if you have to. Tell her you know you're unworthy to kiss the ground she walks on, and that you'll never know a moment's peace if she won't take you."

Perceiving the exaggeration in Dev's declaration—after all, he had to sleep sometimes, and if that wasn't peace Ash didn't know what was—he grumbled, "I don't know about this, Dev."

"Pisht, Ash, you're a hard case. Do as I tell you. You'll regret it forever if you don't."

"I already regret it," Ash muttered. Something occurred to him. "Wait a minute. You keep telling me I'm supposed to make an ass of myself—"

"Nonsense! That isn't true, and you know it!"

"Hmm. At any rate, you keep telling me I'm supposed to tell Georgina I love her—"

"Because it's the truth."

"Hang the truth, dammit! I already admitted that part, didn't I? I'm trying to ask you a question!"

Dev waved an airy hand. *"Ask away."*

"Why the hell don't you go tell Maybelle you love her, if that's all there is to it?"

The ghost seemed to waver and shrink. For a second, Ash's heart soared because he thought he'd finally discovered how to get rid of it without going through the hard part. Unfortunately, Dev came back again after only a moment. *"It's not that easy."*

"No? You keep telling me it's that easy."

"Aye. But you're still alive."

"So what?"

"So, you have an opportunity to tell her now while it'll do you some good. I—ah—had a wee bit of trouble getting the words out when I was alive."

Ash huffed indignantly. "And you don't think I do? For God's sake, Dev, Phoebe about killed me!"

"Don't I know it. But you see, I never quite got around to declarin' myself while I was alive."

"You've told Maybelle you love her since you died, haven't you?"

"Er, not exactly."

"What do you mean, not exactly?"

Dev swooped around in an agitated circle that Ash found difficult to keep up with. *"She won't listen to me, is what I mean! Every time I try to proclaim my everlasting love to her, she throws something at me!"*

"Ha." Ash couldn't help it. He remembered Maybelle heaving shoes at him and Georgina the day he met the train, thought about how the old witch would probably have an even better time heaving things at her dead lover who never quite got around to telling her he loved her, and laughed.

Dev eyed him coldly. *"It's not funny, boyo."*

It was, too. Ash finally managed to choke down his guffaws, but he had to wipe his eyes.

"So you'd better get on with it," Dev said, still fairly chilly. *"I'll hover around and direct you."*

"Lord." Ash wasn't looking forward to that particular threat being fulfilled. "I reckon I have to do it, if that's the only way to get rid of you."

"It is."

"But it's not fair. After I talk to Georgina, you've got to talk to Maybelle."

"I've talked until I'm blue, and the woman won't listen."

Ash peered at the ghost of Devlin O'Rourke and thinned his gaze. "You know something, Dev?"

"What?" Dev swooped back up to his oak branch.

"I think you're as scared as I am to say the words."

"Me? Never!"

"You wouldn't say them in life," Ash pointed out reasonably.

"Aye, perhaps, but I know better now. I've tried since I died, and she won't listen."

"Try again today. She might change her mind when she knows I'm talking to Georgina."

"I don't know, Ash. . . ."

Waffling. This was pure, cowardly waffling on the ghost's part, and Ash resented it. "Dammit, I'm willing to tell Georgina I love her." He shuddered, a reaction that had become automatic to him in recent years whenever he thought about the word *love*. "It's not fair to expect me to do something you're afraid to do yourself. Criminy, Dev! You're a ghost! What can Maybelle do to a ghost?"

"You don't know Maybelle." Dev sounded gloomier than ever.

"I know her well enough to understand your reluctance," Ash conceded. "But I'm not going to let you get away with this, Devlin O'Rourke, because it's not fair. It's not fair to me, and it's not fair to Maybelle. Hell's bells, man, if what I understand is true, you've loved her for years. Why in blazes did you wait so long to tell her?"

The ghost turned his head and muttered something that made the oak leaves flutter.

Ash said, "I didn't hear you."

Dev's head whipped around again. *"Because you're right. I'm a damned coward is why. Because I allowed one woman to rule my behavior for the rest of my life even though she'd been dead for years before I even met Maybelle! I allowed*

Laurinda O'Dell to color my perception of all women. In fact, I'm just like you!''

A protest trembled on the tip of Ash's tongue until he realized the ghost's assessment was correct. Dammit, he hated it when things like that happened. "Well, now's your chance, because I'm not going up there to make a fool of myself in front of three women without you there too." Something occurred to him. "They know about you, don't they?"

"Of course they do."

"Shoot. No wonder Georgina looked so sick the first few weeks she was here."

"If you're sayin' I made the woman sick, I'll take it amiss, Ashley Barrett."

Ash cast a glance at the heavens. "No, no, no. I'm only saying that meeting you for the first time is an unsettling experience."

Dev squinted at him for a moment, but at last appeared mollified. Ash wasn't going to let him off the hook, however. "I mean it, Dev. You're going to that house with me, and you're going to tell Maybelle exactly how you feel about her. Fair's fair."

"Ach! You're a hard man, Ash Barrett."

Immediately Ash's thoughts turned to Georgina. Before he had time to stop himself, he murmured, "Not at the moment I'm not." When he realized what he'd said, he blushed for the second time in twenty years. Dev laughed. *"Jay-sus, you've got it bad, boyo. I suppose I'd better go with you to make sure you don't botch it up."*

A protest bounced around in Ash's brain before he decided not to bother voicing it. If he did, they might be here all day, and he wanted to get this over with and get on with his life.

In the end, Ash walked to the Murphy house with his heart hammering out a funeral dirge in his chest and Dev floating along overhead. He couldn't recall ever being this scared and nervous. Not even when he was in the Dakotas chasing Indians and knowing his life might be blasted out of his body any second had he been this scared and nervous.

He knocked almost timidly. The door whooshed open so fast he uttered a quick "Damn!"

"Are you still here?"

Maybelle held the shotgun and looked mean enough to use it. Ash frowned at her. "You aren't going to need that, Miss Maybelle. I need to speak to Georgina for a minute."

"She doesn't want to speak to you. Go away."

"Listen, Miss Maybelle, I *need* to talk to her. Just for a second or two. It won't take long."

"Christ, man, don't say that. You want these women to think you're going to spend the whole rest of your life making everything up to Georgina."

"Making what up to her? What have I ever done to her?"

"You seduced her, you son of a bitch! If you don't remember that, I'll be damned if I'll let you talk to her now!" Maybelle pulled the lever on the gun, and Ash heard a round chunk into place in the chamber.

"No! No, I didn't mean that!" Damn, he wished Dev would go away.

"You're goin' about this all wrong, Ash." Dev was obviously annoyed with him.

The ghost's annoyance was nothing compared to Ash's. "Dammit, shut up."

"Don't you tell *me* to shut up, you lousy, two-bit, good-for-nothing scoundrel!"

"Not you, Miss Maybelle. I didn't mean you." Ash raked his hand through his hair and wished he were dead.

Maybelle squinted into the sun above Ash's head. "Oh. Is it Dev? Is that pesky damned ghost bothering you?"

Thank God she understood that much, at least. "Yes." Ash felt so relieved, he almost managed a smile. "Yes, Dev's been talking to me."

"Is that why you were out there swinging your arms around and acting like a lunatic?"

Hmm. Ash wasn't sure he appreciated Maybelle's assessment of his prior behavior, no matter how accurate it was. "Yes." He sucked in a huge breath. "*Now* may I please talk to Georgina?"

Maybelle thought for about three seconds. Then she said, "No," and slammed the door in Ash's face for the second time that day.

He stood there, staring at the door, an unremarkable piece of carpentry, and felt at a complete loss. Now what? If he knocked again, the same thing would happen—if, of course,

Maybelle didn't decide to blow a hole through him instead. He glared up at Dev. "All right. What am I supposed to do now?"

"Let me think a minute."

Dev thought. Ash waited. Dev thought some more. After about two or three minutes—they felt like two or three hours—Ash heard Maybelle's witchy voice through the keyhole.

"Get the hell off my front porch, Ash, or I'll shoot you off of it!"

"Good God."

Perceiving no real alternative, since he had no particular wish to die even if Georgina never agreed to see him again—no matter what Dev thought—Ash went down the porch steps. He walked over to Shiloh and stroked his neck. He presumed Dev was still thinking. As for Ash, he was all thought out. He didn't know what to do. As much as he hated himself for making two gigantic mistakes in one short lifetime, he loved Georgina Witherspoon. There was no getting away from it.

And maybe Dev was right. Maybe Georgina wasn't like Phoebe.

Oh, hell, Ash *knew* she wasn't. He supposed his reluctance to snatch her up and marry her was that he feared she might one day turn on him. That's what Phoebe had done. She'd waited until she had him locked up right and tight and then she'd shown him her true colors. According to Dev, Georgina's true colors were the same ones she showed to the world every day, but Ash didn't quite dare believe it for fear he'd tumble headlong into disaster again. He didn't think he could stand to be so disillusioned in a person another time without cracking up.

It galled him that he, a man of the law and a Texan, for the love of God, should be at the mercy of a tiny, little female.

"I don't see any alternative, Ash. You're going to have to do it outside."

Ash looked up, to where Dev had taken to hovering once more. He'd sure be glad to get rid of him. Not that he hadn't always liked Dev, but hell's bells, liking the living man was a whole lot different than putting up with the dead man's ghost. He shook his head and decided he'd be very glad when his world stopped tilting sideways and got back to normal.

"Do what outside?"

"Tell the woman what she means to you."

"How can I do that? If they won't let me inside to talk to her, I can't imagine she'd agree to come outside and talk to me."

Dev eyed Ash as if he were the slowest student in class. *"Pisht, you're a knothead, Ash Barrett. Odd how I never noticed it until now."*

Ash was not amused. He glared at the ghost.

"What you've got to do is declare yourself from out here. They aren't going to let you do it any other way."

Ash blinked at Dev. "You mean holler at her? What kind of god-awful, cockeyed notion is that? I can't stand outside and yell at her!"

"And why not?"

"Because . . . because . . ." Oh, hell.

Ash thought. He knew he couldn't do it, but the explanatory words weren't on the tip of his tongue and he couldn't seem to locate them anywhere else in his head. At last he settled for, "Because it's not . . . right. Or something."

"Hogwash. You're a coward, is what's the matter here."

"Confound it, Dev, quit calling me a coward!"

"And why should I? It's the truth."

"Damn." Ash took a swipe at the ghost of Devlin O'Rourke and nearly got his hand frozen for his effort. Criminy, the substance of the ghost was cold.

"You're being nonsensical, Ash. Just stand under a window and bellow. Why not? The only folks who'll hear you are the three ladies inside the house, and they already hate your guts. What's a little disturbance going to matter?"

"What's it going to matter?" Ash could hardly believe his ears. "I'll humiliate myself beyond redemption, is what! What's the matter with you, anyway?"

"Nothing that doing what you're going to do wouldn't solve in a minute, if Maybelle would only listen to me and reciprocate."

There they were. Apparently there was nothing like dying with unacknowledged love to block one's passage into the hereafter. Well, hell. Ash stroked Shiloh's neck another few times. Then he looked back at the house, scowling. Finally he eyeballed Dev. Hard. "Oh, very well. I reckon they already think I'm crazy."

"Sure, and it's a likely thing."

Ash resented Dev's agreement in this particular instance. Nevertheless, before he could talk himself into some sense, he walked back over to the house. In fact, he walked around the house, trying to determine where the best hollering site might be. Ultimately, he opted for the front porch, right smack in front of the door. If Maybelle aimed to shoot him, he didn't want her to miss a vital organ. Far better he die at once and get it over with than linger in agony for days.

He positioned himself squarely, legs apart, arms at his sides. He removed his hat, just in case—well, he didn't know why, but he did. He licked his lips. He cleared his throat. He wiped his hands on his britches and cupped them around his mouth.

"God damm it, Georgina, I love you!"

"Jay-sus," Dev muttered behind him.

Hmm. All right, so that didn't sound awfully loverlike. Ash tried again. "I've never loved anyone the way I love you!"

That was better. Behind him, Dev snorted. Ash drew his eyebrows together in a frown of concentration. Was he supposed to say more than that?

Aw, hell, this wasn't fair.

He wiped his hands again, cupped his mouth, and bellowed, "I don't want to live without you! I love you! I want to marry you."

Since he'd run out of breath, he paused. He heard not a peep from inside the house. Damn.

"Keep going, boyo. Keep it up until her heart melts."

"It's more likely that Maybelle will shoot me off her front porch," Ash muttered, feeling sorely aggrieved.

Dev only laughed.

Ash gulped more air, and then gathered his strength for the next yelling segment, "I know I made a mess of things yesterday, Georgina! That's because I was scared! I kept thinking you were going to ruin my life like Phoebe did!"

He stopped. Dev swooped down and hovered in front of his face. *"Keep going, you blasted fool! You can't just leave her like that. You've got to tell her why you don't think so any longer."*

"But I'm not sure I don't think so any longer!"

"Jay-sus! You're either as stupid as a rock or as stubborn

as a mule, Ash Barrett! If you don't think it's the truth, then lie, *for the love of Christ!''*

Feeling abused and mistreated, Ash guessed he might as well. Hell, he'd already made a bigger ass of himself than he could ever remember doing. "Georgina! I know you're not like Phoebe! She was a good-for-nothing flibbertigibbet. You're not! You're . . . you're useful! You can cook!'' More or less. Well, hell, she was trying. Ash supposed that was the important part. "You can make butter! You can . . . you can . . .'' Aw, hell, what else could she do?

"She can disarm bandits single-handed,'' Dev suggested.

Good one. "You can disarm bandits!'' Ash shouted. "I know you don't need me! But I need you! Do you hear me? I need you!''

Suddenly someone inside the house yanked a curtain aside and pushed wide open a window to his left. He held his breath until Georgina's pretty head appeared, then he released the breath in a gust. He honestly didn't want Maybelle to shoot him.

"What in the world are you shouting for, Ashley Barrett? Haven't you done enough damage already?''

Damage? Well, he liked that! "Confound it, Georgina, didn't you hear what I said?''

"How could I help but hear what you said? You shouted it to the whole neighborhood!''

As the whole neighborhood consisted of the Murphy farm, a bunch of trees and a few chickens and horses and cows, Ash didn't think her point was at all valid, although he wasn't going to argue about it now. "Listen, Georgina, I love you. I love you, and I want to marry you.''

She squinted at him as if he were something vile and despicable that had taken up residence on her front porch without anyone's permission—a poisonous mushroom or a toad or a rattlesnake, perhaps. "I'm not sure I believe you.''

Aw, hell. Trust a woman.

"Make her believe you, boyo, or you'll never know another moment's peace.''

Ash gritted his teeth. "Why? You gonna haunt me to death?''

"Pisht! I mean you'll regret it if you lose her, boy! You know it's true.''

"I guess so."

"You guess what?" Georgina looked and sounded aggravated.

"I guess I love you! I guess I'll be miserable if you don't agree to marry me! I guess I'm sorry about yesterday! Not because we went to bed together. That part was wonderful. I'm sorry I spoiled it by remembering my marriage. Dammit, Georgina, you don't know what it was like!"

Ignoring the last part of his speech, which Ash figured he should have expected, Georgina seized upon the first part. "What do you mean, you *guess* you love me, Ashley Barrett? You either do or you don't, and if you can't make up your mind, I think we might as well terminate this conversation right now!"

She reached out, Ash presumed to pull the window closed, but she got there first and damned near broke the glass stopping her. As it was she caught his hand between the two frames.

"Ow! Dammit, Georgina, you're squashing my hand!"

"Want me to shoot him, honey?"

Great. There was Maybelle, holding that shotgun, her bird-of-prey eyes sparkling like polished obsidian, and looking as if the greatest pleasure in her life would be shooting Ash. He gave her a murderous scowl, which had about as much effect as anything ever did on Maybelle Murphy.

"Oh, Mother! Please don't shoot the sheriff! I'm sure the law takes a very dim view of such things!"

Good old Vernice. Ash really appreciated her. Georgina finally relented and pushed the window open enough for Ash to withdraw his hand from between the two sides. He shook it hard, wondering if he'd ever recover full use of it. The woman was dangerous.

"Please, Georgina," he said, willing to do as Dev had told him to do and beg if it would help. "I mean it. I do love you. When you said you wouldn't marry me, I—I—I almost died."

Georgina remained silent.

Maybelle snorted.

Vernice sighed deeply, Ash presumed with sentiment.

Dev said, *"Keep going, boyo. You're on the right track."*

Ash took that as encouraging. "And I can't stand the thought of living forever without you."

Georgina squinted at him.

"Please, Georgina. I know I'm not the world's best talker. I know I've made you mad at me because of what I said yesterday, and I'm really sorry. My—my marriage was hell, Georgina. Phoebe acted as if she wanted me before we were married, and then afterwards, she changed."

"Did she?" Georgina sounded as if she didn't believe him.

"Yes." Ash pondered how best to describe Phoebe. "She—she pretended she wanted the same life I did, but she really didn't."

"And what, exactly, kind of life is that?"

Shoot, the woman sounded hard. Ash almost winced when he heard the steel in her voice. What the hell, though. He'd started. He might as well finish. What did he care if the entire universe knew the secrets of his heart? He braced himself and sucked up more air.

"She pretended she wanted to live in the territory with me. She pretended she wanted to make a new life for us out here, away from Galveston. She pretended she was willing to live rough for a few years until I could make a better life for us."

His heart gave a sudden, hard spasm. He'd made a better life, all right, but Phoebe had died before he'd achieved it. And she hadn't wanted to participate in the building of it, either.

"It hurt me, Georgina. It hurt bad. I'm well set up now, but Phoebe didn't want to stick it out until then. I don't know what would have happened if she hadn't died, but I suspect she'd have left me and gone back to Galveston."

At least Georgina had stopped scowling at him. Ash considered that a step in the right direction and unburdened himself some more. What did he care at this point? "She broke my heart, Georgina, and after she died, I swore that I'd never let another women get under my skin like that again." He stopped abruptly, a sudden sick sensation having invaded his innards, then forged onward recklessly. "But you got under my skin in spite of my vigilance."

"Did I?" Her voice didn't sound hard and cold any longer.

A speck of optimism began to burn in Ash's chest. "Yes. Yes! For God's sake, I can't even remember the last time I lost control of myself the way I did with you. That never even happened with Phoebe, even though I was a young buck in those days."

"You're not so awfully old now," Georgina said.

This was very encouraging. "I'm thirty-three, Georgina. I reckon that's a good age. It's an age where I ought to know my own mind. And, I swear to you, that if I hadn't been so badly burned by Phoebe, I wouldn't have had such a hard time coming to grips with you." So to speak. Ash briefly considered more gentlemanly ways of expressing his last sentiment, but gave it up.

She blinked, and Ash feared for a moment that she might even start shedding tears. By God, he thought, he was getting the hang of this. Using the momentum he'd built up, he went on. "I love you, Georgina. I love you madly. Passionately. If I hadn't had my heart busted in pieces by Phoebe, I wouldn't have been so scared to admit it."

"Oh, Ash."

Oh, Ash? The words had come out as a little sigh, and Ash's heart gave a big leap of hope.

"And I'm not putting all the blame on her," he continued, feeling like a man on the edge of a cliff who was grabbing with all his strength to a rocky ledge and trying to lift himself to solid ground. "If I'd had more sense, I'd have seen she was a dedicated city girl who didn't want to leave Galveston. And she was too young to know her mind, really, and I should have known that, too. Hell, she was only seventeen, and had never done a lick of real work in her life.

"But, you see, I loved her. I pretended she was what I wanted because I loved her so damned much. But neither of us were what the other one needed or even wanted, and we didn't realize that until it was too late for both of us."

"Oh, Ash," she said again, this time even breathier than before.

"And you don't have to worry about money, either, Georgina. I've made a lot of money in my uncle's cotton brokerage business in Galveston. I like my job as sheriff here in Picacho Wells, but if I didn't have that job—if I wanted to devote all my time to my ranch—we'd still have lots of money."

"I'm not worried about money, Ash. I have plenty of my own."

He frowned. She wasn't supposed to say things like that. She was supposed to be happy he'd be able to take care of her financially. Besides, he'd really like to know that she needed him as much as he needed her. Or even almost as much.

"But I'm glad you're not a fortune hunter," she added.

A fortune hunter? Good God. "No. I'm rich in my own right."

She heaved a big sigh.

Ash figured it was now or never. He dropped to his knees and lifted his arms in a gesture that would have done Romeo or one of those other old-time Italian bucks proud. "So, please believe me when I tell you I love you. It's not easy for me to say, Georgina. But it's the truth, and if you'll agree to marry me, I swear to you and Maybelle and Vernice and God Himself that I'll never, ever do anything to hurt you."

"Oh, Ash."

The window slammed shut. Ash stared at it for a second, his heart reeling. Then he stood up and dusted off his pants.

Well, shoot, what now? If he'd bared his soul and told all of his deepest, darkest secrets for nothing, he'd be mad as hell. The front door banged open, and he jumped with alarm.

Then Georgina burst out of it and flung herself into his arms, and completed his humiliation by breaking into tears of joy.

Chapter
Nineteen

"Oh, Ash, I love you so much!"

Georgina was laughing and crying and generally in a state the likes of which she'd never experienced before. She was so happy, though. So very, very happy.

"I love you, too, honey."

"And I need you. Oh, how I need you!"

"Thank God."

That seemed to Georgina a rather odd statement, but when she peered at him, he obviously meant it. His arms held her like steel bonds, and the look of relief on his face could be plainly seen.

"Will you marry me, Georgina?"

Georgina thought she detected the thickness of tears in his voice and she was touched beyond measure. "Yes. Oh, yes!"

Then he kissed her. And he kissed her. And she kissed him. And he kissed her. And she kissed him.

And then Maybelle strode out onto the porch, holding her knitting in her fist. "All right, you two. Break it up. I don't allow any fornicating on the front porch."

"Mother!"

"Jay-sus, Maybelle, you're a spoilsport."

"Don't you dare talk to me, Dev!" Maybelle heaved a knitting needle at him.

Ash finally let Georgina go, although he held onto her hand as if he didn't quite dare release her entirely. Georgina didn't mind a bit.

"I'll go make a nice pot of tea and fetch some cookies." Vernice bustled off.

"I'll go to the cellar and get the dandelion wine," Maybelle said after she'd picked up her knitting needle. She glared at Dev, who had backed off a yard or two and was wafting rather unsubstantially in the branches of a nearby cottonwood.

"I don't know if I trust Georgina with wine, Miss Maybelle." Ash hugged Georgina hard.

Georgina laughed. "I promise not to pour it over your head this time." She pondered her statement. "Well, that is to say, I won't pour it over your head unless you say something I don't like."

Ash rolled his eyes.

"And if you get really out of hand, I'll bash you over the head with the decanter after I pour the wine on you. You wouldn't mind that, would you?" She batted her eyelashes. Ash kissed her again.

Dev made himself more material and fluttered down to the porch. He ignored Maybelle. *"She's only feelin' her oats, boyo. Pay her no mind."*

"A lot you know about it," Maybelle grumbled. She swished into the house.

Dev sighed.

Ash finally stopped kissing Georgina, much to her dismay.

"Don't forget that you've still got unfinished business in the house, Dev," Ash told the ghost.

"Oh? What business is that?" Even though her own happiness all but overwhelmed her, Georgina was pleased to know she could still experience interest in the affairs of others. She nearly died from happiness when Ash put his arm around her waist and walked with her into the house.

"He's got unfinished business with Miss Maybelle."

"Oh, that." She wished Ash hadn't brought up her grandmother and Mr. O'Rourke's problems. They tended to put a damper on things.

"Now, Ash, I don't know about this—"

Georgina interrupted. "I've been trying to get Grandmother

to hear him out ever since I got here and realized he was haunting the place.''

"He's going to do it today,'' Ash assured her. "He promised.''

"Now wait a minute, boyo. I didn't exactly promise.''

"You did, too.''

Georgina perceived that Ash was becoming annoyed with the ghost and decided to intervene. It would be just like Devlin, the clever devil, to argue with Ash and then pretend offense and vanish. "I think Ash has a wonderful idea, Mr. O'Rourke. Grandmother was touched by Ash's declaration of love''—she could hardly believe it when sheriff Ashley Barrett, of all rugged western men, blushed—"and I'll bet she'd be more apt to listen to you today than most days.''

"She's touched, all right,'' grumbled Ash, who evidently didn't like having his sentimental moments referred to.

"I don't know about this,'' muttered the ghost.

"You said you would, dammit.''

"Now Ash,'' soothed Georgina. "There's no need to swear at Mr. O'Rourke. He's only frightened.''

"Folderol! I'm not frightened!''

"Well, then, I believe you ought to go to the cellar right this minute and declare your love for Grandmother before she comes back upstairs.''

"Now, Georgina, I'm not sure this is the best—''

"Wait, Georgina, that's not fair,'' Ash cried.

Georgina turned to stare at him. He sounded incensed, and she didn't understand. "Whatever is the matter with him going to the cellar, Ash?''

"Dad blast it, he made me stand outside your door and holler at the top of my lungs. It's not fair that he gets to declare himself in private.''

The ghost's eyes went wide. *"Sure, and the boy's right, isn't he? It would be a lot more private in the cellar.''* And with that, Dev vanished.

"Blast it, this isn't fair!''

Georgina eyed her lover askance. He really did appear to be upset. She shook her head. "Don't be ridiculous, Ash. If a declaration in the cellar will get rid of him, I think you're being petty to haggle.''

He looked unconvinced for several seconds before the good

sense of her statement penetrated his brain. About time, too. Georgina devoutly prayed that Ashley Barrett wasn't a simpleton disguising himself as an intelligent human being or she'd be most displeased.

"Oh, all right. I reckon you're right."

It was strange, she thought, how very dear she found his Texas drawl today. The first time she'd heard it, she'd thought it was too twangy. Now she loved it just as she loved every single thing about him. Even the things that had at first set her off were now precious to her.

She'd originally considered him too tall, but she now found his height comforting. Whereas she'd first thought he should have a mustache, she was now glad he didn't. She was sure mustaches must tickle during kisses, and she didn't think she'd like to be distracted during those delicious moments.

And his name. Today she was very glad he wasn't a Buck or a Kid something-or-other. It would be difficult enough writing her parents and informing them of her impending marriage to a gentleman named Ashley Barrett. If she had to tell them she was marrying a Buck or a Kid, she wasn't sure how they'd react. If her father went off into an apoplectic fit brought on by the shock of her news, she'd never forgive herself.

But Ashley Barrett was such an unexceptionable name; surely her parents wouldn't object to it. And they couldn't object to his occupation, either. After all, sheriff was a responsible and respectable position—and he didn't even need it! He was already rich, in spite of his job.

"Georgina Barrett," she whispered. "Doesn't that sound fine?"

"It sounds terrific."

He put his arms around her and kissed her again. Georgina was thrilled.

They heard a huge crash from the cellar, and released each other. Then the sound of feet tromping up the cellar stairs came to them. Georgina eyed Ash, who eyed her back.

She said, "Oh, dear."

He said, "Yeah."

"I don't want to hear another word out of you!" came Maybelle's voice, as loud and angry as Georgina had ever heard it. She sounded like a gaggle of crows. Or whatever a bunch of crows was called.

"But, Maybelle, you have to hear me out!"

"Damn you, Devlin O'Rourke, I don't have to do anything!"

"But it's true, Maybelle!"

Maybelle appeared at the parlor door, gripping a bottle of dandelion wine by its neck. Recognizing the bottle of wine as an imminently flingable object, Georgina rushed over to her grandmother and took the bottom of the bottle in both hands. Ash hurried over to help her, but he couldn't get so much as a fingertip on the bottle for all the Murphy and Witherspoon fingers already there.

Georgina tugged. Maybelle yanked. Georgina said, "Let me pour the wine into the decanter, Grandmother."

Maybelle hollered, "Be damned if I will! I'm going to throw it at Dev!"

"It won't hurt him, for heaven's sake, and you'll ruin a good bottle of wine. Haven't you learned that by now?"

"Sure, and the girl's right, Maybelle. You can heave things at me forever, and you won't hurt me. The only way you can hurt me is by not hearing what I have to say to you today."

"Not to mention the rest of us," Ash muttered behind Georgina. She loved him so much. He was so . . . so terse. So honest. So ruggedly western.

"Ash has a good point, Grandmother," she said. She didn't dare release her hold on the bottle. She wasn't sure if dandelion wine would stain carpeting and walls, but she didn't aim to find out without a fight.

"Hang Ash Barrett's points! I don't want anything to do with Dev!"

"The best way to get rid of him is to listen to him, then," Georgina pointed out reasonably.

"Bilgewater!"

" 'Tisn't bilgewater! I love you. I've always loved you! I wanted to marry you, but I was afraid to say I love you!"

Maybelle squinted up at the ghost. "I don't believe you."

"For the love of God, Maybelle, why do you think I stayed with you for twenty-five years if I didn't love you?"

"Because you were too lazy to look for work?"

Georgina heard Ash snort behind her and wished she had a hand free so she could whap him.

"That's not true and you know it! I worked like a slave in New York City before we moved out here!"

"Well . . ."

Georgina knew how difficult it was for her grandmother to give up a healthy grudge, and she hoped she could help her. "I didn't know that, Mr. O'Rourke. What was your occupation in New York?"

"He scooped up horseshit from the stables."

"You're mean as a snake, Maybelle Murphy!" Dev was obviously offended by her blunt assessment of his duties in New York. *"I was the chief groom in Maybelle's father's stables, is what I was. It was a responsible position, and it required great skill. Not to mention a knack with horses."*

"Dev's always been a good horseman," Ash said, sounding as if he honestly appreciated Dev's horse skills.

"Oh, very well. He was the head groom and he was good with horses. So what?"

"So what? So, your father was too bullheaded to acknowledge that a man who worked for a living was worthy of his daughter, is so what. Damnation, Maybelle, you know that as well as I do. Your father's prejudices against me were what made you marry that idiot Murphy!"

Maybelle shrugged, although her grip on the bottle loosened sufficiently that Georgina was able to grab it away from her. She quickly transferred it to Ash, who headed to the kitchen without a word. She loved that about him, too: He was so quick to size up a situation and act upon it. "So it was your father who prevented you from marrying the man you loved all those years ago?" She said it as if it came as a surprise to her, although Dev had told her as much already.

"I suppose so." Maybelle didn't sound as if she liked admitting it.

"But you did love Mr. O'Rourke back then, didn't you?"

Her grandmother gave her such a glare that if Georgina had still been the woman she'd been in New York City, she might well have fainted from it. However, she'd developed a good deal of western spunk and gumption since her arrival in the territory and Maybelle's glare didn't move her one bit. "It's no use giving me that baleful look, Grandmother. Just answer my question, if you will."

"You're a sassy bit of goods, you know that, Georgina?"

"Yes indeed. I'm just like my grandmother, in fact."

Maybelle squinted at her. "Which grandmother?"

"Why, Grandmother Witherspoon, of course." Georgina squinted back, not giving an inch. She knew her grandmother too well by this time. Give her an inch, and she'd take the whole yardstick and then hit you over the head with it.

"Ha!" Maybelle snorted derisively. "Like hell. Your Grandmother Witherspoon was as frail as a porcelain rose. And about as useful."

"You're right, of course. According to Ash, I'm just like you."

Her grandmother transferred her scowl to Ash, who reentered the room at that moment and nodded. "I'm sure he didn't mean it as a compliment."

"Of course he didn't."

"Who would?" asked Ash in a friendly voice.

Maybelle huffed.

"Don't let them rile you, Maybelle. You're the most wonderful woman in the entire world, and I know it even if they're too stupid to see it."

"Oh, I am, am I?" Maybelle transferred her squint to Dev. She sounded as if she didn't believe a word he said, never had, and didn't intend to start any time soon.

"Yes, you are."

Georgina wouldn't have believed it if she didn't see it with her own eyes, but she did. Devlin O'Rourke, smooth-talking Irishman and devil-may-care raconteur, crumpled up like a transparent wad of paper and began weeping piteously.

"Oh, God, Maybelle, please don't keep torturing me this way. I'm sorry I didn't say I loved you sooner. You'll never know how much I regret it. I'll regret it for all eternity if you don't relent soon! I don't have much time left to persuade you. I begged for a chance to sway you, Maybelle. I begged until Saint Peter himself let me come back to you."

Maybelle looked appalled. Georgina decided she'd like to have a small chat with Saint Peter and recommend that he exercise greater regard in the future for the breathing human beings who had to live with hauntees.

Ash said, "Good God."

"It's the truth! He said I'd have a year, and no more. If you hadn't relented by then, he said it would be too late, and

I'd have to take what I get on the other side. Oh, Lord, Maybelle!'' His voice rose to an eerie wail.

He actually sounded like a ghost. Georgina wished he didn't because it was quite an upsetting noise. She clapped her hands over her ears to block out the sound.

Vernice appeared in the doorway. ''What is that awful racket?''

''It's only Dev.'' Ash sounded bored.

Vernice said, ''Oh,'' and went back in the kitchen.

''Is that the truth?''

Maybelle didn't sound as if she aimed to relent, but at least she was curious. Georgina took that as a good sign, and decided to add her mite.

''My goodness, Mr. O'Rourke, do you mean you were only given an extra year? To persuade my grandmother?'' She made a show of looking first at Maybelle and then back at Dev. ''Saint Peter must not know her very well.''

Ash snorted again. Georgina aimed a kick at him but missed.

''Aye. I told him it would be a miracle if a year would do it.'' Dev's voice had lowered into a sepulchral rumble. *''He said greater miracles had been achieved in a lot less time. Those miracles had been committed by saints, though, and I'm no saint.''*

''Isn't *that* the truth!'' This time it was Maybelle who snorted.

''But you're trying,'' Georgina encouraged, perceiving the faintest hint of mellowing in her grandmother's tone.

''He's trying, all right,'' muttered Maybelle. ''He's tried me for twenty-five years now.''

Dev sighed. *''Aye, I'm trying my best, and so far I'm havin' no luck at all.''*

''Aw, come on, Maybelle.''

Georgina was so surprised to hear Ash break into the conversation that she spun around. Was he going to try to influence her, too? Merciful heavens.

''You know you love the guy,'' Ash continued. ''You always have. And he's always loved you. It's as plain as the nose on Frank Dunwiddy's face. I don't know why you're both so stubborn about admitting it.''

''*You* don't know why?'' Maybelle's face amply expressed

her sarcasm. "When it took a shotgun and the threat of never seeing Georgina again to drive you to it?"

Ash shuffled uncomfortably. "Yes, I know I was a little hard to convince. But I did it. Now you two need to do it. If you don't, you may never see Dev again in this life or the next, Miss Maybelle. You don't want that, do you?"

"Well . . ."

"The boy's right, Maybelle. There aren't any guarantees otherwise. Saint Peter said that if you agree to tie the knot with me on the other side when you pass over, he'd make the arrangements. If you won't agree to do it, he'll hold our years of living together in sin as proof that we were merely dallying with each other."

"*Dallying* with each other? For twenty-five years?" Maybelle's screech hurt Georgina's ears.

Dev held out his arms. That made him look like an angel, which was, to Georgina's way of thinking even more incongruous than his being a ghost. *"Sure, and twenty-five years is a mere snap of the fingers to God, darlin'. Less than that, even."*

"Hmm. Maybe so."

Georgina and Ash exchanged a look of encouragement.

Dev flung himself on the floor in front of Maybelle. Georgina jumped back because his essence was cold and she was standing in part of it. Fortunately, she bumped into Ash, who put his arms around her, so it worked out all right.

"Please, Maybelle! Please! You've got to say you'll marry me on the other side! You must! I can't bear the notion of eternity without you! Can you imagine it? Can you? You can't want that!"

"Well . . ."

"Oh, God, Maybelle, just say yes. Please! Please! I'll go away and never darken your door again if you'll only say you'll marry me in the hereafter. I love you so much! I never loved anyone the way I love you. I'll love you until the end of time, but if you don't say the words, too, I'll never see you again! I can't bear it. Talk about hell!"

"Is that the truth?" Maybelle appeared very skeptical.

Devlin began weeping again. *"Yes! Yes, it's the truth. I couldn't lie if I wanted to. That was part of the deal I made with Saint Peter."*

"Hmm."

"Maybelle, you have the happiness of my immortal soul in your hands. And yours, too, as you well know. You'd be miserable without me forever. Almost as miserable as I'd be without you."

A silence ensued that lasted until Georgina thought her nerves would shatter. Ash reached for her hand, and she took his gratefully. She felt ever so loved and protected with him.

At last Maybelle heaved a gigantic sigh. "Oh, very well. I love you, and I'll marry you after I die." She looked to one side.

Georgina got the impression she was embarrassed by her admission. As for Georgina, she was so happy, she turned and hugged Ash hard. He hugged her back, just as hard. He also whispered in her ear, "Thank the good Lord!" and Georgina giggled.

"But I resent it, Devlin O'Rourke," Maybelle went on. "If you'd said such nice things while you were alive, you could have spared us both a lot of misery."

"I know it. And I'm sorrier than you can imagine."

Georgina, who hadn't enjoyed being haunted, muttered, "I'll bet *we* can, though."

"So when will you go away?" Ash asked. Georgina smacked his arm to let him know he ought to have a little sensitivity on the matter. He only looked miffed.

"I want one more night with my beloved," the ghost said. *"Then I'll depart."* He sniffled miserably. *"It won't be heaven without you, Maybelle. I hope you die soon."*

Maybelle stiffened. "You miserable louse! What a thing to say!"

"I didn't mean it that way," Dev muttered. *"What I meant was that I'll be lonely without you."*

Maybelle sniffed. "Well, I suppose I'll miss you, too. I anticipated missing you months ago but never got the chance. I suppose it'll be worse now, since you hung around so long as a ghost."

"Perhaps I can have another chat with Saint Peter . . ."

A chorus of *"No's!"* sang through the house. Georgina and Ash looked toward the door of the kitchen, where Vernice stood. Georgina thought it was rather funny that all three of them had had the same reaction to Dev's offer.

"I wouldn't bother you folks any longer," Dev promised. *"If I can work out a deal with Saint Pete, I'll only be visible to Maybelle."*

"Are you sure about that?" Vernice asked in a voice so tough that Georgina almost didn't recognize it. "Because I don't fancy having you pop up all the time the way you've done since you died. I do believe I'd have to have my own chat with Saint Peter."

Dev sighed. *"Aye, spoil it for me, Vernice. I always thought you were the nice one."*

"And exactly what is *that* supposed to mean?" Maybelle glowered at Dev.

Georgina felt Ash tug on her arm. When she turned to see what he wanted, he beckoned her with a finger. He lifted his voice and spoke over her head. "Georgina and I are going for a little ride. Don't wait up for her."

Vernice's eyes went as round as marbles. Dev winked at the two of them. Maybelle looked sour.

Georgina decided her lover was a very wise man. She paused only long enough to fetch her nightgown, robe, and slippers. Then she joined Ash on Shiloh, and they rode together to his ranch house—the perfect little house that Georgina already loved and couldn't wait to move into.

"Do that some more! Oh, please, Ash!"

Ash was positive he'd never been so happy in his life. Phoebe had never let him do this to her. She'd even been shocked when he'd suggested it. Not Georgina. Georgina was delighted to practice all sorts of experiments with him in bed.

He looked up at her now from between her silken thighs. The sight of her dazed with passion was so gorgeous, he nearly lost control of himself. Knowing it was his duty as a man and her future husband to perform well, he ceased watching her and resumed doing what he'd been doing, which involved the expertise with his mouth and tongue.

It didn't take her long, and when she achieved her release, she had to stuff a fist in her mouth so she wouldn't scream. Not that it mattered. They were alone in his ranch house, miles away from another human being. What's more, she aimed to stay the night with him.

Lord above, he loved this woman.

After she had almost recovered herself, Ash climbed aboard and rode her like a stallion. It didn't take him long, either, and when his orgasm came, it was like the end of the world and the beginning of heaven, all rolled into one.

"I love you, Georgina," he whispered into her ear afterwards.

"And I love you, Ash," she panted back.

In fact, they loved each other so much that they decided to prove it again in a very short while. And once more several times after that.

It was, Ash decided in the morning, the finest night of his life.

Chapter
Twenty

"I can't hold my stomach in for a second longer," Georgina gasped. She was nearly squeezing Ash's hand to death.

"It's all right, dear. No one can tell." Vernice patted her on the shoulder.

Georgina smiled at her aunt. She should have expected Vernice to say something of the sort. Vernice was so sweet. Vernice and Evelyn, Georgina's mother, evidently took after their father's side of the family. Georgina had decided some time ago that she herself must be Murphy throwback.

"To hell with your stomach," declared Maybelle in her usual scrappy tone. "If your parents can't tolerate the results human nature, to hell with them, too."

"I agree with her one hundred percent," Ash whispered into her ear.

"You would."

Although she was already experiencing the sickness common to the early stages of pregnancy, her tummy had begun to grow, and she was as anxious as a cat on a hot stove about what her parents were going to think about herself and Ash jumping the marriage gun by several weeks, Georgina was happy as a lark. Knowing she was pregnant—which would have been shocking in New York—only made her happy.

They were going to be a family. She and Ash. Shortly after

they got married. By her reckoning, she was about two months along. They'd had to wait this long to have the wedding in order for her parents and her brother to make arrangements to attend. Ash's uncle from Galveston was due to arrive in a day or so.

Ash had warned her that everything she'd ever heard about Texans being loud and expansive went double for Uncle Bart.

Georgina could hardly wait to meet him. A real Texan! Well, Ash was technically a Texan, too, but he wasn't what she'd call a *real* one. On the other hand, she'd been mistaken before. When she first met Ash, she hadn't believed him to be a really, truly, rugged western sheriff, either. But he was. And she loved him for it—among other things.

Henry Spurling had left for New York City the day after Georgina had spurned him. The letter she wrote to her parents explaining her rejection of Henry and her acceptance of Ash crossed in the mail with the one her parents had written her, advising her to take her time making a decision about whom to marry. Evidently, she surmised, her parents had seen tendencies in their daughter that Georgina hadn't even guessed at before she'd come to the territory.

Payton Pierce had been distant and formal to her for a few weeks after she'd rejected him, and had then begun courting a nice girl who had recently moved to Picacho Wells with her parents and siblings. Her name was Lucy Hyde, and she was every bit as insipid as Mr. Pierce. Georgina thought they would suit each other admirably.

Everyone else in town was ecstatic about her impending nuptials to Ash. Not only did they dearly love their sheriff, but they'd come to love Georgina as well. There wasn't a lady in town who wasn't sure Georgina would be the cure of any lingering ills left over from Ash's disastrous marriage to Phoebe. Georgina agreed.

She'd been moved to tears when the ladies from the quilting society had presented her with a patchwork quilt, worked in the double wedding ring pattern, as a shower gift. They were busily quilting away on baby blankets now, and not a single one of them had seemed to frown upon Georgina for being pregnant without a wedding band on her finger. They understood weddings couldn't be rushed when one had parents in New York City—and they also understood that some marital acts were rushed by common consent when the motivation was strong enough.

Besides, as Betsy Bailey told her, it wasn't at all uncommon for folks in the territory to have to wait months, or even years, for a preacher to come along and marry them, no matter how long they'd been living as man and wife. "We're lucky here in Picacho Wells," Betsy said. "We have our own preacher in town. And even a church. When Sam and I got together, it took two years for a preacher to say the words over us, and by that time we had a baby and another one on the way." All the ladies in the quilting society had laughed gaily.

Georgina had never looked at the matter from a territorial point of view before Betsy's revelation. It made her feel better about everything.

The wedding ceremony was planned for the upcoming Saturday, which was the third one in October. Georgina and her friends in town had been decorating the church for days now with the last of the year's flowers, early fall leaves, fabric garlands, and big fat candles ordered specially from San Antonio.

Considering how small a building the Picacho Wells Church was, and the fact that Georgina had attended Grace Church in New York City, she thought the sanctuary was shaping up nicely. It was a little rustic. So what? Its rusticity would lend a certain charm to everything.

The choir was going to sing at the wedding. Georgina had already warned her parents and her brother about this particular choir. She told her brother, via letter, that if he so much as looked like he was sneering at the singers, she'd shoot him with her derringer. He probably hadn't believed her, but he'd learn.

"Oh, look! I see smoke from the train!" Vernice vibrated with excitement as she pointed toward the east. "I haven't seen Evelyn for so long!" She pulled out a handkerchief and dabbed at her eyes.

"I see it." Georgina was excited herself. "Oh, Ash, I hope you like them!"

"I'm sure I will."

Georgina considered the statement quite gallant of him, considering his opinion of bankers, which he'd shared with her several times.

"I hope they like me," he added.

She squeezed his hand. "They'll like you, never fear."

When she looked up into his eyes, she nearly swooned when she read the expression of love in them. She'd been doing that a lot lately—nearly swooning. She chalked it up to her delicate condition, even though she didn't feel very delicate. Indeed, why should she? She could now churn butter without resting once, put chickens to sleep like a champ, quilt without pricking her fingers, roll out the flakiest piecrusts in the territory, make dumplings, foil desperadoes, and even milk Bossy without hurting her.

She was, in fact, a true western woman, and she was proud to the point of bursting.

"You think so, do you?" Ash sounded doubtful.

"Hell, they'll like you," said Maybelle with one of her witchiest smiles. "As soon as they see Georgina's stomach, they'll beg you to marry their daughter and make an honest woman of her." She went off into a gale of cackles.

"I think your grandmother is crazy," Ash muttered.

"That's why I came out here in the first place, you know," Georgina told him. "Aunt Vernice thought she'd gone off the deep end. Then she discovered Mr. O'Rourke."

"I'm not sure the one negates the other."

She whacked his arm.

The train chugged in and squealed to a stop. Georgina held her breath and nearly burst from excitement. When she saw her mother appear at the head of the steps, looking timid and a little lost, she broke away from Ash.

"Mother! Mother!"

Evelyn blinked and glanced toward the raucous shout, which Georgina was sure she'd never anticipated coming from her daughter's throat. When Evelyn spied Georgina, a smile burst onto her countenance, and she hurried down the stairs.

Georgina nearly knocked her over in her exuberance. "Oh, Mother, I'm so glad you could come!" She was embarrassed when she started to cry.

"God, Georgie, you look wonderful. What have you been doing to yourself?"

Wiping her eyes, Georgina looked up into her older brother's handsome face. He'd always been her hero—well, until she met Ash, who had taken over the position. "Simon!

Oh, Simon!'' And she disengaged herself from her mother and flung herself at her brother, who laughed and hugged her hard. Vernice took over hugging Evelyn.

Her father came next. Georgina knew for a fact that she'd changed almost beyond recognition when she hugged her father. She hadn't hugged her father since she was five or six years old. But she was a westerner now, and her eastern inhibitions had disappeared as completely as Devlin O'Rourke.

In other words, they only showed up occasionally, and today wasn't one of the occasions.

Saturday morning dawned as clear and as sweet as a day in southeastern New Mexico Territory ever dawned. There was the slightest nip in the air, no wind to speak of, and clouds like white horses bounded across a deep-blue sky.

Ash was ready. He wasn't even hardly very much scared.

The last couple of months had cured him. Life with Georgina was a pure treat. She was as unlike Phoebe as a rock was from a puff of eiderdown. Or maybe it was the other way around. Whatever it was, Ash was in love, and he was ready to tie the knot. In fact, he was eager to, especially now that Georgina was expecting.

He wanted a boy. Unless it was a girl, in which case he wanted a girl.

And her parents weren't bad at all. Her father had taken quite a shine to Uncle Bart, so he couldn't be all bad, even if he was a banker and a little bit stuffy. Georgina's mother reminded Ash of Vernice, which figured. And her brother Simon was a brick. Simon had been raising hell with the other young bucks in town ever since his arrival. Ash was sort of glad the Witherspoons would be heading back to New York in a week because he didn't fancy having to arrest Simon for rowdy behavior.

Hell, he probably wouldn't have to arrest him. He'd just let Georgina go after him with her derringer. If that didn't calm Simon down, nothing would.

He straightened his tie and tapped his top hat. He hadn't worn a high beaver since his wedding to Phoebe. He looked better in it today than he had ten years ago. Hell, everything looked better today than it had ten years ago—especially his wife-to-be.

His shoes were polished to perfection. He glanced down at them, glad he was dressing in the choir room so he wouldn't have to walk through the dust outside to get to the church. Frank Dunwiddy and Simon were seeing to last-minute arrangements in the sanctuary. Frank was Ash's best man, and Simon was acting as an attendant, whatever that was. Georgina knew, and that's what counted.

Ash was ready. He was absolutely, pure-D, sure-as-spit ready. He wasn't even nervous. Not even a little tiny bit.

"So, you're going to do it at last. About time, I'd say, Ashley Barrett."

"Ack!" Ash leaped a yard in the air and whirled around, Devlin O'Rourke's voice having nearly caused his heart to stop. "Dammit, Dev! I thought you were gone for good. Well, except for Maybelle."

"A little nervous, are we, boyo?" Dev grinned at him most devilishly, which Ash guessed also figured.

"Nervous? Me? Hell, no. I'm ready. I'm happy, even."

"As well you should be. Georgina's a prize, Ash. You treat her well, or I'll come back and haunt the dickens out of you."

"I don't need your threats, Dev. I aim to treat her well. I love her." Ash couldn't believe he'd said that out loud to Dev. He'd been telling Georgina he loved her pretty much daily, but he hadn't said it to anyone else recently. Not since he'd shrieked it to the skies on Maybelle Murphy's front porch.

"Aye, I believe you, son." The ghost sighed. *"I'll be glad when I can marry Maybelle."*

"Well, you've got her promise now at last."

"Aye, and Saint Pete's blessing. I only wish I'd been as bright as you and done it while I was still alive."

"You should be glad the universe allows second chances, Dev. You're lucky."

"I suppose so. Anyway, I'll be happy to watch you and Georgina tie the knot."

Ash wasn't especially happy to know Dev would be watching, although he didn't suppose it mattered a whole lot. A body could never trust Maybelle not to cut up, and he didn't guess interference from a ghost would be any worse than one of Maybelle's capers.

Lordy, sometimes he thought Georgina was the *only* truly sane member of her family. Ash could handle her, though. It was a damned good thing he'd gotten her instead of one of those other fellows.

Frank Dunwiddy came through the door and Ash whirled around, reaching for the gun that wasn't tucked into his waistband today. Frank laughed.

"Lordamercy, Ash, you're jumpy as frog legs in a skillet."

Ash ran his finger under his collar. "Maybe I'm a little bit skittish, Frank."

"I'd say so. A little bit." Frank laughed again. "Reverend Voorhees is ready, Ash. How about you?"

Ash tugged his tie again, and again tapped his top hat. He inspected his shoes, which were as shiny as they'd been the last time he looked. He pulled out the watch his uncle had given him and checked the time. Eleven thirty. Oh, God, it was time. He snatched up a handkerchief from the table and wiped his brow.

"I'm ready."

"You don't have to sound like you're facing an executioner," Frank told him with yet another laugh. "You're marrying Miss Georgina, who's about the prettiest gal anyone in Picacho Wells has ever seen. And the nicest."

"And the most useful," Ash reported dutifully.

Frank said, "Useful?" in a puzzled-sounding voice.

"Never mind."

Mrs. Voorhees had been playing some tunes on the piano that Ash didn't recognize. All at once, the opening notes of Wagner's "Wedding March" from *Lohengrin* sounded, and he swallowed hard. His heart gave an enormous spasm, and he hoped like hell he wouldn't pass out. How humiliating *that* would be.

He'd contemplated trying to talk Georgina into eloping with him. He'd abandoned the idea when he remembered that most folks in this part of the territory who eloped did so in Picacho Wells because, as Betsy Bailey had informed Georgina, Picacho Wells was one of the few towns in the area with a resident preacher.

As soon as Ash and Frank took their places by Reverend Voorhees, Ash glanced down the aisle, and he saw Georgina on the arm of her father, walking toward him. His nerves smoothed out as if someone had ironed them. There she was.

The most beautiful, wonderful, special woman in the universe, and she was his.

His bride. She was walking down the aisle, straight at him. Georgina, the only woman in the world for him, was coming to him this very minute. She was giving herself over to his care. She trusted him to treat her as a wife should be treated. She was going to be his helpmate, his lover, his friend, and the mother of his children. She loved him.

She loved him. Ash's eyes filled with tears, which he swallowed mercilessly and immediately. Hell's bells, the sheriff of Picacho Wells couldn't cry at his own wedding. It was unheard of.

Georgina and her father reached him, her father handed her over to Ash, and Ash and Georgina turned to face the preacher.

Mrs. Voorhees played another chord, and the choir lifted their voices in "Blest Be the Tie that Binds." By God, they were on key!

Ash decided that if God had wanted to send him a sign that he was doing the right thing, this was it. The very last of his nervous flutters flew out the window.

George Ashley Barrett came into the world with a squawk and a vigorous kick on the ninth day of May, 1897. His mother, Georgina Witherspoon Barrett, came through the ordeal of his birth with flying colors. His father, Ashley Montgomery Barrett, who swore he wasn't one bit nervous, fainted with relief when Maybelle Murphy brought his son to him from the bedroom where Georgina had given birth.

"Shoot, the lad's a sensitive sort, isn't he?" Devlin O'Rourke hovered over Maybelle's head, making cooing noises at the baby, who ignored them.

"Oh, poor Mr. Barrett! I'll get him a little sip of brandy." Vernice bustled off to do so.

Maybelle eyed Ash and shook her head. "Men. They're all alike."

In later years, Georgina was careful never to refer to Ash's undignified behavior on the day of his first son's birth.

Anyhow, he had lots of practice after George was born. The Barrett brood eventually numbered eight, and they were, by anyone's reckoning, as happy a family as the New Mexico Territory had ever seen, especially after Uncle Simon moved to Picacho Wells and set himself up as a hotel keeper.

Ash taught every one of his sons and daughters the fine points of good horsemanship. Dev tried to interfere, but Saint Peter made him stop. Ash also taught them how best to invest money and make it grow.

Their mother taught them all how to shoot, since she was reckoned to be the best shot in the territory.

*Presenting all-new romances—featuring
ghostly heroes and heroines and the
passions they inspire.*

❤ Haunting Hearts ❤

☐ *A SPIRITED SEDUCTION*
  by Casey Claybourne   0-515-12066-9/$5.99

☐ *STARDUST OF YESTERDAY*
  by Lynn Kurland   0-515-11839-7/$6.50

☐ *A GHOST OF A CHANCE*
  by Casey Claybourne   0-515-11857-5/$5.99

☐ *ETERNAL VOWS*
  by Alice Alfonsi   0-515-12002-2/$5.99

☐ *ETERNAL LOVE*
  by Alice Alfonsi   0-515-12207-6/$5.99

☐ *ARRANGED IN HEAVEN*
  by Sara Jarrod   0-515-12275-0/$5.99

Prices slightly higher in Canada

Payable in U.S. funds only. No cash/COD accepted. Postage & handling: U.S /CAN $2.75 for one book, $1.00 for each additional, not to exceed $6.75; Int'l $5.00 for one book, $1.00 each additional. We accept Visa, Amex, MC ($10.00 min.), checks ($15.00 fee for returned checks) and money orders. Call 800-788-6262 or 201-933-9292, fax 201-896-8569; refer to ad # 636 (7/99)

Penguin Putnam Inc.   Bill my: ☐ Visa ☐ MasterCard ☐ Amex _____ (expires)
P.O. Box 12289, Dept. B
Newark, NJ 07101-5289   Card# _____
Please allow 4-6 weeks for delivery   Signature _____
Foreign and Canadian delivery 6-8 weeks

Bill to:
Name _____
Address _____ City _____
State/ZIP _____ Daytime Phone # _____
Ship to:
Name _____ Book Total $ _____
Address _____ Applicable Sales Tax $ _____
City _____ Postage & Handling $ _____
State/ZIP _____ Total Amount Due $ _____

            This offer subject to change without notice.

FRIENDS ROMANCE

Can a man come between friends?

❑ **A TASTE OF HONEY**

by DeWanna Pace   0-515-12387-0

❑ **WHERE THE HEART IS**

by Sheridon Smythe   0-515-12412-5

❑ **LONG WAY HOME**

by Wendy Corsi Staub   0-515-12440-0

All books $5.99